Rave reviews for Po Bronson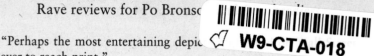

"Perhaps the most entertaining depic[tion] ever to reach print."
—*Business Week*

"A hilarious must-read! The most entertaining work of fiction on Wall Street since *The Bonfire of the Vanities*."
—*USA Today*

"Excellent. The genre of manic black comedy has never been better. In split-second mercurial prose, Bronson combines the echoes of *Glengarry Glenn Ross* and *Catch–22*."
—*The Boston Globe*

"His talent is impressive, his lampooning has the clear, loud ring of truth." —*The Washington Post*

"*Bombardiers* is, in a word, brilliant. It's devastatingly funny, as wise as any Wall Street guru, and bitter as a cup of jet black coffee."
—*The Baltimore Sun*

"A hilarious, distinctly terrifying first novel, told in zippy deadpan prose. *Bombardiers* takes off at Mach 1 and soon approaches light speed." —*Chicago Tribune*

PENGUIN BOOKS

BOMBARDIERS

Po Bronson is a thirty-one-year-old writer with a B.A. in economics from Stanford University and an M.F.A. in creative writing from San Francisco State University. Prior to his current job as associate publisher at Mercury House, he did a stint as a recruit on the salesforce of the First Boston Corporation. He grew up in Seattle and lives in San Francisco.

BOMBARDIERS

PO BRONSON

PENGUIN BOOKS

PENGUIN BOOKS
Published by the Penguin Group
Penguin Books USA Inc., 375 Hudson Street, New York, New York 10014, U.S.A.
Penguin Books Ltd, 27 Wrights Lane, London W8 5TZ, England
Penguin Books Australia Ltd, Ringwood, Victoria, Australia
Penguin Books Canada Ltd, 10 Alcorn Avenue, Toronto, Ontario, Canada M4V 3B2
Penguin Books (N.Z.) Ltd, 182–190 Wairau Road, Auckland 10, New Zealand

Penguin Books Ltd, Registered Offices: Harmondsworth, Middlesex, England

First published in the United States of America by Random House, Inc., 1995
Reprinted by arrangement with Random House, Inc.
Published in Penguin Books 1996

1   3   5   7   9   10   8   6   4   2

PUBLISHER'S NOTE
This is a work of fiction. Names, characters, places, and incidents either are the product
of the author's imagination or are used fictitiously, and any resemblance to actual
persons, living or dead, events, or locales is entirely coincidental.

THE LIBRARY OF CONGRESS HAS CATALOGUED THE HARDCOVER AS FOLLOWS:
Bronson, Po.
Bombardiers/Po Bronson.
p.   cm.
ISBN 0-679-43541-7 (hc.)
ISBN 0 14 02.5450 1 (pbk.)
I. Title.
PS3552.R653B66   1995
813'.54—dc20   94–20610

Printed in the United States of America
Set in Sabon

For Nina

Is it worse to be:
a) unjust?   b) merciless?

—question from Kelrsey Temperament Sorter,
  a common career-counseling tool

ACKNOWLEDGMENTS

Thanks to Nina Schuyler, Peter Ginsberg, Jon Karp, Jim Humes, Ethan Watters, Jean Thompson, and Louise Edmunds for their roles in helping with the manuscript. I owe a great debt to all of you, as well as to those others who have kept me writing over the past many years, including Rick Bass, Bill Brinton, Duncan Bronson, Deborah Bull, Ethan Canin, Michelle Carter, Barbara Himmelman, Howard Junker, and Mitch Radcliffe.

At Random House, I'm grateful to Deborah Aiges, Andy Carpenter, Harold Evans, Ivan Held, Bridget Marmion, and Beth Pearson.

In addition, thanks to my old friends at First Boston who ordered me around relentlessly, particularly Dan Vandivort, Samuel Belk, Dennis Blodgett, Marcia Reynolds, and Mark Kraschel. No hard feelings.

BOMBARDIERS

1 · Filth

IT WAS A filthy profession, but the money was addicting, and one addiction led to another, and they were all going to hell. Turner had gone to hell, and Mike McAfferey had gone to hell. Wes "Green Thumb" Griffin developed a wandering eye, while Antonia Zennario, who used to joke that "all investors were made from Adam's rib," lost her sense of humor, and then her smile, and then her job. Carol Manning miscarried. Coyote Jack began to stutter on his numbers and was moved into management. They had all gone to hell. Sid Geeder hated them all and missed them like crazy. The phone rang constantly and everyone suffered cauliflower ears, neck rashes, and cervical pain, and when the sun came up in the morning and they had already been at their desks two, three hours, they went to the forty-first-floor window and imagined what it would be like to have to ride a bus or find a parking place. The squawk box cackled as traders in London and New York and Chicago bid up the long bond, then it quieted as the dust cleared and they settled in to wait for retail to continue the rally. Green monochrome monitors tinted everyone's face a pasty color, and Lisa Lisa reached for her pancake of low-lustre, firming-action moisture cream. Sidney Geeder drank some coffee. Nickel Sansome massaged his scalp. Sue Marino flipped through a bridal magazine.

When the sun didn't come up and instead their tower was socked in by clouds and fog, the other world existed even less than usual; they could not see the streets below, or most of the shorter buildings, and they were one of the few spaceships in the sky. The next attack could come from anywhere. The economic forecasts were useless. The fundamentals were ignored. The Federal Reserve was unpredictable. Money supply meant nothing in a global market. The Yanks followed the lead of the Japs, and the Japs followed the

Krauts, and the Krauts followed the Yanks. They waited for instructions from the top, but their standing instructions were to sell first and not wait for instructions. Nobody knew where the market was going, but those that knew less than others lost their shirts and had their eyes ripped out and were made to swallow. In the mornings, there was always a chance to make it back. Later, the government would bail them out. But this wasn't later; they got glasses with higher prescriptions and gained weight and rode yellow cabs to work and the market was always the same.

This unmerciful uniformity of their days was always something to joke about. They also joked about Coyote Jack's management wardrobe, especially his leather suspenders and corporate initialed cuff links. And Nelson Dicky's teeth, which were rotting. And the corporation's name, which had been mud on the street after the Euro-Floaters deal and had had to be changed to revive the firm's image. And Lisa Lisa's testicles, which were made of steel and clanged when she sold the flip from mortgages to high-yield corporates. They joked about these things and they wondered what it would be like not to have a paycheck, and though it wasn't easy, they all survived. Then there were things that were not so easy to joke about, such as when Sid Geeder nearly killed himself from drinking coffee. And when Eggs Igino vanished. Or during the Euro-Floaters deal when that kid, Turner, fell asleep and couldn't wake up. They never left their trenches and they did as they were told; they didn't do anything except go to work eleven hours a day, five days a week, for a few years of their lives. They gave 110 percent in service to the firm. In the end, only one of them would be left standing, and everything would be different except the market, which was normal, because it was normal to rub out everything human and leave only the cockroaches and those made of steel. Sid Geeder looked around him at who was left from the old days. Paul DeShews was still there, tipped back in his chair like an astronaut. Clark Kalinov was still there, eating his breakfast and reading the paper as if nothing had happened. Cockroaches, all of them. Sid Geeder slurped his coffee. Nine more months and then he could cash out his company shares and leave here with his head high. He called a customer and sold him $6 million Dai Nippon Floating Rate Notes, which usually would have made Sid feel better. But all his friends were gone, even the ones he hated, and in their place was fresh young meat that believed this would be the last job they ever needed.

Sid's stomach soured and his back stiffened and he began to worry that he was going to develop an ear infection from all the germs that breeded unrestrained in the receiver of his phone.

"Do you see anything in there?" he asked Lisa Lisa, having unscrewed the receiver cap, exposing the resonator drum.

"I don't see anything," she answered, scrutinizing the cap. She poked the end of a paper clip through the holes in the hard plastic.

"I'm thinking of microwaving it," he commented. "Kill 'em off."

"Would that do anything?"

"It couldn't hurt."

Lisa Lisa unplugged her handset from the long cord that ran down under her desk. "Let's go," she whispered. They walked across the sales floor nonchalantly, holding their phone handsets down at thigh level, below the height of the desks. The kitchen was empty. They set the microwave on high, timed for five minutes.

"What do you think?" Sid asked, leaning up against the counter.

"Hard to say."

"You want some coffee?"

Lisa Lisa retrieved two mugs from a cupboard and poured in coffee and milk. They sipped at it slowly.

"Yup," Sid said, drumming his fingers on the countertop. "I have a good feeling about this."

"You think?"

Sid nodded. "Could be the start of a trend." He grinned broadly. "If so, I'll let you take half the credit."

They indeed had started a trend. When the word got around the floor that all the microbes festering in their phone receivers could possibly be eradicated by just five minutes in the microwave, a line formed at the entrance of the kitchen. Out on the sales floor, phone lines rang unanswered as the salesforce stared sullenly at the opened machinery of their handsets. In the kitchen, scuffles broke out as salesmen argued whether putting more phones in the microwave required a commensurate increase in cooking time. Then John White came storming out on the trading floor and asked Sid

Geeder into his office and told everyone else to go back to work. *This is it,* Sid Geeder thought to himself as John White's secretary poured him a fresh cup of coffee. *Now I'm gone too.*

"Jesus fucking Christ, Geeder," John White said. "What's all this about you nuking your goddamn phones?"

"I don't know anything about it," Sid mused delightedly.

"Don't lie to me. This caper has got your name all over it. Who else is so paranoid that they'd worry about germs in a place as clean as this?"

Sid fumbled with a button on his cuff. "I heard about it from Lisa Lisa," he admitted.

"Yeah? Well, she says she heard about it from you."

Sid shrugged and looked down.

John White blew out a deep breath. He shook his head despondently. "If you weren't so goddamn important to this firm, I'd fire you in a second."

"You can't fire me," Sid said. "You need me."

"You're damn right we need you. Look, we've got another big Resolution Trust deal coming down the pipes. The firm's really gone out on a limb on this one, and we're going to need your early support. We can't have you creating diversions like this microbe scare."

"Another Resolution Trust!" Sid balked. "We just did a big deal for them nine months ago. Have they run out of that money already?"

John White leaned back and shook his head in exaggerated disbelief. "That's exactly the sort of monkey business I'm talking about, Geeder. I just mention the deal and already you're criticizing. We need team players on this one."

"Uh-oh. Red alert. Every time you ask me to be a team player it means you're about to announce some major fucking bullshit that you expect me to swallow."

To calm down, John White took a deep, slow inhale through his nose, which he'd heard took the oxygen right into the brain. Sid Geeder always came through in the clutch, but in the month or so between when a deal was announced and when it finally came down, Sid was predictably disruptive. "Look, Sid, we're just asking you not to jump to any conclusions. Try the deal on for size for a while."

"Oh, don't worry about me," Sid said. "I don't have an opinion about the Resolution Trust Corp., despite the fact that the last forty billion—which was supposed to last a couple years, if my memory serves me—appears to have been squandered in just nine months. Boy, those guys at the RTC could teach the Pentagon a lesson. If the Pentagon could build a two-year rocket in just nine months, then they wouldn't be in such hot water all the time."

John White just rubbed his jaw and tried to wait out Sid's rage. "You just be careful what you say out on the floor or to your accounts. And no sneak attacks, either. No sly asides. If something like this microbe scare or that sweatshirt fiasco happens, you're out on your butt."

"What makes you think I was behind that sweatshirt fiasco?" When the firm's name became mud on the street after the Euro-Floaters deal soured, Sid Geeder had called the decal company that printed corporate mugs, calendars, and ashtrays. Sid ordered two dozen extra-large sweatshirts in corporate blue with the firm's recognizable logo of a schooner ship at full sail emblazoned on the front. Above the logo, in the typestyle normally reserved for "First Boston," was silkscreened "Mud on the Street." The sweatshirts were sent anonymously via interdepartment mail to senior management.

"We know more than you think," John White said. "A lot of people wanted you fired. I had to save your ass."

"The only thing that saved my ass was the realization that I make this firm a hell of a lot of money." Sid was quiet for a moment. "Maybe I'm going to quit," he mumbled, suddenly feeling sorry for himself.

"You won't quit. You've got nine more months and then you're cashing out your corporate shares and we all know it."

"That didn't make a difference to Wes Griffin."

John White shook his head remorsefully. "I should have fired you a long time ago, Geeder. We can't let people become invaluable to us."

"That's crazy," Sid said.

"It's not crazy. It's management."

Sid Geeder looked out John White's forty-first-floor window. There was nothing but fog and they were the only spaceship in the sky. There was no way to tell they were in San Francisco—they could be flying over Tokyo or London or Bonn and they wouldn't even know, they were so tuned in to the market. It didn't even matter that they were the Atlantic Pacific Corporation now, they just went right on flying. But the firm was nothing without its trimmings. Sid knew that if you took away the marbled elevators and the mahogany-paneled entranceway and the low-static corporate-blue carpet and the historically correct, proportional-to-scale toy schooners that were the new company logo, the firm would look like any other retail chophouse on the street. If you took away the custom-designed mahogany trading pits and the global clocks and the LED ticker tape running across one wall, it could be any other cost center of any other big downtown business, such as a phone company or an insurance carrier. And if you took away the downtown view and knocked $300 off everyone's suit and put a parking lot outside, it could be any back-office support in Stockton or Sacramento. The jobs weren't much different. The salespeople answered the phone and sent faxes off and stared at their computer monitors and had meetings in the mornings over cream-cheese danishes where they wondered under their breath if there would ever come a time when they didn't have to work so hard.

Therefore Clark Kalinov, the office manager, had a great responsibility. His responsibility was to rebuild the corporate image as the finest selling machine on the planet. His first step in this objective was to secure himself a window office. Clark was a translucent-faced know-it-all with blunt hair like a beaver, and nobody respected him because he hung out in his fluorescent-lit cubicle off the copy room. So Clark requisitioned two hundred reams of stationery, six cases of copier toner, seven thousand corporate-blue ballpoint pens, a cutting board, a second fax machine, a Z3200 Pitney Bowes mail machine, and one thousand interdepartment mail reusable envelopes. Then he wrote out lengthy complaints to the facilities department in New York that they were so packed into their office that copier toner and stationery were piling up in the hallways.

"This place is a mess," Sid Geeder said, trying to squeeze past the overstocked supplies to use the fax machine.

"Call New York and complain," Clark answered.

Sidney Geeder stood over the two fax machines, one of which was busy receiving a very long document and one of which was busy sending a very thick prospectus. He looked at his watch. "Do you think this fax going through is very important?" he asked.

"Extremely important," Clark answered.

Sidney rifled through the prospectus pages looking for a cover letter to see who was sending such a long document, but there was no cover letter. Then he rifled through the incoming pages to look for a cover letter to know how many more pages were coming, but there was no cover letter there either.

"Hey," Sidney Geeder said. "Some idiot accidentally sent this prospectus to our second fax machine."

"It's not an accident," Clark said, not bothering to look up from the office supply catalog he was leafing through.

"Are you testing the new machine?"

"I'm trying to wear it out."

"Why?"

"So I can order a new one."

Sidney Geeder didn't get it, though he was long accustomed to the asinine antics of Kalinov's bureaucracy. But accepting that his fax wouldn't get through was nearly impossible. "If you order a new one, it'll be even more crowded around here. There'll be no space to put anything."

"Exactly!" Clark said, finally looking up from his catalog.

"The phone line has probably been busy for an hour," Sidney reasoned. "What if someone in New York is trying to fax us something important?"

Clark leaned back in his chair and rested his feet on the desktop. "What if they are?"

"They'll think we don't have enough fax machines, that's what," he said with great exasperation.

"Exactly! Now you're getting it."

But Sidney wasn't getting it at all. When he got angry, his back began to stiffen, and when his back stiffened he couldn't think straight. "I can't work without a fax machine," he mumbled.

"Exactly!" Clark laughed. "That's why I'm getting us a third one."

They needed a larger space. After all, the fundamentals for growth were good, despite all the firm had gone through. This was an information economy, and they were in the information business. They sold predictions for the direction of money, and they sold financial instruments designed to take advantage of that direction. There would always be money, and as long as there were markets, money would always have a direction, and a speed, and an acceleration, all of which could be sold. And as long as Atlantic Pacific was selling money, it would burn through stationery and fax machines and employees at an alarming rate, all of which would need wise management. Some of the systems Atlantic Pacific had established to handle the volume of business would break down, such as its self-insured health system or its interdepartment mail system. So sure was Clark Kalinov that the interdepartment mail system would break down that he set out to prove it to facilities in New York. All mail was supposed to get anywhere in the world in two days. Every afternoon, Clark ordered prospectuses and trading reports and closing prices from research departments in New York for each of the salespersons, and every two days later, twelve canvas sacks of Intermail were delivered to the copy room for sorting. Ricky, the simpleminded doughboy of a mail clerk who previously had spent most of his afternoons snacking on Fritos he had stolen from the vending machine in the kitchen, now found himself struggling to enforce corporate policy of two-day Intermail. When he got tired he suffered more paper cuts, which stung horribly and didn't stop bleeding and hurt even worse when the salt from the Fritos got into the wounds. Eventually, Ricky strained the sacroiliac joint in his butt when he tried throwing a canvas sack of Intermail across the room at Clark. Then the self-insured health system broke down too, because sacroiliac stress is difficult to relieve, particularly in the overweight. Intermail took three or four days to reach the salespersons' desks, and by that time it was out of date and entirely worthless.

When the entire forty-second floor upstairs was vacated by an insurance company that moved to Stockton, Clark Kalinov's requests were finally granted. The firm decided that the vast, ethereal, lofty forty-second floor would be a whole lot more impressive than the squat, cramped, tarnished forty-first floor. Clark ordered more mahogany entranceway paneling, fourteen thousand square feet of low-static corporate-blue carpeting, and brass railings for the ramps down to the sales floor, which had forty mahogany-inlaid four-foot-high cubicle/desks organized into platoons for the mortgages, money markets, municipals, and equities departments. Clark had his own office with his own squawk box and his own computer monitors and his own incandescent rose-tinted lighting system and his own window, which had a forty-two-story view of the wall of fog that surrounded the building. Then, because the walls of the sales floor looked barren, he ordered eight identical clocks showing the time in the Atlantic Pacific offices around the world and a twenty-foot-long LED ticker tape that rushed stock quotes by at a manic pace only manic salesmen could read. Coyote Jack, the sales manager, had his own fishbowl office looking out over the sales floor. Managing director John White, who split his time between their office and New York, had an even bigger window office with two couches and a coffee table. It was horribly expensive, but not a single person complained because life on the forty-second floor was the luxury they had always felt entitled to. The doors were wired with a magnetic card-key security system. The kitchen had a microwave, a vending machine full of candy bars, and a refrigerator. The briefing room, where they gathered in the mornings to hear about new bond issues, had a tele-video screen that visually connected them to a similar conference room in midtown Manhattan. The only remaining resemblance to the insurance company that moved to Stockton was the employees, who spent their days faxing and calling and wondering if the future would be any different.

"Will there ever be a time I don't have to work so hard?" Sid Geeder wondered under his breath as he ate around the cream-cheese center of his danish and listened to someone in New York describe the sales mission for the new Resolution Trust Corp. finance package. On the conference table in New York were danishes with strawberry-jam centers, and Sid Geeder kept wanting to reach into the video screen and grab one. He hated cream cheese, especially the yellowy half-melted type in two-day-old danishes; they reminded him of sales mission briefings, which reminded him of having to sell whatever they'd been briefed on, which reminded him of how hard he'd had to work to meet his quota.

"Not if Coyote Jack keeps volunteering us for huge quotas," whispered Eggs Igino, who'd heard Sid Geeder's rhetorical question. He licked his lips and chuckled.

Sid Geeder turned to his left. That new kid Igino was eating a danish with a strawberry center, and a small bit of jam was stuck to his cheek. Sid was dumbfounded.

"Where'd you get that?"

"What?"

"That strawberry danish."

Igino pushed the rest of the danish into his mouth and tried to speak with a full mouth, but Sid Geeder couldn't understand a word.

"What?" Sid said. "I couldn't hear you."

"I said, 'I try not to speak when my mouth is full.' It's bad manners." It had been a very large danish, and Eggs Igino was still chewing.

"But we've never had *any* strawberry danishes here before. Never. Did you get here early?"

"I was the last one here. You're always the first one, Sid, because you work so hard."

Coyote Jack interrupted them. "Shut up, Geeder. Shut up, Igino. Pay attention."

But Sid Geeder couldn't pay any attention at all to the Resolution Trust Corp.'s preposterous intention to borrow a gazillion dollars in order to shut down some thrifts. He kept thinking about the strawberry danish he'd seen the kid eat, and he kept staring at the dab of red gel on the kid's cheek. After the briefing they marched back out onto the sales floor and hunkered down over their desks and settled in for the day's work. The new kid had Wes Griffin's old desk, which was right next to Sid's. Over the squawk box came opening prices on bonds that reflected overnight activity in Tokyo and London. Sid set his broker screens to the mortgage markets and set his trading monitor to the treasury market and set his audio channel to the currency markets. The next move could come from anywhere. It was just before five o'clock in the morning. In a few minutes, the banks of phone panels would light up red.

"So, kid. What's the word of the day?"

"The word?" Eggs Igino repeated.

"You know, *the word*. The news. The story. You gotta have something to say when those phones light up red."

The kid was trying to raise the seat on Wes Griffin's chair. It was only his third day of work, and the first two days he had complained about his hamstrings tightening up from sitting eleven hours straight. All Sid knew about the kid was that he had been a soccer player in college. Sid Geeder had only laughed, because the hamstrings were just the beginning. The kid had a lot to learn. For instance, he had to learn that he would spend the next fifty years of his life sitting all day long. He had to learn to suffer, and he had to learn to live with that suffering. And that was just the beginning.

"Screw it," Igino said.

"Screw you, then," Geeder snapped back.

"Not you. The chair. Screw the chair." Igino pushed the chair on its little plastic wheels back toward the window.

Sid Geeder smirked. "Tell me about the danish."

"You mean where I got it?"

"Sure."

"What will you give me for it?"

"For what?"

Now Igino laughed. Eggs Igino was a quirky, jovial smart aleck with bad taste in ties. He was too young to have suffered, and he was too intelligent to be corrupted. He had a freckled face and an athlete's casual slouch and globular, walnut-sized, muscular jowls that stirred as he spoke. "For the information. The information about the danish. I just can't give that to you for free. It's valuable information that I could sell for a lot of money."

"Just tell me, kid. I'm dying to know."

"Then you ought to be willing to pay for it."

"All right, then. Two dollars."

Igino snorted and chuckled. "Two lousy dollars? Are you kidding?"

"But that's about what a danish costs."

"But I can get them for free. You could too, if you had the information. You could get a strawberry danish every time we had a briefing on a new sales mission. You and I could be eating strawberry danishes while everyone else chews around the center of their half-melted cream-cheese danishes. You could drive everyone crazy, even Coyote Jack, and suddenly those quotas wouldn't be so imposing." Igino leaned his hip up against his desk and stretched his calf muscle out behind him. "You would be in control."

Sid Geeder considered that scenario. For four years he'd been briefed on sales missions and been given quotas that he worked so hard to meet. And every time he met his quota, Coyote Jack raised the quota the next time, so Sid had to work even harder. All he'd ever done was do what he was told, and none of it had ever gotten easier. Even though he was known as the King of Mortgages, he'd never felt in control. It seemed impossible that a little berry-flavored red glycerin could change that vicious cycle. But the kid was a heck of a salesman—Sid could tell that already. Anybody who could make you believe a little red jelly would change your life was going to go a long way in this business.

"Naw," Sid said.

"Fine. Then I'll tell Nickel Sansome and he can drive you crazy."

"I'm already crazy."

"Think about it," Igino said.

"All right! Ten dollars."

"I don't want your money." Again Igino scoffed at Geeder's offer.

"Then what *do* you want?"

"Information. *Quid pro quo.* Tell me something I don't already know."

"Like what? Like gossip, or more like tricks of the trade?"

"Either."

Sid considered what he could say. There was so much and yet there was so little. He could warn the kid about how Coyote Jack would probably grill him this afternoon for talking aloud during the mission briefing. He could warn the kid to never go see the self-insurance company shrink, Helmet Fisher, as Wes Griffin had done, and instead to always go see the company doctor, Ivana Perkova, whose gentle, pearly fingers always made you feel better even if they couldn't cure your problems. He could detail the absurdity of the Resolution Trust system. Or he could scare the kid by telling him how Paine Webber had laid off its entire mortgage department and on Coyote Jack's desk were stacked hundreds of résumés, all wanting the kid's job. In a moment, the phones would start ringing, and they wouldn't stop for eleven hours.

"I'll tell you what," Eggs Igino said. "I'll tell you about the danishes if you let me patch in to your sales calls today. Let me hear how you work your clients."

"How about I give you some advice: a salesman never lets anyone listen in on his calls. Our mouths are all we've got."

"Just one day."

"No chance, kiddo. The only thing that separates me from the other morons on this floor is my technique. If I let you in on it, how do I know you won't share it with Nickel Sansome tomorrow?"

Eggs Igino wound his fingers through his phone cord. "How do I know that if I tell you where I get my danishes you won't go tell Lisa Lisa?"

"You don't," Sid answered meanly.

"You can trust me."

That made Sid laugh with foolish delight. The phones started ringing. Sid turned his back and went to work, making a first round of calls to his top accounts, briefing them on overnight trading and reading off opening prices in the mortgage markets, giving commentary on each price—noting the spread between coupons, what looked rich or poor, what might be under buying pressure. It was these subtleties that made Sidney Geeder the King of Mortgages—anyone could read off opening prices or repeat the short commentary the traders gave out to influence the market, but only Sid Geeder had his own opinions on each of the various mortgage products.

Eggs Igino, who on his third day still hadn't been given any accounts of his own to call, had nothing better to do than to listen to everything Sid was saying and try to jot a bit of it down. He wasn't accustomed to being awake at five in the morning, and his throat was so dry that a small line of white paste caked his lips. He reached into his file cabinet and removed a crumpled grocery bag full of strawberry danishes. He nibbled his way through danish after danish, causing crumbs of hardened sugar to coat his desktop and float unmercifully into Sidney's lap. Sidney couldn't help but get a jealous ache in his stomach and in the split second between calls dab at the crumbs of sugar with his fingers and pop them onto his tongue. He saw Eggs Igino listening in, so he sat backward on his chair, facing out toward the huge window behind them.

Still, Eggs Igino could hear everything, because Sid had to yell into his mouthpiece to overcome the noise on the floor. Eggs heard how Sid made a second round of calls, going over the numbers that would be announced that week—the quarterly trade deficit, the Year bill auction, the consumer confidence index, the 11th district Cost of Funds. He reminded them that it was the third of the month—the Fed would be loaning in the market that afternoon to compensate for the drain of thirty million Social Security checks being cashed that day at banks around the country. His mouth never stopped moving, and at least one line was on hold at all times.

"All right, just give me a fucking danish," Sid spat. "You've been listening in to my calls anyway."

"No I'm not," Eggs said innocently. "I'm just standing here trying not to look foolish. If you gave me an account to call on, then I'd be on the phone and I couldn't hear anything you were saying."

"*Give you an account?* Now you've really gone over the deep end!" Sid picked up his phones again. As he talked, his voice changed, became softer. His shoulders rounded out, and he leaned back in his chair, propping his feet on his trash can. He rolled his shirtsleeves up to the forearms. Then he dropped the news. "Well, it looks like our buddies at the old RTC have been working harder than we expected. It seems they've already managed to spend all that money you loaned them nine months ago. At this rate, the savings and loan crisis will be over before we know it and we can all go back to owning T-notes."

"Oh, yeah, I heard you guys were coming out with another offering," the trust manager at World Savings sighed.

Sid bolted upright in his chair. "You heard it already! It's *our* deal. How in the hell did you hear about it?"

"From Goldman," the trust manager brooded quietly. "They

said the only reason you got this deal over them was you agreed to price it rich."

Sid couldn't believe Goldman was maligning their deal. "Yeah, well, they lost the deal," Sid argued quickly. "They're bad sports. Of course they're going to dis it now."

"Well, they say the bonds stink."

"Don't be ridiculous. Do you think the Office of Thrift Supervision would have given us this deal if we were pricing it unrealistically?" Sid countered. He hadn't heard anything yet about the pricing—he was just arguing without the facts.

"Don't get mad at me. I'm just telling you what they said."

"All right," Sid agreed. "But for god's sakes, just don't jump to any conclusions. Try the deal on for size for a while." He jumped off the line and punched the button to another of his accounts.

"You talk to Goldman this morning?" Sid asked bluntly.

"We talk to them every morning."

"They say anything about our Resolution deal?"

"Not much. The usual."

"What the fuck'd they say?"

"They stink. But hey—these deals always stink. The only reason we buy them is because they're our regulators. We *have* to buy them."

Sid put down his phone in a rage and kicked at his trash can.

"What's wrong?" Eggs Igino asked him.

"Wouldn't you like to know?" he retorted angrily.

"What the hell's the matter with you!" Coyote Jack screamed when Sidney Geeder burst into his office and started pacing back and forth.

"What the hell's the matter with *you*," Sid shot back. "How come Goldman knows about our pricing on the RTC deal before I do? You would think a sales manager would let his salesforce be prepared to defend a rich pricing."

"Whoa, hold on there. Calm down, Geeder. Do you think the Office of Thrift Supervision would have awarded us this deal if we were going to price it unrealistically?"

"That doesn't work with me," Sid said. "Don't you get it? If Goldman is telling the market that the deal stinks, then they're obviously not going to be part of the syndicate. And if the syndicate is weak, then we're in deep shit. The market has had about all the Resolution Trust bonds it can take. Fuck!" He swung his arms at the air in frustration. He was too old for this bullshit.

Coyote Jack played it calm. He rolled a corporate-blue ballpoint pen in his fingers. "Relax, Sid. Your accounts *have* to buy these bonds. The RTC is their regulating body."

"But nobody says how much they have to buy. There's a big difference between twenty million and two. Now I want you to fill me in on the pricing strategy or I tell my accounts to skip this deal. I've got my reputation to protect."

"All in due time," Coyote Jack yawned.

"Damnit!" Sid hollered so loudly that out on the sales floor all heads turned toward the glass window of Coyote Jack's office.

"If I tell you," Coyote Jack explained casually, "then all you're going to do is complain. I've got enough to worry about already with this deal priced so rich and Goldman dropping from the syndicate. The last thing I need is you throwing tantrums."

"Fine," Sid agreed. "I'll go tell my accounts to skip this deal."

Coyote Jack reached out and patted the stack of résumés on the corner of his desk. "You tell them that and I'll have you out of here so fast . . ."

Sid headed for the door.

Coyote Jack cut him off. "Tell that kid Igino to get in here. I've got to terrorize him for talking during the morning meeting."

2 · Numbers

THE NUMBERS TOLD the story. It was a business that came down to numbers, as all businesses do, and each of the salespersons had his or her own favorite numbers to watch. Paul "Goody" De-Shews, a short-term money market salesman who had managed to retain his faith in the aristocratic worthiness of their profession, liked to watch the interest rates on Japanese banker's acceptances because he believed the Japanese controlled most of the discretionary world income. Regis Reed, who came in to work fifteen minutes early every morning to shave in the bathroom, tracked the rate spread between mortgages and treasuries, an indicator of market confidence and market worry. Eggs Igino, who had never taken an afternoon class during college or graduate school, watched the eight clocks on the wall for three o'clock PST, at which point he left the building to get some sunshine regardless of unfinished business or Coyote Jack's glares.

Nickel Sansome's number was $20 million, which was the quota of Resolution Trust bonds Coyote Jack had given him. Nickel was a sad, balding preppie without a single chip on his shoulder or an ax to grind who couldn't sell umbrellas in a rainstorm. Since the morning briefing, Nickel Sansome had not been able to think about anything except the twenty million gullible dollars he was supposed to find out there in a market full of worry and caution. Nickel calculated how much commission he would earn if he could somehow manage to find so much gullible money, and for a moment his life looked brighter. So he switched numbers. Now his number was the amount of commission he would earn, and he thought about how good it would sound to call his father and say, "Father, I'm rich!" even though Nickel would never really say that because his father was already far richer than Nickel could even hope to be. Nickel's father had just established an emeritus chair at the graduate business school Nickel had graduated from. The family money had put Nickel at a great disadvantage in the market, because Nickel wasn't greedy for money. He already knew money had solved nothing for his father or any of his father's three wives or any of Nickel's two older brothers. Without greed, the only thing to drive him was fear: fear of failure, fear of poverty, fear of disappointing. Nickel was not very confident that fear alone could find $20 million in his hodgepodge of small thrifts, regional banks, county treasurers, and utility companies. Nickel knew that if he'd been poor, he'd be rich by now.

Lisa Lisa's number was thirty, which was the age she was going to become in November. Her other, equally important number was the seven digits of her new boyfriend's home telephone. Lisa Lisa had been hoping that these two numbers might somehow merge: that, as one fantasy went, she might be married before March, or maybe engaged, or at least sharing the same home phone number. She wrote out his seven digits in her trading notebook and wished that they were hers. Sid Geeder watched her do this and laughed. She had a lot to learn.

Sid Geeder's number was 1,127, which was the number of days he'd worked for Atlantic Pacific since he'd first arrived in 1989. He kept a hash-mark tally on the unfinished mahogany well of his desk drawer. Every afternoon he opened his drawer and while pretending to look for something among his trading notes, he scratched another mark in the wood with a paper clip. On Fridays he scratched diagonally, knocking off another week. It was his one act of industrial sabotage, his only revenge upon the company that made him rich and miserable, and he didn't let anyone know about it, not even his ambitious sales assistant, Jackie, who had shiny brunette hair to her waist and a round bunny nose and rail-thin, butter-smooth, honey-colored legs that Sidney Geeder could often not peel his eyes from.

Sidney Geeder's sales assistant was so beautiful that people frequently had the urge to confess to her just to get her attention. If she wasn't so ambitious Sid might have been lured into giving her exactly what she wanted, which was the secrets to his trade. She had learned to brief his accounts on overnight trading, and then she had learned to run down the weekly numbers. Always in the name of helping him, but he knew she was stealing from him. She was stealing his sales pitches and his know-how and his unconventional wisdom. When Sidney caught on, he restationed her across the floor and stopped giving her work. As a consequence she was taken advantage of by the other salespeople, few of whom had sales assistants of their own. They kissed up to her, asking her how Sid had sold the Euro-Floaters or Freddie Mac Adjustables. Jackie was a liberal-minded girl who rode the express bus in the mornings and reread Kundera and Nietzsche on her lunch hour. Always eager to please, she did whatever was asked of her, including go out to lunch with Nickel Sansome at the Ming Garden on his corporate expense account.

"You better not have charged the firm for that lunch," Sidney warned Nickel when the two came strolling back on the floor in the late afternoon, yawning and patting their stomachs.

"What do you care?" Nickel said defensively.

Sid Geeder hated waste on principle, and he felt that if the sales-force just stopped padding its expense accounts he wouldn't be trying to sell those damn Resolutions above market. "Let me see your credit card receipts," Sid demanded.

"I paid in cash," Nickel answered.

"Like hell you did. I'm on to you, Sansome. You feed her a fancy meal, give her a glass of wine, and then start asking how I'm prep-ping my accounts on the Resolutions."

"I didn't tell him anything," Jackie protested when Sid cornered her later that day. "How could I tell him anything when you don't give me a chance to help you? I could make your life a lot easier."

"I don't need any help."

"I could be running numbers on the Resolutions for you."

"For me and for who else?"

The numbers on the Resolution Trust offering totaled $145 bil-lion, which was to help shut down a few dozen bankrupt savings and loans. All of the unpayable debt was being moved off the bal-ance sheets of the government-insured thrifts and into the fine-print footnotes of the government-backed Resolution Trust. It was a perfectly legal accounting transaction that would make the S&Ls' embarrassing $145 billion loss disappear from the public eye, and though the government had done nothing yet to figure out how it was going to pay back the bonds, it did discover that the Federal Reserve could print enough money to pay the interest until it was all figured out. The bonds didn't come due for thirty years, and everyone had confidence that by the year 2024 the United States government would be such a bloated, gargantuan scarfing pig that it'd never notice this little $145 billion invoice. That would be loose change in 2024. It would be nothing compared to the radioactive-uranium storage barrels, which were scheduled to be dug out of the Utah desert in 2020 and atomically defused. It would seem like small potatoes compared to the cost of cleaning up all our rivers and lakes, which private industry had polluted for 110 years before the government stepped in and told them that what they were doing was perfectly legal. Heck, the S&Ls had only five or six years to pollute the financial system before the government stepped in and told them that it would bail out all their losses. But still, $145 billion was such a gargantuan, monstrous, scandalous sum that the salespeople couldn't take it seriously and joked about how the RTC ate money like Godzilla ate Tokyo.

"They're asking for a gillion zillions," Lisa Lisa explained to Honolulu Federal.

"A jillion trillions," surmised Regis Reed.

"A dillion fillions," Nickel Sansome piped in proudly.

"There's no such thing as a dillion," Regis Reed shot back. "Or a fillion."

"Oh yes there is," Nickel blathered, "A dillion is a thousand fillions."

"Then what's a fillion?" Reed quizzed him.

"A thousand magillions."

"Magillions! Christ, Sansome, you're an idiot."

"What does it matter?" Nickel wondered rhetorically. "All that matters is that I have to sell twenty million or Coyote Jack will give my job to one of those geeks from Paine Webber."

"Twenty million! Is that all?" Regis Reed sneered disgustedly. "I could do twenty million in my sleep."

"What's your quota?" Nickel asked him, suddenly somber.

"Twenty-five."

Nickel paused and glanced around, then bent over and whispered in Reed's direction, "I hear that in Los Angeles, nobody has a quota more than fifteen."

"Fifteen! My grandma could sell fifteen. She could sell fifteen in her sleep! What gives?"

"It's Coyote Jack," Nickel suggested. "He must be up for a promotion or something again."

"Oh, man," Regis Reed said with angst, slouching his shoulders. "My life was going along just fine until this damn Resolution Trust deal. I'll never be able to do twenty-five million," he admitted. "Fucking Coyote. The numbers don't mean anything anymore to him. He doesn't care. As soon as it looks like I might make twenty, he raises me to twenty-five."

Coyote Jack had lost his numbers entirely. Back in the old days, four or five years previously, Coyote Jack had been the King of

Mortgages. This was before Sid Geeder, and even before Wes Griffin. Mortgage bonds were brand-new and nobody understood them, so they were easy to sell, because no client wanted to admit he lacked the intellectual brainpower to understand these complex, variable cash flows. Coyote Jack threw numbers around to make it sound as if he understood the bonds, but he really had no idea either. One day he began to stutter, but just on his numbers. All the other lies came out fine. Panicking, he took a vacation alone to Hawaii, but even there he had trouble saying aloud the temperature and his golf score and his hotel room and the Sun Protection Factor of his sunscreen. He continued to go to hell. He was relegated to the driving range, where he bashed drives "out past that sign out there," because he couldn't say "220." He couldn't order room service, because it required him to state his room number. Coyote Jack was a fat man with a thin skin. He didn't know what to do. He swam in the evenings when the air was cool and he drank dark rum out of coconuts in the hotel bar until it closed and then he went up to his room with a woman from Cleveland. Coyote Jack was a devout Catholic who for the first time in fifteen years made a prayer to God. He knelt on the shag rug of his bathroom and bowed his head. "Please, please, God," he said. "Numbers are the way of the future. I'll die without them. I'll never be able to work again." Coyote Jack was drunk and he began to wonder if maybe God controlled words while numbers were in the domain of the Devil. "Please, please, Devil. I'll never be able to do your dirty work without them." Then he went out into his bedroom and continued to explain to the woman from Cleveland (who he didn't believe for one moment was from Cleveland) that he was an aerospace engineer from Pasadena working on solar-powered cars for General Motors. When he returned to the sales floor the next Monday, Coyote Jack was afraid. He was afraid of failure, and afraid of poverty, and afraid of embarrassment. They had a morning briefing and then hunkered down over their desks and waited for the phones to ring. Coyote Jack's shirt was already pitted out. His elastic suspenders were yanking his trousers up into his balls. There was a hammering in his ears and his eyes were watering and he couldn't control any of it. Then John White, who back then was the sales manager, came out on the sales floor and asked Coyote

Jack into his office. *This is it,* Coyote Jack thought, as John White's secretary poured him a cup of coffee. John White didn't waste any time. "You're being promoted to sales manager, Coyote. Nobody did any work when you were gone. You're way too valuable to us to be playing such an important role. I'm going to be splitting my time here and New York. That new kid Geeder will take your accounts. Kick Kalinov out of his office and put him in a cubicle off the copy room. You'll get a free parking spot in the garage. And for chrissake, get some decent suspenders and some nice cuff links and shirts with French cuffs. You dress like a goddamn salesman."

Coyote Jack couldn't believe it.

"It's true," Eggs Igino protested. "I know I was talking during the briefing. But all I said to him was that I couldn't talk because my mouth was full."

Coyote Jack continued to grill the kid. "But you *would* have talked if your mouth hadn't been full."

"Not exactly, sir. I put the danish in my mouth so that I couldn't talk. I used the danish to avoid talking aloud during the briefing. It was the only way not to be rude to Geeder, who had just asked me a question and expected an answer."

"And what did he ask you?"

"He asked me if I thought it was rude that he was speaking aloud during the meeting. It was clearly some ploy to get me to speak out and get in trouble."

"So you're blaming Geeder, huh. And how long have you worked here?"

"Three days."

"Sid Geeder is the King of Mortgages. The King. He could sell sand to the Arabs."

"I'm aware of that, sir. I don't think his ploy was malicious. It was educational. I have a lot to learn from Sidney. Today was just the beginning."

Coyote Jack stared at the kid. He had a bright ruddy aura about him that Coyote Jack was jealous of and wanted to squelch. The kid sat with his arm over the back of the couch and one leg kicked over the other like he was having a good time. There wasn't even a mist of perspiration on his brow. He had huge jowls that would never wear out from talking all day. And in ten minutes the kid hadn't given a single straight answer. He was clearly going to be a great salesman and upset the balance of power. Low heart rate under pressure, honest-looking, a quick mind comfortable with contradiction. Good god, Coyote Jack almost *believed* that the kid hadn't been talking during the briefing. Maybe the kid was ready for a quota on the RTCs. Coyote Jack needed somebody to back up Sansome. Sansome wasn't greedy enough to sell bonds so overpriced.

"You were down in Mexico for a while, weren't you, Igino? Zihuatanejo, right? Where is that?"

"If you're looking for a vacation spot, there's other places that are more your style."

"Naw, I'm just making conversation. Why'd you go down there, anyway?"

Eggs Igino looked away. "It has a quiet bay and a steady gentle wind. Good for windsurfing beginners."

"Uh huh. I mean, I'm not prying—don't get me wrong. I just like to know who's working for me. I mean, why just go to Mexico?"

"Well, it's pretty clear that Spanish is going to be an important job skill in the borderless future."

Coyote Jack could tell the kid wasn't going to cough up the truth. "What's your father do for a living, Igino? He a lawyer or something?"

"He's in the seafood business."

"He own a restaurant?"

"Not exactly. He's a shift manager at a clam chowder canning plant."

"Wow." The kid had been lucky enough to have grown up poor. Probably been mowing lawns since the third grade. "What d'you think of those Resolution Trust bonds, Igino?"

"What do you mean, sir?"

"What do you *think* of them? Are they a good buy?"

"They'll add yield to a stable portfolio. They'll add stability to a high-yield portfolio."

"In other words, they're a piece of shit."

"I didn't say that, sir."

"Don't you think they're a little overpriced?"

Eggs Igino couldn't tell if Coyote Jack wanted him to be honest.

"They're backed by the full faith and credit of the U.S. government. The price seems fair."

"Of course they're overpriced, Igino. They're always overpriced. The only reason we got this deal over Merrill and Goldman is we agreed to force our customers to buy them at an inflated price. Don't you agree?"

Eggs Igino shook his head. "Everything is overpriced these days. Compared to everything else, these bonds look pretty good." He knew Coyote Jack was just testing him. Of course the bonds were a piece of shit; otherwise the firm wouldn't be working so hard to sell them and wouldn't be offering such a high commission. But he also knew that he was never to admit this out loud, unless he felt like being fired or wanted his pay docked. If a salesperson ever admitted it out loud, he might accidentally admit it to a customer. It was better to talk in circles than to talk straight, just as it was better to sound sensible than to be sensible. It was an insensible undertaking to try to make sense of the savings and loan bailout. Better to use a deep, calm, confident voice, and to quote well-respected economists, and to pretend the market was not already swamped with debt. And when the words start to fail, switch to numbers. It was no coincidence to Eggs Igino that a great deal of cheating occurred in a business based on numbers, because even in the post-Newtonian age people *still* had the foolish, completely innocent notion that numbers do not lie and could therefore be trusted.

That was the opinion of Paul DeShews. "They can't lie," he quibbled, when he overheard Sid Geeder complaining to a customer about the reliability of the performance forecasts on the Resolutions. "They're *numbers*. They're raw data. Facts, ground zero—they're gospel." It was vital to Paul DeShews that he live a moral, honest life, and he had grown up believing that business, which always came down to numbers, was a respectable, proper career for a man.

"Hogwash!" Sid Geeder spat back, holding down the mute button on his phone. "I didn't know the Boy Scouts were visiting us today."

Paul DeShews stood his ground. "Don't tell me you have it in for the Boy Scouts, too." Paul was a scout leader who took his boys car-camping in the Sierras on weekends. "You're so negative, Geeder. You have it in for everybody, don't you?"

"Those brainwashed ducklings in poplin culottes and scarves? No, I don't have anything against them."

"Those aren't *scarves*. They're neckties."

"They're scarves."

"Neckties!"

"Culottes!"

Paul DeShews scrunched his face and plugged both ears with his fingertips and rocked back and forth. "Stop it! Stop it! You *never* make any sense, Geeder. What do Boy Scouts have to do with numbers? . . . Nothing. They have nothing to do with numbers."

Geeder waved his arms and stomped up and down to frighten DeShews. "Oh yes they do. They have very much in common. Believing in them requires a callow, naive, boneheaded faith in the government that compiles and publishes those numbers."

DeShews bit down on his teeth and winced in disgust. "I knew you had it in for the government. I *knew* it."

"Those conniving, myopic barrel-rollers in thousand-dollar Italian suits and lizard-skin shoes? No, I don't have it in for them."

"Arrrgghh!" DeShews blew out steam and forced himself to walk away, to turn the cheek. Geeder had been made a rich man and had his government to thank, but Geeder didn't have a thankful bone in his muscly, squat body. Guys like him were ruining the profession.

Geeder just laughed. He enjoyed making DeShews squirm. Paul DeShews was the closest thing to having an actual congressman in the office to use as a punching bag. Geeder really did wish he had a congressman in the office to yell at—because there were all sorts of things to yell about. Letter writing wasn't good enough—it was too quiet, too passive. So instead Geeder worked to overthrow the government by sellings its bonds to whoever didn't want to buy them. He pretended to be the most loyal foot soldier in the military, consistently raising money to be spent on Ostrich helicopters and Stealth bombers and other things that couldn't fly. He was also the most loyal social worker in the safety-net welfare system, consistently raising money to be spent on farming credits, Social Security, residential housing projects, and other giveaways that weakened society. The Resolution Trust bonds were a perfect example: he was helping to undermine the government by giving it the money to make a fool of itself. He hoped that if he helped build the government into a bloated, gobbling, scarfing pig, one day it would topple under its own weight. It was the only way he could enjoy his job.

But Eggs Igino liked his job. He knew he wasn't supposed to like it. He knew it was supposed to be hell. But everything the others hated, Eggs Igino enjoyed. He enjoyed the malleability of numbers. He enjoyed the sounds, the shouting and the ringing. He enjoyed the hubbub of grown men and women zipping about, carrying reports to the fax machines and spreadsheets back from the laser printer. Eggs Igino even liked waking up at 3:45 A.M. each morning, when the rest of the world was still asleep. It made him feel less like just another gray suit, and it didn't make sense to waste the sunlight hours indoors anyways. He knew Coyote Jack was ruthless and rotten and never lifted a finger if there wasn't something in it for him, but—crazy as it was—Eggs Igino got a kick out of Coyote Jack. Coyote Jack was funny. He was hilarious, prowling the aisles of the sales floor with his eyes roving side to side, pushing those Resolution Trusts. And Sid Geeder! Wound up like a knot, sprung tight like a toy. Eggs Igino had to fight the urge to laugh whenever Sid stomped across the floor with the tail of his shirt hanging down to his thighs.

With the tail of his shirt hanging out, Sid Geeder stomped across the sales floor to give his assistant a list of research reports to pull for his accounts. But his assistant was nowhere to be seen, and just then his phone lit up red. Sid sat down at her desk and answered it. As he started to brief the caller on the advantages of adjustable-rate mortgages, he reached into her desk for a pen to take notes. To his surprise, he found a stack of forged Atlantic Pacific business cards, falsely stating her position as "Sales Associate."

"I'm sorry, Sid," she pleaded when she got his note to come see her. His note was scribbled on the back of one of the business cards and had been stuck with saliva to her Quotron monitor. "They're just for my family and friends."

"You're fired!" he yelled. "You're a thief."

"What are you talking about? I haven't stolen anything," she protested. "I've never touched your stuff."

"My *stuff*? What do you mean, my *stuff*? My stuff is worthless. Everything except this Cross pen is absolutely valueless. Or maybe you want to take it, too?" He pushed the Cross pen into her hands.

"Sid, you're not making any sense. It's been a long day."

"Of course I'm not making any sense! If I made sense, then you would understand the situation. And if you understood it, then you could steal that understanding!"

"Sid, please!"

"Don't you get it? The market is chaotic. I make some sense of the chaos. That's how I earn my living. And you *can't have it anymore*. Go make your own sense of the world!"

"But—" she cried.

"I said, 'You're fired.' I'm leaving now, and I don't want anything on your desk when I come back in the morning. Leave your magnetic card-key and NASDAQ pass on your chair." He didn't say anything more. He grabbed his empty briefcase from under his desk and pulled his suit coat out of the closet and limped out the back door to the elevator, where he descended to the parking garage. His ears popped. His back was suddenly killing him. Sid Geeder was a burly fireplug of a man who had wrestled in college and had never been suited to the physical demands of the modern economy. Whenever he used the clutch with his left foot, his right leg went momentarily numb and he had a tingling sensation in his thumbs. The downtown traffic required him to hold down the clutch constantly. He couldn't stand it.

"It feels like a small fire has been lit at the base of my vertebrae," he said to Ivana Perkova, to whom he had driven right away for an examination. Her office was on the ground floor of an old apartment building. Large-paned windows looked out on a fern garden. She had a padded leather orthopedic bench in a convex crescent-moon shape that Sid loved to lie face down on. The blood pooled in his face and feet. His spinal column unknotted. "It could be the sacroiliac, I think."

"I see," she said, gently setting her hand down on Sid's lumbar region.

As Sid let out a deep, worried sigh, Dr. Perkova applied pressure. She was a young second-generation Romanian with wiry brown hair who'd studied orthopedics and Rolfing and had a natural gift for laying on of hands. She had a dream of returning to her family's old village in Transylvania to deliver babies, set broken bones, and milk cows. Her voice was hoarse but kind. She wore stretch pants under her smock, which he would sometimes entice her into removing after her aides had gone home for the night.

"I don't think it's your sacroiliac, Sidney. Your symptoms aren't localized."

"Then maybe L-four/L-five."

"I don't think it's that, either. Here, squeeze my fingers with each hand."

Sid took her fingers in his hands and squeezed. Her fingers were long and smooth, the nails rounded and polished. He didn't want to hurt them, but he didn't want to let go either.

"Does that make you feel any better?" she asked.

"Significantly," Sid said.

"Sidney, there's no anatomical reason your back should feel better when you squeeze my fingers. Your symptoms are clearly stress-related. You really ought to be seeing Helmet Fisher."

"Helmet Fisher? The shrink? I'd have to be crazy to go see him."

"He's not just for raving lunatics. He could help you relax."

Sid gagged at the thought. "Help me? Like he helped Wes Griffin?"

"What happened to Wes?"

"Wes is gone."

"Gone?"

Sid explained. "He went to see Helmet Fisher. Started talking about breathing exercises and self-guided visualization. Then just didn't show up for work one day."

Dr. Perkova circled around to the other side and began to work Sidney's shoulders. "Maybe he's happier."

"Happier? Wes was only six months away from cashing out his corporate shares. Six more months and he could have doubled his net worth."

"Big deal. He has plenty of money. You *all* have plenty of money."

"It's not the money, it's the victory. Wes was a foot soldier. He was in the trenches every day at four-thirty in the morning, five days a week. He was loyal to his firm and to his country. He was going to walk out with his head high. Then they got him."

"Who's 'they'?"

"They *wanted* him to go see Helmet Fisher. They didn't want to give him those shares. What other company in their right mind would pay for psychiatric care? He's even more expensive than you are."

"Sidney, who's '*they*'?"

"I don't know!" Sid closed his eyes and breathed in the leather smell from the couch. He didn't want to be taught to inhale from his gut, and he didn't want to guide himself on a walking tour of a mountain meadow. He wasn't going to let anyone inside his head. Everything he owned was in there. Everything that had made him happy, and everything that had made him successful. Four years of market data were in there. His sense of humor was in there. His dreams and his fantasies, many of which involved Dr. Perkova. His sense of judgment. All of his elementary school, middle school, high school, college, and business school education was in there. They were all in there. He would have to be crazy to let a shrink on the firm's payroll inside his head. The company had already stolen so much. They'd stolen his sales pitches and trading analyses. They'd stolen his poise. They'd stolen his trust in mankind, and they couldn't give it back. It was like believing in Santa Claus. It was like virginity. It was a one-way street.

Lisa Lisa stood in the street, waiting for her boyfriend to drive up in his Jaguar and whisk her away from a world that rewarded her for thinking like a man and punished her for acting like a woman. After work, she'd gone into the rest room and removed her blouse under her suit coat. She'd left her briefcase under her desk and moved her valuables into a black patent-leather handbag that she now clutched to her side with her elbow. Her boyfriend's name was Gary or Peter or David—it didn't matter to her story: he would leave her before she had a chance to get used to him. He would leave her because he too had some important downtown white-collar job and he needed an escape. He needed a woman who looked upon the skyscraper world with awe and respect, who thought he was a bigshot-to-be. He needed someone with soft edges and round curves and elegant skin. He needed someone with high-society contacts from a blue-collar background with a graduate degree in humanities and the sexual frankness of a common whore. Lisa Lisa could never compete with the nonexistent women these men were waiting for, even though she had a graduate degree from Carnegie Mellon University and walked about the sales floor flashing her cleavage and thighs like a common whore. Lisa Lisa's fundamental weakness was that she was strong. She could yell on the phone and drag herself out of bed at 4:00 A.M. and make men masturbate with her in mind. She could run four miles in twenty-three minutes and hail a taxi and down a martini without wincing. Lisa Lisa had so many strengths that she was weak with desperation. She was the oldest of three brown-haired sisters, but she was the only one not yet married. She'd dated a patent attorney and a direct-mail marketer and the sportscaster on the Channel 5 news. All of them had "cut their losses."

Gary (or Peter or David), though, was different: he'd been married previously, so he'd learned where serious relationships fall apart. And he had his own six-figure income, so he wouldn't compete or feel threatened by her whopping semiannual bonuses. And he'd slept with many women since his divorce, so he wouldn't still need to sow his oats. He ate at restaurants almost every night, so he wouldn't expect her to put dinner on the table. He'd seen a therapist every Wednesday morning for two years, so he had dealt with his overbearing mother and distant father. He'd already lost most of his hair, so he was no longer obsessed with baldness. He'd gone through AA in college, so he wasn't going to fall into a rut drinking martinis every evening. Nothing could go wrong. They were too similar to have differences of opinion. They were too different to have their territory threatened. It didn't make any sense, which proved it must really be love. Oh, it was all useless. Someday she'd meet a man that didn't require a string of rationalizations to love, a man with a kind gift in his eyes and a body not stiff-jointed with male bravado. Someday she'd meet a man whose hands roamed but didn't grab, and who believed love made him stronger, not weaker. Someday it would make sense why she'd become what she'd become, because she didn't come this way to be alone.

3 · Survival

IT WAS NOT a surprise that working in such a profession they
developed manic obsessions with cleanliness. The air was maintained at sixty-eight degrees exactly, the humidity at a very un-
sweaty 20 percent, and the carpets were vacuumed twice daily, by
two different maids, with two different makes of vacuum. It was a
profession of dirty tricks and muddied moralities and soiled aspira-
tions, but they did their best to keep their uniforms clean. Every
man kept an extra tie in his desk, plus a razor and nail clippers, an
Ace comb, a toothbrush, and tins of Kiwi shoe wax in black and
mahogany. That was bare minimum. Most kept extra cuff links,
hairspray, antiperspirant, spare belt, floss, lint tape, and two
brand-new, plastic-wrapped pinpoint cotton dress shirts with
fused collars. Nelson Dicky, who's teeth were rotting, kept a Water
Pik and antibacterial Listerine. Nickel Sansome, who had trouble
breathing, kept an albuterol inhaler that was prescribed by Dr. Perkova. When everyone realized Wes Griffin had had enough and
was never coming back to work, they found in his desk all of the
above, plus extra-long shoelaces, high-powered zoom binoculars,
duct tape, and a tube of grease-cutting soap. On nights that he
couldn't sleep he had worked on his car, a 350 GTO geared for
quick acceleration, and he'd come to work with axle grease under
his fingernails. Eggs Igino inherited the stash, and he was particularly tickled to get a roll of duct tape, which was sure to come in
handy in a world that appeared to be coming unglued. They all
kept umbrellas. Several men kept spare tropical wool suits in the
hallway closet. Their shoes always had double-welt construction.
When the money was moving fast and the markets were hopping
and the pressure to be in front of them was greatest, they could yell
and curse and play Nerf basketball and piss in a cup (rather than

leave the trading floor), but they could never be seen with un-trimmed cuticles. They broke the rules against talking with invest-ment bankers downstairs, they broke the rules against discussing among each other the amount of their semiannual bonuses, and they broke the rules against admitting to customers that their bonds were overpriced, but they never broke the rule against show-ing up with wet hair. Though it wasn't easy, they all survived.

Sid Geeder had lasted four years, but he was an old man, nearly thirty-four, and he intended to leave soon. Nelson Dicky had lasted three and a half years, Lisa Lisa and Nickel Sansome three, Sue Marino two, and Regis Reed one. That kid Turner had been there only three weeks before they found him collapsed on his desk with his face in his fruit salad, causing conjecture that he'd choked on a hunk of melon. Thom Slavonika had been there twenty-two years, but he had to floss his teeth after every sale, maybe fifteen times a day, cuspids through molars, top and bottom, working that waxed string through gums that five times had been repaired with a skin graft from his hip. If he did not floss he could not sell—those were the rules he played by, and he never broke them. They all survived, at least until Eggs Igino came in on his fourth day with his hair dripping onto his unstarched shoulders, the loose curls falling down into his eyes.

The cleanliness was not for professional image or good manners or upper-class habit. The cleanliness was to assuage guilt, to pre-tend they were above the fray, and it intensified during major sales campaigns. Sales missions differed from daily trading in one im-portant respect: the price was fixed. In the secondary markets, prices fluctuated to reflect a bond's worth, and the salespersons profited whether the market went up or down. The price was al-ways determined by the market. Times were good, the money was good, and nobody went to hell. But in the primary market of new bond issues, it was the salesman's job to justify the preset price to the customer. They dreaded it. The salesmen spent weeks earning the trust of their customers with fair prices from the secondary markets, and then they blew this trust with one large block of over-priced new-issue bonds. For weeks they faxed research reports and called five times a day and took customers to lunch at the Ming Garden and sent them watches on their birthday. Then they cashed in. According to Sid Geeder, who did this better than anyone, success was only a question of how much they could lie before they felt guilty, and then how much guilt they could take before they suffered psychological malfunction.

Sid Geeder didn't feel guilty, because he considered it a matter of self-defense. All of his customers were greedy, glory-hungry hacks pretending they were good at numbers who kept coming back for more because he was the King of Mortgages. They wanted his secrets. They kept calling for the contents of his head. *Gimme, gimme.* It was a war out there, and his lies were his only ammunition. His lies were well-constructed bombs that blew up a few years down the road. Examples included the Euro-Floaters, the Freddie Mac Adjustables, and the Resolution Trust bonds. The lies took many forms, but invariably the lies involved the promise that the bonds would always be highly liquid and actively traded, meaning that Atlantic Pacific would always be willing to buy them back at a reasonable price, which was never true. They wouldn't have been selling them if they wanted to buy them back. Sid Geeder, who had been on the sales floor longer than everyone but Thom Slavonika, falsely maintained that in his long career Atlantic Pacific had never stopped actively trading the bonds it had put in the market. Sid Geeder was a bombardier who pushed the button on command. He had constructed an odd psychological profile that Dr. Perkova considered bordered on psychological malfunction: as revenge against being made to sell bonds, he sold even *more* bonds. He had no confidence in the debt instruments he was selling, and so to assuage his guilt he sold them to everyone he hated. He trained himself to hate everyone he sold to, so he suffered no guilt and avoided psychological malfunction.

"But *who* are you fighting?" Dr. Perkova said, after Sid Geeder had been given a $100 million quota on the Resolution Trust bonds and needed his back unknotted.

"I don't know!" Sid Geeder yelled, his face buried in the leather.

"I don't know," Sid Geeder had said when Coyote Jack asked him if the kid was ready for a quota on the Resolution Trust bonds.

"I think he's ready," Coyote Jack said.

"The bonds are a piece of shit," Sid Geeder let out. "I don't think even I can sell any."

"You always say that. The more you say it, the more you end up selling."

"That's only because I hate selling them so much that I sell them to everybody."

"Exactly. That's why I've got you down for f-f-fifty million."

"Fifty million!"

"The bonds are worthless. So worthless that you'll sell that much easy."

"Stop it!"

"You've picked up Wes Griffin's best accounts. You've got World Savings. You've got Ingenesis Corp. You've got Franklin Mutual."

"Franklin Mutual's on credit hold! World won't buy anything that we won't buy back from them!"

"We'll buy them back. We'll be actively trading those bonds for decades."

"That's crazy, Coyote. The money from the bonds is going to shut down savings and loans. When the Resolution Trust is done shutting them down, they're going to stop borrowing, and then there'll be no active market for the bonds."

Coyote Jack laughed. "What makes you think the government is going to stop shutting them down? Shutting down unprofitable savings and loans has become a very profitable business for us. We made money turning the savings and loans unprofitable, and now we make money shutting them down. The Resolution Trust will be borrowing for at least th-th-thirty years."

"Just like the Euro-Floaters and Freddie Mac Adjustables."

"These bonds are different."

"How are they different?"

"This time the government is involved."

"I have no faith in the government. The government created this problem in the first place."

"Exactly! So how can you have any faith that they'll be able to fix it?"

Sid was struck silent with grief.

"You really hate these bonds, don't you?" Coyote Jack said peacefully, suddenly sympathetic.

"Yes! I hate them! I hate them with every single molecule of my being!"

"Then I suppose I should put you down for a h-h-hundred million."

"Go ahead! Hah! One hundred million. I'll just go tell my customers that the government is a safe investment because we can count on them to never solve their problems."

"If you don't want to tell them, then I'm sure that kid Igino will be happy to do it for you."

"What's that supposed to mean?"

"You've got a half-dozen accounts you're too busy even to call. Why don't you let Igino have a crack at a few of them? He needs to get started somewhere."

As much as he hated giving an inch, Sid knew this request was inevitable. When he was first starting out, he'd cut his teeth on Coyote Jack's accounts. "Is Nelson Dicky giving him any accounts?"

Coyote Jack nodded.

"So who were you thinking?" Sid asked.

"Give him AmeriTrust. Give him Walnut Creek."

"AmeriTrust's on credit hold. Walnut Creek doesn't trust investment banks."

"So I guess it's no skin off your back," Coyote Jack concluded.

"It still hurts," Sid answered, shuffling out of Coyote Jack's office.

Coyote Jack leaned back in his chair. He hadn't felt this good in years. Coyote Jack had a ballooning face that strained at the limits of the skin. His neck was bloated and hung over his collar. His eyelids puffed up to where his eyes were in a constant squint. But his leather suspenders didn't bother him one bit, and his neck rash didn't itch, and he owed it all to Wes Griffin, who had not shown up for work one day and made Coyote Jack miserable. Mark Igino had taken Wes Griffin's place. Wes Griffin had been a good salesman, but Igino was the prototype salesman of the future: boyish, trustworthy, great with numbers. In that morning's Intermail had finally arrived the reports from the New York training program on Igino, which said that he was a rebellious crank who disobeyed orders and had created a market among the trainees for lecture notes. The report recommended that he be sent to some distant, insignificant office far away from New York where he could do the least damage. Coyote Jack had never read such a promising report. In a world of unmerciful uniformity, rebels were hard to come by. Those willing to be the first to break rules were rare. Those willing to disregard orders were even scarcer. Rebels had built this business, and rebels had continued to redefine it. Wasserstein had been a rebel. Milken had been a rebel. Coyote Jack went to his fishbowl window and looked out over the pits where thirty-seven salespeople slaved under his command. The evidence of Igino's blatant disregard for authority was already in evidence on only his fourth day of work. He had gotten rid of his chair entirely and was standing up while he worked the phones. And his hair was wet! Two days ago Coyote Jack had told him to get it cut, which he hadn't done, and now he showed up with it wet and entirely unstyled. Coyote Jack couldn't have been happier. A market for lecture notes!

Coyote Jack had been terrified to hear that the syndicate was falling apart behind the Resolutions. It was a bad omen for the firm that made Coyote Jack seriously consider putting his ranch house in Sonoma on the market. But now he realized it was a great opportunity for someone to be a hero. Coyote Jack was going to ride Sid Geeder and Mark Igino all the way to managing director. Coyote Jack was seriously considering putting in a pool at his ranch house in Sonoma. He called the syndicate desk in New York and told them he was upping the office's quota on the Resolution Trust bonds. Then he called Stormin' Norman Walker, the personal tax accountant the firm paid to make sure all the salesmen were cheating on their taxes, and told him to come in to the office the next day. Then he told his secretary to go into Clark Kalinov's office and drive him crazy. Coyote Jack hadn't heard any trouble from Kalinov in several days and wondered what he was up to. Kalinov was probably burying the new kid in health forms and tax forms and noncompete agreements and purchase requisition procedures. Kalinov was a problem, a stitch in the saddle, and Coyote Jack didn't know what to do about it except have his secretary drive him crazy.

Coyote Jack's secretary was an incompetent woman who had

failed all of her filing, typing, and coffee-making tests and could therefore do her job perfectly. She had robust hips, great motherly breasts, plump arms, and sweet-smelling pillowy hair, which made her perfect for her role. Coyote Jack, whose only responsibility was to make sure that his salesforce was miserable, had none of his own work to give her. Her sole responsibility was to drive Kalinov crazy, which she did by volunteering to do his filing and typing and making him coffee. Clark Kalinov was obsessed with order and had established an intricate empire of health forms, tax forms, noncompete agreements, and purchase requisition procedures that kept anything from getting accomplished and therefore ensured that there was always work to be done. There was always a huge stack of paper in his in-box, hundreds of Post-Its in his To Do pile, and dozens of phone calls that he never returned. Coyote Jack's secretary ignored his systems and procedures entirely; Kalinov tried to keep her from doing his work, but each morning, as he went to any one of the downtown health clubs he was testing out for a corporate membership, she came into his office and did it anyway. At the afternoon lull, when Clark was digesting his lunch, she brought him coffee that was always weak or oily or too heavily sugared. He said nothing, though, because he lost his words every time she sauntered into his office in blouses too small for her breasts. She volunteered to file and mail the stack of paper in his out-box, and he managed to whimper that that would be fine.

Clark had recently commissioned a lengthy employee training manual on gender sensitivity to make sure that the men and women didn't openly drool over each other. It would do her good to read it, because it discouraged enticing clothing and leading behavior. The manual had been on his desk for several weeks. He pointed to it for her to photocopy, collate, and spiral-bind, and as she leaned over his desk to get it he drooled into his oily coffee without knowing. Flustered, he tried to cover up his unease by gulping his coffee, which was worse than ever. Clark had implemented very strict thirteen-point rules against socialization among the employees in order to keep himself from socializing with her and possibly bringing down his empire. Clark had studied empires over the centuries, and they were all brought down by either greed or women, and sometimes greed over women. Alexander the

Great. Napoleon. The Ming Dynasty. Trying to resist her was driving him crazy. He thought about her as he rode the Exercycle at the health club in the morning. He thought about her as he took supply inventory in the afternoon. He thought about her as he made love to his girlfriend at night. If she had been his secretary, he would have fired her long ago to avoid harassing her. But she was Coyote Jack's secretary, and he didn't know how to get even except continue to bury Coyote Jack's salesforce under tax forms and new regulations. He sat back down at his desk and penciled out a draft of a memo to Mark Igino asking why he had not responded to his memo of two days previous. Kalinov knew why Igino hadn't responded to his memo—it was because he hadn't gotten it yet. Clark had sent it Intermail, which sat in Ricky's mailroom for two days even when it just needed to go across the sales floor. Two days was corporate policy. Kalinov had wanted to know what Igino thought would happen to the firm if every salesperson started acting like he did and got rid of their chairs. Clark went to his window and looked out at the fog. Didn't the kid appreciate his great view of the fog? Didn't he appreciate the polished mahogany wood his sales pit was made of? Didn't he appreciate the low-static carpet that he stood on all day?

"What's this!" Eggs Igino yelled, suddenly appearing in the doorway to Kalinov's office and waving a piece of corporate letterhead.

Clark whirled around. "What?"

"I can damn well stand up if I want to."

"Where did you get that?"

"You *sent* it to me. It's dated yesterday."

"But . . ."

"Coyote Jack's secretary put it on my desk."

Kalinov winced. That woman. "Yes, well, what if everyone took your example and stood up all day just because it's more comfortable?"

"What if they did?" Igino snapped back.

"It's a slippery slope, Igino. What if they then decided it was more comfortable to wear jogging shoes?"

"That's not a bad idea."

"What's next? Blue jeans? Desk lamps?"

"How about get rid of that LCD ticker tape running across the wall? It gives us headaches."

Kalinov turned his back to Igino and faced the window as he spoke. It was a power move he'd learned from a book on body language. "Clients are impressed by that ticker tape. Just as they're impressed by our uniforms and the meticulous order of our sales floor, with everyone sitting at their desk. I have to protect our corporate image. Without that image, we're no different from any chophouse on the street."

"Well, I'm not sitting," he said emphatically.

"Don't be a crank, Igino. I can make it hard on you. . . ." Clark Kalinov turned back around and saw that Igino had already left his office and was headed back to the sales floor.

Eggs Igino had too much to bother with already. He'd inherited a dozen accounts to call upon, most of which were tiny consumer banks or county treasurers without any real money to spend. The only accounts of any size were the previous salesman's savings and loans, but they were so bankrupt that the credit department considered them too risky to do business with—they might never have the cash to pay for the bonds they promised to buy. Coyote Jack had given him a $20 million quota on the Resolution Trust bonds, which were due to be issued in a couple of days. Eggs Igino figured he could move a fifth of that if he was lucky. Selling a little was easy—there was always some pension fund of an obscure labor union that wanted more yield than treasuries but less risk than mortgages. Selling a lot was going to be impossible, especially without any lead time for his accounts to learn to trust him.

Even though he was brand, spanking new to the sales floor, Eggs Igino wasn't intimidated by selling. He'd been selling one thing or another for most of his life as he worked his way through school: morning newspapers when he was nine; organic, grain-fed bacon at a butcher's shop when he was thirteen; his talents as a computer programmer when he was seventeen; an economics curriculum for high schools he'd developed with Katie when he was twenty-two; windsurfing lessons on a beach in Zihuatanejo, Mexico, when he was twenty-three. Now it was his predictions for the direction of money, and financial instruments designed to take advantage of that direction. So Eggs Igino got on the horn and started teaching his accounts to trust his opinion on where the market was going.

"It's going to hell," he said to a very sad voice at a little bank of Sid Geeder's who seemed willing to hear him out. "Not going down or up necessarily, but just becoming more volatile. It's a long-run trend. We've got twenty-four-hour-a-day trading, program trading, new versions of mutual funds being offered by banks. We've got computers up the wazoo, all instantaneously deciphering news. It's made the market more volatile than ever. Information is far more volatile than industry. With industry, companies had inventory and long-term labor contracts and product loyalty, all of which kept those companies stable. But nobody inventories information, and they don't manufacture it, and consumers don't have any more loyalty. It's the Third Law of Information Economics: Knowledge has no shelf life. Market share can vanish in a single day. All of this leads to greater volatility."

"So what should I be doing?" the sad voice asked. "Every time I buy, the market goes down. Every time I sell, the market goes up."

"You have to stop thinking about up *or* down. It's going to do both. You have to think of how to profit from up *and* down. You have to profit from the volatility."

"How?"

"Buy investments that do well in volatile times. Buy Atlantic Pacific stock, for instance; we make a killing every time the market goes up, and we make a killing every time it goes down. We lose our shirts when it stays in one place."

"It never stays in one place," the sad voice said.

"It's going to hell," Lisa Lisa said, after she overheard Eggs Igino sell a large block of company stock to a tiny bank in Walnut Creek. She was talking to Mike Kohanamoku, the head trader and tribal chief of Honolulu Federal. She could barely read her notes. She winged it. "It's the Third Law of Information Economics: Knowledge has no shelf life—you have to eat it off the vine. You have to learn to profit from the volatility."

"It's going to hell," Nelson Dicky said, after he overheard Lisa Lisa sell a large block of company stock to a thrift in Hawaii. He was talking to the state treasurer of Utah, who normally traded only in treasury bonds because everything else was too unstable. "Nobody carries inventory anymore. Knowledge is on the vine. That's the Third Law of Information Economics. It's a long-term trend, and you've got to get on board."

"It's going to hell," Nickel Sansome said, after the State of Utah bought something other than treasury bonds for the first time in two years. He was talking to a very wealthy investor who also happened to be his father. "It's an information economy, and money grows on trees again. You just have to reach up and take it. That's the Third Law of Information Economics." Nickel Sansome always tried out his new sales pitches on his father to build up confidence.

"The Third Law of Information Economics? That's kind of catchy. What did you say it was again?"

Nickel stammered for a moment, looking at his notes. "Knowledge is like a tree, and the big money is on the highest branches," he improvised, faking a professorial tone. "That's the nutshell version. What do you think?"

"Anything that reminds people to go to graduate school is okay by me."

"It's going to hell," Nickel said to his father when he asked about his love life. "Nobody fits my criteria."

"Which are?"

"Loose."

"Sexually? Oh, there're many women like that."

"Not that have master's degrees in contemporary literature."

"I suppose not."

"And know how to cook fried apples like Mom."

Nickel's father took a deep breath. "Don't you think you're being too limited?"

"I've had a lot of time to develop my criteria. Criteria are important, otherwise I waste too much time dating women I wouldn't want to marry. I was starting to see someone for a while. I took her to lunch a few times at this restaurant we go to to impress our clients. She'd read Kant and Nietzsche on her lunch hour and we'd secretly talk about philosophy over the phone in the afternoons. We'd talk so passionately about passion that it looked like we were getting a lot of work done."

"What happened to her?"

"She got fired."

"She *worked* with you? Never wash your hands in your drinking water, son. Never."

"It's the only place I spend enough time with women to get to know them. Meeting women is impossible."

"Maybe you should see a psychiatrist," his father suggested.

"What for?"

"I'm worried what my divorces have done to you."

"Then quit getting divorced."

"But my marriages are awful."

"Then quit getting married!"

"I don't want to limit myself like that."

After calling his father, Nickel felt depressed and decided he needed a lift. Making it look like he had misplaced something in his desk drawer, he pulled out an oversized Cadbury chocolate bar he kept inside an Intermail envelope. Then he stood up, pushed his chair back in, and guiltily marched out the back door to the bathroom, where he sat in the stall and scratched his scalp with one hand as he held his Cadbury bar to his lips with the other. He knew Coyote Jack had seen him march off the sales floor. He knew his addiction to sweets was psychosomatic and had nothing to do with glucose deficiencies he sometimes told people he suffered from. It was an information economy, and knowledge was supposed to give him power, but it didn't work that way. Nickel Sansome felt much more powerful without knowledge. As an ignorant boy he had been an overconfident bully, but over the years he had matured into an intelligent, worldly man with self-esteem in the cellar. Knowledge had led to paralysis. Examples included knowing that his father encouraged his wives to sleep with young men. And knowing that his quota of Resolution Trust bonds had been raised to $25 million. And reading in the morning's *Wall Street Journal* that in the Dominican Republic there was a mountain of garbage three miles across, and that gangs of desperate youths killed each other over the right to scavenge it for recyclables. And hearing from Regis Reed that he and Sid Geeder's old assistant used to snort coke off the polished glass lens of the monster photocopier. Nickel had been about to call her for a date when he heard the news from Reed. Knowledge only drove Nickel Sansome out of the real world and into his own. He sat on the toilet with his pants around his ankles and gnawed at his Cadbury bar, trying to take deep breaths, remembering how Sid Geeder's assistant, who worked only ten feet away, would call him on the phone and wonder whether true Dread could be known in an artificial age. They had longed to go to Prague together, to sit in the Magic Lantern Theater where Havel made his speeches and to sit in the coffeehouses among people who appreciated their freedom.

Sid Geeder dreaded talking to Clark Kalinov. Clark Kalinov was like those cream-cheese danishes, half melted. Physically, they were the same—limp and pale. Physiologically, they caused the same reaction in Sid—they made him puke. For two weeks Sid and Clark had been exchanging memos as a way of avoiding confrontation. These were aggressive, bitter memos that pulled no punches and confronted the issue directly. The issue was Sid Geeder's assistant, who Clark maintained still worked for Sid even though Sid had fired her. As facilities manager of the West Coast office, Clark Kalinov had memoed Geeder that he was solely responsible for all office equipment, office furniture, health insurance, and nonsales personnel—including the power to hire and fire all nonsales personnel. He included documentation, including his official job description—which he had written and sneaked under John White's signature—and the above-mentioned assistant's W-2 tax forms, which showed she was not an employee of Geeder but rather of the corporation. Geeder had countered with his own memo on his vice president stationery referencing three bonus checks he had written to the assistant out of his own personal bank account that totaled 300 percent of the firm's piddling salary. Enclosed were copies of 1099 tax forms and photocopies of the three checks, as well as one of the above-mentioned assistant's business cards, with her title printed as "Sales Associate," indicating she was in the sales department and under the jurisdiction of Coyote Jack. It was a covert dogfight, a perfectly safe eye-gouging, hair-pulling brawl over inconsequential turf that mattered to them both immensely. They communicated entirely through Intermail, with their letters sitting on Ricky's desk for two days each time, causing them to stew over their words to the point of being sour and cranky to everyone else

on the floor. Kalinov took the psychological advantage momentarily when he processed payroll for the assistant, sending a check for
her hourly wage to her home address and cc'ing Geeder on his note
to her, which said he was sorry she had been ill and hoped she
would be back soon. Kalinov had never been so happy. Every single one of Geeder's memos followed corporate guidelines for spac-
ing, typestyle, and format. Kalinov had no idea how Geeder had
learned the rules, let alone managed to abide by them. The empire
he had created had never proved itself so efficient at redirecting
aggression into passive channels. Then Geeder shot back with an
invoice for one silver-plated blue-ink Cross pen that previously
mentioned employee had stolen. It totaled $279.38, which in-
cluded a finance charge for five weeks' interest, and was addressed
to the accounting department in New York with a copy to Kalinov.
Kalinov had never been so miserable. He had never been able to
block a payment once it had been sent to the accounting department. He immediately ran downstairs to the mailroom, where
Ricky was kicking back in his chair with his feet on his desk, eating
Fritos and gazing through an office supply catalog. But it was no
use—Geeder's invoice had made it to New York faster than it had
made it across the sales floor. He immediately ran back to his office, but when he got there, Coyote Jack's secretary was digging
through his out-box.

"I brought you some coffee," she said in a luxurious, sickeningly
cheery way, as if she had brought him breakfast in bed.

"That'll be fine," he said stiffly, trying to hold back his shoulders
and suck in his gut underneath his pinpoint cotton dress shirt.
"You ought to make Sid Geeder coffee sometime. He drinks coffee
constantly."

"Sid Geeder hates my coffee. He spit it into his wastebasket the
one time I took him a cup. He said it was oily. You're the only one
that loves my coffee."

"Well, it's an acquired taste." He smiled and tried to look satisfied. "Is there anything else?"

"I was going to type out this memo to Mr. Igino for you. Something about not responding to a previous memo."

"That'll be fine," he said again, even though the last thing he wanted was for Igino to confront him directly like that again. Hadn't the kid learned anything yet from Geeder?

"This is just the beginning," Eggs Igino added, after explaining to Sid Geeder how he'd gotten the corporate stock to rise two points in just a few hours and had moved his tiny Walnut Creek bank into Australian Euros at a huge profit. "I still have lots to learn from you."

"Walnut Creek! That's impressive," Geeder said, shaking his head in wonder. He'd been a bond salesman for four years and he'd never even thought of selling stocks. Of course, selling any stock other than company stock would have been illegal, but Igino had sold company stock, and the company certainly couldn't be upset with that. "By the way, which Aussies did you put them in?"

"The 8s of '03."

"You sold the 8s of '03! Those bonds should be illegal. We've been sitting on that position for over a year."

Eggs Igino agreed. "They're a piece of shit, all right. They're so bad that the Resolution Trust bonds will look like gems in comparison."

Sid Geeder guffawed. "You *dog,* you. Ripping their eyes out already. You'll be selling ice to the Eskimos in no time. Wow—AP stock for the '03 Aussies. How in the hell did you manage that?"

A huge, irresistible grin came over Eggs Igino's face. "Wouldn't you like to know," he laughed.

"Well, you owe me something for giving you that account," Sid reminded him.

Eggs Igino reached under his trading notebook and lifted away another strawberry danish, which he began to gnaw on as he talked, scattering crumbs in every direction. "You know, that bank in Walnut Creek hates you. They said you called them shit-for-brains and refused to talk to them for months."

Sid gazed at the danish entering and exiting Igino's mouth, getting smaller each time. "Well, they bought the '03 Aussies. How smart can they be?"

"For a bank in their position it's not a bad buy," Eggs stated.

"How so?"

"Oh, I'm not going to tell you. Why don't you give them a call and ask them why they bought the Aussies? I'm sure ol' shit-for-brains would be glad to hear from you."

"Aw, c'mon. I've had a long day. Just tell me."

Eggs Igino took a particularly large bite of the danish, a strand of which curled out of his mouth and touched his chin. "Do you think it bothers my accounts that I talk with my mouth full? Coyote Jack says I'd better watch it."

"Beats me."

"I think they *like* to know I'm eating," Eggs speculated. "I think they'll trust me more if they know I'm not some machine, that I have to eat. I'd like my accounts to answer the phone and hear a little gnawing on the other end of the line and know right away it's ol' Igino calling." He chuckled at his own thought and ponderously ground away on a knot of dough that had, through excessive chewing, turned into the indigestible consistency of gum. He turned and spit a huge loogie into the wastebasket between them.

"Well, Christ, if you're just going to spit it out, then let me have some," Sid cried, then immediately wished he hadn't.

"Hungry, are you?" the kid asked him in a self-satisfied tone, relishing Sid's misery.

"I'm not hungry at all!" Sid yelled back. "It's just impossible to stand here watching you eat!"

Eggs Igino paused. He opened the oily-walled grocery bag and stared down at its contents. "Do you realize how crazy Nickel Sansome would get if we sat here eating strawberry danishes every morning?"

"Oh no, not this again."

"Just let me listen in tomorrow. Just one day. I'll tape down the mute button. They'll never know I'm there."

"I should have known this was coming. Don't you realize I just fired my sales assistant for snooping on me?"

"Sure, but you can trust me." Eggs forced a wide, clownish smile.

"Why can I trust you?"

"Because I appreciate your art. Subtleties that would be lost on the others."

"Quit conning me. You can never sell a salesman."

Eggs cut to the chase. "So we have a deal?"

"No!" But Sid was laughing.

"Gotcha!"

"I shouldn't do this. I'm going to regret it."

But the deal was done. Eggs Igino explained that Clark Kalinov, in his continuous effort to test the Intermail system, ordered the morning danishes from New York. In New York they nuked the danishes to make them steamy, but the process turned the cream cheese yellow. Nobody ever ate those danishes, so they were shipped to the West Coast. Two days old when they arrived, they were nuked again to look fresh. The small Mexican maid who cleaned the kitchen every afternoon explained this to Igino on his very first day on the job. In Spanish. So Eggs Igino had a friend in New York put a strawberry danish in an Intermail box every afternoon. "They're great if you nuke 'em," he added, while promising to up his daily order to two danishes.

"Brilliant," Sid said admiringly, shaking his head with delight at the thought of undermining Clark Kalinov. "What do you say we go nuke a few right now and have ourselves a feast?"

"You go ahead," Igino said, handing over the crumpled bag. "I'm going home." So Eggs Igino, on only his third week on the job, left the office an hour early, without carrying a briefcase or an umbrella or an overcoat, and without acknowledging the bewildered stares of the other salespersons, who couldn't imagine leaving early under so much peer pressure to stay late.

Later, Sid rode the elevator with Lisa Lisa. She was carrying bundles of research reports under her arms. Sid had a rule against bringing work home—he feared the business already had too much control over his mind. He would rather stay late at the office than study at his kitchen table. He watched Lisa Lisa attempt, in the dull shine of the elevator's marbled walls, to even out her lipstick by smacking her lips together.

"Would you hold these for a moment?" she said, holding out an armful of the reports.

"Not a chance," he answered.

She frowned. "Is my lipstick uneven?" she asked, turning her head and shaking her hair slightly, then pausing to model for him.

He looked at her. "Looks okay to me."

Lisa Lisa relaxed. She looked at him thankfully, but he was looking down at the carpet. She noticed grease stains and bits of white substance on the apron of his tie.

"You've got some grease stains on that tie," she let him know politely.

"I'd rather have grease stains on my tie than uneven lipstick."

They rode the rest of the way silently, then crossed the lobby together and took another elevator to the parking garage.

"Why are you so mean to me?" she cried as they walked to their cars.

"Because now I don't have a sales assistant, on account of you."

"Me? What did I do?"

"You were using her to get information."

"But I didn't get anything out of her. She never told me anything!"

"That's because there's nothing to tell."

"If there's nothing to tell, then why are you so secretive?"

"None of your business."

They reached Sid's car. Lisa Lisa set her bundles of reports down on his hood.

"If you told me," she said, "then maybe we could work out an arrangement. I'll pay you a part of any commissions I earn."

"You'll *what*?"

"You heard me. How much do you want—twenty percent?"

"*What for?*"

"For letting me in on the secret to selling the Resolutions."

"There isn't any secret!"

"Thirty percent, then," Lisa Lisa persisted.

"You're out of your mind!" he yelled, pushing her arm aside and climbing into his car. She knocked on the window. He backed out of the narrow slot, spilling her reports on the pavement, and drove off.

4 · Addictions

THEY COULD NEVER catch up. There was always more work to do. There was always someone smarter, sharper, and richer who made them feel inconsequential in comparison. They had worked too hard to accept being inconsequential, so they worked even harder to even less effect. They grew accustomed to the constant chatter and whir of urban life, and they fell into a malaise when the world fell silent. But the world rarely fell silent, because they carried the whir home with them, like a headache, and it kept up its chatter throughout the night. It was the scream of the modern world, the background pitch of so many voices, and they couldn't sleep without it. Nor could they sleep with it, because they had sold yen for dollars on the eve of the trade deficit figure, and they had sold those dollars for sterling as the British voted for the Maastricht Treaty, and they had moved that sterling into an offshore bank likely to be hurt by new tax policies in Bonn. The economy whirred twenty-four hours a day, and it was an economy of the brain (rather than the body), so the brain whirred twenty-four hours a day and they rarely slept at all without pills or alcohol or drugs of some kind. Soon they were addicted to drink, or pills, and they couldn't get started in the morning without large transfusions of caffeine, which they also became addicted to. Once in a cycle of addiction, every cure was a future addiction. Every ladder pointed up. Every rope pointed down.

The salespeople, who knew that addictions were inescapable, tried to draw a line between malignant addictions and benign ones. Regis Reed had both. He was addicted to drugs, though not to any drug in particular. He was addicted to chemical peace, and he avoided taking the same drug two afternoons straight to escape their death grip. He had become as good a chemist as he was a salesman: gamma-aminobutyric acid on Mondays; coca on Tuesdays; cannabis sativa on Wednesdays; crystal menthalamine on Thursdays; lysergic-diethylamide on Fridays. He was also, very weirdly, addicted to shaving. Perhaps because of the drugs, Regis Reed had unbelievably thin and sensitive skin. He could not shave when he awoke in the morning because his hands shook, so he drove to work and shaved in the bathroom. All day his face itched with razor burn, and when he daydreamed, which was often, he found himself picking at the stubble that was trying to grow back. As soon as he got home he shaved again. He beat back that stubble and kept his face flushed with a boyish, innocent glow caused by razor burn. Regis Reed was also, arguably, addicted to risk. In college he had illegally taken out student loans, which he had invested in the futures market to try to beat the interest he was paying on the loans. He was smart as a whip but never slept and gave the impression of having been spoiled as a boy. Regis Reed had never known happiness and never intended to. He had wanted to run away to the marines, but there were no wars to fight, so he joined Atlantic Pacific, which had been impressed that a college kid had covered the spread on his student loans.

In comparison, Sidney Geeder was a strapping, able-bodied, wholesome man. He was only addicted to caffeine, an addiction that he openly admitted and did not try to cure with something that could lead to worse. He was also, arguably, addicted to his late-afternoon romps with Ivana Perkova, but the last thing Sid wanted was for her to fix his back. He had survived just fine with these low-level sufferings, and he didn't want them replaced by more severe disasters. His back was his pressure valve. His paranoia was his regulator. Ivana Perkova had tried to convince him that he was addicted to selling bonds—it fit the profile of addictive psychosis perfectly: his solution to having to sell overpriced bonds was to sell more of them to whomever he hated, which was everyone who ever called him on the phone to steal his secrets. She had been digging into his rhomboids as she talked, and as her hand hit the supraspinatus muscle running through the shoulder, he changed the subject by admitting he loved her.

"You don't love me," she said calmly, trying to remain professional. "You just think you do."

"What's the difference?" Sid demanded to know.

Dr. Perkova was quick with her answer. "Love is based on knowledge. Infatuation is based on fantasy. You don't know anything about me."

"I'm a salesman," Sid said. "I trust my intuition."

"How convenient," she said.

"Hey, I don't like it any more than you do. The last thing I wanted to do was fall in love—I've survived just fine being loveless."

Dr. Perkova kept her hands on his back and her voice even-toned and clinical. "Infatuation is a common reaction to an overload of stress. Your condition will wear off after the Resolution Trust deal, I'm sure."

"You think so?"

"I'm sure of it."

Sid blew out a sigh of relief.

Nelson Dicky wished he could find such an easy answer to his rotting teeth. He too had gone to see Ivana Perkova, who had referred him to a dentist. The dentist had X-rayed every tooth and X-rayed his cervical vertebrae but found nothing to substantiate Nelson's claim that his teeth were soft and itched. The dentist had never heard anyone complain of teeth that itched, and he could find no reference in his medical encyclopedias. The dentist had seen few teeth to compare with Nelson's. They were prosperous, rock-hard, milky-colored examples of what teeth could be like if a man gave up coffee, drugs, alcohol, and sweets. The dentist took Polaroids to use as motivation for his other patients who were addicted to acidic foods and sweets. Still, Nelson kept coming back. "You have to find something," he pleaded. "I've been chewing on popsicle sticks all afternoon to stop the itching." But there was nothing to find. Every tooth checked out, cuspids through molars. Eventually, the dentist recommended Nelson see a psychiatrist to find the origin of his pain. So Nelson returned to Dr. Perkova, and she sent him to Helmet Fisher, the firm psychiatrist, who was intrigued by his malady and charged the firm in six-minute increments to figure it out for them. Helmet Fisher was a Jungian who applied archetypes and mythology to contemporary existence, imparting exaggerated significance to the salespersons' feeble lives. He had a subdued personality that reflected his patients like a mirror. Every Tuesday afternoon for eight weeks, Nelson Dicky sat in Helmet Fisher's overstuffed armchair and explained his devotions to God, family, and country. Helmet heard stories of growing up in Lewiston, Idaho, the son of a potato farmer. He heard stories of playing shooting guard for the Eastern Washington State Ellensburg Cougars, averaging nineteen points and seven assists a game for the Western Athletic Conference repeat champions. He heard the early origins of a successful career in the Provo, Utah, county treasurer's office. He heard how much Nelson loved his job and considered it an upstanding, respectable position. Helmet Fisher nodded and hummed and listened intently, but at the end of eight weeks he found no reason why Nelson Dicky's teeth should itch. Nelson was a well-adjusted, spiritually centered, emotionally capable individual with a modest sense of humor. He was a walking and talking example of what a mind could accomplish if it gave up coffee, alcohol, drugs, and sweets. Helmet Fisher was, on principle, reluctant to admit that Nelson's problem might be purely physical rather than some psychosomatic manifestation of a profound, complex, and costly pathological condition. But his only advice to Nelson was to buy a Water Pik.

Addictions were somehow a necessary part of surviving. The only one without an addiction was Turner, and look what happened to him.

"Look what happened to him," Nelson Dicky had said during the Euro-Floaters deal, pointing at the kid slumped over in his chair.

"Hey, kid, wake up!" Sid Geeder shouted, tossing a wad of paper at the kid's head. The wad of paper landed in Turner's breakfast of fruit salad and splashed pineapple syrup up on his nose. "He's asleep," Sid surmised.

Nelson Dicky rocked the kid's shoulder. "Should we let him sleep it off?"

But a half hour later, when Coyote Jack came through the aisle, Turner hadn't moved. "Yo! Homeboy!" Coyote Jack grabbed him by the shirt collar and shook him fiercely, to no effect.

"You killed him," Sid said from several feet away.

Coyote Jack whirled around. "I didn't touch him! He was already like that!"

Sid shook his head. "We all saw it. You're going to the slammer."

"Hasn't anyone called the ambulance?" Coyote Jack yelled back.

The ambulance came in about an hour. "Is he dead?" Coyote Jack begged the orderlies. They said that he wasn't dead yet, and then wheeled him away.

" 'Yet'! What's 'yet' supposed to mean?"

"It means you're going to jail," Wes Griffin agreed. "That was quite a shake you gave him. You must have broken his neck."

"I barely touched him!" Coyote Jack protested fearfully.

Sid chipped in, "Just like Lennie and the girl in that Steinbeck book. What was its name?"

"*Of Mice and Men,*" Wes Griffin answered.

"That's the one," Sid concurred. He put his wrists together and wrenched them, making a cracking sound with his mouth. "You'd better leave town," he advised Coyote Jack.

"You guys are crazy," Coyote Jack said, then turned and ran back to his office, where he hid for a week.

Lisa Lisa believed she was addicted to love. It was her second-greatest weakness, after being too strong. The more love gave her trouble, the more she craved its peaceful grip. Most of the salespersons would have considered love a benign addiction, but Lisa Lisa, who was too tough to coexist with weakness, wished she could rub away that needy part of her. Love had brought down centuries of women. For a woman in the workplace, the need for constant affirmation was often the most threatening addiction of all. Symptoms included checking one's answering machine frequently and sleeping with a pillow between the legs, both of which she was guilty of. Lisa Lisa felt guilty every time she felt the natural urge to lie down with a man. These thoughts ran through her head constantly, a second channel of white noise in the background, constantly reminding her that both her younger sisters were married, Nelson Dicky was married, Paul DeShews was married—even Coyote Jack was married. On some days Lisa Lisa might argue with the noise, telling herself that she didn't need anyone but herself to be happy. In the afternoons she ran along the Embarcadero, dodging tourists and horse-drawn carts and the outstretched hands of the homeless, circling back over Russian Hill, a four-mile loop in less than twenty-three minutes, her lungs chugging the polluted air, her legs churning against the lactic-acid ache of her muscles. Then she pampered herself in the bathroom for an hour before snuggling up to a copy of Friedrich Nietzsche's *Thus Spake Zarathustra* that Sid Geeder's assistant had loaned her. It attacked the Christian idealization of weakness, preaching instead the Superman, the *Übermensch*. It was the philosophical partner to Darwinism, and it made her feel good about being independent and conquering the material world. On other days she gave in to the pressure, and she drooled over Sid Geeder's burly Popeye forearms and Eggs Igino's tree-trunk thighs and Regis Reed's thin, flushed face. She took pleasure in the overtures the garage parking attendant made to her each morning, and she enjoyed the turned heads of the security men as she entered the building.

She could deny it or accept it, but the white noise was always there in the background, except when it rose into the foreground, as when Sue Marino returned from her vacation in Scotland with a radiant blissful glow to her face and announced that she had gotten engaged. She wore a flowered print dress with a thigh-high slit up the side. Her body language had changed completely: she sauntered in to her desk and crossed her legs in her chair and turned away from the phone lines as she talked, so as not to be interrupted by their blinking lights. All the men on the floor stared at her and made kind comments and brought her coffee. Sue spoke more slowly, and some of her cowgirl dialect had returned. She giggled when Nickel Sansome joked that the firm ought to open up a Scotland office. She smiled when Coyote Jack welcomed her back with a $20 million quota on the Resolution Trusts. Sue Marino was only twenty-eight years old, and her fiancé had an established OB-GYN practice at Children's Hospital in Pacific Heights. Lisa Lisa tried to be happy for her. Women in the business needed to stick together. It was their nature to cooperate, supposedly. But Lisa Lisa could only simmer with envy and found it difficult to welcome her back. All morning Lisa Lisa remained on the phone and avoided walking the twenty paces to Sue Marino's desk. She knew she had to do something, so to hide her jealousy she went downstairs to the flower shop in the lobby and ordered a huge bouquet of snapdragons and gladiolas in a skirt of heather, which was delivered an hour later with a card full of mushy congratulations.

"It's beautiful," Sue Marino said, walking over to Lisa Lisa's desk.

"I'm so happy for you," Lisa Lisa managed to get out. "So when's the date?"

"June," she answered, squeezing everything out of the word as if it were an orange. "I'm still in a daze," Sue admitted.

"Enjoy it while it lasts."

"I feel like I've been gone three months." Sue giggled. "Do I *really* work here?"

"This is the place. Your dysfunctional family. Home for most of your waking hours. You'll pick it all back up in a few days."

"That's what I'm afraid of."

"Well . . ." But Lisa Lisa couldn't think of anything else to say. "Well . . . back to work, I guess."

"Yes, back to work." And Lisa Lisa picked up her phone, which had been ringing for thirty seconds.

"Back to work!" Coyote Jack yelled into the phone. "You two women have been lollygagging around out there for twenty minutes."

Lisa Lisa gazed across the sales floor at Coyote Jack standing erect at the window of his fishbowl. He was leering back at her with a scowlish, daunting, bigoted stare that he had perfected by practicing for hours at the bathroom mirror. A sales manager had a huge responsibility but almost no actual work to do. His responsibility was to keep his salespeople motivated. His tools to achieve this fell into two main camps. The first camp was Fear, which included intimidation, anxiety, dread, guilt, browbeating, bullying, misery, shame, and panic. The second camp was Greed, which included temptation, seduction, ambition, competition, envy, enticement, and glory. These were the prime motivators of our animal ancestors, the flight-or-fight genetic coding that every salesperson had inherited, the core programming that salespeople could not override. Coyote Jack played upon that vulnerability. He stalked the aisleways with his hands behind his back and his nose in everybody's business, clucking his tongue, a stern, militant cast to his face, growling at those who stopped to savor their breakfast or comb their hair. He sat in the back during the televideo conferences, his oversized hands intertwined at their hairy knuckles in front of his face. When in his fishbowl he was cool and sly and manipulative, moving with slow, assured gestures that implied his mind was busy plotting his next cruel ploy. He wore garish watches and pointed shoes and starch-hardened shirt collars that caused a rash.

He gave the salespeople enough encouragement to want more, but never so much as to make their heads swell. On quiet Fridays he called a Cajun joint on the waterfront and ordered buckets of baby bareback spareribs, which the salespeople, famished for praise, gorged upon. He gave corporate watches to the big hitters and money clips to the also-rans. He handed out the paychecks, which were advances against expected commissions, and he awarded the semiannual "bonuses," which weren't bonuses at all—they were the commissions the salesmen had earned, but Coyote Jack made them seem like a gift from the firm, an act of graciousness, or a favor to be returned. He assigned each of them quotas to shoot for on the new issues, and he berated them or fired them if they fell short. He listened to Sid's phone calls and wrote down his trade ideas to give them to the research department in New York, where they were posted on the Quotron. Coyote Jack didn't care about the research department—he did this just to make Sid angry, because Sidney Geeder was a better salesman when he was angry.

"I think someone's listening to my phone calls," Sidney Geeder complained to Eggs Igino. "My trades keep appearing on the research department's Quotron screen."

"You'd better tell Coyote Jack," Eggs Igino advised.

"I think someone's listening to my phone calls," Sidney Geeder moaned to Coyote Jack. "My trades keep appearing on the research department's Quotron screen."

"That's ridiculous," Coyote Jack responded, wiggling his fingers underneath his desk in sheer delight as his face solemnly weighed

Sid's worry. "Surveillance checks this place for wiretaps every month."

"Maybe the surveillance department is in on it too."

"You're paranoid, Geeder. If the research department wanted to know your trade ideas, all they'd have to do is call me and I'd order you to tell them."

"I'd never tell those thieves a word!"

"Oh yes you would, because I've got you in my back pocket, Geeder. You've got seven more months and you're not going to try anything that will screw it up."

"You can't fire me," Geeder scoffed. "You'd never make your quota on the Resolutions with just those ragtags out there. Now call the research department and tell them to back off."

Coyote Jack only laughed, and then he called the research department to tell them that Sidney Geeder was fuming and was surely about to come up with some good trade ideas.

Now and then Coyote Jack made examples of one of them for the purpose of keeping the others in line. He fined someone for bad-mouthing the firm to customers, or he ridiculed one of them during the videoconference by asking trick questions he or she couldn't answer, or he fired a salesman who had been doing a perfectly good job. It kept them all on their toes. It kept them awake nights. It kept them threatened, and they either sold bonds out of fear or they sold bonds to prove they were tough. Nickel Sansome sold bonds out of fear. Sid Geeder sold bonds in self-defense. Nelson Dicky and Goody DeShews sold bonds because it was a respectable, admirable, honorable profession. Lisa Lisa sold bonds to prove she was as strong and smart as any man on the floor. Regis Reed sold bonds because it was the closest thing in modern society to the conventional trench warfare he'd been born fifty years too late to enjoy. They all had a reason, and Coyote Jack knew their reasons. All except Eggs Igino. Coyote Jack didn't know why the kid liked it. The kid was too new to have any addictions yet, and he was too calm to feel intimidated, and Coyote Jack wasn't going to rest until the kid was locked into his seat.

Coyote Jack needed them all locked in to make sure they wouldn't wake up one day and decide they'd had enough. For example, Sid Geeder was after his corporate shares. Nelson Dicky needed his money for the private school tuitions of his seven children. Regis Reed needed his money to support his cocaine habit. Lisa Lisa needed her money because she was a woman and carried the female gender's long history of oppression. Nickel Sansome needed his money because being rich was what was expected of a man in his family. They all needed their jobs, no matter how much they bitched and moaned. They would all show up for work tomorrow. None of them would call it quits, as Wes Griffin had done. But the kid . . . Coyote Jack suffered a lightness in his stomach when he imagined such brute brainpower just not coming in to work one day.

"How's that stomach of yours?" Stormin' Norman said, offering Coyote a pink stick of Pepto-Bismol gum. Stormin' Norman was the personal accountant for most of the salespeople. The firm hired him so they would know where the salespeople put their money to use, know why the salespeople came in to work each day. Norman Walker was a hot-tempered Southern gentleman who'd been a yacht salesman in South Carolina until he read a book about avoiding taxes and discovered his role in the information economy. Norman billed the firm in ten-minute increments to tell the salespeople what they could get out of a book for $20 or out of government pamphlets for free. It was a thriving practice with excellent fundamentals: every year, Congress opened a few tax loopholes and closed a few others and, in the process, gave the personal accountants a reason to exist.

"Okay," Stormin' Norman said, taking a seat on the couch. "Where's the warm body?"

"The kid near the window, standing next to Geeder." Coyote Jack moved to the intercom on his desk and ordered his secretary to escort Eggs Igino into his office.

Norman gazed out the window. "What's with his hair?"

"Kid's got a mind of his own."

"So? What's that have to do with hair?"

"Just sending a signal, I think. Staking his turf. Don't push him too hard."

Stormin' Norman bristled. "Don't tell me how to do my business. I know my business. I'll put thoughts in his head."

Eggs Igino appeared in the doorway. Coyote Jack introduced him as "the future of the firm," and he introduced Norman Walker as "the man who can find a tax break in a candy bar." They shook hands. Eggs Igino remained standing. Then Coyote Jack handed Igino an envelope. "That's your first paycheck, kid. Go buy a house."

"There must be some mistake," Igino admitted, looking at the check. "This is twice what I was supposed to draw."

Coyote Jack laughed nonchalantly. "Don't worry, kid. You'll be selling vodka to the Russians in no time. You're good for the money." Then he asked the two if they wanted coffee, and Stormin' Norman, on cue, said "no cream." Coyote Jack complained about his secretary's coffee and said he would be right back, leaving the two men alone together. They exchanged glances, then Stormin' Norman offered Igino a seat on the couch.

"I'm just fine standing. Thanks."

"Really. Take a seat."

"I'd rather not," he said coldly, avoiding Norman Walker's eyes, which were yellowy and bloodshot and painful to look at. Igino could smell the cigarette smoke on Walker's pale gray suit from across the room.

Their conversation halted for a moment. Norman tried to draw the kid out, to get his opinion on Michigan's chances in the Big Ten, and whether he'd yet viewed Nickel Sansome's videotape of the 1982 Rose Bowl matchup between the Wolverines and the Washington Huskies, where, in the closing moments of the national broadcast, Lisa Lisa cries into her pom-poms.

"She was a cheerleader?" Eggs Igino was amazed.

"Flashing her crotch on national TV," Walker affirmed with a snicker.

"He's got it on videotape?"

"She looked great back then. What a doll! Don't tell her, though—she doesn't have any idea that every one of her accounts has seen the tape. Poor girl, going to hell and all. Deducts her deslackening agent from her taxes, though."

"Deslackening agent?"

"Her Retin-A. It's a skin-care product. Girl's gotta have good skin to be a success in the business. Deslackening agents are a legitimate business expense. Same as Nickel Sansome's candy bars. Tell you what—you know why the firm pays you commission instead of a salary?"

Eggs Igino gave the obvious answer. "To avoid paying Social Security taxes to the government?"

"Social Security is loose change," Walker corrected him with a sneer. "Social Security is three thousand bucks a year, tops. You're on commission so you can *deduct*. Being a salesman's a one-man business, and you're entitled to the same expenses as any other business. For example: What kind of car do you drive to work?"

"I take the bus."

"Buy a car, kid. Deduct it from your taxes. Cost you only sixty cents on the dollar. Deduct it all: your suits; dentist bills; shoeshines. Haircuts." Walker's drawl grew more pronounced and his eyes started blinking constantly. "Hey—a salesman doesn't have any tools, or any inventory. He's got two things: his head and his image. Taking care of that image is a legitimate expense. You know why Regis Reed lives at the Excelsior?"

Eggs Igino was stunned. "Regis Reed lives in a hotel?"

"Hotel bills are a legitimate expense! Regis Reed's business is incorporated in my home state of South Carolina. He's been here on legitimate business travel for twelve months. Deducts eighty-five percent of the Excelsior bill, sixty percent of the cost of eating dinner in its penthouse restaurant, and one hundred percent of his airfare to fly to South Carolina to see my daughter, who adores him."

"That's not illegal?" Eggs Igino groaned.

"Might be. Reed likes the risk, though. Thrives on it. The boy's not comfortable unless he's under fire." Walker chuckled and rubbed his closed eyes with his knuckles. "Hell of a boy—my daughter can pick 'em. I got three daughters, all keen as a bloodhound. You married, kid?"

"I'm not interested." Igino looked out over the sales floor. The salespeople were congregating around Paul DeShews's desk, and it looked as if Sid Geeder might hit someone.

"Not for my daughters—for your taxes. In your bracket, being married is great for taxes. You ought to get married, Igino. Put a ring on her finger. Tell the world who's your girl," he urged.

"That's none of your business."

"Wait till April, when it's time to cut that IRS check. Shit, nobody likes paying taxes. You'll be looking for deductions, believe me. You'll be wondering what you can write off, but you can't write off anything unless we incorporate you. You gotta plan. You gotta think ahead. You got life insurance, kid?"

"Nope." Eggs Igino wanted to leave, but he sensed it was almost over.

"You got any health problems?"

"I take a lot of vitamins," he offered.

"Vitamins! Perfect! Write those off. What else? You belong to a health club?"

"Clark Kalinov says we're going to have a corporate membership soon."

"He's been saying that for twelve months. Soon as he loses ten pounds, he'll drop the subject. Look—you're a busy man. I'll send you some forms to sign. Meanwhile, you put that paycheck in a smart place. Buy some vitamins. Hell, buy some vitamin stock. . . ."

But Eggs Igino was gone. Eggs Igino was only twenty-four years old and hadn't learned to enjoy worrying as the others salespeople did, although he was learning very quickly with the prospect of moving the Resolutions.

"I'll never be able to sell thirty million Resolutions," Eggs Igino complained, when the market took a moment to settle.

Sid Geeder looked up at the kid. "Thirty million! I thought your quota was twenty."

"Coyote Jack raised it."

"Hah! Just tell your customers that the government is a safe investment because we can count on them to never fix their problems."

"I don't have any customers," Eggs Igino explained dejectedly. "They're all on credit hold. The credit department won't let me sell them anything."

"Then buy something from them."

"I'd like to, but when they sell a bond they have to mark its price to market and officially record how much money they've lost.

Once the Resolution Trust sees how much money they've lost, it will come in to shut them down. They'll lose their jobs."

"Believe me, I'd like to," Morgan Gorman whispered over the phone line, "but I'll lose my job if I sell you those bonds. I bought them at ninety-six. Now they're at eighty-four. I lost my shirt on those bonds." He was the mortgage trader at AmeriTrust Savings and enjoyed talking with Eggs Igino about vitamins and weight lifting. His voice was jolly and mischievous—he cynically called Igino "Sunny," on account of his gloomy forecasts about the market veering toward nonsense.

"Who sold them to you?" Eggs Igino asked.

"Wes Griffin did. I tried to sell them back, but the price kept dropping, and now it's too late. We'll have to wait until the bonds mature until we have any money to reinvest."

"That's in two years!" Igino bleated. "Don't you have *any* bonds you can sell me?"

"Sure I do," Morgan Gorman laughed. "I could sell you the rare ones that have gone up in price. But why sell them when they're doing so well?"

"Maybe we should have lunch," Eggs Igino offered. "We have a nice place . . ."

"I hate the Ming Garden," Gorman interjected. "That damn set menu they have. Too much soy on their vegetables, and they give you beer whether you ask or not, and always something with pork. Pork pot stickers. Barbecued pork rinds. Spicy pork soup. Green beans stuffed with pork . . ."

So Eggs Igino and Morgan Gorman met in the late afternoon at the YMCA, where Gorman was a regular. Igino had bought a silly pair of nylon shorts and a tank top from a tourist shop. They started out in the hips and stomach on the crunch machine, then moved to the hamstrings and calves before hitting the sled. They talked only a little, instead focusing on their breathing and fluids and concentration. Gorman was thirty-five years old and built like a barrel, all chest, with comparatively twiggish legs and arms. He'd been a sprint swimmer for a few years after college and still held the 50-freestyle record for the Y in the over-thirty division. But his legs were weak. Igino kept adding iron to the sled, surprised at how easy it was to press so much weight, and Gorman tried to keep up.

He groaned and grimaced and shook with the strain of the lift, then surrendered when Igino reached for another twenty-five-pound plate. They hit the showers and then shared a blackberry-banana fruitshake on the patio overlooking the Bay Bridge. "I know what you're after, Sunny. But maybe you ought to think of coming to work for me," Gorman announced. "I can't pay you as much, but it's an easier life."

"It's the damn credit limits," Sid Geeder complained the next afternoon to Coyote Jack, after Franklin Mutual had complained over lunch at the Ming Garden. "I sold everyone so much shit the past few years, now everyone's on credit hold."

"You'll figure it out," Coyote Jack retorted.

"I don't think I will," Sidney answered. "I think you've gone too far on this one."

"You're bluffing," Coyote Jack challenged. "The kid will think of something."

"He might," Sid affirmed. "But the deal's in a couple days. What if he thinks of quitting?"

"Quitting?" Coyote sniped. "The kid's not a quitter. You're reading him wrong."

"Morgan Gorman offered him a job."

"That asshole."

"Talk to the credit department," Sid reasoned. "Talk to management. Get John White's help. Do something."

Coyote Jack was bewildered. He couldn't believe it. He *didn't* believe it. "The kid won't go to AmeriTrust. He'll make three times as much money here."

"Not if all his accounts are on credit hold." Sid was glum at the prospect. "Besides, I'm not sure he's interested in money yet."

"Well, of course he's not interested in money—he's never had any! We've got to give him some to get used to it."

"Tell it to the credit department."

"I will. I will! I *will*!"

5 · Information Economics

THE INFORMATION ECONOMY was a Ponzi scheme spiraling out of control. The investment bankers got rich slaving away, so they called in their tax accountants, who got so rich filing government forms that they called their investment bankers back for advice about where to invest their surging wealth. The investment bankers were also miserable, so they called their therapists, who billed them by the hour to listen like a good friend and assure them they weren't crazy. They worked so hard they neglected their families, so many of which ended up in divorce. They called their divorce lawyers. The lawyers worked even harder than the investment bankers and suffered physical maladies that the doctors charged them ridiculous fees to attempt to cure. The doctors, worried about being sued by the lawyers, called their insurance brokers for malpractice coverage. The engineers built computer systems that helped all of them speed up this cycle so they could call and bill at a faster pace. The engineers that didn't build computers worked in the military industry at the request of the politicians, who were worried the Iranians might invade Florida. The politicians kept changing the laws so the lawyers could keep busy, and they kept changing the tax code so the accountants could keep busy, and they kept borrowing money to keep the investment bankers busy. This was the Third Law of Information Economics at work, and it was the way of the future. A young person could either go to college and become an expert and learn to play along, or he could work part-time answering phones for someone who had gone to college and learned to play along. They all profited from the increasing disarray of the information glut. So many experts led to so many theories, and they needed an expert to sort them all out. They needed a gynecologist and an obstetrician and an ophthalmologist and an internist and a dentist, as well as a dozen books on their ailments to make sure they weren't being ripped off. They needed a tax accountant and a stockbroker and a personal banker and an insurance broker, plus a few business magazines to cover the bases. They needed a therapist and an aerobics class and several volunteer projects to assuage their guilt, as well as a stack of books beside their bed to help explain the unexplainable. Then, to stay up on it all, they needed the *New York Times,* the *McLaughlin Group,* the *MacNeil/Lehrer NewsHour,* the local daily, the local weekly, *Morning Edition,* and several insider newsletters to cover what the others had missed. Everyone needed each other, and it all went around faster and faster in the name of efficiency. Everyone in the economy worked the phones. Their many voices raised up into a frenetic, urgent pitch, the whir of the machinery of the modern economy. The sound wouldn't go away, so they grew to like it instead, and couldn't relax without knowing there was lots for them to do. For brief periods life grew more hopeful, which meant it was even more disappointing when the volatility failed to subside.

The salespeople made money when bond prices went up. The bond prices went up when interest rates went down. The Fed pushed interest rates down when the economy softened and bordered on a recession, which it kept doing because it was so saddled with debt. The economy remained soft, interest rates kept going lower, and the salespeople kept making money. They disguised it all with numbers. They bought and sold money, and every year the Fed pumped more money into the economy for them to buy and sell. They paid for the money they had bought with money they had sold. They paid for a little bit of long-term money with a lot of short-term money. They paid for a little low-risk money with a lot of high-risk money. The savings and loans, which tried to play along, were taken to the cleaners and had their eyes ripped out and were made to swallow, then they went on credit hold until the government bailed them out. Money had a direction, and a speed, and an acceleration. The acceleration was always increasing with the benefit of computers and the politicians, who gave the markets free rein in the name of efficiency. It was the most efficient system in the world at making the rich richer. It was a far better system than entrepreneurism—that antiquated way of starting a business from scratch and growing it a little every year without borrowing, which sometimes took decades to make a rich man richer. The money was in sales, and the real money was in selling money. In a very short time, a man could make a great deal of money selling money. Coyote Jack did. Sid Geeder did. Wes Griffin did. Eggs Igino was trying, but the credit department was in the way.

The credit department was the top echelon of back-office employees who had worked at Atlantic Pacific since the seventies. For most of that time, they had been ordered about by the often much younger salesmen, doing them favors and getting nothing in return. They wired money, sent claim forms, and tracked down mismailed interest payments. They were old men from New Jersey who had spent their college-age years getting an education on the job about how pompous college grads can be. They smoked and drank and scorned the flashy attire of the salespeople, preferring instead to stick with their poly-blend suits that no longer fit in the rear. They gambled on cards and ponies, and not a single one of them was divorced. When they made it to the credit department, they finally had a chance to get back at the salesmen who had berated them every time money had been slow wiring out to a customer. It was the credit department's job to protect the firm, but it was also its creed to protect its turf. It didn't take kindly to Coyote's call. It remembered him from a few years before, right before he was made sales manager—all the amounts on his trade tickets were wrong. He was gone on vacation in Hawaii or Fiji, unavailable to straighten out his trades. It was a mess. Nobody got any work done for a week.

But every sales manager in every office had called the credit department to complain on the eve of the Resolution Trust deal, and several of them had called the syndicate desk to suggest they could up their quota if the credit limits were lifted, even if for only a few hours. Then the syndicate desk was calling the credit department too, and the men there couldn't finish their poker game because the phone was ringing off the hook. The syndicate desk also called the president and each member of the board of directors, who knew how important it was for the Resolutions to move smoothly. They'd taken so much heat when the Euro-Floaters deal soured, and they didn't want it to happen again. They gathered for a closed-door meeting in the penthouse apartment atop the firm's 49th Street tower. They sat about on the white couches with drinks in their hands and worried about the profitable business they had carved out helping the government shut down unprofitable savings and loans. It would all go to hell if the Resolution deal didn't sell. This was a highly secretive, clandestine, top-brass-only, late-night debate that was successfully leaked onto the front page of the next morning's *Wall Street Journal*.

"It doesn't make any sense," Eggs Igino uttered to nobody in particular, reading the front-page news at five o'clock the next morning. "If you think about it, it doesn't make any sense at all."

Paul DeShews was walking past with a bowl of Cheerios. "What doesn't make sense, Igino?"

"Our top brass announcing that the savings and loan crisis is over."

"It's hard to believe, isn't it? What a relief. Seems like we were paying to clean them up for years."

"But it doesn't make sense!"

"The war's over, kid. You missed the action. Count yourself lucky."

"But how can they say the crisis is over on the eve of selling a gazillion bonds to shut down another hundred savings and loans?"

"Just a little last-minute cleanup. A light dusting. I hear it's over. Even the credit department has relaxed trading limits."

"That's idiotic." Eggs Igino suddenly felt the urge to sock De-Shews right across the nose.

"The credit department and our top brass and the *Journal* can't all be wrong, can they, Igino?"

"But what about the Resolution Trusts?"

"They look pretty cheap now that the crisis is over. Like war bonds, sort of. I think they'll move like hotcakes."

It was a well-reasoned message of optimism and renewal that the firm expected to go over sensationally, because even though it made no sense it was what everyone wanted to hear. The public, which had been ignoring this little festering scratch from the beginning, was glad to hear it. The savings and loans, which had been the butt of too many jokes and highbrow analyses, were relieved to hear it. The salesforce, which now could borrow from the savings and loans in order to loan it right back to them (less commissions), was ecstatic to hear it. Now that the savings and loan crisis was over, the Resolutions—which had been priced at one-half percent interest rate higher than treasury bonds—were a darn good buy. The risk of the whole system's coming down under a domino of bankruptcies, foreclosures, and loan defaults had passed, and now that the government was going to finish up with a little $145 billion dust-mopping on the remaining few hundred worst bankruptcies, everyone ought to do his patriotic part to help.

So excited was the firm about the new turn of events and the bright prospect for the Resolutions that every ambitious sales manager in every worldwide office immediately volunteered to speak to the salesforce at the next morning's briefing. Each of the sales managers studied the *Journal* article in hopeful preparation and ran to the bathroom to act out his leading role in front of the mirror. Coyote Jack needed the bathroom to himself, so he stalked the sales floor for ten minutes, scowling at Lisa Lisa when she paused to reapply her lipstick and sternly narrowing his eyes at Nickel Sansome after he got off the phone with his father, so that none of the salesforce would risk his wrath and pause for a piss. Then he marched back to his office, and when nobody was looking he went out the back exit to the luxurious marbled rest room with tall ceilings, automated toilets, and lotion dispensers. The bathroom was the most relaxing, calm space in the building, and everyone secretly nurtured his time there. The brown marble walls blocked out all the sounds from the sales floor, even the sound of Lisa Lisa screaming at her customers, and it trapped the sounds within the bathroom and made them echo like reverb on an amplifier. Coyote Jack loved the sound of the automatic urinals flushing water down their pipes, and his own voice sounded most authoritative echoing off the walls. Coyote boomed out a stanza of propaganda, then paused on cue as the urinals flushed in unison like a roaring crowd. Even if the firm didn't let him address the worldwide salesforce, he intended to give his own short chalk talk after the televideo screens were turned off. He planted himself in front of the mirror, where in the dim, rose-tinted overhead lighting his facial blotchiness was unnoticeable. He tucked his hands behind his back, which kept his shoulders broad and his gut tucked, then, to emphasize certain phrases, he aggressively leaned on the sink, balanced on the palms of his hands like an ape. Satisfied, he scrubbed his hands, combed back his hair under another coating of gel, and returned to his fishbowl to call the syndicate desk and see if his request to brief the salesforce had been granted. As long as he had them on the phone, he beefed up his office quota another 5 percent.

"Everybody's upping their quota five percent," a gruff, impatient voice yapped back. "You're only staying even."

"Double it then!" Coyote Jack offered without thinking.

"To two hundred percent, or to ten percent?" the voice asked.

"The latter," Coyote Jack answered, avoiding the troubling digits.

"Ten percent San Fran," the voice summarized, before hopping off the line.

"That's one hundred and ten million dollars!" Sid Geeder wailed when Coyote Jack informed him the next morning, on the way into the final briefing, that his quota had been raised. Sid Geeder was always the first to arrive because he hated his job more than the others. He was always this recalcitrant before a big offering—during the Euro-Floaters deal, he had knocked an open thermos of coffee onto the warm plate of cream-cheese danishes in the center of the table just to get attention. Now, Sid Geeder paused at the window and looked down into the darkness at the blurred lights of the city and wondered what would happen if the deal didn't go well. Coyote Jack stood by the door as the salesforce filed in, their faces gloomy and despondent. This was it. The test of the mettle of the man, and Coyote Jack was up to it. He was wearing his lucky cowhide suspenders and managing-director-style sheer white-on-white-striped tab-collar shirt, which he had purchased on his last trip to Manhattan for several hundred dollars.

"Nice shirt!" Eggs Igino said cheerily, his mouth full and chomping away. Bits of danish dough and frosting were stuck to the outsides of his thick, expressive lips, which smacked and slurped as he chatted. "Well, this is it, huh! The big kahuna. The blue monster. The test of the mettle in the man. Everything I ever studied, every final exam and SAT and honors paper and GMAT and Series 63 test, all leading up to this single, primal challenge." He chuckled, slapped Coyote on the shoulder, and took a seat inches away from the televideo screen. Sid Geeder had warned him of Coyote Jack's speeches, variations on Knute Rockne–style tests of manhood that never failed to inspire Lisa Lisa.

Lisa Lisa showed up in full corporate uniform and in an exhausted, ill-tempered mood that Coyote Jack mistakenly assumed was the deadpan seriousness of a foot soldier before battle. She wore the camouflage of the trade, which blended her in seamlessly to corporate America. She wore a gray wool suit and a white silk blouse and the stiff spine of a faithful employee. She wore the flesh-colored pancake foundation and the pale blue eye shadow and the terse mouth of a hired gun. She walked in dim, low-heeled pumps and sheer nylons and the strut of a seasoned warrior. But to Coyote Jack, Lisa Lisa always looked five years younger when away from the pasty light of the green monochrome monitors, and she was less dumpy when standing up, walking around. He could see a little of the pom-pom girl in tears he'd seen in Nickel Sansome's videotape of the 1982 Rose Bowl, a little of the sprightly go-getter in snug sweater and vented skirt.

All thirty-seven salespeople filed into the briefing. Sue Marino, who wasn't yet up to speed on her corporate image, arrived in a tan dress with a red belt. Nelson Dicky arrived with the boggle-eyed jitteriness of a man under pressure. Regis Reed, who feared nothing, waited until the last possible moment before he exited the copy room, wiping his nose and clenching his jaw and rolling his tongue across his lips in smug overconfidence. Thom Slavonika took the same back-corner seat he'd taken since John White had been a rookie money-market salesman in the mid-seventies. Managing director John White arrived unannounced, fresh off the red-eye from La Guardia with crease marks in his cheeks and dents in his helmet of preppy hair.

"Morning, Coyote," John White said in forced formality.

"To what do we owe the pleasure, J.W.?" Coyote asked.

"Thought I'd give my own little pep talk after the main teleconference," John White answered, though he avoided Coyote's eyes, because he knew that Coyote had also petitioned the syndicate desk for the opportunity to address the salesforce. It was a safe role to volunteer for, because the syndicate desk never let anyone do it but themselves. It was so safe that on every big, successfully positioned deal, every sales manager in the world requested to take the credit on worldwide closed-circuit television, and they were all summarily denied. Nobody was going to take credit for the successful deals but the syndicate desk, and since the Resolution Trust offering had gone from a dog with fleas to a no-brainer in a single day, John White's and Coyote Jack's proposals were flatly rejected.

They all knew the routine. The firm armed the salesforce with hollow slogans and schlocky metaphors to help communicate optimism to their customers. *The storm has lifted. The rising tide has eased. The coast is clear.* These sounded nebulous and infantile in the midst of a high-tech videoconference, but they were easy to remember, and in the tense pauses of a sales call could, if imparted with confidence and urgency, sway clients to overlook their natural sense of restraint. Every salesperson except Sidney Geeder dutifully penned them down in the margins of their trading notes, where they could easily be found in a pinch.

Sidney Geeder didn't write down anything that had been announced in the sales mission briefings during the past month. He didn't write down that this $145 billion deal was more than twice the size of the 1992 Resolution deal, or that it was five times the size of a normal quarterly treasury offering. He didn't write down that the Japanese were going to wake up early to get their share, or that the Germans were staying late at their Bonn offices to put in their bids. It was perfect timing—the Japanese would be groggy and easily fooled, while the Germans would be drunk and easily deluded. He didn't write down that in overnight trading the British had hammered the long bond in an unsuccessful attempt to knock up the coupon rate on the Resolutions they intended to buy.

Sid Geeder hadn't written down anything during mission briefings since his assistant had walked out with the $36 Cross pen that he had charged the firm $275 to replace, plus interest. Sid Geeder was protesting. He wasn't going to write down anything that he could store in his head instead. If he wrote it down, the firm could come in during the middle of the night to Xerox it, transfer it to microfiche, and have their top-level, overpaid economists examine it under microscope for ideas to steal. Sid Geeder was paid to sell the firm's bonds—they didn't pay him enough to take his ideas, too. They could never pay him enough for that. Ideas were all he had. His trade ideas. His ideas on the shakedown of the information economy. His ideas about human frailty and the condition of modern man. If the firm stole those, it would steal the meaning from his life. To make his protest obvious, Sid Geeder sat right in front of the two-way video screen, so that everyone in New York could see what he didn't write down. He sat directly across from Eggs Igino, who sat in front of the screen so that everyone in New York could see the sweet glaze and realistic strawberry jam and whisper of steam coming off the danishes he was scarfing down. There hadn't been a predawn briefing mission for several days, so Eggs Igino had stashed plenty of strawberry danishes in his brief-case underneath the table, within easy reach of Sid Geeder. They made an obvious show of their strawberry danishes, savoring each morsel, tearing off ribbons of the flaky dough, letting the crumbs fall into their coffee, all to a point where the other salespeople in the room couldn't concentrate on the speeches being broadcast directly from the syndicate desk.

The syndicate desk was the foxhole to beat all foxholes. Most salesperson's "desks" were a dressed-up hybrid of a table and a cubicle, with a small amount of horizontal desk space flanked by sloping panels in which computer monitors and audio speakers were sunk and banks of phone lines were laid. The average two-person desk had 180 phone buttons, each an instant direct dial to an account, as well as a special series of buttons to patch in to the squawk box, the "Hoot 'n' Holler," the global walkie-talkie. But the five-man syndicate desk was a monstrous eight-foot-tall fortress of central command that imparted the great seriousness of the impending deal, the whopping dependence of the modern economy on this dubious medicine being swallowed smoothly by the financial system.

Sue Marino had a hard time swallowing her cream-cheese danish, watching those two boys in the front row gorge upon strawberry filling. She also had a hard time not being the temptation in every man's eye, a feeling she had grown to like over the two days since her return. She'd been beaten out by a pastry. She made a note in her trading book to show up early at the next briefing and grab a chair in front. "Red silk blouse," she wrote immediately below, then underlined that three times.

"All right," John White said, after the syndicate desk had signed off. He stood up and paced in front of the window as he spoke. "You're all professionals. You know the routine. I don't need to remind you how significantly the future of the firm hangs on the success of your efforts today. You've all been notified by Coyote how much we're estimating you will sell, and you all know that these are merely estimates and not strict quotas or even goals. You just do your best." He paused for a moment, tucked his arms behind his back, and then approached the table and leaned on it like an ape. "But I'm not taking any excuses—no 'it's the credit department,' no 'luck's not with me,' no goddamn lies about 'the ones that got away.' You're all a horde of sniveling amateurs when the pressure is on, and you'd better not crumble under the cooker. The firm needs this one. Some of you will earn as much as a quarter of your annual bonus today, and those that don't shouldn't bother to show up for work tomorrow. Those quotas are strict, and don't you forget it!"

The salesforce double-timed out of the room on cue, Nickel Sansome in the lead, and took their positions behind their desks. It was two minutes to five in the morning. Some tiptoed off to the bathrooms. They all began to jot down a list of the order in which they were going to call their accounts. Their handwriting was shaky and anxious. People nervously tapped their feet. They eyed the clock. Nickel Sansome stole the dental floss out of Thom Slavonika's drawer, then took three quick blasts off his antihistamine inhaler. Sid Geeder brought a thermos of coffee out to his desk. Lisa Lisa, eyeing the reflection of her face in the green monochrome monitor, reapplied her lucky lipstick. Eggs Igino had received—from his old girlfriend's kindergarten students—twenty-two "Good Luck!" letters cut to the shape of turtles, which he spread across his desk. Regis Reed ran off to the copy room again. Paul DeShews set a tiny toy American flag and flagpole above his phone panel. Nelson Dicky turned all seven framed pictures of his children toward DeShews's flagpole in mock allegiance. Sue Marino held back the urge to burst out in tears at how sad life had so quickly become.

Thom Slavonika opened his drawer to get his dental floss. Coyote Jack, still smarting from John White's ambush, angrily hobbled up and down the narrow aisles, spitting at people who ran back in from the bathrooms.

They turned up the volume on their squawk boxes until the hoarse feedback made the worn-out speakers hiss and pop. They all gazed into the dark night clouds that rattled and bowed the enormous, wall-high windowpanes. Several of them jumped when the air-filtering vents overhead clicked on with a churning grumble. The heating element on the monster photocopier in the back room sucked in a rush of electricity that made the fluorescent bulbs above momentarily dim. The control panel on the central laser printer flashed through its self-test operation. The fax machine spit out and chopped off its hourly activity report. At five o'clock, the building's machinery automatically activated through a single timed power switch hidden deep in the bowels below the parking garages. Then the phone banks went red.

"Incoming!" screamed Nickel Sansome.

"Who has floss!" screamed Thom Slavonika.

"Sell the Aussies!" screamed Eggs Igino.

"It's patriotic!" screamed Paul DeShews.

"More yield than treasuries!" screamed Nelson Dicky.

"Back to work!" screamed Coyote Jack.

"Of course we'll buy them back!" Sidney Geeder screamed.

"Syndicate! Syndicate!" Lisa Lisa screamed.

"The coast is clear!" Sue Marino screamed, when she couldn't think of anything else to fill the pauses in her sales pitch, of which there were many. Sue Marino was out of practice. She was trying to make sense of the bonds, rather than just jam them down her customer's throat with a line about how fast the bonds were moving and you'd better not miss out. That "get 'em while they're hot" angle had to be pitched with conviction, and with the trust developed from a month's worth of loyal trading updates, pricings, and faxed analyses. But for the past month, Sue Marino had been in Scotland, and many of her accounts had developed dependence upon Solly or Merrill. She couldn't beg or get angry. As much as she wanted to, she couldn't get into it. She kept thinking about this museum she had been to in Aberdeen where, among the landscape paintings and stringed instruments, five live sheep were kept on pedestals. From afar they looked stuffed, but they weren't—they were chained to their pedestals, and they seemed perfectly happy to be scratched by the visitors. Sue Marino kept thinking about those sheep.

She uncrossed her legs and turned back to the phone lines and tried to concentrate, but she just wasn't dressed for it. Panic swept over her, and suddenly she was moist everywhere with sweat. The acrylic material of her dress clung to her sides and began to stain at her armpits and in the small of her back, where it was bunched against her skin by her red belt. She tried to loosen the belt, but she was already using the last notched hole—it was a dress/belt tandem she'd worn in college, and though she'd managed to drop seven pounds hiking around Scotland, she wasn't her old self anymore. Without the belt, the dress unfurled around her chair embarrassingly, like a parachute, and it didn't do anything to stop the sweat stains at her armpits or the origin of the sweat itself, which was the realization that now that she was engaged she had lost her edge and couldn't sell mittens in a snowstorm. She clutched her hands over her ears to block out the sounds of so many people screaming and so much machinery whirring. She peered over the top of her foxhole at the other salespeople, all of whom were ranting away furiously, even Lisa Lisa, who had patched into the Hoot 'n' Holler twice already to announce she'd moved Resolutions in size. An idea popped into Sue Marino's head, a desperate inspiration. She jumped out of her chair and scuttled inconspicuously around the outside aisles of the sales floor, avoiding Coyote Jack's myopic eyesight; he was too absorbed in his browbeating of Regis Reed to notice Sue Marino stealing Lisa Lisa's spare blouse and wool suit out of the hallway closet. Sue Marino tucked the clothes into a ball and ran toward the back exit, where she practically knocked over Thom Slavonika in her panic to prove she hadn't lost her edge. In the bathroom she yanked the flimsy dress over her head in one pull and jammed it into the small garbage canister below the sink. She moistened a wad of paper napkins and ran it up and down her arms and over her breasts and onto the parts of her back that she could reach, leaving shreds of wet paper in its path, which she then furiously patted off her skin. Then she hopped into Lisa Lisa's uniform, which—to her chagrin—wasn't too big for her in either the rear, waist, or shoulders, but was too large across the chest. She drew her hair behind her head with a rubber band, washed her hands once, and then charged back onto the sales floor, where she almost collided with the small Mexican maid who was delivering the cart of preordered breakfast. Sue Marino squatted on her chair and turned up the volume on her squawk box and pushed the direct line to her top account and begged him to please, *please,* just buy the fucking bonds, asshole, after all I've done for you the past two years . . . and so he did—as an engagement present.

"Syndicate! Syndicate!" she hollered, trying to announce her sale on the squawk box amid the flurry of trading. "Syndicate: five million in San Fran. Syndicate!"

All thirty-seven salespeople in the West Coast office worked the phones except Thom Slavonika, who was raging through his drawer looking for floss. "Who has floss?" he yelled out in vain, but the salesmen couldn't help him, even those with floss, because they were on the phone and under stress and it was survival of the fittest. He dumped out his desk drawer on the floor and kicked it into the aisleway. Then he dumped out his file drawer, and flipped over his organized stack of trading tips, and pulled his chair away from his desk to see if a piece of floss on the floor had escaped the eye of the Mexican maids who scoured the office each evening. He pounded on his desk and then collapsed on it with his head in his hands, thinking. He ran off the sales floor to the desks of the management secretaries, who didn't show up until long after the sun came up. He found lipstick and calligraphic pens and spare change, but no dental floss. Then he barged into Clark Kalinov's office and rifled through his desk, and found a sewing kit that Clark used to sew designer labels onto the backs of his ties. In the sewing kit was a spool of thick black thread, which he pushed into his pocket as he ran back out onto the sales floor, nearly bowling over Sue Marino, who was on her way to the bathroom to change out of her sweaty dress. Thom Slavonika didn't bother to reassemble his desk. He picked up his phone and sold to the same accounts he'd been eye-gouging for twenty-two years, his mouth pausing only for intermittent scrubdowns with black sewing thread, which he found worked quite well. After each sale he patched into the squawk box and told the syndicate desk he'd moved another few million Resolution Trusts. That was the greatest feeling, to have every salesperson in every Atlantic Pacific office around the world hear that you had just made a sale. For just a moment, every salesperson in the world was jealous. It was a glorious, gratifying feeling that made it all seem worthwhile, and it was a feeling Thom Slavonika was addicted to.

Every moment was a battle. There was the battle to persuade a customer to abandon common sense. There was the battle to keep one's composure under pressure, and to resist admitting to one's client that the bonds were overpriced, and to not think about that three-mile-wide mountain of garbage in the Dominican Republic, or those barrels of radioactive uranium in Utah, or the day the bonds came due. There was the battle to not be the first to break down and rush to the kitchen for breakfast. There was the battle to not drool over Coyote Jack's secretary as she arrived late and ambled past the sales pits, fumbling through her handbag for a breath mint. There was the battle against the accelerated aging of the human body caused by sitting eleven hours a day, five days a week, for a few years of their lives. There was the battle to not just bust out crying at how surreal their battles had become.

"It's all so surreal," admired Eggs Igino, who was witnessing postmilitary combat for the very first time. He stood by the thundering windows and gazed across the sales floor.

"It's burglary!" Sid Geeder screamed back. They'd stolen his peace of mind, right when he most needed it. The financial system lurched and buckled and blew its fuses under the surge of so many new bonds rushing in, and one of those fuses was Sid Geeder, who was concentrating on how much he hated the innocent trade manager at World Savings. Sid dwelled on the time he'd offered the trade manager his two tickets to the Stanford-Cal football game, and the trade manager had been so greedy as to accept his offer and go to the game, which ended in a dramatic last-second Hail Mary touchdown. Sid ruminated on the time the trade manager had expressed a naive, boneheaded faith in the capacity of the U.S. military to successfully convert the mothballed B-2 Stealth technology into productive civilian uses, like a better razor blade. Sid recalled the time the trade manager had asked him to fax the entire prospec-

tus on the Euro-Floater deal before buying it. Sid struggled in his
seat thinking of these things. That man had made Sid miserable
over the past few months. That man had also been so stupid as to
actually buy the Euro-Floaters, and anybody so stupid should be
forced to buy the Resolutions as punishment.

World Savings was one of the few profitable and well-capital-
ized savings and loans in the country, despite Sid Geeder's relent-
less efforts to make it take losses on sizable positions of new, highly
speculative bonds. It was wisecrack thrifts like World that were
preventing the government from just folding up the whole savings
and loan system in its entirety. Sidney despised World. It was his
best account, and since he'd been miserable only since he'd become
rich, it was largely to blame. He'd talked with the trade manager
three times already that morning and was waiting for a return call.
Three times was Sid's limit; if they didn't bite in three pitches, that
was it. Sid didn't beg. Sid had never begged. He was the King of
Mortgages and he didn't have to. Then he called the trade manager
at World a fourth time and wound his way through the fortress of
voice mail, secretaries, and assistants so that he could remind the
jerk once again that in his nearly four years with Atlantic Pacific,
they had never stopped actively trading bonds they had put in the
market.

Eggs Igino was still gawking. Occasionally he flipped through
his paper turtles. For once he wasn't stretching his calves or hamstrings in some yoga position. He was just standing there, being
knocked about by the crossfire of yelps, cusses, and pitches.

"You'll get used to it, kid," Sidney Geeder offered.

"It's all coming true," he giggled.

"Stop giggling, kid—you're getting rich and you'll be miserable
before you know it. Get back on the phone. You called Gorman
yet?"

"He goes to the Y before work. He'll be in at nine."

"Go get me some breakfast then. I'm starving here. Those
danishes put me on a sugar elevator."

"You'll get used to them," Eggs Igino said, wandering off to the
kitchen in a dust cloud, completely ignoring the bewildered stares
of the other salespersons, who couldn't imagine getting their free
breakfast while under so much peer pressure to stay at their desks.

Eggs Igino was enjoying the whole thing and didn't see the harm in any of it. He didn't think there was any harm because the whole world was trending toward disorder anyway. Eggs Igino had been studying economics for six years, and he'd never seen such a perfect display of the Third Law. He sat down at the small round table in the kitchen and tried to gather his thoughts. The First Law of Information Economics was simple: Knowledge is power. The Second Law was only a little more complicated: Knowledge is not a candy bar. If you eat a candy bar, the candy bar is gone. And if you give it to a friend, then he gets to eat it and you don't. But with knowledge, you can't use it up, and you can't get rid of it by giving it away. This leads to the corollary to the Second Law: Word travels fast. Knowledge spreads much faster and more easily than any physical product, mostly because telling your friends doesn't make you poorer. If knowledge spreads effortlessly to everyone, and if knowledge is power, then one logical conclusion was that everyone would have power. The other logical conclusion was that the power of knowledge was fleeting and temporary and we would all be powerless. Eggs Igino pulled a paper napkin off the breakfast cart and wrote on it with one of the corporate pens in light blue ink:

1. Knowledge is Power!
2. Knowledge is not a Candy Bar.
2(b). Word Travels Fast.

He stared at his theories. He underlined each of them twice as he rehearsed their logic. It was just so beautiful to see the salespeople so powerless and their world going to hell. For an intellectual like Igino, it was as beautiful as mitochondria in a petri dish or a mouse in a maze. Then he wrote below the other lines in large, energetic, slashing letters:

3. Power is Temporary!!!

"You'll get used to it, kid," said Clark Kalinov, in a moment of rare compassion. He had walked into the kitchen to get his scrambled eggs and rye toast. Clark had spent an hour on the Exercycle that morning and was famished.

"Get used to what?" Eggs Igino asked, tucking the napkin into his pocket.

"The stress. It's horrible on days like this."

"Oh, I'm already used to it. I'm so used to it, in fact, that I don't feel stressful at all. In fact, I'm perfectly amused."

Kalinov didn't seem to hear him. "Well, eat something and you'll feel better."

"Oh, this isn't for me—this is for Sid. He's feeling very stressed."

"Well, he'll get used to it," Kalinov mumbled unconsciously as he left the kitchen.

Paul DeShews was trying to get used to the new chair he'd brought in to work with him that morning. It was an ergonomically correct pretzel of alloy frame and sorbothane padding that he was supposed to wrap himself around. Dr. Perkova had prescribed it to prevent further degeneration of his carpal tunnels. The chair had wheels, but because his legs were buckled under his body and not even touching the floor, the only way he could move about his desk was by tugging himself around with his hands, like a paraplegic. Without his legs, he couldn't rise up an inch to peer over the edge of his desk at Coyote Jack's secretary as she strolled in late.

"Look at that," Sid Geeder snickered, pointing at Paul DeShews when Eggs Igino returned to their desk with fruit cups and unbuttered toast. Sid Geeder poured them each a cup of coffee out of his thermos. He was trying to cheer the kid up. "Look at that," he repeated, pointing at Coyote Jack's secretary as she passed through the trenches like a ghost of health and beauty. Sidney let his tongue hang out and panted like a dog. He grabbed his balls through his wool trousers. It was a crude gesture, but it was a sane reaction to feeling the flush in the groin. It was a far more human reaction than Nickel Sansome's, which was to try to deny how much he fantasized about her lying down naked on the monster photocopier and masturbating as the salesmen remained chained to their desks. It was a lengthy fantasy that he added to each night as he lay in bed trying to sleep. Thinking about sex was often the only way he could block out the rest of the world and pass into his dreams. He thought about receiving the pornographic photocopies in an Intermail envelope two days later, sent by her to all the salesmen to drive them crazy. He thought about Regis Reed going in there and laying down a line of cocaine on the glass ahead of time. The coke would inflame her genitals and make her rage upon the glass, all of which would be captured in photocopies delivered two days later by the simpleminded mail clerk, who had no idea how he was involved in her conspiracy to drive the men insane. It would have been a perfectly human sexual fantasy if Nickel Sansome had only let himself think about it during work and maybe mention it to Sid Geeder or Thom Slavonika, who had fantasies just as weird and cruel. But Nickel denied himself; he repressed it, drove it out of his mind—but it only came back at night in a perverted way to haunt him. It came back every night as he lay in his bed with his hand on his boner. Coyote Jack's secretary was a perfectly nice, friendly girl whom Nickel guiltily avoided during the days. He was often curt with her, even rude, and she had no idea why he always treated her so. She always smiled at him and tried to bring him coffee and offered to refile his research reports alphabetically and otherwise tried to make him like her, but he was always evasive.

"Syndicate desk?" Eggs Igino had patched in to the Hoot.

"Syndicate here," a voice came back.

For a moment the trading quieted as everyone paused to hear who had sold how much to whom.

"Syndicate, this is San Fran."

"Go ahead, San Fran."

Paul DeShews untwined his legs from his chair and leaned forward to peer over the edge of his desk at Igino.

"I've made a sale to AmeriTrust," Igino offered.

"Roger that, San Fran. How much?"

Coyote Jack, who was in his fishbowl, went to the window to watch the kid.

"Fifty million."

"Fifty million! Way to go, San Fran. Who am I talking to?"

Eggs paused. Every salesman and every sales manager in every worldwide office was listening. "This is Mark Igino."

"Ladies and gentlemen," the voice broadcast in a barker's inflection, "Mark Igino in San Fran just moved fifty million Resolutions. Now get off your butts and follow his lead!" The Hoot went quiet for a moment, and then the trading started back up again.

It had been easy. Eggs Igino had simply phoned Morgan Gorman, told him he was off credit hold, and offered the Resolutions. Gorman, who had a tremendous amount of pent-up desire to trade bonds, a desire that had been constrained by the trading limits every single investment bank had inflicted upon him, went gang-busters on the Resolutions. He took fifty, and he had a hankering to take more. And now that he had spent $50 million that he didn't have, he needed to sell an equivalent amount of something that he also didn't have. So Morgan Gorman called back Sunny Igino and shorted $50 million Freddie Mac 9.5 mortgage-backed securities. He'd sold as much as he'd bought and he was back in the market and he was happy. It was great to be trading again. He didn't care about making money anymore, he just wanted to participate. The investment banks had stonewalled him ever since the rumor spread that AmeriTrust was going to be shut down by the Resolution Trust. The Resolution Trust Corp. had caused Morgan Gorman so much trouble, so in defense he bought the Resolutions, the bonds. This meant that if the RTC ever came to close him down, it would in effect be eating its own bonds, at a loss. Nobody in the financial system ever bought back his own bonds. Atlantic Pacific had never done it. Chase Manhattan had never done it. Dai Nippon had never done it. Morgan Gorman was counting on the pattern hold-ing. He was counting on the RTC being too embarrassed to admit publicly that what had made AmeriTrust go bankrupt was exces-sive purchase of bonds the RTC had issued. Morgan Gorman was counting on the fear of a public relations nightmare, which for government agencies was far more damaging than financial hem-orrhage or ineffective programs.

"Look at that!" Sid Geeder laughed. It was the lunch hour al-ready, and the market had slowed to let the dust settle. He was pointing across the floor at Lisa Lisa, who was chewing out one of her customers as her bald-headed boyfriend sat around waiting to take her to lunch. He had a red face inconsistent with his smug posture and natty attire, which included a thin gold chain around his tie that made Sid Geeder want to storm across the floor and sock him between the eyes. Lisa Lisa couldn't get off the phone, though—it sounded as if the client had promised to buy the bonds today but now was backing out. Something about the Federal Re-serve about to raise the discount rate. "Greenspan's a peckerhead!" she screamed. The boyfriend kept waiting. Then Coyote Jack's secretary came back out on the floor and offered him some coffee, which he accepted in a graceful, mischievous, erudite way that made Eggs Igino want to dash across the sales floor and kick him in the shins. The guy's eyes were all over Coyote Jack's secretary as she walked into the kitchen, and they were groping her again when she came back with coffee and offered to let him wait in Clark Kalinov's office, where it was quieter. So he traipsed off the floor behind her, his eyes already having undressed her to her lingerie.

"Lisa Lisa's dead," Sid Geeder observed.

"Never should have called Greenspan a peckerhead," Eggs Igino agreed. "Most guys don't like that in a woman."

"I do," Geeder countered. "I love it. Chicks with dicks, man—I like a woman with *cojones,* gusto, power."

Finally, Lisa Lisa patched in to the squawk box. She stood up and arched her back. "Syndicate. Syndicate, this is San Fran."

"Look at that," Sid Geeder said with admiration. "Steel balls on that gal. Hear them clanging." But then his phone rang and he was back to work. Eggs Igino's selling so many bonds was just the kick in the pants that Geeder needed to prove that he was still top dog around here. No hotshot kid was going to sell more ice to the Eskimos than Sid Geeder. Sid Geeder hated these bonds, even more than the Euro-Floaters or Freddie Mac Adjustables, and so he loved to sell them. These had a far better chance of bringing down the entire financial system under its own buffoonery, and so he did his best to make sure every last penny of the $145 billion was in a place where it could do the most damage. Ingenesis Corp., which had recently secured an enormous government military contract to engineer a better razor blade, had plenty of government cash lying around, and so Sidney helped Ingenesis loan $25 million of it right back to the government, less commissions. Sid found this hilarious, and he had great confidence that some journalist would one day pick up on the nonsense and get the whole story wrong. Franklin Mutual, which had just come off credit hold, took $30 million. They would never be able to pay for the bonds, of course—that's why they had been on credit hold—and so the RTC would have to shut them down in order to step in and buy their own bonds from

Atlantic Pacific, less commissions. Sid Geeder got such a good laugh out of this that he did it again to Prudential Federal for another $10 million, and after that he had to take a break because his belly hurt. He'd never had so much fun getting rich, and being miserable had never been so painless. Then the trade manager at World called, asking to see a prospectus, and Sid knew that World would soon do its patriotic part in helping to improve the government by making it worse.

It had been a good day all around. It had been a huge success that left everyone feeling hollow and confused, particularly Thom Slavonika, whose successful streak of twenty-two years almost ended over running out of dental floss. Now his hands trembled as he sawed Clark Kalinov's unwaxed sewing thread into his gums. He knew Coyote Jack was watching him from behind his fishbowl window, and a hollow feeling struck him as Coyote Jack's finger popped up and beckoned Slavonika into his office.

Thom Slavonika took a seat on Coyote Jack's couch.

"Close the door, will you, Flossman?"

Thom Slavonika got up and closed the door.

Coyote Jack looked down at a yellow notepad and made a notation. He cleared his throat. "Secretariat was the greatest racehorse of all time, Flossman. A Triple Crown winner. You remember her?"

"Aww, Christ," Thom Slavonika cried. "Don't do this to me, Coyote."

"You know how old she was when they had to put her to sleep?"

"I had a bad day, Coyote."

"She was twenty-two years old. Came down with a bad case of laminitis. Intense pain in the hooves."

Thom Slavonika held his head in his hands. "Oh, please, Coyote."

"I'm giving you a fucking compliment, Flossman! You want to do it the hard way or do you want to do it the easy way?" Coyote Jack walked over to his file cabinet and opened it. He pulled a manila folder and set it down on his desk, then sat back down and opened the folder. "It's not just today, and you know it. Who are you kidding? You've got to pass the mantle sometime. You ain't got it anymore. It's time for greener pastures."

"Quit comparing me to a goddamn horse! Twenty-two years I give this firm, and you compare me to a goddamn horse!"

"It's a compliment!" Coyote Jack yelled. "I'm trying to tell you that you're a legend."

"Oh, that's really fucking generous of you, Coyote: 'You're a legend, and by the way—you're fired.'"

"Quit being a crybaby about it. I'm giving your accounts to Igino. You saw what he did out there with AmeriTrust today. The accounts trust him."

"What do I care?!" Thom Slavonika screeched, ripping his tie out of his shirt collar and throwing it into the wastebasket beside Coyote's couch.

Coyote Jack shook his head. "I'm telling you that this is a natural process. Pass the torch, Flossman. Let it happen. You know how this works: I can call security, and you can go out kicking and screaming, and we'll ship you the contents of your desk in a box. Or you can go clean out your desk, be real nice and quiet about it, and save yourself the humiliation."

"That's some choice you're giving me. A real nice set of options."

"Take your pick," Coyote Jack shot back as he reached for the phone to call security.

Thom Slavonika got up from the couch and went to the door. "You're an asshole, Coyote. In the old days I never would have been treated this way. Never." Thom Slavonika traipsed back to his desk for the last time. He kept a garment bag in the hallway closet, and he began to fill it with his personal items. His arms and shoulders were heavy with exhaustion. He sank to his knees as he went through his filing cabinet.

"What gives, Flossman?" It was Sid Geeder, standing behind him with a warm cup of coffee in his hand.

Thom Slavonika didn't look up. "They're giving my accounts to Igino."

"Say that again?" Eggs Igino coughed, after Coyote Jack invited him into his office.

"You've got Slavonika's accounts, starting tomorrow."

"Tomorrow? You're not even giving him two weeks?" Eggs Igino was horrified.

"What in the world would we give him two weeks for?" Coyote Jack said with curt disdain. "He'd be a lame duck. He'd be worthless."

"But you can't just fire him, can you?" Eggs Igino asked.

Coyote Jack cut him off. "We already fired him. He's gone. Put it out of your head. It's not your job to show sympathy for other salesmen. Go through his desk and take home his trading notebooks. Get acquainted. Memorize his accounts' portfolios."

"I can't believe it," Eggs Igino panted, when he got back to his desk and sat down with his back to the window.

"What did you expect?" Sidney Geeder asked.

"Everyone will hate me now," Igino predicted.

"Don't take it so personally. Flossman's days were numbered. He was an antique."

"What am I supposed to do now?" Eggs Igino wondered.

"If I were you," Sidney answered, looking at the clock on the wall, "I would quit while I still had the chance."

"Quit?"

"Go back to Mexico. Do what you love. While you still have the chance."

"Mexico wasn't what I loved. I'd go back if it was."

"Aha—I sense a woman in your past."

Eggs paused. "Isn't that true of every man?"

"For some people it's truer than others. Did she hurt you, or did you hurt her?"

Eggs gulped, thinking about it, but didn't say anything.

Sid answered himself. "I guess it's never that simple."

Eggs nodded, holding in his emotions.

"I'll tell you one thing," Sid said. "You'll never find *it* here."

"Find what?"

"You know what I meant."

Eggs nodded again.

"Like I said," Sid repeated. "While you still have the chance."

6 · Escapes

THEY NEEDED A Paris, or a Rome, or a Seoul, or a Bangkok—a muggy, pillowed den of purely physical pleasure to bring the common world back into focus. They needed three-day drunken sprees that landed them with a venereal disease and a night in jail being tormented by a jailer who spoke no English. They needed to bury themselves in sand and sunburn their skin and loll about in tepid waves, then jog down the beach as foreign boys tried to sell them an hour with their older sisters. They needed dim lights and mysterious hands and bad music and an adventure into their other selves. Whatever it took to forget. They needed to lose themselves in order to shed the salesman's skin and find the man inside. The last thing they needed was to go home to their wives, who had married them because they were upstanding, wealthy businessmen with a reserve that reminded the wives of their fathers, and who expected them to act that way after the long, tortuous commute back from the city. The next-to-last thing they needed was a bunch of children around who expected them to use jesting baby talk and get excited about the model airplane they had built from popsicle sticks that really looked like an oil rig. The third-to-last thing they needed was an exclusive downtown club of wealthy, civic-minded aristocrats who sat about in smoke-tainted leather chairs reading the international newspapers and gabbing about which congressman would buckle under the pressure of those special-interest environmental fanatics. None of those were escapes, not really, because they expected the financier to still be a financier when he left the office.

Sid Geeder, who understood this, attributed his survival in the business to never falling in love, never having children, and never befriending farty old stooges who invited him to their clubs. Therefore, his growing love for Ivana Perkova was an acute threat to what had made him rich and miserable and was going to award him 100,000 shares of company stock currently trading at 42⅛. As long as it was just fascination with her long, pink fingernails that could gouge his flesh as he lay out vulnerably, half naked, then Sid would last. As long as it was just infatuation with the encyclopedic knowledge she carried of the human anatomy, then he would hang in there. As long as his sexual fantasies never came true, especially the one of her bathing him in an emerald-colored pool of water so salty that the human body merely floated, then he would survive. But Sidney Geeder gravely feared what these enamorations added up to, and so he tried desperately not to think of the way her curly brown hair would feel upon his neck. He cursed the urge to invite her to a romantic sunset picnic upon the huge sand dune at Baker Beach, where they could loll around on a wool blanket and she would tell him funny stories about studying Rolfing at an institute in Big Sur. He struggled against the impulse to bring her a bouquet of the daffodils that grew relentlessly in his backyard because of favorable soil conditions produced by the neighborhood dogs that used it as a latrine.

"Close the door," Ivana Perkova directed, as Sidney Geeder came into her office carrying a bouquet of daffodils. "You shouldn't have brought these," she said.

"I know I shouldn't," Sid exclaimed, grabbing Ivana Perkova by the hips and sliding his numb hands under her smock, where they skirted the silky, luscious, fervent flesh of her tummy and ribs and unconsciously groped at her little breasts as he mashed his mouth onto hers and slid his tongue between her teeth. "And I tried desperately not to."

Ivana Perkova uncontrollably opened her legs just enough to grind her crotch against Sidney Geeder's bulky, knotted thigh. Her skinny legs clenched him in desperate urgency and twined about his until she was no longer touching the carpet. She gasped for air and tossed her hair back with a flip of her neck. "I can't afford to get involved with you, Sid," she grunted hungrily.

"You think you've got a problem," Sid laughed, falling off balance and staggering about her room as his blunt fingers attempted to wriggle themselves inside the waistband of her tights. "I'm already bordering on psychological malfunction. You said it yourself. Thinking about you is practically driving me crazy." And with that they toppled wildly, landing in a mangled heap on Ivana Perkova's down-stuffed velveteen couch, where they caressed each other voraciously.

Ivana Perkova, who had been trained to display a reserve appropriate to her profession, couldn't resist Sidney Geeder's absolute disregard for propriety, and despite her better judgment and fear of impending doom she nearly let herself get carried away in their act. She raised her hips, hoping to get off quickly. With a smidgen of restraint she managed to blurt, "You don't know what I'm talking about."

"The hell I don't," Sidney whooped. The glorious feeling of Ivana Perkova's lithe, taut, squirming body against his nearly brought tears of joy to his eyes. "After this I'll never get any work done."

She squeezed his shoulders. "If they see the flowers, they'll know you've been here."

"Who will?" Sid said, biting her ear.

"Whoever's been coming in at night and searching through my office." Ivana Perkova sighed with pleasure as she pinched Sidney's nipples and tugged at the hair on his chest.

"Maybe it was the research department," Sid giggled, drawing a line down one clavicle and up the other with his tongue.

"Sid, I'm serious!" she cried, kicking at his legs anxiously with the heels of her feet until she had rolled up on top of him and could grab his face and look him in the eyes.

Her long hair draped into his mouth. He sucked it in through his lips and tasted her shampoo. "I'm serious too. I wish I could catch them in the act."

She tucked her hair behind her ears and sat up with her hands holding him down by the shoulders. "Sid, one of my files is gone!"

"Whose file?" he drawled lazily, trying to reach her breasts with his mouth.

"Yours!" she screamed.

"Oh my god!" Sid wailed, shaking his head maniacally. "Why didn't you tell me?"

"That's what I've been trying to tell you!" she hollered, beating on his chest with clenched fists. Sidney spun in agony, and suddenly there were white stars everywhere. Thousands of wispy white stars filled the air about them, covering their naked bodies like snowflakes, and Ivana Perkova stared as if she had just entered a dream. The white stars landed on Sidney's wet mouth and clung to his lips and tongue when he opened his mouth to cry out in anxious bewilderment. He could not understand what had happened, and he swung at the air frantically, causing the white stars to swirl up in a cloud.

"Why are you laughing?!" he yelled at Ivana Perkova, who was indeed giggling and clutching her sides as she pointed at Sidney's down-covered face.

"You popped the couch!" she squealed, reaching down behind Sid to a tear in the velveteen. She grabbed a fistful of white down and dumped it on Sidney's black hair. Sidney rolled over, and the pressure on the down caused another cloud to rise from the tear. He sat up in agony and attempted to spit the bits of goose down from his mouth. He ran naked across the office to the water cooler. He filled his mouth and swished the feathers, then spat angrily into the garbage can. He stood there plucking the fluff from his eyelashes and shaking it from his hair.

"Put some clothes on, please," Ivana Perkova laughed.

Sidney clumped back to the couch and slid into his underwear.

"What's in the file?" he asked with resignation.

"Just records of your visits. Sid, I'm worried."

"You don't have anything to worry about. It's me they're after."

"Then why are they bothering with me? There's nothing in your files except X-rays and medical notes. It's like they're trying to send a message. Even though they've got your file, they keep coming back. This morning, the furniture was rearranged. They *want* me to know they were here."

"Who's *they*?"

"I don't have any idea." She bit on her lower lip. "Sid, we can't see each other anymore."

"Are you kidding?" Sid said. "You're my only escape. Without you, I'll really go crazy. I'll be lost in the maze."

"Sid, I'm serious."

"I'm serious too," he stammered. "I've never been more serious in my life."

"Well, we can't fight them."

"Fight *who*? Who the hell are they?"

"It could be anybody," Ivana Perkova muttered.

"Maybe they want me to quit," Sidney guessed. "Like Wes Griffin. They don't want me to get my hundred thousand shares."

"Maybe they want *me* to quit," Ivana Perkova speculated.

"You? What do you have to do with this?"

"I wish I knew," she submitted.

But Sid was sure it had to do with his 100,000 shares of Atlantic Pacific stock that had traded up 3 points after the success of the Resolution deal.

"You should have bought them last week when I told you to," Nickel Sansome bravely told his father, after he double-checked the price in the afternoon paper.

Nickel's father leaned forward out of his smoky leather chair and pushed aside the international newspaper he was studying. "Should have bought what, son?"

"Atlantic Pacific. Jumped another point today."

Nickel's father considered this. "Well, that doesn't do me much good, does it? Is that what you do to your clients, Albert—call them up to tell them how stupid they are?"

"No, I don't do that." But he did do that. It was a sales technique he'd stolen from Sidney Geeder, who regularly intimidated his clients to make them feel intellectually inferior and lucky to even be talking to the King of Mortgages.

"So should I buy them now, Albert?"

"Buy what?"

"Atlantic Pacific. Now that it's gone up three points, should I buy it or sell it?"

Nickel really had no idea. "I'd recommend a hold strategy shortterm. Let the flippers take their profits, then snap it up with the bottom-feeders."

"Well, you just let me know when that time comes," his father said in a stuffy, pompous way that reminded Nickel of how much he hated his father and his father's exclusive downtown club, which admitted only men (the three women members were fictional composites fabricated to ward off nosy journalists), and then only men who either had reason to donate money to politicians or were extremely skilled backgammon players. Every year Nickel's father's club matched sixteen players against the Olympic Golf and Country Club in a wide-open, no-holds-barred backgammon tournament to once-and-for-all settle the long-standing feud over bragging rights. Nickel's father had raised young Albert Sansome to be the world's best backgammon player. As a boy, Nickel had been thrust into tournaments against men ten times his age to learn to keep his cool under pressure. Young Nickel had been quizzed on possible defense strategies at the dinner table, and the bathroom—where he seemed to spend much of his time—had been wallpapered with advice columns from Arab backgammon masters. Even though he still competed, Nickel had long ago lost his love of the game. He came to his father's club only because his father invited him and because he was developing an incurable longing for the Korean girl who brought finger sandwiches out to the backgammon table.

Nickel ate like a glutton as he played, wolfing down plates of tiny triangled club sandwiches continuously, to the point where the Korean girl needed to remain at his side and anticipate his next order. In her presence, he feigned a gambler's slick confidence and often looked her in the eyes before tossing his die. She became his lucky official sandwich-maker, and Nickel began to insist that she travel with him to tournaments at the Olympic Club. She was a dainty twenty-three-year-old who knew only enough English to take orders off the lunch menu and watch *Dick Van Dyke Show* reruns on late-night UHF television. She had a small heart-shaped tattoo on the underside of her left biceps. Nickel didn't want to protect her or console her or adore her—he suspected the tattoo meant she had worked as a whore for Japanese businessmen on an island off Japan, a slavery she had fled from once her age began to show. Nickel had read somewhere about the tattoo's meaning, and he was pretty sure he was correct. He suspected she had far more mettle than he did, as Coyote Jack would say. Nickel wanted to learn from her how to survive. He forced the club to buy her dresses and camisoles and nylons and hats out of its petty cash fund, and then he forced his father to buy her a necklace that would make the unknowing Olympic Club maids look upon her with envy. John White belonged to the Olympic Club and was a decent backgammon player, though by no means of championship caliber. Several years before, John White had made the mistake of thinking a young man so capable of calculating die combinations would be a whiz with bonds. Nickel Sansome really was a geek with numbers, but his mind went fuzzy when the numbers had dollar signs preceding them. He couldn't help it, and he couldn't stop it.

When John White was in town, as he was following the Resolutions deal, he entered in the tournament, and Nickel Sansome made absolutely sure that in the random drawing he was pitted against his boss for the opening round. Winners were the first players to win ten games, with double-games counting. Nickel, with his lucky sandwich-maker at his elbow, took four of the first five with ease. But John White was a crafty gentleman schooled in old-style manipulations—he wouldn't give in so easily. After a three-minute break, John White returned from the rest room and announced he had just bet Nickel's father $5,000 on the match. Nickel retained his cocky attitude and tried to ignore the distraction by staring at the heart tattoo on his good-luck charm. After the next break, with Nickel up seven to three, John White whispered he'd raised the wager to $25,000 and received two-to-one odds. John White was a shrewd, patriarchal mentor who wasn't going to let his professional status as Nickel's father figure be challenged, even by Nickel's father. With so much money involved, Nickel began to struggle with his breathing, losing his concentration, and when the $50,000 was lost he grabbed his Korean girl by the wrist and ran out of the building and tried to get as far, far away from it all as humanly possible. An hour later he was drunk on plum wine and sitting on the Korean girl's bed, laughing hysterically as Dick Van Dyke tripped over the buckle in the hallway rug.

Nickel Sansome, of course, couldn't escape his hatred for his father, just as he couldn't escape the truth that John White would always be able to squash him if necessary. Nor could he escape the urge to rub his bald scalp, an urge that intensified whenever he ignored Coyote Jack's secretary. This was a totally unconscious, vulgar, masturbatory image that was frighteningly obvious to Sid Geeder and Eggs Igino, who watched it from across the floor. But Nickel Sansome never made the connection.

"What are you guys laughing at?" he chuckled, because their howls were contagious.

Sid Geeder climbed off the floor. "Nothing, man, just nothing. Go back to work."

"Come on, tell me," Nickel persisted. "What's so funny?"

"Don't worry about it," Igino piped up. "No big deal. Nothing that doesn't happen every day." And that sent the two of them into hysterics again, as Nickel Sansome nervously tittered and scanned the floor for whatever might be such a good joke that it would put two grown men on the floor.

"I gotta get my phone," Sid Geeder said, hitting the red light, which had been blinking for five seconds.

"Back to work!" Coyote Jack yelled into the phone. "You guys have been prancing around out there for ten minutes!"

They could not escape far in the thirteen hours between the end of one day's work and the beginning of another. If they could have, the firm would have lengthened the workday to prevent it. There was not meant to be an escape, because escapes were the antidote to addictions. Addictions were necessary in order to sell, particularly the addiction to work—the sense that work provided the meaning to their lives, and therefore, in order to make life more meaningful, bust butt to be promoted to assistant vice president. Though they were all salespeople, the firm kept a very clear pecking order with a tall list of job titles to lend an artificial sense of importance to jobs that were always the same. John White was managing director with lifetime tenure unless he was fired. Coyote Jack was executive vice president. Sid Geeder and Nelson Dicky were senior vice presidents, just as Thom Slavonika and Wes Griffin had been. The majority of salespeople were simply vice presidents, as was Nickel Sansome, though Lisa Lisa was only an associate vice president, because Coyote Jack didn't trust that she would stick it out. He had seen her cry once, on national TV even, and he was convinced that despite being strong, she was brittle and would crack. A vice president had to be both strong and solid, without any weak veins. It also helped to be a man. Sue Marino was an assistant vice president, and Regis Reed was up for the same title in two weeks. Eggs Igino still hadn't received his business cards proving that he was a vice salesman, because he'd never filled out Clark Kalinov's absurd noncompete agreement which stated that he would never move to Shearson or Merrill to clean Atlantic Pacific's clocks.

"There's no escaping it," Clark Kalinov said the next afternoon to Eggs Igino, after Coyote Jack's secretary had left the office.

"Escaping what?" Eggs Igino demanded.

Kalinov took a stack of papers out of his To Do pile and re-stacked them more neatly. "Getting rid of your chair is one thing, Igino. But you underestimate my influence here."

"I'm busy, Kalinov. Get to the point."

"I'm busy, too, Igino. Look at all this work that has to be done." He backed away from his desk and took a deep breath. "I'm speaking of the noncompete agreement that was sent to you last week."

Eggs Igino chortled. "That dumb thing?"

"Why haven't I received it back from you yet?"

"Because it's stupid!" Igino vented. "How can you ask me to not compete against you if I leave?"

"It's a standard agreement, Igino. Everybody signs one. We know you're loyal to the firm," he insinuated, "but this is just in case."

"But I don't ask *you* to not hire other salesmen if you decide to fire me."

"That's ridiculous, Igino. This is our business. Of course we'll hire someone else if we decide to fire you. We can do what we want," Clark pronounced.

"Then I'm going to do what I want. This is my business, too. It's how I make my living. You can't tell me not to do it."

Clark went to the window again, turning his back on Eggs Igino. He had planned out this conversation at length, strategized on what buttons to push. He would offer the carrot first: "I'm not forcing you to do anything. This is a completely voluntary program that you're not obligated to sign, and it wouldn't hold in a court of law unless we decided to sue your ass off. But let's just say it enti-tles you to a few privileges that I control."

"What privileges?"

"Perks, let's call them. A wide cache of Atlantic Pacific perks that don't fall in the domain of the sales department."

"Such as?" Eggs fired back.

"Do you want me to start at the top or at the bottom?"

"How about just hit the highlights?"

"Okay, a few highlights. Breakfast, for instance. There's not a single mention of free breakfast in the corporate manual, but every morning the salesmen enjoy a warm breakfast prepared to standing order."

"Who cares? I could pay for my own breakfast to be delivered each morning. In fact, I could have the whole mortgage desk's breakfast delivered right out to our desks for less than it costs you. Who knows what you're extorting out of them?" he improvised.

"Don't get any ideas, Igino. Breakfast is loose change. You're going to need a sales assistant soon. But my sales assistant budget is tight."

"Sid Geeder gets along without an assistant," he argued.

"And he's never been so miserable. He's working a half hour longer on each end of the day to make up for it." The kid was too smart to not see the sense in Clark's offer. "Come on, face the music, Igino. Time to grow up. Let's make a deal."

But Igino stonewalled him. He loved to see Kalinov squirm. "I'm not signing your form."

"Don't be a crank, Igino. What's John White going to think when he hears you have no loyalty to the firm? John White's been around a long time. He's still the old guard—business done on a handshake, that sort of thing. . . . Am I making myself clear? You hear what I'm saying?"

Kalinov turned back around and saw that Igino had already left his office and was headed back toward the kitchen. It seemed the world was going in circles. He was glad, though, that the kid hadn't given in, because it gave Kalinov a reason for teaching them all a lesson about ignoring their Intermail. In a move of sheer bureaucratic brilliance, Clark Kalinov had drawn up a new breakfast order form listing all of the choices for free breakfast. At the bottom was a notice that if a salesman's form was not returned in four days via Intermail—meaning the salesman had to read it and fill it out and return it on the same day he received it—he would receive the default breakfast, Cream of Wheat with raisins. Clark had personally made thirty-seven photocopies, one for each salesperson, and had locked the master form in the office safe. He sat down at his desk and began sliding each of the photocopies into an old, worn beige Intermail envelope that looked like it had been around the world a hundred times. It gave him intense, snide pleasure, and he relished each envelope, carefully looping the sealing string around the button cleat and typing in the salesperson's name at the bottom of the routing table, then neatly stacking the package in his out-box. He went through the salesmen in alphabetical order, and he chuckled to himself in cruel amusement as he scratched their names off his To Do list. He was on Mark Igino's envelope, snickering at the image of Igino stewing over a bowl of Cream of Wheat with raisins, when Coyote Jack's secretary walked into his office without knocking, surprising him and making him leap to his feet in fury.

"I thought I told you to knock," he whined, stifling his rage.

"You told me to tell Mark Igino to knock before he storms into your office again," she corrected him shyly.

"Well," he shot back in a meek, trebled voice. "It would apply to you as well. I'm a very busy man."

"But I never storm into your office," she observed.

"What about just now?" he argued, pointing to the door and trying to avoid her eyes.

"I *strolled* in," she huffed. "I certainly did not storm in. I do not storm anywhere. Have you ever seen me storming?"

"I haven't," he admitted, debating to himself whether to apologize and regain her kindness or to piss her off further in order to keep her out of his business. Clark Kalinov was a shrewd plotter who could see how crucial this moment would be in the Great Scheme of his empire. He would not make the same mistake as Alexander the Great, who took a harem of women with him during his conquest into Persia. "But I don't want you entering here without knocking, period. And quit bringing me your coffee. It tastes like industrial sludge."

Coyote Jack's secretary's eyes widened and then narrowed, and her hand tightened its grip on the fistful of Kalinov's pencils that she'd just sharpened for him. Then she twisted around with a snoot and stormed out of his office, letting him return to his thoughts of Mark Igino.

Eggs Igino had run off to the kitchen because he'd just had an excellent idea that was ripe for immediate implementation. He found the Mexican maid who brought out breakfast and asked her how much breakfast would cost him if he had it brought right out to the mortgage desk from the catering service in the basement of the building. She assured him that if he didn't put it on the corporate account, his prices would be far less than the markups the catering service socked to the high-flying investment banking firm that every service worker in the building absolutely hated. She was excited that Eggs Igino spoke Spanish, and she tried to tell him everything she knew. She told him how the catering chef had to special-order low-salt sausages for Nickel Sansome. She told him how Clark Kalinov demanded that the air supply repairmen climb into the ceiling to change the recirculation filters every other Monday. She told him how Coyote Jack ordered the shoe-shine man, who had once been a tribal warrior in Kenya, to remove the laces from his shoes before shining them, so as not to get wax on the laces. Finally she told him the prices, which Eggs Igino jotted down on a napkin.

"Sidney! Sidney!" he heckled his partner, who was already on the phone to two accounts, one on each ear, alternating the mute buttons. Sidney tried to wave him away. He already had a horrible, unexplainable headache that felt as if his skull had been cracked in a huge garlic press and then Tabasco sauce had been poured into the wound. He was busy telling each of his accounts exactly how this headache felt. He'd tell one client, and then he would hold down the mute button and tell the other as the first one responded with his own war stories of headaches caused by drinking, exposure to enamel paints, and sunstroke.

"Sidney! Sidney!" Eggs Igino heckled.

Sidney tried to kick at Igino, and then he threw a trading report at Igino's face.

"But Sidney, we can get breakfast delivered right out onto the sales floor."

Geeder couldn't hear him. Both his clients were talking, and there were too many voices in his already swollen head.

"But Sidney—"

Sid Geeder had gone into a crouch and ducked his head into the crawl space below his desk. The tail of his shirt had yanked out of his waistbelt and a pale, hairy swatch of his bruised lumbar region was sticking up in the air. It was an ugly sight that made Eggs Igino turn his head and stifle a bellyaching laugh.

Eggs Igino hadn't had so much fun since Weston Bank tried to make him type up his trainee notes. Weston Bank was an old Atlantic Pacific executive's son who had been raised by his father to be one of the world's great sniveling nincompoops. Weston Bank, Sr., had spent all of his clout getting his prodigy into the prestigious Atlantic Pacific training program, and there was no clout left to get him out of it. The Atlantic Pacific heavy hitters, who wouldn't trust Weston Bank with a role of any significance, were so unimpressed by his mastery of financial terminology that they promoted him quickly to dean of the prestigious training program, where the most damage he could do was teach them accounting. Weston Bank was a stickler for detail and a true believer in education by repetition. His one goal in life was to get transferred to the research department, where he could get all the glory of correctly predicting the market while avoiding the financial risk that comes with putting your own money on the line. Weston Bank was a nasal-toned supply-sider with a buzz-cut hairstyle and a gift for raising the hackles of the incoming trainees. They resisted his authority and rebelled against him with great regularity, and they were the most prepared crop of young foot soldiers on the street. Since Weston Bank had taken over the training program, its trainees were much quicker to break laws and ignore regulations and abuse the trust of their customers and do all the other things that made a young salesman a heavy hitter. By being the most asinine, unrealistic educator on the street, he made his trainees keen to the absurdist realities of high finance, and they didn't flinch when First Boston declared itself bankrupt after the troubled Euro-Floaters deal, and they didn't blink when the company reemerged later the same day as the new and improved Atlantic Pacific Corporation.

Weston Bank had meticulously outlined all of his lectures and provided photocopies for the trainees to make sure they followed along. When Eggs Igino failed to stay awake during Weston Bank's lecture on the tax advantages of Real Estate Investment Trusts, Weston Bank countered with a new policy that all trainees turn in their own typed lecture notes the following morning, and he made

sure that his lectures strayed far and wide from the assigned reading so that cheats like Igino couldn't type up outlines from the
textbooks. Eggs Igino, always on the lookout for useful applica-
tions of the trading techniques Bank had taught him, decided to
purchase inexpensively two photocopies of the lecture notes be-
longing to a young coed who had been attempting all summer to
get Eggs Igino to sleep with her. Igino kept one copy for himself
and sold the second copy for $40 to a drunk from Princeton who
added gin to his orange-flavored soda pop at the inception of every
Bank lecture. This was repeated the next day, and then on the third
day Igino bought five copies, each printed out in a different font on
a different bond paper to prevent the appearance of a market glut
of lecture notes. Weston Bank didn't yet know how Eggs Igino
slept through two days on the Federal Farm Credit System and still
managed to jot down all of the significant information on how
grain subsidy vouchers meant to prop up the Romanian food supply were being resold by the Romanians in Miami for American
blue jeans sewn in Puerto Rico. But he found out the next day,
when Eggs Igino took his infant market public and taped a sign to
the swivel arm of his chair: "Lecture Notes, Bought and Sold."
Bank was so flustered he failed to stray from the assigned reading
at all.

Throughout the lecture, trainees wandered back to Igino's back-
row chair, whispered something in his ear, and then walked out the
back door of the small auditorium. There was so much demand for
the lecture notes that Eggs Igino kept raising the price without any
resistance. He knew he could tap his supply only so many times
without angering her, so he developed a second source: a Japanese
MBA destined for the Tokyo office who didn't fear retribution and
needed the cash to support his penchant for great slabs of oak-
wood-grilled T-bone steak. But the young coed hadn't given up on
Igino yet, and soon she was lowering her price to beat out the for-
eigner. Igino's spread kept broadening, and his billfold thickened.
Every night the coed invited him to pick up the notes at her apartment, and every night when he arrived she mentioned how she'd
just had three glasses of Sambuca liqueur and was up for a party. It
was better than having to sit through long dinners with the overweight Japanese MBA in the dimly lit Tudor Room three floors

below the Chrysler Building. Then the drunk from Princeton, who was running out of cash and had to drink at home rather than go to bars just to support his dependence on Igino's lecture notes, got the idea of satisfying the longing gaze in the young coed's eye. He showed up at her apartment right after she'd just had four glasses of Sambuca liqueur. She was vulnerable. He screwed her, took her to a party, and bought three copies of her trading notes, two of which he sold the next day at a price $5 below Igino's.

Open competition had begun just as Weston Bank raised the courage to clamp down on this blatant profiteering. He called Igino into his office and attempted to grill the kid into a blabbering crybaby, but instead Igino offered Bank a $3 "Lecture Tax" on all transactions. There were sixty trainees in the program, at least half of whom were involved in Igino's market and no longer bothered to attend any of the lectures. Weston Bank was caught so off guard that he almost accepted Igino's offer, but then he summoned the principles and the integrity and the courage to demand a $6 tax and a 10 percent royalty as the author. Eggs Igino laughed, shook his head, and bluffed that competition was too stiff to allow such extortion. He explained how the other trainees were raiding his market and how supply was becoming more difficult to guarantee. Eggs Igino offered Weston Bank a sweet deal: If he, Weston Bank, could guarantee a supply of typed trading notes—the same sort of thing he used to hand out for free—Eggs Igino would pay $12 per copy *plus* a $4 tax and an 8 percent royalty. College professors did it all the time, Igino reasoned. Soon Weston Bank was back to his old lectures, never straying from his meticulously detailed notes, and collecting $19 for every trainee who was too bored to show up. Weston Bank was extremely skilled at being boring. He drove them all right out of the auditorium. Then Eggs Igino sold his market share to a consortium of Yale grads who were tired of forking out $40 every day just for skipping lectures and decided they ought to profit from the deal. They talked Weston Bank, who suspected that Igino had bluffed him into a low price, into taking a 30 percent share in the consortium for only $1,500. They bought Igino's market share for $3,000, but forgot to force him to sign a noncompete agreement. They were MBAs who'd been in school far, far too long, and all they could think about was margins and market share. They were all headed to the research department. They didn't know how to connive or sucker or bluff. Eggs Igino drank three cups of coffee during each lecture for the next few days, managed to jot down the high points of Bank's lectures, and flooded the market with free photocopies. The bottom dropped out in futures contracts. The price fell through the floor, from $40 to less than $2.

In revenge, Weston Bank, who was out $1,500, stayed up all night typing out the most scathing, critical evaluation of Eggs Igino he could think of and copied in several of the heavy hitters, warning them of this insolent boat rocker. Two days later, when the evaluation hit their desks, there was a flurry of bidding for Eggs Igino's talent among the New York high-yield desk, the London syndicate desk, and the Los Angeles mortgage research department. But Eggs Igino, who hated Manhattan and knew every jogging trail in Central Park, missed the Pacific Coast. Five months was far, far too long to be away. So Eggs Igino, who never graduated from the prestigious training program he'd almost crippled, left Manhattan four weeks early, completely ignoring the lonesome gaze of the smitten coed and the anxious pleas of his back-row buddies, who feared the fun was over.

In the late afternoons, when the market had closed, when the others went to their wives and their clubs and their bars and tried to pretend they were still familiar with the outside world, Eggs Igino went home to run. Sometimes he would run in the park, ignoring trails, slashing through the trees, those thick legs of his breathing the world back into him. Then he would go on the roof of his apartment building. This was on the east side of the city, where the sun shined often but the landscape was thick with smokestacks and warehouses and tall apartment buildings. He sat on the roof drinking lemonade mixed with sloe gin and talked with the girl next door about how it would be to live nearer the ocean. Soon they were making trips out to the beach and carrying plastic bags of sand back, which they dumped out on one downsloping corner of the rooftop. When the neighbors moved, Eggs bought one of their wooden chairs, sawed the legs down to five-inch stubs, and set it in the middle of his rooftop beach. He hung a wind chime on a pole. He looked out over the city on three sides, and on the fourth side he looked into an upper floor of a seniors' hospital, where Eggs could see the patients drift past the windows in their wrinkled white smocks. Sometimes, if it was the kind of day that got Nickel Sansome rubbing his scalp and Sidney Geeder chugging coffee and Coyote Jack stammering on his numbers—if, for instance, they were long treasury strips when the Fed raised the discount rate, or they were in Euros for yield when the dollar reversed its slide—Eggs would turn his beach chair toward the hospital and watch the weakened patients in the windows. He'd raise his sloe gin lemonade and wave, and sometimes, slowly, one of the patients' hands might rise in return.

Every afternoon at five, the Southern Pacific freight train arrived at the switching station from Los Angeles, and he watched as cars were removed and added. He'd had a girlfriend that he loved terribly, once, before he'd gone away to Mexico. Katie always took L-glutamine in silver-speckled capsules to stimulate her brain activity, along with echinacea concentrate, which was a syrupy extract from some flower that grew in the Santa Cruz Mountains. She made Eggs swallow a drop of it whenever his throat was sore. Eggs Igino loved her because she was always saying things like "The air feels perfect for new ideas today." She'd believed the clouds and the weather, which affected the static electricity levels in the air, made thoughts—as electrical impulses—more likely to travel the axon-dendrite nerve bridges in their brains. With the fog coming in was the best time, she'd always said. The time for discoveries, for insights. Eggs thought about her and got up out of his beach chair and faced the oncoming fog, and watched it eclipse the sun, and swallow his building. The city around it disappeared. He waited for the big thoughts to come. No more smokestacks, no more warehouses. No railroad yard or cantilever bridges. Only the hospital patients and him. When Eggs turned around, they'd all be standing in the windows, sometimes two deep, with the nurses behind them trying to keep them from getting too close.

7 · Time

1993. TIME SLIPPED away, and it slipped away some more, and there was never enough even though there was plenty in the years ahead. In fact, there was so much time in the future that, under the laws of supply and demand, time in the future was absolutely worthless. The salesmen and saleswomen kept postponing things into the future—falling in love, getting into good physical condition, reading a book, taking a trip—without ever pressuring the future's schedule. The future was never booked up. It always took a rain check, was always willing to reschedule. It was always willing to make a deal. Time in the present, however, had them over a barrel. There was just so damn little of it—and then the little bit of time that was there kept slipping away before they could use it. It was a tough negotiator, but most of the salesmen had struck one deal or another. Sidney Geeder expected this to be the last job he ever needed; he was trading five years now for the rest of his life in the future, even though he'd never given much thought to what he'd do when that day came. He wanted to experience life's simpler pleasures, slow the pace down to a crawl. He wanted to really taste his food and enjoy deep dreams and feel true love for a woman— something more than this unbalanced, uncontrollable lust he developed for anything with hips. He wanted to go a week without screaming at someone, and a month without counting the hours until Friday. He wanted to wake up without dread and go to bed wishing the day never ended. He wanted to lose track of time.

Time in the past, by comparison, was virtually nonexistent, even though there was incredible demand for it. Everyone obsessed about the times they could have over again, and how they would do it differently, such as the time during the Euro-Floaters deal when Sid Geeder hid below his desk, or the time Lisa Lisa called

Alan Greenspan a peckerhead in front of her boyfriend, or the time Nickel Sansome let John White beat him at backgammon. Their obsession with the past, though, was quite selective, because they were generally ignorant of history and always failed to learn from it. They were in fact quite skilled at disregarding history, and when the firm leaked that its next big bond idea involved sending fax machines, insurance, and Michael Jackson to Romania in exchange for crude oil and timber, the salesforce had little trouble ignoring the pesky little details of Romania's long history of oppression—by the Romans in the second century, the Mongols in the thirteenth, the Hungarians in the fourteenth, the Ottomans in the fifteenth, the Greeks in the sixteenth, the Turks in the nineteenth, and the Soviets in the twentieth. Romania was a hot potato, but all the salesforce needed to know was that they were rescuing this poor country rich with natural resources from the throes of post-communist economic inefficiency. The horrors of Soviet-style command economics were practically unspeakable. For instance, the Romanian forests of Transylvania, which covered 27 percent of the land, produced only 1.1 million tons of softwood pulp in 1993. And if that weren't awful enough, Romanian Power and Energy was capable of drilling only 13.4 million barrels of crude oil from under the Black Sea. "Can you believe that?" Lisa Lisa scoffed incredulously to Mike Kohanamoku at Honolulu Federal. "Only thirteen point four million barrels! Those communists— they had the golden goose but couldn't get it to lay the egg. They don't call it the Black Sea for its windsurfing." Romania's twenty-first century belonged to Wall Street. Eastern Europe was the last frontier. America was the marshal and Atlantic Pacific the Lone Ranger, rolling into town slinging double-entry accounting, jury trials, and health insurance.

When the firm then leaked that the cornerstone of this package of deals involved loaning money directly to the single, newly privatized Romanian central bank, the salesforce managed to overlook the huge loans that had been made to the newly privatized central banks of Chile, Peru, Brazil, Uruguay, and Mexico in the late 1970s under the urging of President Carter. Those loans hadn't "performed" very well, meaning that they'd never been paid back, and the U.S. money banks that made the loans had been writing them off ever since. Romania was different, according to the memorandums the salesforce committed to memory; in the 1970s those South American countries had just shaken off years of *socialism*, while the Romanians were now shaking off decades of *communism*.

"You see," Nickel Sansome clarified to Bonnie Hao at the Bank of Canton, "socialist government is very different. They have prime ministers and parliaments. The communists, on the other hand, have premiers and politburos. They're really not the same at all. Apples and oranges, so to speak." What evolved was a line of reasoning that said the communists had been far more oppressive and really ravaged their economies, so the citizens there were far more *hungry* than the South Americans. The South Americans hadn't been oppressed enough to be hungry enough to get rich enough to pay back the loans.

"They weren't!" Coyote Jack testified at the morning briefing, when Eggs Igino brought up the economic history he had studied. "Don't even think about the past," Coyote Jack ordered. "Think about the future."

"Okay," Eggs Igino said. "What if, in the future, the price of crude oil goes back down, like it seems to do every few years—won't the Romanian economy crumble under the staggering debt it has to repay?"

"Well, I don't see why we would be selling these bonds if that was a risk we really had to concern ourselves with," Coyote Jack answered smoothly. "We have our reputation as a successful manager of risky financial deals on the line."

Everyone wrote that down. As Coyote Jack knew, the success of the deal was in the timing, and there was no doubt that this was a good time for the deal. Eastern Europe had been getting so much press since the revolutions. Honest-to-god political revolutions didn't come around that many times a century, and Atlantic Pacific wasn't going to miss a rare chance to cash in on the momentary spike in global goodwill. It might have been more prudent to wait another decade before throwing private money after the United Nations grants and loans already in place, but Atlantic Pacific hadn't yet figured out how to take a commission on UN relief missions and World Bank redevelopment grants. The only way Atlantic Pacific could take a cut was if private banks and companies were persuaded that the United Nations shouldn't be the only one taking the credit for saving the Eastern bloc from the brink of economic ruin. It didn't matter that Romania was still undercapitalized, polluted, and corrupt—the accounts would never know, and the salesmen would never know: Romania was all the way on the other side of the earth. And the press was so head-over-heels about the do-good opportunities there that it would be several years before it would get around to reporting how the Danube was toxic and the air over Bucharest was dark with coal dust. Deals were done when they could be sold, not when they made sense. Making sense had never been a prerequisite for doing a deal, and Atlantic Pacific wasn't going to break with precedent.

Though the firm was still cagey about the deal's specifics—none of the salesmen knew how big a deal it would be or how the bonds were collateralized—Sidney Geeder developed an immediate distaste for the bonds. The United States government had been a good example of how money could be made by mortgaging the future, and now the idea was being exported. It was a highly exportable concept, and in an effort to improve the trade deficit many other countries, such as Canada and France, had been persuaded to mortgage their futures by floating bonds. "Why not Romania?" argued Paul DeShews.

"You don't know a thing about Romania," Sidney charged.

"I know their lumber mills are producing fewer than a million tons of softwood board a year," Paul DeShews snickered superiorly. "They're really in need of help."

"Oh, that's really terrible," Sidney Geeder chided sarcastically. "I had no idea life in Romania was so deprived."

"You're just complaining so Coyote Jack will raise the commissions," Paul said. "You always complain and threaten not to sell the bonds until Coyote Jack increases our cut, and then you never fail to sell them. I'm on to you. It's really quite an act you put on. You deserve an Oscar for that fit you threw over the Freddie Mac Adjustables. Coming in to work that day wearing a dog muzzle." Paul chuckled, remembering. "Brilliant, really brilliant. Sometimes I'm fooled into believing you really do hate this job."

"But I do hate it!" Sidney spluttered. "I despise it! I'm only here long enough to get my shares, then I'm gone."

"Beautiful, just sensational," Paul DeShews pandered, shaking his head in admiration. "Really quite convincing."

"I'm gone in six months!"

"Then there's no time to waste," Paul smirked.

There sure wasn't time to waste. Time was money, and the money was addicting, and so they kept trading away the best years of their lives to satisfy their addictions. Those who made the most money had the least amount of time, while those who had the most time to lounge around chatting and remembered to call their mothers once a month made the least amount of money. If they spent their time wisely, this could be the last job they ever needed. Every moment counted. According to Sidney Geeder, success depended upon their innate ability to shift between time's three dimensions, any of which could be at stake simultaneously: the Here and Now, the Foreseeable Future, and the Great Scheme of Things. Most salesmen lived primarily in the Here and Now; when they walked out on that sales floor in the morning the rest of their lives fell away under the onslaught of numbers and market jolts and phone calls. It was nearly impossible to stay up with the market, let alone stand back and make plausible predictions about the Foreseeable Future. The Foreseeable Future was primarily the role of the research departments, which provided reports for the salesmen to arm them with predictions. In turn, the Great Scheme of Things was the chore of management, who sat around in their fishbowl offices worrying whether Salomon or Merrill or Drexel or Shearson was about to clean their clocks. This division of responsibilities inevitably failed, because management ignored obvious data affecting the Foreseeable Future, such as when Coyote Jack didn't notice that Regis Reed took a stack of research reports home with him every evening but didn't bring them back in the morning. And then the salesmen completely forgot the Great Scheme of Things, such as how they ignored the economic cycles that had led, in the past year, to seven San Francisco salespeople being laid off, five being fired, one having quit, and one having been cooked into a vegetable from lack of oxygen. Sidney Geeder, who didn't trust the researchers and despised management, relied on his own visions of the Foreseeable Future and the Great Scheme of Things.

"What's your secret?" Sue Marino begged him as they rode up the marbled elevator at four-thirty one morning.

"My secret is that I think for myself," Sid Geeder responded quickly. "You ought to try it."

"I will," she answered tentatively. "I'll give it a try. So what should I think about?"

Sid Geeder slapped his forehead. "I can't tell you what to think about!"

"Why not?" Sue Marino pleaded, clutching her briefcase to her chest.

"Because then you wouldn't be thinking for yourself!" he howled, glancing up at the floor light to see how soon he could escape being imprisoned with an ignoramus.

Sue Marino was quiet for a moment, forlorn. She shrugged her shoulders. When the floor bell dinged and the steel doors parted, she mumbled, "I knew you were going to keep it a secret."

"Arrrgghh!" Sidney Geeder bawled, losing all control momentarily. He ran into the office and over to his desk, where he slid into the crawl space below it and closed his eyes and had the vertigo sensation of falling backward into space.

"Sidney! Sidney, wake up!"

Sidney Geeder snapped open his eyes. He was looking at a pair of toothpick-skinny ankles, slightly knotty, that descended into a pair of forest-green T-strap pumps. They were beautiful ankles, a work of art, and it broke Sid's heart to think about how Lisa Lisa was balanced so precariously on such delicate bones.

"Are you awake?" Lisa Lisa asked, her voice full of worry and fright.

"What's wrong?" Sid said.

Lisa Lisa got down on her knees. She had a furtive expression on her face and seemed about to cry.

"What is it?" he said, laughing uneasily.

"It's Ivana Perkova, the doctor," Lisa Lisa whimpered.

"What about her?" Sid said quickly.

Lisa Lisa began to snap her teeth on the frayed edges of her cuticles. "I heard Clark Kalinov and John White talking about her when I was in the kitchen."

"What'd they say?"

"That she can't be trusted."

"Jesus," Sid mumbled.

"What's it mean?" Lisa Lisa pleaded fearfully. "Are they going to do something to her?"

"Of course not," Sid reassured her, patting her ankles. "Why in the world would they do something to her?"

"How do I know?" Lisa Lisa cried. "I'm telling you all I heard."

"I'm sorry," Sid apologized.

"I trusted her," Lisa Lisa wept. "I told her everything. She told me not to tell her, but I couldn't help it. I just had to talk to someone."

"It's all right," Sidney said firmly. "Go back to your desk and get to work. I'll take care of it."

Lisa Lisa slumped back to her desk as Sidney plopped down in his chair and turned to the window, wiping a mist of sweat off his brow with one of Eggs Igino's napkins.

"Dr. Perkova, please," he said to the nurse who always intercepted Ivana's calls.

"Yes, Mr. Geeder. Dr. Vandivort is taking her calls. I'll put you through to him."

"No—wait!" Sidney interrupted. "I don't want to talk to anyone but Dr. Perkova. Is she with a patient?"

The nurse paused for a moment. "Your case has been reassigned to Dr. Vandivort. You should speak to him about it. Dr. Perkova is not available."

Before Sidney could object, the line began to ring again until a male voice answered in a kind, mellifluous, soothing tone that made Sidney wish he were there to bite the guy's nose off.

"Hello, you've reached Dr. Vandivort. To whom am I speaking?"

"I'm looking for Ivana Perkova," Sidney inserted gruffly. "Put her through."

"Dr. Perkova is no longer available. All of her cases have been reassigned. Shall I assume I am talking to one of her patients?"

"Hell yes, I'm one of her patients. Where the fuck is she? What does 'not available' mean?"

"And your name is, sir?"

"Quit bullshitting me. I'll tell you my name if you tell me what's happened to Dr. Perkova."

"We don't know what's happened to Dr. Perkova. All I know is that I have been retained to take over her industrial practice. We have to assume that she was fired by the firm that had retained her."

"Fired? What for?"

"I really have no idea, and I wouldn't want to prejudice her reputation by conjecturing. I've never met the doctor. Now, would you like to schedule an appointment?"

"What for?" Sidney screamed at Clark Kalinov, when he had run into Kalinov's office and pulled the plug on Kalinov's phone to get his attention.

Clark Kalinov leaned back in his chair mischievously, taking inhuman pleasure at Sidney Geeder's angst. "Something upsetting you, Geeder?"

"You know damn well what's going on! Why did you fire Dr. Perkova?"

"But I didn't fire her," Clark Kalinov tittered, drawing out the moment. "And I'm going to have to dock your pay for that telephone jack you just destroyed. PacTel's labor charge starts at ninety dollars an hour."

"Then where is she?"

"How do I know where she is?" Clark Kalinov laughed. "Boy, this has really got your goat, hasn't it? I wish I'd thought of it."

"Thought of what?"

"Oh, you'll have to ask John White. I'm not authorized to say anything to just a mere salesman."

"What for?!" Sidney yelled at John White, when he had run into White's office and it had been explained that Dr. Perkova had been relieved of her duties.

John White leaned back in his chair and stuck a pencil over one ear. "What's the big deal, Geeder? We put another doctor in her place. I hear he has an orthopedics specialty. He ought to be able to help your back."

"But he won't relieve it at all! It wasn't medicine that relieved the nervous tension in my spine. It wasn't MRIs or ultrasound or electromagnetic stimulation. It wasn't acetaminophen, codeine, or Ben-Gay. The only thing able to fix my back was being in the sympathetic hands of an omniscient foreign temptress who knew nothing of the spiritual hellhole I slave away in all day and night."

"Hell, Sidney, we can get you a whore if that's what you need. Coyote Jack's got a service we use for clients and visiting management. He'll give you the number."

"It's not the same!" Sidney squawked, clenching his fists and hunching his shoulders in a rage. It was amazing Sidney was so good a salesman, considering how inefficient his emotions were and how little control he had over them. "Why was she fired?!" he yelled, doing it again.

John White bristled. "Who said she was fired? Dr. Perkova was not fired."

"But you just said she was fired!"

"I did not. I said she was relieved of her duties. Her contract was up, and we decided not to renew it. It was all handled out of New York. I really don't know many details. Internal surveillance gave her a thumbs-down on the renewal. The report's classified; what I know is only rumor. She knew too much. Her patients talked. Maybe she was getting inside information, calling her stockbroker after every Atlantic Pacific patient whined about the next deal on the block. Who knows? If her patients wanted to talk, she was supposed to send them to Helmet Fisher. Helmet Fisher has a much higher security clearance. He's prepared to handle patients who talk. This is a very information-sensitive business, Sidney. We pay our salesforce to talk all day long, but we also pay them to shut up when they leave the forty-second floor. What with the Romanians and all, I don't think we could take any chances."

"The Romanians! This was all about her being Romanian, wasn't it?"

"We can't have our salesforce get afflicted with that kind of guilt, can we, Sidney? Guilt of that strain can spread like an epidemic. We had to take preventive measures. It was sound medicine.

Nipped it in the butt, so to speak. Dr. Perkova was developing some awfully close relationships with her patients. It was an unhealthy situation, a veritable breeding ground for shame and contrition. This is an extremely important deal to the firm, what with the Sprint and Canadian Petroleum deals following the Romanians. We just couldn't afford to take any chances."

"You're sick, White. You're really fucking diseased. You really ought to see a doctor. You really ought to be strapped to a bed and hooked up to an IV and have your ethics flushed for about three years."

John White was amused. "Thanks for the advice, Sidney. I'll take it under consideration."

"Anytime," Sidney Geeder retorted, marching out of the room, off the sales floor, and out of the building, where he stormed around the block, sucking in car exhaust and airborne dust and the chaff of the system, the dirty details of downtown—the meter maids, the neon eye-grabbing signage, the mini-tornadoes of litter that whipped up at intersections, the shoves of urgent pedestrians, the intrusive hands offering pizza coupons, the scribbled pleas of homeless seeking work. It was enough to drive a man indoors. Sidney Geeder usually avoided the street level entirely—he kept his commute to the parking garage, the tower lobby, and the forty-second floor. The street level was a disgusting thoroughfare of so many small minds trafficking in petty necessities, a buzzing reminder to Sidney of the mundaneness of the world he was trapped in. Just six more months and he could leave it all behind, bow out from the provincial scuffles of bureaucratic maneuvering, abandon the inexpressive mask atop the haughty uniform, forget the incessant cattle drive to sell sell sell information nobody truly needed even though they begged him for it.

He walked down into the parking garage and drove his truck away from the megalopolis to Ivana Perkova's office. He had to find her. Sidney double-parked, left the motor running, and popped into what was now Dr. Vandivort's office, staying only long enough to put the receptionist in tears with a tyrannical rant while Dr. Vandivort called the police. Sidney charged out of the office, hopped back in his truck, and drove the half mile to her flat, which she rented from an old Dutch woman who lived downstairs.

Sidney pounded on Ivana's door, and when he got no answer he pounded on the old Dutch woman's door.

"What do you want?" she said through the security chain.

"Have you seen Ivana?"

"Who are you?"

"I'm an old boyfriend. I was also a patient. Please, I need to get in touch with her."

The old lady considered his request. "Talk to the company."

"What company?"

"The corporation."

"Which one?"

"The one that pays her rent here."

"But I work with the company!"

"Then why are you bothering me?"

"Arrrgghh!" Sidney wailed when the salesmen marched out of the morning briefing on the Romanian deal the next morning. "Why me?"

"But it's not just you," Paul DeShews reasoned cheerily, walking behind him. "We all have to sell the bonds."

"Wait until we get our quotas," Sidney bawled, holding his head in his hands. "Mine will be larger than the entire money market desk's."

"We all have to do our part to promote democracy," DeShews stated patriotically.

"No we don't," Sidney objected. "One of the great privileges of living in a democracy is that we can't be forced to lift a hand in its defense."

"But a democracy is the best part of our government!" Paul De-Shews shouted.

"No," Sid Geeder shouted back. "The best thing about our government is that it's perfectly legal to try to overthrow it."

"You ought to be straitjacketed and thrown in a padded cell, Geeder."

Sid Geeder whirled around, pushing his face right up to Paul DeShews's chin. "If you weren't a girl, Goody, I would sock you."

"But I'm not a girl," he answered.

And so Sid Geeder socked him. Sid Geeder threw an uppercut that grazed DeShews's jaw and sent him spinning to the carpet.

Then he turned away, straightened his tie, and continued walking out to his desk. The rest of the salesmen were too stunned to do anything. They hadn't seen anybody throw a punch in years. Some of them—the assholes, bullshitters, and bullies—couldn't help laughing crudely and making smart-aleck asides to each other. Paul DeShews was too stunned to do anything but rub his jaw dreamily and try to remember how he ended up on the floor. He had been in the sales briefing and then . . .

"His jaw?" Coyote Jack incredulously asked Sid Geeder several hours later, when the dust raised from the morning activity took a moment to settle. "Not his nose?"

"Why would I punch him in the nose?" Sid Geeder shrugged. "His nose is of no use to him. He does not need to smell the bonds in order to sell them. But his jaw—a salesman needs his jaw like he needs his confidence. Besides, I only grazed him. Consider it a warning shot across his bow."

Coyote Jack paused, considering Geeder's explanation. Then he broke out giggling with the same sheer joy that had overcome him when he'd first heard that Goody Two Shoes had been dropped to the carpet. It was not pleasure that DeShews was hurt—it was glee that the Romanians had really pushed Geeder's buttons. "You really hate these bonds, don't you?" he said.

"I abhor them," Sidney stated emphatically, fidgeting in his seat, trying not to lose control.

"Well, then I have a very good feeling about this deal," Coyote Jack concluded, rolling a pencil between his fingers. "You've never failed to unload bonds you dislike."

"This is different," Sid Geeder warned. "I don't just dislike these bonds—I wouldn't use them for fertilizer. Management has gone completely wacko. These bonds will be entirely worthless in three years. We won't loan money to Mexico—why would we loan it to Romania?"

"What's the matter, Sidney? You usually take great pleasure in having a chance to destroy the financial system."

"But they don't have a financial system in Romania! They don't have a government! They're innocent folk who have absolutely no idea what they're getting into."

"Nobody's innocent," Coyote Jack retorted, steeling his eyes seriously. "They're in this for the money, just like we are. The revolution has unleashed a rabid greed that's been muted for fifty years. They'll be the most power-hungry, money-eyed, backstabbing, miserly, gluttonous culture in the world for the next twenty years. If you knew anything about greed, Sidney, you'd understand that it can't be stifled, it can't be repressed, and it can't be denied. The totalitarian regime in Romania was the most oppressive in all of the communist bloc. Those people are chomping at the chance to make a buck. Mexico's had a democracy since 1917; all of their pent-up energy has dissipated."

"But we've had a democracy since 1787!" Sidney cried painfully. "Does that mean we're a bad investment?"

"Hell no," Coyote Jack spit back. "This country's full of immigrants fleeing repression who want a chance to make a buck. We've kept the doors open the whole time, and as long as we continue we'll always have a thriving economy. Next week it'll be the Afghanskis or the Sudanese or the Amazonians, whoever. Long as they've been repressed and oppressed and depressed, we'll take 'em. Shit, Geeder, haven't you studied history? Always some new immigrant population willing to work for peanuts, keeping those of us who arrived earlier honest, making us look over our shoulders and work our asses off. All the really, really gutsy Romanians already made it here. We skimmed the talent off the top already. It's America, man. As long as there's oppression somewhere else in the world—as long as people elsewhere are being forced to sleep twelve to a blanket and eat ants and drink pisswater—we'll be kings of the world. You know what's going on in the Dominican Republic? I cut out this article," and Coyote Jack, who was showing the skill with words that had earned him his nickname, pulled a *Journal* clipping from his desk drawer. "A mountain of garbage three miles across. Gangs of kids killing each other over the turf to scavenge for recyclable bottles and cans." He pushed the article into Sid Geeder's lap. "The last thing we should have done was stop General Balaguer from oppressing those people. We were getting some damn fine talent off of that island before we restored democracy." He reached into his desk for another, this one a photograph and caption, which described it as soldiers of the Dominican Liberation Party sitting outside a bar, getting drunk. "Look at these bums. They get a little freedom, and what do they do? They go get loaded."

"You're crazy," Sid Geeder accused. "You're really fucking crazy, Coyote. You're one greedy bastard that doesn't know how to say *when*."

"Grow up, Geeder. You may be the King of Mortgages, but when it comes to management you're still a virgin," Coyote barked.

"You can't move these bonds without me," Sidney challenged, his hackles raised and his competitive spirit flushed.

"And you won't make it to the end of the year without moving your quota of these bonds."

"What's that supposed to mean?"

"The firm's going out on a limb here. These bonds are crucial to our future. We've got a whole sequence of deals planned for private firms to go into Romania, all of which need money to make the investment. Hilton Hotels has a deal with the Athenée Palace in Bucharest. Sprint has a deal for a telephone switching system. Canadian Petroleum will be drilling oil. We're looking for somebody to chop the trees. Hell, even Ingenesis has got a military contract to send in an army of robotic foot soldiers."

"Ingenesis! They're not in on it, too!"

"Of course they are," Coyote Jack said. "You think they're going to let a good opportunity like this pass them by?"

Sidney Geeder couldn't take it anymore. He'd grown weary of his world, and he'd lost his knack for making sense of it. He missed the good old days, when he was just a salesman of bonds, just a greaseman keeping the financial machine running smoothly, when the money was good and the bonds were straightforward and everyone got what he had coming to him and nobody suddenly disappeared or unexpectedly got pressure-cooked into a vegetable. His eyelids hung half-mast, his shoulders hunched forward, and he shaved lazily, sometimes missing entire swatches of beard on his eerily white cheeks. He felt clammy all day long under his clothes and feared he'd given himself a mysterious case of athlete's foot, because his feet were red and cracked. But Sidney Geeder's feet were numb and if it really was a case of athlete's foot he couldn't tell because his toes were as hard as golf balls.

Sidney desperately wanted to rediscover life, to regain the sense of order and custom, to understand the X's and O's as life unfolded. Most of all, he wanted to know where the hell Ivana Perkova had gone, and in a futile attempt to find out he called up the short-haired private investigator who had a pierced "outie" belly button and whom he used to date. Sidney was weak with guilt and overworn with hard work and completely vulnerable to the dog tags she hung from her belly-button ring, which he had loved to suckle in extended foreplay as she whispered the strange secrets of her trade. She kept a dingy apartment near the ocean. She had removed all the interior doors and replaced them with translucent, wispy batik curtains so that the treble tones of the opera music she blasted constantly—Wagner, Conrad Susa, Dvořák—could be heard equally in every room. The private investigator had served twenty months in the navy and had grown accustomed to sleeping in small, airtight bunkrooms, so she'd put her king-size bed on the floor of the walk-in closet. The mattress butted into the walls on two sides and curled up vertically on the others. The ocean air was humid and had made their skin sticky. It was a muggy, pillowed den of purely physical pleasure that brought the common world back into focus. It was a padded cell where a man could go ahead and whack out without hurting himself, and as soon as Sidney Geeder went to see her about Ivana Perkova, he had the irresistible urge to strip down to his underwear and climb in.

"You're driving me crazy," Geeder moaned, as the private investigator teased him by delaying the climax of her story, which involved a divorced woman the ex-husband had hired the private investigator to follow.

"So the divorcée calls his office and asks his assistant to bring over a file. The assistant shows up and the divorcée gets him a drink. Then she not so accidentally spills the drink on herself."

"And where were you?" Sid Geeder babbled, staring at the sweater covering her stomach as he wondered if the dog tags were hanging underneath. The taste of metal entered his mouth from memory.

"I'm across the street in the car, watching it all through binoculars."

"The curtains aren't drawn?"

The private investigator stroked Sidney's hair. "She wants the whole world to know. She's trying to get attention. She probably even knew I was watching. She was getting even at her husband."

"You can't see into a house at night with binoculars," he challenged.

"They have a polarizing lens."

"You're making this up."

The private investigator laughed at Sidney's innocence. "This stuff happens so often it's boring. Everybody knows that."

But Sid Geeder could never be bored hearing how the divorcée then removed her blouse and invited the assistant to see whether her skin tasted like gin, and how the assistant sucked his olive into his mouth and moved across the room to make a martini, even if the story was entirely invented and all the private investigator did during the day was pore over old phone bills. Sid Geeder loved sappy tales of sexual romance, and he wanted the private investigator to take him by the ears and order him to make her a martini.

"So do you love this doctor?" the private investigator asked quite seriously.

"What difference does that make?"

"I'm trying to understand whether you're asking me to investigate a lover's squabble or a case of international corporate kidnapping."

"Maybe the firm had her deported," Sidney said, rolling onto his back.

"You sure your girlfriend didn't just skip town because she doesn't want you chasing after her?" the private investigator teased.

"She's not my girlfriend! And I don't love her!" Sid bawled, pounding the pillow in histrionic frustration.

"Well, I don't see why else she wouldn't just call you and tell you where she is, even if she were in Romania," the private investigator reasoned.

"I don't get it either," Sid agreed with subdued resignation. "That's why I came to you. It doesn't make any sense."

"You said they took your file out of her office. Maybe she's not contacting you because it will only get you into more trouble. Maybe she knows it's best for you if the two of you don't communicate." The private investigator ran her fingers through Sidney's thick black hair, and Sidney groaned.

"What are you getting at?" Sid mumbled into his pillow.

"That maybe you should just leave it all alone."

Sid shook his head. "Please, just try to find something out," he begged.

"I don't know," she said. "I kind of like having you back in my life. But I guess you'll only call me again if I look for her, huh?"

"Oh, I don't know," Sid replied. "You're twisting this in a way I didn't intend."

"And what did you expect? The red-carpet treatment? This is a little awkward, don't you think?"

"Pleeeze. I think she may be in trouble. I've been worrying myself sick. I can't just let her disappear."

8 · Language

THEIRS WAS A bastard language, the illegitimate offspring of technical financial terminology and forty years of pop Americana, littered with ill-chosen metaphors and living acronyms. The Romanian bonds had a current yield and a strike yield and a yield book and a yield to maturity, all of which Sid Geeder tossed out to Kenny Whitlash at Ingenesis in order to convince him the bonds were a decent buy. But the Romanians also had a "marshmallow-creme center" under a "buffalo-hide cover," with a "knuckleball's seam" that caused them, when the market was moving, to "float in the wind." They also had "integrity" and "durability" and were "new and improved" over the undercapitalized and unsecured South American deals of the seventies. They were "amphibious," meaning they were supposed to perform well in either up or down markets. The Romanians had an average duration and an implicit call option and a single monthly mortality and a dollar-weighted-return, none of which Lisa Lisa really understood. But she rattled the phrases off with sincere confidence, and her customer, Mike Kohanamoku at Honolulu Federal Savings, didn't want to admit to her that he had slept through his graduate-school lectures on fixed-income securities. He pretended he understood completely. The bonds were a sure thing, a layup, a gimme putt, an extra point, and a turkey shoot. Kohanamoku understood this, and then to prove that he understood he was prepared to put his money where his mouth was.

It was an office in the sky assembled entirely from high technology. It was technology without moving parts: the computers didn't move, the digital LCD screens didn't move, the telephones didn't move, the microwave didn't move, and the building didn't move—although when the clouds rushed past the windows it often seemed as if they were flying through the air at terrific speeds. The only moving parts in the Atlantic Pacific machine were the salesmen, and of all their moving parts the ones that moved most were their mouths. They never stopped talking. They talked themselves into a zone, into a fever, into a spell. In a lull they might say anything just to keep the words flowing, to stay in the groove. If they said something stupid—"test of the mettle in the man" or "the coast is clear," for instance—they just repeated it often enough until it became self-mockery, satire, communication by negation.

When they hung up the phone they still kept talking. They recounted their stories to each other. These were tall tales. War stories. Fish stories. Oral folklore, which they insisted was 100 percent true. Their diction lent meaning to an otherwise passive, nontactile, purely digital environment. They fabricated an aggressive, visceral, tangible secondary reality to record the apparent decay. If they had made many trades in a single day, as Sid Geeder managed almost every day, he was "whipping them and driving them." If they had sold a position that a trader had been unable to move, as Eggs Igino did when he sold the Aussie 8s of '03, he had "unloaded his bombs." If they browbeat and lied to a customer in order to convince him to buy, as Nickel Sansome did when he sold the Resolutions to the innocent Bank of Canton, he had "jammed bonds"—jammed them down his customer's throat. Nickel felt horrible afterward and wanted forgiveness, so he momentarily wandered toward Geeder's desk to listen as Sidney ripped the eyes out of Franklin Mutual.

Selling a customer on a new bond often took a dozen phone calls to gradually prevail upon a customer's sense of greed. It was a slow dance, a cat-and-mouse game. If the customer was a woman, the first step was to "goose" her, meaning to "touch her soft spot," "get her wet," and "make her want it." Even Lisa Lisa, who hated the sexual innuendo of their language, couldn't help herself from bragging to Regis Reed that she'd just goosed Hewlett-Packard. If the customer was a man, the first step was to "sink the hook in deep" and then "let the line out until he gets tired." If, on the other hand, they failed entirely, as Regis Reed did when he tried to move the Aussie 8s of '03 to the Plumbers and Pipefitters Pension Plan, he "cut bait," or "grounded out to second." When Nelson Dicky, who gave most of his money to his church because he felt guilty for never being able to convert his fellow salesmen to the Latter-Day Saints, couldn't persuade First Nationwide to invest in the Euro-Floaters, it was a day of "unanswered prayers" spent "journeying across the desert."

Above all, it was war. They humped out to their foxholes, hunkered down, got combat-ready, dropped their bombs, waited for the faceless enemy. At the end of the day, when tallying up their trading tickets, they were "counting scalps." The 1987 stock market crash was the Bomb, and time was measured Before the Bomb/After the Bomb, as if the market had never rebounded from that ominous day. The money market desk was staffed by grunts, while Green Berets roved the mortgage desk. Coyote Jack was frequently referred to as General William Tecumseh Sherman, and John White as President Eisenhower, while the bond market was their "theater of command." It wasn't war at all, not really, but it helped them to understand a vague and obscure world more than quantitative analysis, which explained "rate anticipation components" and "horizon induction" but couldn't explain why Lisa Lisa received a jockstrap at the Secret Santa Christmas party. It couldn't explain at all how humiliated she felt when she tore off the green tissue paper and everyone began to laugh. It didn't explain why she wanted to bust out in tears when Regis Reed asked her to model it for them. It didn't explain why

Sue Marino, who should have supported her in such a time of crisis, said that the jockstrap didn't look big enough. Lisa Lisa had drunk two glasses of low-fat eggnog and could feel the heat of the rum in her face. She tried to be a good sport and chuckle, but her smile was weak and her pain obvious.

Everybody else had been ridiculed too, but not nearly so severely. Coyote Jack received a cheap pair of clown suspenders that were long enough to reach his knees. Nickel Sansome received a bottle of Vitalis hair oil. Lisa Lisa could have been really mean to Clark Kalinov, but instead she bought him a toy anchor and a history book on the rise and fall of the Roman Empire. Lisa Lisa realized that there was a fine line between good fun and ridicule. And there was an even finer line between letting out tension and harassment. But a jockstrap! It was insensitive, inhuman, and unexplainable.

"Let me explain," Nickel Sansome said, when Sidney Geeder had cornered him in the copy room. "It was meant in admiration. It was her admittance to the club. She's joined the team!"

"Bullshit," Geeder countered, popping his finger down hard on Sansome's chest. "You just wanted to humiliate her."

"I swear it, Sid," Nickel blubbered. "I didn't mean to hurt her feelings."

Geeder wanted to throw Sansome to the ground and tear his arms out of their sockets. "You're just jealous because she's tougher than you and makes twice as much money as you do."

"I didn't think she'd take it so hard."

"How do you expect her to take it? She's a woman!"

Nickel stammered and tried to take a step forward from the crate of corporate letterhead. "Everyone got jabbed a little."

"A dirty trick, Sansome. She doesn't even know who did it—you aren't giving her a chance to get even. It's lowbrow, Nickel. A sneak attack at a vulnerable time. You ought to apologize."

"All right, I'll apologize. Big fucking deal."

Lisa Lisa was indeed quite crushed and heartfallen. Christmas was always a hard time for her. Like everyone else, Lisa Lisa wanted to escape into the spell of love, but men didn't really love her, and they hadn't for several years now. In retrospect, the Channel 5 sportscaster hadn't loved her any more than the patent attorney or the direct-mail marketer. Not real love, love that breathes, love that gives confidence. But Lisa Lisa had nobody to blame but herself. Kundera had taught her that her dependence on love was only a symptom of failing to love herself. Nietzsche had taught her that if she loved herself she would rise above good and evil and petty office politics. Lisa Lisa blamed herself for being caught in petty office politics, and she blamed herself for the fact that men could only love their mothers. Her blame got in the way of her self-love, and then she hated herself for always blaming herself. The more she tried to love herself, the more she was filled with self-hate and a whopping sense of hollowness and despair.

She hated herself for thinking it, but she really just wanted a man to sweep her far, far away from it all. When the urge was strongest, she ran from it. She filled a knapsack with a pair of jeans and a sweater, slipped into her jogging outfit, and ran up and down three San Francisco hills to a bathhouse near the ocean. It was a small place with only three private rooms hidden from the street by a latticework fence overgrown with ferns and purple ivy. Each room had a stereo, a shower, and a hot mineral pool fed from an underground stream. All of the walls, including the pool, were covered in emerald tiles. Lisa Lisa would arrive sweaty and jittery. She would put a tape in the stereo that boomed the sounds of a rain-forest thunderstorm, complete with tittering monkeys and screeching macaws. She would turn out all the lights except the underwater bulbs in the pool. She would step into the shower with her jogging clothes on so she wouldn't have to wash them at home later. When clean, she would roll into the pool and float in the water for an hour until all of her nail polish had melted off and her swollen feet had drained of whatever fluids made them bloat. She closed her eyes and let the water embrace her. Her hands roamed her body. She gave a wet kiss to the tender skin of her shoulder. This was her escape, and she had told nobody about it, absolutely nobody, except for that one time she let it slip to Sid Geeder's assistant, who had in turn let it leak to Nickel Sansome.

Nickel Sansome drove over to Lisa Lisa's apartment after work to apologize. He double-parked, not expecting it to take long. She had the top-story apartment, and he was slightly winded when he reached her door. He knocked. He heard her soft footsteps come down the hallway. She asked who was there, and he said his name. A minute later she unlocked the door and let him in. Her hair wasn't wet. She wore only a short unbelted kimono that immediately made him begin to rub his scalp. Red and green lit candles were scattered throughout the apartment. She offered him a beer, and then he followed her into the kitchen, which opened out onto a balcony and a view of downtown. Away from the harsh brutality of the sales floor, Lisa Lisa had many of the qualities about her that Nickel Sansome had adored in his videotape of the 1982 Rose Bowl.

"I was just checking on you," he said softly. "After today."

Lisa Lisa leaned against the refrigerator. "That's sweet of you, Nickel. I didn't know you were so kind."

"Well, I saw that your feelings were hurt and . . . I just wanted to make sure you were okay."

They were quiet for a moment. Lisa Lisa took a sip from her glass. "You don't think of me that way, do you Nickel?"

"What way?"

"You know—needing a jockstrap and all."

Nickel gulped. "No, I, uh, I don't think of you that way at all."

"Well, what do you think of me?" She turned toward him and looked him in the eyes.

"Well, I think that, uh, you're a beautiful woman."

"Am I?"

"Sure," he said, putting his fingernails to his scalp nonchalantly as he looked her over. "Not bad at all."

"That's sweet," she said again. She went over to the refrigerator. "Are you hungry?" she asked.

Nickel said that he wasn't, but when Lisa Lisa offered to reheat some delicious chicken mole tamales that she'd made, his stomach growled and he sat down at her kitchen table. He began to play with the lit candles, boyishly flashing his finger through the flame. She brought him another beer. When she bent over to check the oven, he gawked at the curve of her hamstrings. Unconsciously his hand moved to his scalp and began to rub at the fine hair on the edges of his bald spot, involuntarily plucking out what was left of his nap.

"My father says that Atlantic Pacific is going to lay off two hundred of us," Nickel blurted out, attempting to gain control of himself by changing the subject. "That's the word on the street, at least."

Lisa Lisa leaned her hip against the oven with her arms crossed to keep her kimono closed. "From what department?"

"Who knows? My father says it's just to help push the stock up a little bit before Christmas bonuses. They announce some cost cuts, the stock goes up, and the firm sells reserve shares at the inflated price to raise the cash for bonuses."

"That's sick," Lisa Lisa said dejectedly, dropping her shoulders. "It's just so, so . . ."

"Wrongheaded."

"No, *cannibalistic.*"

"Eating someone to save yourself."

"Exactly," she said. "We're always the last ones to hear about it, too. Christ, tell me some good news, please." She pulled the tamales from the oven and slid them onto a plate, which she set down in front of Nickel. He dove into them with his fork.

She asked if he liked them and he nodded with his mouth full.

"Nickel, do you have a girlfriend?"

"Not really," he lied.

"We've known each other for how long? Two years? Has it been two years or three? Two, right? Anyway, a long time. So you can be honest with me, right?"

"Sure," Nickel agreed, not looking up from his plate, because he thought she was about to accuse him of giving her the jockstrap.

"Then what's wrong with me, Nickel? I mean, really—I mean this. From a man's point of view, is there something about me that men just don't like?"

Nickel looked up.

"I mean," she went on, "tell me the truth. Why haven't you ever hit on me? I'm not asking you to, I'm just trying to understand exactly what it is about me."

"Well, jeez, Lisa. We work together."

"But you slept with Sidney Geeder's assistant when you were working with her."

"She was different."

"How so? How, exactly?"

"Aw, Christ. I'd hit on you if I thought you'd allow it. But you got a huge chip on your shoulder that guys can feel from across the floor."

"I do? I don't mean to." She was about to cry. Her lower lip pouted as she sniffled through her nose.

Nickel stood up and gave her a hug. "Aww, I'm sorry. I shouldn't have said that." Lisa Lisa put her face into Nickel's soft chest and slid her arms around his mushy girth and squeezed him back. As she squeezed, her kimono slid open a little and her naked body was pressed against him.

"I think I ought to get going," Nickel slobbered, setting his beer down on the stove.

"Oh, I don't mind," she said, rewrapping herself. "I don't get many visitors."

"Well, we'll do it again sometime," he offered, suddenly wheezing uncomfortably. He made his way to the door. "I'll let myself out." He ran down the stairs and got back in his car and drove to his Korean girlfriend's apartment, where he showered and ate three candy bars and balled his host while an image of Lisa Lisa in a short unbelted kimono ran through his mind. Nickel Sansome felt humiliated, but he couldn't help himself. The next day he got even with Sidney Geeder by replacing the coffee in Sid's thermos with decaf. Then he told Lisa Lisa what he had done, and together they got a great laugh when Sid began to rant to his customers about how his brain matter was going to start oozing out of his ears. Whenever Sid felt a headache like this it meant he wasn't getting enough coffee, so every hour he poured himself another cup out of his thermos. But the headache persisted. Sid found aspirin and Advil in the kitchen and took three of each, but it did no good. He ate a big lunch, but to no effect.

"I told you so," Nickel Sansome told him, leaning over his desk. "It's psychosomatic. It's stress. It's not a physical manifestation at all."

"Shut up, Sansome, or I'll hang you by your tie."

"You really ought to go see Helmet Fisher," Nickel joked. "He solved your buddy Wes Griffin's wandering eye."

Sidney Geeder didn't want to be reminded again of how Wes Griffin had gone to the company shrink and ended up calling it kaput, even though Sidney Geeder felt it was absolutely crucial not to forget the details of history and took great pride in reminding every new kid who walked through the front door how much they looked like that boy Turner, who had trouble breathing and now worked at the Ghirardelli Square McDonald's busing tables. Geeder wasn't really sure that it was Turner who was busing tables the last time he went for a Big Mac, but the boy he saw sure looked like Turner, or at least his memory of Turner.

Sidney Geeder fell into a deep emotional void and swam about the day in isolation, not talking to anybody and avoiding eye contact. Sidney Geeder burned with hatred for the pudgy, sweaty faces of so many salespeople, even though he adored all of them individually and couldn't bear to think about how every single one of them would probably get fired or laid off within just a few short years. He tried not to think of all the pain that they would suffer, collectively, or of how shocked they would be to learn their lives were being cut short. Sidney Geeder couldn't bear to watch as they worked the phones so innocently, unaware of the fate that lay ahead. Time moved so painfully slowly. In agony, Sidney Geeder hid in the crawl space under his desk and made his phone calls until three o'clock, at which point he called the private investigator with the outside belly button and invited her to a romantic sunset picnic atop the huge sand dune at Baker Beach, and she eagerly accepted.

The private investigator was not the romantic type, and Sid Geeder hoped that the evening would fail miserably—that without their clothes off they would have nothing to talk about, and that the lack of magic would simultaneously keep them from falling in love and smash apart Sidney's long-standing preconception that a sand dune was romantic. But Sid Geeder grossly miscalculated the private investigator with the outside belly button's willingness to bare her body in public, and instead they frolicked on the scratchy wool blanket and sang television theme songs as duet rounds and got drunk slurping from a flask of mescal. By the time they collapsed in a sweaty heap on the king-size mattress in her walk-in closet, Sidney Geeder was dangerously bordering on some type of temporary, summer-camp love that would never last. He dove under the covers and snuggled up against her warm belly as she massaged his neck. He clutched at her and pouted into her warm

skin until her petting relaxed him so much that he fell sound asleep
entwined about her middle. It was a gorgeous, feathery, baby-
babbling sleep. His dreams were exorbitant and completely free of
any references to selling bombs or being chased by Coyote Jack.

When her alarm woke him at six in the morning he burst out of
bed anxiously and kissed her tummy goodbye and hopped in his
truck carrying his clothes under one arm. He gunned himself
downtown. At stoplights he climbed back into his clothes, leaving
the buttons and zippers and snaps and laces for later. He screeched
into the parking lot and skidded to a stop in his stall and ran to the
elevator, which took him to the lobby, where he signed in and took
another elevator to the forty-second floor. Sidney Geeder was the
King of Mortgages and he'd never been late to work or called in
sick. He was a loyal bombardier who always found a way to show
up. He knew falling in love would do this to him. He knew getting
up to go to work would be that much harder if he had to leave the
embrace of a lover. At thirteen minutes after six he exploded
through the front doors and charged out onto the sales floor,
which was entirely empty except for Eggs Igino, who was at his
desk calmly chatting to an account and stretching his hamstring by
propping his foot up on Sidney Geeder's chair. The phones were
going crazy, but nobody was answering them.

"Where is everybody?" he inquired, reaching into his file cabinet
for a fresh shirt and unwrinkled tie, then momentarily unplugging
the Quotron so he could plug in his electric razor.

"In the kitchen," Eggs Igino said nonchalantly, holding down
the mute button.

"What are they doing in there?" Sidney asked, running the razor
over his chin with one hand as he buttoned his shirt with the other.

"Mutiny," Eggs Igino laughed.

"Huh?"

"Civil war," he snickered, taking his leg off Geeder's chair.

"What?"

"The workers unite!" he chortled. "Rebellion!"

And so Sidney Geeder had to go see for himself as soon as he'd
combed a little gel into his hair and slapped aftershave on his face
and squirted half a bottle of eyedrops into his eyes and rifled
through Nickel Sansome's desk to steal the nickel he hid taped to

the underside of the drawer. Then he stormed into the kitchen, where everybody was shouting and pushing against each other angrily and occasionally surging en masse upon Paul DeShews and a few of the retail salesmen, who were guarding the breakfast cart. Sidney couldn't figure out what the hell was happening. He hadn't drunk any coffee yet and he was growing light-headed and foggy and kept having the physical sensation of falling backward. Paul DeShews nervously clutched a bowl of strawberries in one hand and a plate of pancakes in the other; each time he made a break for the door the crowd of salespeople cut him off, vehemently shouting at him to share his meal. Eventually they closed in on him and grabbed the food from his arms and passed it back into the crowd, where it was devoured instantly. Then they went after the other retail salesmen, took their food, and scarfed it down too. Then they ripped apart the box that usually contained their breakfast except this time all that was in it was thirty-four Styrofoam bowls of hot Cream of Wheat with raisins. Over each bowl was a little Saran Wrap, held by a rubber band. Several of the bowls tipped over onto the floor. People shouted suggestions, but the mob had a mind of its own. Each of the salespersons grabbed a bowl of Cream of Wheat and they all marched through the hallways to Clark Kalinov's office, where they dumped the cereal on the proportional-to-scale corporate toy schooner, snapping the mizzenmast and caving in the poop deck. Raisins stuck to the gaffsail. Then they filed back out onto the sales floor, taking positions at their desks and jumping back on the phones, furiously shouting and cursing and grumbling.

"Unbelievable," Sidney Geeder exclaimed, when he'd returned to his desk after filling his thermos with coffee.

"You just wait." Eggs Igino grinned wolfishly, smirking to himself giddily and rubbing his palms together greedily.

"Gimme a strawberry danish, will you?" Sid Geeder asked, putting out his hand.

"Trust me," Eggs Igino responded. "Just wait."

"I don't trust anybody. If there's anything this job has taught me, it's not to trust an Atlantic Pacific salesman."

"Give me half an hour."

A half hour later, Clark Kalinov snuck in the back door, went to his office, and then came running out onto the sales floor, demanding to know who had drowned his ship in porridge.

But the salespeople were too busy to scream back at him. Kalinov ran from desk to desk, petitioning them one by one. They all said they hadn't seen anything and didn't have the faintest idea what he was talking about. So he went to Paul DeShews, who was so mad at Clark Kalinov for singling him out by giving him a special breakfast that he lied and testified he hadn't seen anything, that he'd eaten his bowl of strawberries and pancakes without a glitch.

Just then the little Mexican maid pushed another breakfast cart past them, down the aisle, and toward the window, where she engaged the wheel stop and pulled the tablecloth away to reveal two plates of *huevos rancheros* with hash browns and highball glasses of fresh-squeezed grapefruit juice. The din of the sales floor quieted as she set the plates in front of Eggs Igino and Sidney Geeder, followed by cloth napkins and silverware. Then the little Mexican maid unclicked the wheel stop and pushed the cart back up the aisle, right past Clark Kalinov, who stood there with his mouth agape.

"Wait a minute," he called out, thrusting his arm in the air.

"No hablo inglés," she lied, wheeling the cart through the back door and disappearing.

Clark Kalinov spun about and headed down the aisle in Eggs Igino's direction, then he hesitated, turned a corner, and ran off to Coyote Jack's office to complain.

"Let's eat!" Sidney exclaimed, flaring his nostrils and inhaling a big sniff of the warm food. He encircled his plate with his bulky arms as he fed himself. "Good eats," he mumbled, reaching for his glass of grapefruit juice. When Nickel Sansome looked at him with the flat, drooping expression of a beggar, Sidney shot back a growl like that of a dog defending its bone.

"You like French toast?" Eggs Igino asked, chomping away with a full mouth. "Let's have French toast tomorrow."

Sidney began to chuckle, and his mouth spat out bits of food. "Can you get powdered sugar? Maple syrup and powdered sugar?"

"Of course," Eggs Igino answered, beginning to giggle along with Geeder, whose laugh was contagious and brought Nickel Sansome over.

"What's so funny, guys?" Nickel asked.

"Nothing, man," Sidney said, holding himself by the rib cage. "Go back to work."

"Let me in on it," Nickel pleaded. "Come on, I need a good laugh."

"You wouldn't get it," Eggs Igino guffawed, holding his cloth napkin over his nose to make sure he didn't laugh his food up through his sinuses.

"Try me," Nickel insisted cheerily, chortling a little. He looked over his shoulder to see what they might be laughing at. "You going to eat the rest of those hash browns?" he inquired of Eggs, pointing down at the portion that Eggs couldn't get into his mouth because he was afraid he would cough it back up.

Eggs nodded his head.

"Is that fresh-squeezed juice? I'll bet it's just from a can."

"It's fresh-squeezed," Eggs assured him, bits of hash brown flying from his mouth as he chewed.

"If you gave me a little taste I could tell for sure," Nickel tried. "I can tell the difference in just one sip." He reached toward Eggs's glass.

"Get your paws away from here!" Sidney piped up, jabbing at Sansome's hand with his fork. "Shoo."

Nickel turned and crept away despondently.

And so Mark Igino got his nickname. They all had nicknames. Nicknames lent subtext and drama and direction to a normally chaotic world victimized by market spikes and unforeseeable global crises. The nicknames recorded history and fanned rumors and made their years in the pits into one long story, a chapter in their lives with a beginning, middle, and end. Their nicknames changed with time: during the many years he could not resist marrying women in order to cure his problems, Thom Slavonika had been Dear Thom, Alimony Thom, and Onion "Makin' Me Cry" Thom. When he finally kicked the habit and turned to dental floss, he was known as Flossman, Gums, and CzechoSlavonika—or just "Checkie."

The nicknames predicted their destiny. Regis Reed's real name was Duncan Reed; *regis* was what Sue Marino testified was Greek for "king." When he had first come to the sales floor, Coyote Jack and Stormin' Norman began the rumor that Reed would be the next King of Mortgages, after Sidney Geeder. Several nicknames floated around—Prince Reed, Royal Reed, Regal Reed, Rex Reed, Rey Reed—until Sue Marino's monicker won out. Nobody bothered to question whether *regis* was really "king" in Greek, because Eggs Igino had burst upon the scene and leapfrogged all the senior vice presidents, vice presidents, associate vice presidents, and salesmen in the pecking order, even though he still had no business cards.

They would never have questioned it even if Eggs Igino had not suddenly materialized and altered the status quo, because they were far, far too busy to bother. With all the financial terminology, acronyms, and customer names to memorize, they rarely had time to question any of it. They frequently used acronyms without having ever learned what the letters stood for, just as they had never really bothered to comprehend a risk-weighted return or an interest-rate swap. For instance, Lisa Lisa had always been Lisa Lisa—few of the salesmen could tell you her real surname, and most of them had their own theories as to how she'd been awarded a double name. Sue Marino thought it was the double life she lived as salesperson and woman. Regis Reed thought it was like "New York, New York"—the heart of the heart of the woman. Nelson Dicky thought Sidney Geeder had given her the nickname, but Sidney Geeder couldn't remember exactly why or when he'd started to call her that. He was pretty sure Coyote Jack had crowned her, but Coyote Jack thought it was Nelson Dicky. Only Clark Kalinov knew, but he didn't tell anybody because nobody asked him. When she was a young saleswoman, Lisa Lisa had incorrectly filled out her stationery requisition form, idiotically typing her first name where she should have put her surname. Her middle initial was A., and Kalinov decided to teach her a lesson by printing two thousand business cards with "Lisa A. Lisa" as her name, and she'd had no usable business cards until she'd received a promotion fifteen months later. She'd complained uselessly to Kalinov, but she'd never mentioned it to Coyote Jack or Wes Griffin or John White because she was so self-conscious about being a woman in a man's business and maintaining a faultless professional image. As yet the cards were still buried in the rear of her desk drawer right next to the bunion pads and the measuring tape that tracked the swelling of her feet.

"It's psychosomatic," Nickel insisted, removing the measuring tape from Lisa Lisa's foot. "They're the exact same size they were this morning."

"They don't *feel* psychosomatic," Lisa Lisa rebutted, looking down at her feet. There were creases in the skin from the cuff of her pumps, and her toes were pale and bloodless, and the calluses on the spurs of her heels were hot and red.

"I swear to it," Nickel repeated. "Not a millimeter of difference."

"Then how come I can't fit in my shoes?" Lisa Lisa wept. "How come I can't get them back on?"

"Maybe you don't want to get them back on," Nickel suggested shrewdly.

"Maybe the shoes shrink during the day."

"Not likely."

"This is horrible," Lisa Lisa cried. "Don't they even *look* bigger to you? They look bigger to me."

The nicknames injected humor, making the grind slightly bearable. Every afternoon in the lull right after the New York Stock Exchange closed, Albert Sansome bought a king-size chocolate bar from the vending machine in the kitchen. It was his ritual, his small moment of peace, his single act of self-nurture, an innocent act of self-defense against the unraveling of his life. The chocolate bar cost $1.05, and though it took dollar bills the machine wouldn't return change, because Kalinov had a cruel sense of humor. Very rarely did Nickel carry any change, and so on most days he either had to insert two dollar bills and ruminate about how he'd just been ripped off, or humiliate himself and walk desk to desk begging a nickel off the salespeople who earned a quarter of a million dollars in commission annually. A bankroll of nickels had relieved the situation until the nickels disappeared from his desk drawer. Nickel was pretty sure Sidney Geeder had stolen the roll, because when Nickel begged for a nickel Sidney Geeder always had one.

Nickel hated to cave in to Sidney Geeder and come begging, but he equally hated the idea of abandoning his self-protective ritual. He didn't really love the candy bar, but it became a matter of principle. He hid loose change around his desk—wedged in the crack between the mahogany and the lateral filing cabinet, slipped underneath his keyboard, folded inside his quarterly research reports. But these nickels unnervingly disappeared, and Nickel suffered the inevitable consequences. He suffered Coyote Jack's scorn by running across the street for change, or he suffered a humbling cackle from whichever salesperson loaned him five cents, or he suffered remorse for failing to carry out his one act of self-preservation. Either way, he suffered a spike of guilt and self-hatred that often revived a cycle of disgust and malignant psychological dry rot that led him to be mean and crude to his Korean girlfriend, telling her he would probably marry her if her nose was straighter and her face not quite so round and her lower teeth not crooked. Then he proceeded to drink half a bottle of brandy on her bed and apologize profusely and tell her he liked her just the way she was and begin to pet her jet-black hair with one hand while his other ran up and down the soft skin of her inner arm where her tattoo sang of woes far deeper and wider than his.

Sidney Geeder popped the direct phone line to Morgan Gorman at AmeriTrust to spread the news about Igino's new nickname. "Eggs Igino!" he shouted as the phone rang and rang and nobody picked up on the other end. "Come on, pick up, Gorman!" he hollered, banging his headset on the mahogany desktop and gouging a dent in the beveled trim. The line continued to ring.

Finally there was a small click on the other end of someone picking up the phone and setting it back in its cradle.

"He cut me off!" Geeder announced. "What's going on over there?" He backed up to the window and tried to look through the fog to the AmeriTrust Tower building to try and spot if they were maybe in a meeting on the AmeriTrust trading desk. "Igino! Get Wes Griffin's field binoculars out of your desk!"

Igino handed the prism binoculars to Geeder, who slung the strap over his shoulder and peered through the mist, past the Wide World Tower and the Merrill Lynch Tower to the trading room at AmeriTrust six blocks away.

"Jesus," Geeder cried. "The place is crawling with suits. Call over there again, Eggs."

Eggs Igino hopped on the line and waited for someone to pick up. "They're not picking up," he said.

"I don't get it," Sidney said. "I don't recognize any of them."

Finally, the phone was picked up. "What do you want?" an unknown voice answered gruffly.

"Who is this?" Eggs Igino demanded.

"Who is *this*?" the voice retorted.

"This is Merrill Lynch," Igino lied, altering his voice an octave. Then he turned and whispered to Geeder to describe suits on the phone. "I'm trying to test our two-way trading screens. Where's Morgan Gorman?" he asked the voice.

"Gorman doesn't work here anymore."

"Is this AmeriTrust Savings?" Eggs asked to be sure.

The voice hesitated. "AmeriTrust Savings and Loan doesn't exist anymore."

Geeder whispered that the only man on the phone had black curly hair, a brown suit, a mustache, and octagonal rimless glasses.

Eggs Igino let go of his mute button. "Those are nice rimless glasses you have. I'm looking for a pair like that."

"How do you know I have glasses?" the voice implored.

"I told you," Eggs Igino said. "I can see you through the monitor."

"Is there a camera in there?"

"In the Quotron. Are you the Feds?"

"We're the Resolution Trust Corporation."

"I didn't think the Feds had mustaches," Igino jested.

"What did you say your name was?"

"I didn't say. Am I in trouble?"

Geeder held back a laugh and whispered that the Fed was peering into his Quotron.

"Don't stand so close," Igino shouted.

The suit jumped back and took his suit coat off and hung it over the Quotron monitor.

"Hey, who turned out the lights?" Eggs bellowed, then unplugged the phone and fell into hysterical convulsions on the floor, where he was joined by Sidney Geeder when the RTC men began to unscrew the bolts on the Quotron housing. Eggs and Sidney pounded the carpet and kicked their file cabinets and rolled into their crawl spaces where their howls were muted. Then they sat up against their lateral filing cabinets and brooded about the loss of AmeriTrust Savings to the RTC.

"No advance warning," Geeder lamented.

"Just like *that*." Igino snapped his fingers. "Boom. Gone."

"He didn't even get to say goodbye."

"What will they do to him?" Eggs wondered.

"Take away his Series 63 and his right to vote. Make an example out of him. Throw him in some white-collar slammer for a few years, probably. Let him work on his memoirs and his tennis serve."

"Just like *that*," Igino repeated.

"Just like that. Good old Gorman."

"Be working for the government now at eighty cents an hour stamping license plates. G-man Gorman."

And then Coyote Jack came out on the floor and ordered them to get back to work.

9 · The Art of Selling

ACCORDING TO EGGS Igino, in the second stage of history power was attained through wealth. In this three-thousand-year period of commerce, tradable commodities typically were physical objects: land, copper, gold, currency, crops, oil. The realm of ideas was left to art and education, and though they had their own small commercial aspects, ideas had intrinsic value beyond their value in land, gold, or oil. But in the third stage of history, power is attained through knowledge—through ideas and information. Art, then, lacks any obvious distinction from commerce. Art becomes commerce, in the sense that selling music to the Romanians was driven by commercial goals, not artistic ones. And vice versa: commerce becomes art, in the sense that there was an art to selling bonds, just as there was an art to law or an art to teaching or an art to being a doctor, all of which imparted ideas to the public for a fee. They were the best-paid monologuists in the arts. Coyote Jack, who had not been the King of Mortgages for nothing, believed that art depended entirely upon confidence, and that overconfident, self-righteous, greedy bastards such as himself made the best artists. Regis Reed, who didn't have the confidence yet to tell Coyote Jack he was quitting, believed that art was in timing, in waiting for the right moment. Lisa Lisa, who was looking for a man, believed the art was in knowing when to ease off, to present yourself and then let the situation sell itself.

But nothing sold itself, certainly not the $800 million of bonds Atlantic Pacific intended to issue for the Finance Bank of Romania. Atlantic Pacific had been watching Eastern Europe very carefully since it first appeared that a financial killing could be made rebuilding its economy. In March of 1990, the Romanian democratic government mandated an instant free market economy with Decree 54, and then, in its first stroke of capitalist plunder, purchased 100 percent of the common stock of the newly formed Bank of Romania, Romanian Power and Energy, and Romanian Telephone companies. With the long-awaited outbreak of a free market, these were surely to be extremely profitable corporations, and the government made a shrewd investment in order to make sure all of the profits drained back into the government coffers. Now the Finance Bank of Romania, in order to profit from loans it wanted to make to Romanian Power, Inc., and ROMTELECOM, Inc., just needed some money to loan to them, and to do this it came to Sidney Geeder, who in turn went to Ingenesis Corporation.

"You're ripping their eyes out!" he howled at Kenny Whitlash, who had bragged again about the government contract they'd received to build a better razor blade.

"It's perfectly legal, Sidney. In fact, it's quite patriotic to be part of the job retraining programs."

"It's armed robbery!"

Kenny Whitlash was a tough-as-nails ex-lawyer with a bass voice and an unexplainable soft spot for Sidney Geeder, who was a little too much of a bleeding heart for Whitlash's taste. Ingenesis Corp. was a hush-hush military subcontractor that kept its name out of the papers and the courts by charging back the government 30 percent overhead to cover a top-flight security force. No trade secrets leaked from Ingenesis unintentionally, and Kenny Whitlash—who was paid tens of thousands of tax-free dollars to discreetly leak information to investment banks—needed Sid Geeder as much as vice versa. In exchange for Sid Geeder's blatant rumormongering, Kenny Whitlash bought whatever Sidney sold and charged back the government for any losses incurred. When the Euro-Floaters deal went sour, for instance, Ingenesis added another 3 percent overhead to its cost of capital component. When the secondary junk market fell through the floor, Ingenesis wrote down 60 percent of the losses against profits on parts it made for the Osprey helicopter, which were embarrassingly high. Ingenesis was one of the most efficient private companies at helping the government sweep its inefficiencies off the balance sheets and into the finely printed footnotes. It always needed losses to tame its profits and avoid a public relations scandal, so Kenny Whitlash listened whenever Sidney Geeder talked. Sid Geeder was never sure what to do with Ingenesis. He hated them on principle and wanted to bring them down even more than the government, but he knew if he brought them down the entire cost of their bailout would go to the government, and then the government would come back to Sidney Geeder to sell more bailout bonds. Sidney wanted to punish Ingenesis, and the only way he could think of to do it was to repeat everything Whitlash told him in strict confidence. He spread every rumor Whitlash ever told him never to repeat, including the ridiculous assertion that Ingenesis had invented a robotic foot soldier and was on the verge of securing a $14 billion contract to mass-produce them.

"Preposterous," Geeder mumbled, taking notes.

"Not at all," Whitlash asserted. "It conspicuously infiltrates the target country, then plugs into their phone system."

"Their phone system?"

"Yes, their phone network. Completely destroys government control of propaganda."

"It ought to work at least as well as that Stealth radar-jamming device you designed."

"No, it's far more effective than that. If you don't believe me, you ought to come see it for yourself. You ought to drive right down here and get a look."

"Ohhh . . . I don't feel strong enough to do that."

"Well, what would make you stronger?"

So Sid Geeder sold Whitlash $6 million Taio Kobe Floating Rate Notes from the secondary market, which momentarily made him feel strong enough to get in his truck and drive fifty miles south to the heart of Silicon Valley, where the Ingenesis complex was buried twenty feet below the golden Santa Clara foothills. A security booth and gate guarded a lonesome stretch of road that circled a knob and then burrowed into a thick clump of scrub oak and sorrel, at which point it descended into the earth in a long, heavily armored tunnel. A snappy young corporal in a U.S. Army uniform escorted Geeder from the parking lot to a shuttle subway that was operated by voice print. The shuttle dumped him out onto an escalator that took him up to Whitlash's control center, where there were three more guards, who frisked Geeder and took his beeper and his wallet calculator and his pen and his waistbelt and his shoelaces. Whitlash slapped him on the back and apologized for the security precautions but warned him never to tell anyone about the $14 billion robotic foot soldier he was about to see demonstrated. They made him sign several clearance forms that required him to testify he'd never considered trying to overthrow his government, never snorted cocaine, shot heroin, or smoked marijuana, and never committed a felony. Then the five of them marched through the building, down two flights of stairs, past a row of uniformed women at desks, and through numerous electronic doors. Finally they reached an electronics lab littered with computer peripherals and telephone wires and testing equipment. The guards stood at the door. At a table in the middle of the room were two men in lab coats installing plastic paper feeders into a blue plastic box that had a numeric keypad on the top and a small LCD display window flashing an error message.

"There it is," Whitlash laughed. "The foot soldier of the future. The post–Cold War fighting machine. The greatest weapon of land invasion since the Bradley tank. We're mass-producing half a million of these little buggers at less than eight thousand dollars per."

"It looks just like a fax machine," Sidney observed.

"It *is* a fax machine," Whitlash answered, giggling a little.

Geeder was perplexed. "Is it a bomb or something?"

Whitlash shook his head. "No, it just sends and receives faxes."

"Does it use poisonous paper or leak gas or something?"

"No, but it does allow you to program up to ten different phone numbers by speed dial, and it prints out an activity report every hour automatically. We're working on a special add-on utility that wires it into the old telephone jacks still prevalent in North Korea."

"Now let me get this right . . . it doesn't secretly make copies of the faxes and send them back to the Pentagon?"

"No, but it uses just about any kind of paper. Paper is a very scarce commodity in Romania."

"You mean it's just a *fax machine*?"

"That's right. A fax machine. We also have a robotic bombardier project that is remarkably similar to a consumer satellite dish. In fact, it *is* just a consumer satellite dish, except ours cost three times as much to assemble because of the security precautions we have to take."

"What good is a fax machine?!"

"The Chinese can stop tanks and missiles and battleships, but they can't stop airwaves. Arm the citizens with fax machines and you have the makings of a revolution. Suddenly they can talk to each other, and we can send them pictures of rock stars and pornography and the Declaration of Independence."

"That's crazy!" Sidney stammered.

"It's not crazy at all. It's modern warfare, Geeder. Grow up. The military has found a role to play in the post–Cold War economy. Everybody's been wondering what we're going to do now that we don't need all that weaponry. This little fax machine and those satellite dishes will accomplish more in five years than forty years of missile-pointing and battleship-maneuvering. Once the Pakistanis get naked twat coming over the phone line, Muslim fundamentalism will crumble. Once those Azerbaijanis start watching American television, their government will never be able to get control of the people again. The military's in the export business, Geeder. Missiles are obsolete. We're the information military. We're dropping feminism on the North Koreans, firing football at the Romanians, shooting adolescence at the Chinese. We're attacking the Hungarians with basketball and the Iranians with rock and roll. Words and pictures are our soldiers; sounds and movies are our ammunition. It's a new world, Geeder."

Sidney felt pressure building inside his head. "But why do you want to take over Romania? They're not hurting anybody. They're not shooting at the Croatians or bullying the Hungarians or scuffling with the Ukrainians. They're not polluting the Black Sea. It's a peaceful little country of peasants and miners and old churches and vampire myths. They have their own music and their own religion and their own folklore. What are you doing there?"

"Well, the military has to do *something*, Geeder. We can't get away with building bombs and storing them underneath South Dakota for too many more years. People are beginning to realize which country those bombs are really threatening. They're beginning to realize how much we've been siphoning out the bottom and skimming off the top all these years. It's gotten so bad that our triple-A credit rating has been rumored for a downgrade at Moody's. And if I can't borrow at four percent and reinvest at seven percent, then we're really going to be unprofitable and our bond rating is going to drop even farther. Pretty soon the whole military-industrial complex is going to be like the savings and loans, and the government is going to have to bail us out. And you know who they're going to come to to bail us out—"

"Me! They'll be coming after me!"

"We'll come get you out of retirement if we have to."

"They'll never find me. I'll be long gone by then. I'll be living on a beach in the South Pacific by then. I'll own my personal island in Alaska. I'll be wrestling with the native women every afternoon."

"We'll find you. We'll find your Swiss bank account and find whoever you have manage your money, or find whatever mutual fund you invest in, and then we'll go to them and sell them Peace Bonds, which will be a piece of shit but will have the full faith and credit of the U.S. government behind them and add yield to a stable portfolio. There's no escape, Geeder. The money stays in the system—you can't take it out of the system unless you want to put eight million dollars in a mattress."

"Can't you just leave Romania out of it?" Sidney pleaded.

"Romania has more forests than Oregon and more oil than Arkansas. The Black Sea is the next Panama Canal—every freighter full of cars and computers and Coca-Cola headed for southern Russia will be going through there. We'll be sending more money to Romania in a couple years than to Turkey and Israel combined. Romania's going to be an American cultural colony in a blink of an eye. An outpost of crass consumerism and mordant commercialism and vulgar capitalism. The Pentagon loves it. The senators love it. Washington loves it. It's a sellable idea, Geeder. 'The U.S. Armed Forces: pioneers on the economic frontier.' Get used to it—you'll be hearing it often."

It was just another thing to get used to in a long list of things to get used to. It was just another wave in the flood of the future, and it hit high finance long before it hit the supermarkets or the newspapers or the streets. Time could be measured in seconds or in decades, but the financial markets were always in front. Everything in America made its way into dollars, and every dollar was part of the system that hissed and popped and crackled and rattled as it absorbed whatever was the next thing to get used to. Everything in America required money except falling in love, and every Atlantic Pacific salesman was on the front line of all those dollars whizzing into their new uses and out of their old ones. On the front line the future was vague and incomprehensible and distorted into numbers, so it was harder to read than a balance sheet. It was like a ghost, a faceless enemy, and they hunkered down over their desks and gazed into their monitors and tried to see the future in the numbers that were always moving. The future was like the clouds that whipped past the building and rattled the windows, and the salesmen stared out at the clouds and tried to recognize the shapes in the clouds, the faces and animals and furniture. When they got confused, as they always did, they looked to the past for clues, but the past was often just as foggy.

The past fifty years of oppression in Romania stirred a great deal of sympathy among the salesforce for that country's redevelopment, but investors did not bet money on their sympathies. Investment was not a basketball pool. Investors bet on greed. So the entire history of Romania had been rewritten by Atlantic Pacific to emphasize its capitalist, commercial roots. Romania was used to having its history rewritten—the communists did it at every change of power, replacing the Turkish castles and Hungarian statues and Greek mausoleums erected by previous oppressors with monuments to the dictator currently in vogue. Now, new monuments of capitalist power were being erected, including a Hilton Hotel, a soccer stadium, wireless cellular radio transmitters on every mountaintop, a Canadian Petroleum oil refinery on the shores of the Black Sea, and a forty-foot-high likeness of Michael Jackson in downtown Bucharest, where he had given a concert before sixty thousand screaming fanatics in October of 1991. Atlantic Pacific's confidential memo had made repeated positive comparisons between Romania and America, including their vast natural resources, their ethnic diversity, and their democratic constitutions. Little mention was made of Romania's history of violence and turmoil, the inexhaustible corruption of the foreign-controlled governments for three hundred years, its failed agricultural economy, or its periods of anti-Semitic barbarianism. It was a heavy sell job that the firm devoted great resources to, including morning briefings every day for a week, but still the salesforce was unconfident and reluctant until the firm raised the commission rate that the salesforce would earn, at which point most of the salesforce fell into line and began to buzz about "the pent-up greed of the oppressed" and vacationing that summer at "Club Med Bucharest." Even then, Coyote Jack took it upon himself to interrogate each of the salespeople individually and ensure that they would not be soft on the bonds. Each afternoon he ordered another salesman into his office and grilled him on current pulp and paper mill capacities in the Transylvanian forests and the various market opportunities that would be created by a surge in silver ore supply.

"I don't give a shit about silver ore," Regis Reed shot back, clutching at his chair's armrests. "I'm quitting." Regis Reed hadn't told Coyote Jack yet that he'd accepted a job offer from one of his customers, because he was trying to steal a comprehensive library of research reports in order to try to clean Atlantic Pacific's clocks from the other side. Ever since Eggs Igino had suddenly arrived on the scene, Coyote Jack had stopped grilling Regis Reed about whether he would get married or buy a house or take out life insurance or invest his salary in a closed-end mutual fund. And Sid Geeder had stopped sharing tips on how to make his customers feel intellectually inferior. And Coyote Jack's secretary had stopped bringing him her coffee. Of course, Regis Reed had once told her that he would rather drink battery acid, but still, the Foreseeable Future was obvious—he was not the Prince of Mortgages anymore.

"Now you're sounding like Sidney Geeder," Coyote Jack observed. "Since when did you become a patron of Romanian folk art?"

"I don't give a shit about Romanian folk art, either," Regis Reed said. "I've had enough."

"These bonds are nothing to quit over. They'll be gone and then you can go back to tracking the rate spread between treasuries and mortgages."

"I'm not quitting over these bonds. I'm just quitting."

Coyote Jack narrowed his eyes and concentrated for a moment. "Bullshit," he laughed. "You're bluffing. What is it you want? You want a sales assistant? You want a promotion? You want a parking space?"

"I want my commission since January."

"Jesus," Coyote Jack realized. "You're serious." Coyote Jack immediately picked up the phone and called downstairs to building security, asking that several security guards be sent upstairs immediately. Then he stood up and strolled to his fishbowl window, stalling for time to think. This would not look good in New York, to hear that a salesman had quit on him. Not look good at all. The timing was horrible. Just yesterday, John White had notified him that Coyote Jack was secretly being considered as managing director for a new Honolulu office. Now this!

Coyote Jack momentarily considered the Foreseeable Future, and he perceived only one option: fire Regis Reed and make an example of him. "You're not owed any bonus," Coyote Jack lied. "You've been drawing a salary since January."

Regis Reed was ready for this, so he was cool and decisive. He rotated his watchband about his wrist. "I've got complete records of how much commission I've earned."

"Correction—you've got records of your sales credit earned, but the rate of commission we pay on those sales credits, well, that's entirely up to the discretion of the firm."

Regis Reed wasn't fazed. "A couple of letters from my lawyer will clear this up, I'm sure."

Coyote Jack laughed. "Don't be so cocky, Reed. Stormin' Norman and Whiskey Phillips know every single thing about you. I'm sure they'll find a technicality in all the fine print you've signed over the years to keep you from seeing another dime out of this place. You've been a shady character ever since you arrived here. I don't think any judge is going to find against a respectable Wall Street house and for a con man who illegally took out student loans and reinvested them in the options market."

"That's long in the past," Regis Reed said a little nervously. "It has nothing to do with my commissions."

"The hell it doesn't," Coyote Jack charged. "Ever since you first bragged during your early job interviews that you'd ripped off the government, the firm has had valuable information to use against you in situations just like this. We've got an entire internal security department that's devoted to finding dirt on our employees. I've got a whole file on you filled with photocopies of your student loan papers, the cashed loan checks, even a trading history of your account from your old broker." Coyote Jack pulled out of his drawer a manila file folder with Regis Reed's name typed across the tab. "I thought you were smarter than that, Reed. Do you think we would have let you become so valuable to us if we didn't have something to use against you?"

Regis Reed squirmed in his seat anxiously. "You'll never get away with it," he feebly argued, his voice suddenly cracking with stress. "You owe me over seventy thousand dollars," he stammered.

"You should have thought of that before you quit." Coyote Jack grinned.

Three security guards arrived at the door. Coyote Jack waved them in and ordered them to escort Regis Reed across the sales floor to his desk, where he would be given five minutes to remove only his personal toiletries. All of his research reports, trading notebooks, and customer lists would stay. The locks on all the doors would be changed that night, so it was no use for him to try to steal his magnetic security card. He was not to be given a chance to say goodbye or to talk to the other salespeople. If he tried to say anything he should be dragged out the front door and escorted out of the building. If he was seen in the building in the next month he was to be detained and charged with trespassing. Coyote Jack spoke to the guards as if Regis Reed were already out of the room.

When they put their hands onto Regis Reed's shoulders to yank him out of his chair, Coyote Jack went back to his fishbowl window and surveyed the layout of the sales pits. A spot on the mortgage desk would be open. Coyote Jack could try to fill the spot, but more likely he would give all of Regis Reed's accounts to Eggs Igino. Coyote Jack smiled at the thought of what Eggs Igino could do with Sierra Prudential and the Bank of Sacramento. There was a lot of money going into Sacramento, a lot of development up there, and a lot of cash ending up in the local banks. Coyote Jack knew that some of Eggs Igino's success was a gimmick, the impression of great honesty he made on his clients with his youth and cleanliness. They trusted him, sure, in a way they could never trust someone whose teeth were rotting, or who stammered, or whose face twitched. But Eggs Igino was *smart,* a rocket scientist if there ever was one. As Coyote Jack watched Regis Reed be escorted to his desk by the security men, he realized how Reed's early departure was really a lucky break. It would play well in New York for Eggs Igino to start posting big monthly numbers with Regis Reed's accounts. It would look downright prescient that Coyote Jack had fired Reed. With that Honolulu deal in the works, the timing couldn't be better. Now he just had to make sure John White didn't try to take credit for it.

Out on the sales floor the activity paused as Regis Reed collected his personal belongings. The security men, who'd been through this routine before, wouldn't even let him open his file cabinet. Regis Reed, who'd suddenly lost his confidence that he'd be able to get his bonus check out of the firm, behaved himself, hoping it might help his chances if he went quietly. He gave Lisa Lisa a momentary scowl to hurt her feelings, which she returned with a cold, disinterested gaze to convey that she had no remorse for him. Then his time was up, and the three young security men put their hands on his elbows and forcibly pushed him toward the exit. The sales floor was hushed.

Coyote Jack marched out into the aisles. "Let's go," he barked, slapping the backs of their chairs and throwing the telephone handsets into their laps. "Let's go, let's go! Back to work!"

Uneasily, they picked up their phones and punched up their trading screens and gazed into the future, but they could imagine no future without their jobs to come to every morning and their accounts to harangue all day long and those whopping bonus checks every six months which never seemed to make up for all the shit they'd been through. Nelson Dicky went back to exaggerating the Romanian economy. Nickel Sansome went back to persuading the State of Nevada to sell its tax-free Hoover Dam 4.5s of '07 for General Motors Australia 12s of '97. Lisa Lisa went back to persuading Honolulu Pacific to sell its General Motors Australia 12s of '97 for tax-free Hoover Dam 4.5s of '07. Sidney Geeder went back to considering whether to punish Ingenesis for getting $8,000 from the taxpayers for every fax machine it shipped to Romania.

Sidney was distraught because the private investigator hadn't been able to find anything out about Ivana Perkova. The firm had been paying for her apartment and her office and her medical association fees and anything else that would be trackable. The AMA had a listing for an old address in New York, where the firm had first discovered her. The private investigator had inquired into her immigration status, but she wouldn't hear for a while. Sid sat there stewing at his desk while he watched the price of Ingenesis continue to rise on the leak that it had secured some wildly profitable military contract. Disgusted, he went into the kitchen to eat, where he bumped into Dave Rennaker, one of the equities salesmen, specializing in aerospace stocks. Sidney hunkered down over a bowl of All-Bran and began to ramble. "Boy, have you seen Ingenesis's stock? It keeps climbing all day," he mumbled.

"It'll go at least to sixty," Dave Rennaker predicted. "That robotic foot soldier sounds amazing. Imagine—it plugs itself into the phone system and receives data from the Pentagon."

"Is that what's causing the rally?" Sidney scoffed, putting down his spoon. "Gosh, I would have thought the market would have heard by now."

"Heard what?"

"About the investigation."

"What investigation?"

"You haven't heard either? Christ, I thought the whole market would have known by now. I've known for two days."

"What?" Dave Rennaker pleaded. "Jeez, Sid, let me in on it."

"Kenny Whitlash was just telling me all about it. I guess it's serious. The GAO is subpoenaing all their records, and I guess some Feds are onsite in Santa Clara, making sure nothing gets accidentally shredded."

"Is Ingenesis under investigation?" Dave Rennaker guessed.

"Isn't that what I've been saying?"

"What did they do?"

"Well, what do you think military contractors get investigated for? I'll give you a hint: it's not jaywalking."

"Bid-rigging? Is that it—they're getting busted for rigging a bid, aren't they?"

"Dang, Rennaker—you're a genius. How did you figure that out?"

But Dave Rennaker didn't answer. He dropped his breakfast and ran to the phone, where he called all his accounts and begged them to sell Ingenesis, and then he called the aerospace trader in New York and gamely notified him of the impending investigation into Ingenesis's improprieties. Sidney went back to his desk and popped up Ingenesis stock on his Quotron. It was down 2 already, and as Sidney watched the news spread through the market, the stock fell through 50, where it had started the day, and now it was at 46 and rumors were rampant. There was a rumor that Ingenesis had lost the contract and was being blocked from bidding on any other government work for three years. There was a rumor that they were being profiled on *60 Minutes* that Sunday for bid-rigging. There was a rumor that a bomb had gone off underground at the Ingenesis compound, blowing up evidence and killing two federal accountants. Sidney decided it was time to call Whitlash.

"What the hell's going on down there?" Sidney laughed. "Christ, I heard from the Equities desk that a bomb went off."

"Holy cow, Sid. It's horrible. These rumors are killing us. No bomb went off at all. I guess someone got the story wrong about one of our robotic foot soldiers that short-circuited. I've been fending off calls all day. Dang, there was even a call from *60 Minutes*. The GAO office called and started asking questions. Some senator got a tip that we controlled the bidding for those eight-thousand-dollar fax machines, wants to appoint a special prosecutor. I've got to sell some bonds to raise some cash."

"What do you need cash for?" Sidney asked, pretending to be naive.

"To buy our stock! Somebody's got to convince the market that this is all rumor. I've got to unload some of those Resolutions you sold me."

"The Resolutions! You want me to buy them back?"

"It's either that or some Euro-Floaters."

"If I had wanted to buy them back, I wouldn't have sold them to you in the first place," Sid said on cue.

"Hey, Sidney. Come on. Unless you've got fifteen million dollars you can loan me, bid those Resolutions."

"Fifteen million!"

"I've got to prop up our stock price. Just for a few days, to get it back over fifty."

"I don't make any commission when we buy bonds from you, do you understand that? I don't make squat, and the traders begin to hate me."

"I'll buy them back in a few days! You'll get a commission then!"

"You have a point there," Sidney admitted facetiously, for he had seen this all along. So he called the trader and asked him to sit on $15 million Resolutions for a few days, and then he switched Kenny Whitlash over to Dave Rennaker, who sold Ingenesis $15 million of its own stock, less commission, and then they reversed the trade a few days later, less commissions.

It was an information economy, and its fundamental flaw was that information didn't have to be true to be sold. Rumor alone could drive a stock up 70 percent and force a company into borrowing to save itself. Every single idea was bought and sold, and usually the farthest-out ideas—such as that two ounces of deslackening agent could reverse thirty years of aging—garnered the highest price. The economy continued to flourish, but it would have crashed if there had been a simple requirement that it be based on truth. Most ideas, such as the one that the Resolutions would be actively traded for thirty years, were only partially true, or possibly true, and the difference was up to the salesmen. In the information economy, every idea that was bought had to be sold, and it had to be sold hard. Every third worker in the information economy was a salesman of one sort or another—a publicist, a PR man, an advertiser, a reporter, a newscaster, an account executive, a sales rep, a politician. The economy hinged upon their success in selling the next new thing. There were more ideas than ever, but very, very few of them sold themselves. Almost none were true enough to make it without a handle and a slogan and advance media coverage and a good story for the sales rep to tell. It was a propaganda economy, an advice economy, a possibility economy, a rumor economy—an economy of tall tales, fish stories, and oral folklore. The fundamental value—the truth—was questionable, and the only way to find out the truth was to wait and see what happened. But they couldn't wait, because time was money. The window of opportunity to take advantage of Eastern Europe was closing. The firm didn't have the ten years it would take to see if the government of Romania really was a safe investment, and so they winged it and hoped nobody would notice.

"What did you say?" Coyote Jack bellowed, leaning on the conference table like an ape and glowering at Eggs Igino. The morning briefing was just about to begin, and New York was coming in on the closed-circuit feed.

Eggs Igino twiddled his finger in his danish filling and poked it into his mouth. "I said, 'Hey! There's a mistake in the numbers on the Romanians.'"

"We don't pay you to question the numbers, Igino."

"Have I sent you a bill?"

Sid Geeder stopped scarfing down his strawberry danish. Lisa Lisa stopped running her fingers up and down the neckline of her blouse.

The age spots on Coyote Jack's forehead were turning red. "We have an entire research department to generate the numbers and an entire legal department to testify to their accurateness."

"Well, they've made a mistake. It's so obvious it's insane."

"I think *you've* made a mistake, Igino!"

"The bonds have a longer average life! There's a miscalculation on how the underlying loans pay the four tranches." The FB Romanians had been structured to have underlying loans to Romanian Power and Energy and ROMTELECOM as collateral. As those loans were paid back, the FB Romanians would pay back each of the four tranche sections in order. It was difficult for even the salesmen to understand, but few admitted it for fear of looking foolish.

Coyote Jack didn't want to look foolish discussing numbers on international television, so he ordered Eggs Igino to put a clamp on it until after the briefing, during which slides were shown of the newly created Bucharest Security Exchange in a renovated Corinthian temple that had previously housed a useless old museum of Transylvanian folklore. Then the senior researcher of telephone stocks got on to detail the joint venture Sprint had struck with ROMTELECOM to install Intelsat digital satellite circuits, followed by a junk-food researcher who announced that Coca-Cola had shipped its ten millionth crate of Coke into Romania earlier that month. But nobody in the San Francisco office could pay attention, because they were still shocked to hear that the numbers were wrong and had begun to have a glimmer of hope that maybe they wouldn't have to sell these bonds after all. None of them were comfortable selling the Romanians. They had begun to think it strange that they were loaning money to Sprint so that it could send satellites into the sky over Moldavia, while at the same time they were loaning money indirectly to ROMTELECOM so that it could pay back Sprint for use of the satellites. That didn't make any more sense than loaning money to Ingenesis to build an army of $8,000 fax machines so that it could sell them to the U.S. military, while at the same time they loaned money to the U.S. Treasury so that the government could pay Ingenesis for the fax machines. They were propping up both sides of the market, and it looked a whole lot like what they had done to the savings and loans ten years before, when they had loaned money to the savings and loans to issue mortgages, while at the same time they had loaned money to government agencies to buy those mortgages from the savings and loans. A lot of people had gone to jail over it, and as much as the salesmen wanted to get filthy rich stealing the shirt off the back of the Romanian public, they didn't want to go to jail.

"It's a glaring error," Eggs Igino insisted, when he and Coyote Jack had gathered in John White's office. "It's on page three in the report, page nine in the prospectus, page two in our in-house memo. I wasn't trying to embarrass you. I just spotted it right then."

John White opened the prospectus to a table of numbers in tiny print. It looked just like every other table of meaningless numbers that was in every memo, report, and prospectus put out by Atlantic Pacific. "It looks fine to me," he said.

"It's not fine!" Eggs Igino repeated, pacing back and forth behind the couch where Coyote Jack hunched forward, propping his chin under his knuckled hands. "Just look at the columns across the bottom. Four columns, four tranches—it's how much of the collateral cash flow goes to pay the bonds."

John White glanced at the totals running the four columns.

"Add them up," Eggs Igino said. "They're supposed to equal one hundred percent."

Coyote Jack interjected, but John White waved him off. He took a pencil and began to jot down the numbers on a Post-It note, but then he tore up the Post-It note and instead wrote the numbers in a column on a stack of white paper napkins he kept for all-important, potentially incriminating information. During the Justice Department's crackdown on high finance in the past few years, all manner of documentation—including Post-It notes—had been subpoenaed for discovery, so the salesforce had been taught to write down secret information on paper napkins, which couldn't yet be subpoenaed as evidence. Every salesman ran around with several paper napkins in his pockets and folded up carefully in his wallet, which could quickly be sneezed into if the Feds came snooping. So John White wrote:

Tranche 1: 46%
Tranche 2: 31%
Tranche 3: 19%
<u>Tranche 4: 14%</u>

"Go ahead," Eggs Igino prodded. "Add them up."

John White looked up momentarily, then bent down over the numbers. He licked the fingertips of his writing hand and began the math by first adding 46 and 31, then adding 19 and 14. It had been a long time since he'd had to do any math, and he wanted to make sure he made no mistake. His brow furrowed in concentration.

"There must be a mistake," he said. "Let me use my calculator." He popped the speaker button on his phone set and buzzed his secretary, asking her to use her calculator and add up the four numbers.

"Okay, now what?" she asked, her voice fizzing with static.

"That's all. Just tell me what the numbers add up to."

"They add up to one hundred and ten."

"So what!" Coyote Jack raged, jumping off the couch and jerking his arms about like a maniac. "So the collateral gives one hundred and ten percent? Big deal! We all give one hundred and ten percent around here! One hundred and ten percent is what it takes in this business! The salesmen will just have to give one hundred and ten percent effort to move those bonds!"

But it was not that simple, and John White knew it, because although as much as they might like to think the collateral gave 110 percent, such a thing was monetarily impossible. If there was a way to magically transform $100 into $110, he surely would have heard about it. Not even the closely guarded New Product department could have kept the lid on a secret that powerful. He would have to call New York and pass the buck on to somebody who could take the heat for it.

But the rumor mill had already started, and the word had already gone around the world that there was a mistake in the numbers on the Romanians. There was a rumor that the European Bank for Reconstruction and Development had pulled its letter of credit on the fourth tranche. There was a rumor that Salomon Brothers was doing a deal for nearby Bulgaria that was priced 50 basis points higher. There was a rumor that the Romanian president, Ion Iliescu, had been arrested at a whorehouse in Italy. The rumors had even swung around to Ingenesis, which called Sidney Geeder to ask if it was true that there'd been an earthquake in Bucharest. New York management was going crazy fielding phone calls and trying to restore the confidence in the deal, which had suddenly disappeared without their having any idea why. There was a rumor that it had started in San Francisco, and so they called John White just as John White was calling them.

10 · Propaganda

THE CORRUPTION OF language and the manipulation of time and the distortion of numbers were all part of the art of selling. The salesforce created illusions, and in the process had visions of prophecy and grandeur, just like any other artists. It was a slippery business, a slimy profession, and the degree of sliminess was itself a slippery slope: little white lies; minor, benign addictions; a prick of guilt; slight exaggerations; short-term debt. These all got out of hand, and they fed on each other, and the salesmen completely lost their vantage point, their ability to discriminate, their capacity to stop themselves from suggesting that the Finance Bank of Romania was partly owned by the European Bank for Reconstruction and Development, or that Romania was a nonvoting member of the European Community, or that the Royal Princess's Cruise Lines had begun a six-day/five-night pleasure cruise circling the Black Sea. In the heat of the sale, they needed to keep talking, and they said whatever came to them, as long as they didn't blatantly lie, as long as it was just color commentary, as long as the fictions were just part of the overall fabric.

The factual truth was not as relevant as the true essence, and as long as they retained the true essence—of which they were the arbiter—then they saw nothing wrong. In the case of the Romanians, their true essence was that they were a good buy, a safe investment, a smart move. As long as the salesmen didn't testify that the bonds were a bad buy, a risky investment, or a dumb move, they were free to embroider the factual data with fictional anecdotes that made a good story. It was all in service to the story. A good story could keep the customer on the phone for an hour. The Royal Princess cruise was a good anecdote—it made a good story. Nobody was sure who had started it: Lisa Lisa had overheard Sidney Geeder tell Franklin Mutual that the ship had 540 beds and four pools. She assumed he wouldn't be lying to Franklin, and so when she called Mike Kohanamoku at Honolulu Federal, she added that the ship began in Athens, sailed northeast through the Sea of Marmara, and anchored for the night in the Bay of Istanbul. Nickel Sansome, who'd overheard Lisa Lisa, explained to the Bank of Canton that every dinner served the best local cuisine, from Crimean roasted fish-cakes to Odessan pork-stuffed cabbage to Moldavian chocolate-covered pears flambé. Roasted fishcakes! It just came out of his mouth. It made a good story. It was a lot easier for Bonnie Hao at the Bank of Canton to imagine sitting on a starlit aft deck eating roasted fishcakes while watching the twinkling skyline of Crimea than it was to study the Finance Bank of Romania 11s of '24 in a motion analysis versus Eurobonds or a reinvested port-folio of CMOs. The Royal Princess anecdote was so often re-peated in the Taxable Fixed Income sales floor that it took on the weight of fact, and even Sidney Geeder—who had started the whole thing—found himself daydreaming of sitting on the starlit aft deck with Dr. Perkova, eating roasted fishcakes and looking out over her twinkling homeland.

Although it was easy to cheat by telling stories, it was even easier to cheat by manipulating numbers. If the raw data were erratic, they published the moving average. If the average yield looked bad, they published the yield-to-maturity, and if that number was too low they substituted the yield-to-horizon, which assumed they would be able to sell the bond back to Atlantic Pacific at a profit in three years—itself an erroneous assumption. The salesman had a computer program that would print out three-dimensional bar charts, pie charts, and X-Y graphs for any security over any time frame, and it was easy to adjust the time frame to withhold data or to distort the visual perspective to exaggerate spreads. If the salesman was thinking for himself, he would have investigated every hidden assumption to verify the published numbers, but most of them trusted the division of labor that left number-crunching to the research department. Even Sidney Geeder—who often discovered errors in the reports—knew how hopeless it would be to fight the corporate momentum; only a complete fool would confront the research department, as Eggs Igino had done.

"I'm sorry—he's on the phone right now," the woman repeated, after John White urgently begged to speak to the Executive Managing Director for Capital Markets.

"I'm sorry—he's on the phone right now," John White's secretary repeated, putting on hold the Executive Managing Director for Capital Markets.

Eventually they got connected and John White was ordered to grab the next flight to New York. He ran out of the room and took the express elevator downstairs to a waiting cab, which rushed him to the airport so he could grab the next plane to Newark. John White was a seasoned executive with over 260,000 frequent flier miles in the bank plus eight free round-trip tickets to Europe and Asia that he never had time to use. John White was the old guard: he had become an executive in the prehistoric days before fax machines and computerized trading, which meant he was accustomed to long periods of boring nothingness interrupted only occasionally by momentary phases of mere tedium. It was an important executive skill that came in handy on the trip to Newark: he was excellent at sitting still in his first-class padded chair for five hours straight. He didn't suffer back spasms or hamstring cramps or thinning blood from the altitude. John White was a less-than-average man in all physical respects, so he fit easily into car and airplane seats. Sitting behind a desk, he made the desk and the office seem vast and spacious. His chin had receded, but his hairline, rather than receding, had actually begun to sprout its way down his forehead toward his bushy eyebrows, so it seemed that his head was always turned down toward the floor, even when it wasn't. This constant deferent posture made him nonthreatening to upper management, who trusted him as one of their own. He didn't drink and he didn't embarrass the firm by bragging about the deals he was involved in to the stewardesses. He sat patiently twiddling his thumbs until he reached Newark, where a helicopter was waiting to rush him to the heliport atop Two World Trade Center. He took another elevator and climbed into another cab and was rushed across town, at which point he realized he'd forgotten his notes and had to call his secretary and order her to fax him his napkins. But the fax machine shredded the napkin in its rollers, and John White had to attend the meeting in the penthouse above midtown without any notes. He sat down on a white couch among the board of directors and tried to explain that one of his salesmen had discovered that the Romanian bonds gave 110 percent.

"Of course they give one hundred and ten percent!" the Senior Executive President for International Markets responded. "We all give one hundred and ten percent! One hundred and ten percent is SOP. One hundred and ten percent is normal."

"It doesn't matter what the bonds give," the Executive-in-Chief of Legal Affairs broke in. "It's a matter of restoring the dwindling confidence in the deal. We've invested a lot of energy propping up both sides of this market. The Sprint deal and the Coke deal and the Canadian Petroleum deal and the Ingenesis deal all count on this deal going smoothly!"

"Of course it matters what the bonds give," the Executive Director of Internal Surveillance objected. "If there's any truth that Salomon's got a Bulgarian deal, then our bonds—which were already fifty basis points lower—are really going to look like a piece of shit when we readjust for there being less collateral."

"But there isn't *less* collateral," the Senior Executive President for International Markets stressed. "Let's just say there's *more* collateral: ten percent more. Let's announce that the deal was going so well that FB Romania found ten percent more collateral, and with the lowered credit risk we have an excuse for the bonds being expensive," he suggested.

"I say let's just fire the pesky salesman who started this whole thing," the Senior Director of Facilities interrupted.

"That goes without saying," the Executive Director of Internal Surveillance agreed.

"Absolutely," the Chief of Internal Affairs said. "He's already been fired, hasn't he, Jack?"

John White shook his head. "We can't fire him," he noted regretfully. "We've got him down for a fifty million quota on the deal. That's six percent of the entire deal. If we fire him, then we might be dooming the deal."

"Then let's fire him after the deal!" the Senior Director of Facilities charged.

"That goes without saying," the Executive Director of Internal Surveillance agreed again.

"You can't fire him if he's just sold six percent of the deal," the Executive-in-Chief of Legal Affairs broke in. "The salesforce will declare mutiny if we fire someone for selling bonds that we told them to sell."

"We have to fire him right now."

"We can't—we need him!" John White argued.

"Give Geeder his quota."

"Geeder's already got fifty million!"

"Fifty million! What the hell is Coyote Jack thinking? Nobody can sell fifty million."

John White shook his head. "Coyote's going crazy on the quotas ever since I told him he's in consideration to manage the new Honolulu office."

"What Honolulu office? We don't have a Honolulu office in the works!"

John White defended his ploy. "Yeah, well, so what? He *thinks* there's a Honolulu office in the works, and because of it we're selling a lot of bonds. Do you have a problem with that?"

"Well, we have to fire somebody," the Executive Director of Internal Surveillance reasoned. "We can't let this happen without some sort of scapegoat."

"Why don't we just promote the kid for finding the extra ten percent in collateral?" the Senior Executive President for International Markets exhorted with his peculiar style of illogic. "Then we reprice the deal to be a little longer in maturity and a little richer because the demand is so great that we can get away with it."

"But there isn't ten percent more collateral!"

"Of course there is! Add up the numbers! It equals one hundred and ten percent."

"That doesn't mean anything!"

"The numbers don't lie," the Senior Executive President of International Markets stated coolly.

"What should we promote him to?" the Director of Personnel asked.

"What's he now, some VP?"

"He's a vice salesman," John White answered.

"Hell, make him Senior Vice President!" the Senior Executive President for International Markets proposed. "Leapfrog him past everyone else in line. That'll teach the salesforce how important his contribution has been to this crucial deal. The kid gave one hundred and ten percent effort, went above and beyond the call of duty to discover that we were about to give away those Romanians much too cheaply."

Eventually it was decided that nothing could be done other than to promote Eggs Igino to Senior Vice President, assign him a stall in the parking garage, mail him a gold corporate watch, add him to the firm's disability insurance policy, and increase his allowable vacation time that he wasn't supposed to take by two weeks. He was to be given a new security clearance level, magnetic access cards to private executive facilities within the Atlantic Pacific buildings around the world, an Amex Platinum card, and forty thousand frequent flier miles from the firm's mileage bank. The firm really saw no other way out of it. They had no choice but for the Chief of Internal Affairs to call a *Wall Street Journal* reporter at home and leak a story that an up-and-coming young salesman from the San Francisco office had studied the numbers and mathematically proved that Atlantic Pacific's Romanian deal had 10 percent more collateral than previously thought. The bonds would be priced with a lower coupon and the net result was that Central Europe would be able to secure cheaper financing for its reconstruction than previously believed. The Chief of Internal Affairs got a little carried away. He let slip that Mark Igino was the Michael Milken of the nineties—in an era of volunteerism and goodwill, Mark Igino was reducing the cost of rebuilding the post-communist countries. Mark Igino was everything to Hope that Milken was to Greed. It was a sappy story with almost no basis in truth, but the *Wall Street Journal* reporter—who had been ordered by his editor to find stories about morally conscious companies to set a tone for the nineties—had been hooked. It would run on the front page: everyone in the global financial community was going to be ecstatic to hear that rebuilding the Soviet Union wasn't going to cost as much as they had feared. And every politician was going to be overjoyed to hear that private money was going into the communist bloc, because it would ease the pressure on the politicians to spend taxpayer money on a Marshall Plan. At the newspapers, everything was in service to the story, and it was too hot a story to check all the facts—the *Journal* didn't want to get scooped by the *Times* or *Institutional Investor* or *Barron's*. The Chief of Internal Affairs faxed over a photograph of Eggs Igino that had run the previous summer in the trainee directory, which the *Journal* transformed into its peculiar unflattering but unmistakable style of pointillist portrait. The picture had been sent in by Eggs Igino when he applied for the job because he got bored renting Windsurfers in Zihuatanejo. It had been taken by some woman when they were drunk and Eggs's hair was wild in the wind and he wasn't wearing any clothes; *The Wall Street Journal* loved it. It made a good story. It was everything that the old-bald-man photos they had run in the eighties weren't. It was the story of the nineties, the spin of the new era: long wild hair, mischievous grin, bare shoulders. It would run page one, left column, and it would be waiting at the desks of the salesmen in the San Francisco office in the morning to be read with their coffee.

Coyote Jack had fretted the entire night, never managing to fall asleep until right before three-thirty, when his alarm startled him so frighteningly that he jerked awake so abruptly that he pinched a muscle in his neck. He drove to work in the right lane on the highway because he couldn't check the blind spot over his right shoulder or even tip his head in that direction to glance at the rearview mirror. As he drove, he considered the great scheme of things. He knew he never should have fired Regis Reed. Regis Reed had cheated on his student loans, which had been well documented by the surveillance department, and he had a drug habit, which had also been well documented by the surveillance department. Atlantic Pacific had two great reasons to fire Regis Reed at any time, and for that very reason they never should have fired him. They had control over him, and once they fired him they lost control. In contrast, they had no control over Eggs Igino, nothing to prevent him from mumbling to the other salesmen that there was a mathematical error on the Romanians. It went without saying that Coyote Jack was going to have to fire Eggs Igino as soon as he walked in the door that morning. Coyote Jack didn't want to do it—he still had hope that Eggs Igino would make them all rich—but he saw no other option unless he could quickly think of some good reason to fire Igino, at which point they wouldn't have to fire him at all. But Eggs Igino had no secrets to be used against him. He'd never committed a crime. He'd never touched any woman but his girlfriend. He'd never cheated in school. The surveillance department had run a complete check on him, but Igino was clean. The surveillance department had dug deep: interviewed professors, investigated potential drug connections in Zihuatanejo, spied on him after work. They knew he bought his bus passes at a liquor store around the corner from his apartment, where he also bought a flask of sloe gin and four cans of reconstituted lemonade. They knew he kept a journal, and often wrote in it on the way to work, though on the way home he merely stared out the window. They knew he didn't eat meat, though Coyote Jack didn't really believe that the most promising young salesman in the firm was a vegetarian. The only other story they could come up with was that when Eggs Igino was about to begin his All-Pac-Ten senior season for the Stanford Cardinal, that top goal-getter of the previous year met a woman named Katie, fell in love, and quit the team. A few years later, when something went wrong, the kid took off for Mexico. Coyote Jack saw neither the fear nor the greed in living in a fishing village in Mexico, or in quitting one's All-Pac-Ten senior season for a woman. But Coyote Jack understood the pattern: the kid had a soft heart, and he could quit again.

When Coyote Jack got to the office he poured himself two mugs of coffee and carried them into his office to consider whether the rest of the salesforce would revolt if he fired Igino visibly, out on the sales floor, before he even had a chance to sit down. It was unfair, of course, to fire him—but it was always fruitful to teach the salesforce that fairness had nothing to do with their job. Whenever the salespeople felt abused and victimized by their profession, they suffered less guilt jamming bonds. According to Coyote Jack, Sidney Geeder was the best salesman because he felt constantly terrorized by the firm. Perhaps watching Eggs Igino get fired would be just the kick the salesforce needed to move the Romanians, if the deal wasn't dead by now. Satisfied with his reasoning, Coyote Jack leaned forward in his chair and pulled out of his desk an Atlantic Pacific employee evaluation form. In the boxes across the top he scribbled in Mark Igino's name, Social Security number, and NASDAQ pass code. Below that he jotted the date of five days previous. Coyote Jack grunted and put X's in low-numbered boxes, railing Eggs Igino for his lack of leadership, poise, respect for superiors, and fulfillment of quotas. With that Honolulu promotion on the line, it was crucial that Coyote Jack find a way to not be blamed for having kept such a rebellious crank on the floor, where he could have nearly doomed the Romanian deal, and so he intended to show management that he'd recommended last week that Eggs Igino be fired—and if only John White had acted upon Coyote Jack's recommendation sooner, none of this would have happened.

Doubly satisfied, Coyote Jack sat back in his chair and kicked his legs onto his desk and picked up the morning paper, where he immediately saw Eggs Igino's face below the keyline—*Igino: Giving 110%*—and read that his youngest vice salesman had just been promoted to senior vice president. Coyote Jack leaped up in shock, and then immediately ran out of his office to retrieve the job evaluation he'd buried in John White's To Do pile. Returning to his office, Coyote Jack pulled out another job evaluation form and gave Eggs Igino the highest marks for leadership, poise, respect for superiors, and fulfillment of quotas. With that Honolulu promotion up for grabs, it was imperative that Coyote Jack find a way to take credit for having kept such a rebellious crank on the sales floor long enough for him to discover a way to improve upon the Romanian deal. He intended to show management that he'd recommended last week that Eggs Igino be leapfrogged past all the other salespeople—and if only John White had acted upon Coyote Jack's recommendation sooner, they wouldn't have been caught off guard by Igino's genius.

"Sensational," Sidney Geeder laughed, slapping his deskmate on the shoulder with his folded-up paper.

"But it doesn't make any sense!" Eggs Igino shouted back in vain, looking down again at his image and continuing to read all manner of lies about his role in rebuilding Eastern Europe and bailing out the financial pressure on NATO countries.

"Did you get your watch yet?" Nickel Sansome chuckled, walking up with the paper under his arm. "You're not really a senior VP until you get your watch."

"What do I need a watch for?" Eggs Igino howled in protest. "I've got eight clocks along the wall here to tell me the time everywhere in the world! There's a digital clock running on every broker screen!"

"I wish I had a watch," Nickel Sansome admitted. "Maybe you'll let me borrow yours."

"Can I borrow your parking place when you take the bus?" Sue Marino begged, clipping the story out so that she could fax it to all of her customers.

"But I don't need a parking space!" Igino bellowed, scrinching his eyes and pounding his desk in exasperation. "I don't deserve any of this."

"You deserve it a lot more than the rest of us," Sid Geeder kidded. "It wasn't me who discovered ten percent more collateral."

"It's not *more* collateral—it's *less*!"

"The numbers don't lie," chirped Paul DeShews, holding a stack of enlarged photocopies of Igino's mug shot. "And neither does *The Wall Street Journal*. If it says you deserve it, then you deserve it."

Then the little Mexican maid came wheeling down the aisle with breakfast for the desk—all of whom had paid Eggs Igino in advance—and Clark Kalinov came running across the floor in fury.

"I order you to not eat that food," Clark Kalinov barked, as firmly and dauntingly as possible.

"You can't order him to do anything," Sid Geeder responded, his mouth full of pancakes and whipped cream. "He outranks you now." Geeder shoved a copy of the article into Kalinov's hands.

Clark Kalinov saw the headline and stammered on his words, hopping up and down and gritting his teeth in agony. Eggs Igino chuckled a little. Finally, Kalinov spun around and marched back into his office.

Not one to pass up an opportunity, Eggs Igino had begun to offer a three-item menu to the entire thirty-seven-member sales-force, most of whom were happy to participate in anything that undermined Kalinov's power. John White, who was a Libertarian, was happy to see a part of the bureaucracy privatized. Coyote Jack supported the breakfasts because it meant the salesforce wasn't leaving their desks to run into the kitchen or pop downstairs to the diner. With the greater volume, Eggs Igino also created a futures market for breakfasts, so that salesmen could buy several months' worth of breakfasts. Eggs reprogrammed the Quotron to get his bid-and-ask prices on one of the internal screens. Now the price moved with demand, and Eggs made some side money buying and selling dishes off his three-item menu. The salesforce began enjoy-ing trading in breakfast futures, and it instantly became more pop-ular than gambling on Nerf as a way to blow off steam. Even though only thirty-seven breakfasts were delivered onto the sales floor each morning, Eggs might broker more than ninety trades each day. The salesforce used the phone rather than calling out across the floor. To Coyote Jack, who stood at his fishbowl win-dow watching his workers, it seemed that they were much more productive since Eggs Igino began feeding them. Eggs Igino en-joyed it tremendously. He stood at his desk all day giggling and jubilantly twittering over how much fun work had become, which drove Sid Geeder crazy with chagrin.

"Stop enjoying yourself!" he would howl, wanting to kick Igino in the kneecaps.

"What for?" Igino chuckled, unwrapping a cherry Tootsie Pop and suckling it with his tongue.

"Don't you get it? To you it's like there's no difference between French toast and Romanian bonds. You're making a mockery of what's going to happen."

Eggs Igino moved the Tootsie Pop into his cheek. "Of course I'm making a mockery of it. That's the whole point."

"But you're enjoying it! You have fun mocking it, which isn't an honest reaction at all. Just because you've taken a satirical view of it all doesn't mean you're excused from your responsibility. You're as bad as they are," Sid said, pointing across the sales floor, indicating the other salespeople.

"You're one to talk. Mr. King of Mortgages, never saw a bond he didn't like."

Sidney waved his arms and howled and lashed out by selling Eggs Igino twenty-five French toasts in June, hoping to knock down the price and make a killing. But over the course of the day, Eggs Igino didn't lower his price and maintained he would have no trouble keeping the market liquid. So Sid Geeder duplicated the trade, twice, pretty sure that such heavy selling would depress the price. Eggs had no trouble turning the trade to Nickel Sansome, who was bullish on the French toasts and believed there would be a shortage in June that would drive prices way up. Near the end of the day, Sidney began to realize he'd made a mistake and thought he'd better cover his position. He went desk to desk secretly, hoping to buy a few June contracts without the whole market finding out there was a big buyer in June. But the phones lit up red and the word got around that someone had shorted French toasts in size and had to cover. They all watched their Quotrons as the price bid up, then slowly June holders of French toast swapped down to omelettes and smoked country sausage. By the time Sidney had repurchased all seventy-five, the contract price was up $6 and smoked country sausage was rallying.

Coyote Jack watched with unbearable pleasure. To have Sidney Geeder howling angry and Eggs Igino wildly insubordinate was the perfect market condition for selling bonds, and Coyote Jack sincerely hoped that the Romanians would take advantage of the clear skies and drop soon. Coyote Jack took the moment to call the syndicate desk and push up his quotas another notch. Then Coyote Jack's secretary interrupted his musing on the intercom. Coyote Jack barked at her, reminding her never to interrupt him when he was all alone in his office. She apologized profusely but relayed a message to call John White immediately. Eggs Igino was in Mr. White's office at the moment and there was some trouble. So Coyote Jack dialed John White's extension and got his own secretary right back again; she had nothing to do but answer John White's phone. She buzzed John White on the intercom, and John White barked at her for interrupting him, reminding her never to interrupt him when he was in a meeting. She apologized profusely but relayed that Coyote Jack was holding for him.

"What's the trouble, J.W.?" Coyote Jack inquired mockingly.

"It's Eggs Igino."

"What's happened to him?"

"He wants to see a bond."

"He wants to see a what?"

"A bond. Any kind of bond. He says he can't sell bonds anymore if he's never seen one."

"You want to what?" Coyote Jack rasped bitterly, suddenly poking his head into John White's office, where Eggs Igino was reclining on John White's sofa and John White was digging through his desk, dumping out the contents.

"I want to see a bond," Eggs Igino remarked flatly.

Coyote Jack's shoulders dropped. "What the fuck for? J.W., he's shitting us, right?"

"I thought I had one in my desk somewhere here," John White mumbled as he dug into a drawer.

Eggs looked down and picked under the fingernail of one hand with the other. "I've sold billions of dollars of bonds. I think it's time I got to know what I was selling."

"You're selling them just fine without ever having seen one!" Coyote Jack blurted in frustration.

John White sighed. "It's just a piece of fucking paper with a bunch of colors and words printed on it. It's like a goddamn Publishers Clearinghouse Sweepstakes coupon."

"I'd still like to see one. I would sleep better at night knowing I wasn't part of some big hoax. I'd like to know they really exist."

"Of course they exist!"

"Do they? They're really just on the Fed's computer, aren't they? How do we really know?"

Coyote Jack ranted hotly, "But nobody uses the pieces of paper anymore! They're inefficient!"

"We used to use the pieces of paper," John White remarked. "Hell, that was a long time ago. When you sold a bond, little old men in Wall Street would go pick it up, sign for it, and place it in a leather satchel bag. They would walk across the street and deliver it. We used to take lunches back then. You'd go out for lunch and all these little old men would be walking around with leather satchel bags. I saw a bunch of bonds, once, when one of these little old men tripped on the curb and fell on the pavement and his leather satchel bag flew open, spilling millions of dollars into the gutter."

"This is stupid," Coyote Jack gasped. "It's idiotic."

"Why don't you just go over to the window at the Federal Reserve branch across the street and buy one?" Eggs Igino suggested. "Just get me a little thousand-dollar-face-value T-note. I just want to see *one*. It doesn't sound like so much to ask."

Coyote Jack and John White stared at each other, realizing they had no choice.

"I ought to fire you," Coyote Jack faltered. "I ought to bust your ass right back down to vice salesman."

Eggs Igino glanced at John White knowingly and only laughed.

So Coyote Jack had no choice. All of the firm's money was handled out of New York, so Coyote Jack had to go to the downtown branch of his bank and withdraw a money order for $1,000, which he carried across the street to the Federal Reserve Bank. He swore and spit and glared menacingly at every walker-by. Coyote Jack hated the street level. The street level was for couriers and secretaries on their lunch hour and laid-off salesmen. He found the window at the Federal Reserve, set down the money order, and asked for the current ten-year note. The teller requested his checking account number so that the bond could be credited to his account. But Coyote Jack didn't want it credited; he wanted to walk out with it. The teller stared at him curiously. He told her he wanted to stuff it inside his mattress. She said that such a thing was no longer possible—they had to have a bank account to wire interest payments to. He asked for them to be mailed, by check. Such a thing was not an option. Finally, he admitted that all he really needed was something that looked official, something that would serve as proof of ownership, even if it wasn't the bond itself. She gave him a receipt, stamped with the embossed seal of the Fed and a printed signature of Alan Greenspan testifying that the bond was backed by the full faith and credit of the U.S. government. But it was no bigger than a credit-card carbon, and the embossed seal was only a three-dimensionalized graphic, and it came in black ink on greenish paper. It could have been Monopoly money. For $1,000, he really thought he was getting ripped off. Coyote Jack marched back to the sales floor and threw it down on Eggs Igino's desk with a show of resentment.

"What do you got there?" Sidney Geeder inquired, leaning over.

Eggs Igino removed the receipt from its brown envelope. "It's a bond," he said happily, though he was unsatisfied with its unassuming appearance.

"No shit. A real bond? Can I see it?"

Eggs Igino held the bond up to the light to see if it had some hologram on it, or colored thread—something to be sure it was real. "Haven't you seen one before?" he asked Geeder.

"Me? Naw. When would I have seen one?"

"I just thought you've been selling them for almost five years, you might have seen one before." Eggs Igino put it down on the desk and scratched at the black type with the point of a paper clip to see how it was printed.

"Nope. Let me see it, huh? What issue is it?"

"The ten-year note. It's Coyote Jack's."

"What have you got there?" Nelson Dicky leaned over the edge of Sidney's desk and stared at the paper in Igino's hand.

"What's the matter, Nelson?" Sidney joked wryly. "Haven't you ever seen a bond before?"

"Sure I have," Nelson Dicky lied. "It's just been a while."

"Bullshit," Sidney challenged. "When have you seen a bond?"

"Hey," Lisa Lisa saluted, crossing over behind Eggs Igino. "What's everyone looking at?"

Nelson Dicky snickered. "Boy, Lisa Lisa—haven't you ever seen a bond before?"

"*That's* a bond?" Lisa Lisa repeated with chagrin. "It's not very impressive."

"Well, what did you expect?" Sidney scoffed. "A brick of gold?"

"I thought it would be bigger, at least," she answered, leaning over Eggs Igino's shoulder. "Can I feel it?"

"Get your own," Sidney Geeder jeered.

"I'll buy it from you," Lisa Lisa stated. She looked at the Telerate screen for the ten-year note, which was trading 98-2 bid. "I'll give you 2+ for it."

"98-4," Nelson Dicky bid, in a plain, poker-faced grunt.

"It's Coyote Jack's," Eggs Igino explained. "I can't sell it to you. Besides, I wouldn't sell a *real* bond for less than 99. There's an authenticity factor you've got to add in."

"I'll give you 99," Sue Marino put in. "It had better be real, though."

"99-4," Nickel Sansome bid, standing behind Nelson Dicky.

"He already sold it to me at 99," Sue Marino maintained.

"No I didn't," Eggs Igino retorted. "The price is moving. Show me another bid."

"99-4+," Sue tendered.

Eggs shook his head ruefully, conveying a brilliant disgust at Sue Marino's inability to get ahold of the market.

"I could just go across the street and buy one," Sue responded.

Eggs shrugged his shoulders.

"99-8," Nickel proffered excitedly.

"Done!" Eggs Igino pronounced. "Sold to the man in the flesh-colored skullcap." His hands flew out to his bond calculator and tapped the keys, figuring the number of days between interest payments and how much was owed. "Make a check out to Coyote for $1,082.46," he said, handing over the piece of paper.

Nickel Sansome beamed proudly, examining the snippet of paper carefully. He wrote the check out for Eggs Igino, who took it into Coyote Jack's office and handed it over.

"What's this?" Coyote Jack inquired, staring at the check.

"I made you a little profit," Eggs said.

"How did you do that?"

Eggs Igino shrugged his shoulders. "I really just wanted to see a bond."

"Sure you did," Coyote Jack said. "You know what you are? You're a fucking genius, Igino. You could sell venom to a snake."

"Fuck you."

"Hey, I'm paying you a compliment!"

"It's not something to be proud of."

"Well, it's true. You're the A-team, a regular Green Beret."

"I don't like that any better."

"Christ." Coyote Jack shook his head. "You've been listening to

Geeder too much. Relax. Shit. Hey, let me ask you something. I've been thinking. Can I ask you something?"

"I guess." Eggs looked away.

"Don't get so defensive. Shit, I'm just talking. You look like I'm going to ask if I can fuck your mother."

"Jesus . . ."

"So, let me ask you. You used to live down in Mexico, right? You liked it there, spent your days on the beaches, climbed palm trees, et cetera. Am I right? You think about it, don't you? You look at all this shit, all this toil, all these buildings, and your mind starts wandering to the surf-and-sand landscape, right?"

"Sure. What's your point?"

"My point is, there's talk about a Honolulu office."

"There is?"

"*Hawaii*. You and me, kiddo. Luaus, volcanos, Polynesian girls with big hooters."

Eggs didn't say anything. Hawaii would be nice, but he had no intention of spending the rest of his twenties with Coyote Jack breathing down his neck.

"Ah ha!" Coyote Jack grinned. "I can see this has some appeal to you."

"Not really," Eggs bluffed, not wanting to give an inch, to be vulnerable.

"You think about it, Igino. That's all I'm asking. Right now, we're just talking. There's nothing on the table. We're just in the positioning stage."

When Eggs Igino left his office, Coyote Jack phoned the syndicate desk to ask for an update on the Romanians. Then he called Lisa Lisa and ordered her to prepare for a grilling on the Romanians. Lisa Lisa was covering Hawaii, and Coyote Jack didn't trust Lisa Lisa, didn't trust her at all. Coyote Jack needed big numbers out of the Hawaiian accounts. He needed size. Coyote Jack began to wonder why he didn't just fire Lisa Lisa and give her accounts to Eggs Igino. If Eggs Igino had done well with Thom Slavonika's and Regis Reed's accounts, he didn't see why he wouldn't do even better with Lisa Lisa's business.

"I *tried* to line them up," Lisa Lisa said, when Coyote Jack wondered why Kern County wasn't on her list of buyers for the Romanians. Lisa Lisa squirmed. Her feet snaked around the legposts of her chair. "But Coyote—they're a county pension. They don't buy high-yield."

"Since when?" he barked, sticking his nose just barely into her hair. She could feel his breath on her neck. "Carol Manning sold them the mortgage strips. Antonia Zennario sold them the Nabiscos. Now you're fucking telling me you can't sell them just three lousy million of the Romanians? Shit. Kern County's been buying high-yield for years."

"They have new bylaws, Coyote." Lisa Lisa turned her head around, but Coyote Jack circled out her view. She turned the other way, but he dodged back behind her.

"Are you in a hurry?" Coyote Jack snickered.

"I'd like to get back to work."

"Like hell you would. You'd like to go home and sit in a bubble bath and prance about in silk pajamas. You're getting lazy, Lisa. You learned a year ago that Kern County wouldn't buy the Euro-Floaters, and you haven't even tried them on high-yield since then. You wrote them off."

"That's not true!" she insisted.

Coyote Jack gruffed, setting his hands down on the back of Lisa Lisa's chair and speaking into the back of her head. "Did you even sell them the Resolutions?"

"I tried," she whined exhaustedly, falling forward in her chair.

"Thom Slavonika sold Humboldt County the Resolutions. How come they bought the Resolutions and Kern County didn't? Humboldt County has bylaws."

"How do I know? I don't know anything about Humboldt County," Lisa Lisa reasoned.

"Correction," Coyote Jack snapped. "You don't know anything about Kern County. You wrote them off. You think just because HonFed bails you out all the time, you don't have to keep working. Isn't that right?"

"I call Kern every day," she insisted.

"What's their phone number?"

"They're on the speed dial, Coyote. I don't know the number. Star fucking seventeen star, that's their speed dial."

"You call them every day, but you don't even know their phone number?"

"It's on my speed dial!"

"Did you call them this morning?"

"Yes!"

"What did you sell them?"

"We did a little overnight cash, and some thirty-day commercial paper."

"That's money market bullshit. You think we make any money on that money market bullshit? You're on the *mortgage* desk. Why do you think we have Kern County assigned to the mortgage desk—huh? What do you think? You think we gave Kern County to you so you could sell them money markets?"

"I sold them a CMO last week."

"Last week? What about this week? You taking a vacation this week? You doing the bubble bath this week? You daydreaming about living in the country? You thinking about buying a dog? You're so fucking predictable. The whole goddamn lot of you, think you're the first salesman on the planet. Think you're the first woman to get swollen feet."

Lisa Lisa waited. "Are we done now?" she asked.

"Hell no we're not done. I want to hear you sell Kern County the Romanians."

"I said I'll try, Coyote."

"You're damn right you'll try. But that's not what I'm talking about. I want to hear your pitch. I want to hear what you're going to say."

"You want me to say it out loud?"

"Right here, right now."

"It's not the same," she complained.

"Who gives a shit? Let me hear it."

"Well, first I give a rundown on the market, overnight trading, et cetera. Then maybe I pick a few bonds out of their portfolio and try to convince them that those bonds will be going downhill shortly and they ought to liquidate."

"Like what kind of bonds?"

"I'd have to look at their portfolio."

"You don't know their portfolio?" he asked incredulously, tearing at his long, sleek, graying hair.

"I have it on paper at my desk. I have it written down."

Coyote Jack was furious, practically spitting. "You think Sid Geeder doesn't know his accounts' portfolios? You think Nelson Dicky doesn't know every fucking bond he's sold Inter-Power the past three years? You think Eggs Igino uses crib notes? I'll bet I could call Carol Manning at home right now and ask her what she sold Kern County in the two years in your seat. She would tell me. She would tell me without blinking. It would be on the tip of her tongue, like her kid's name. She wouldn't even have to think about it. It would be automatic. It would be like two plus two equals four. Boom, right there."

"I'm sorry, Coyote. I know most of it. I'll be prepared by the time the Romanians come out of the pipes."

"You think you're entitled to that seat on the mortgage desk? You aren't royalty. This ain't no monarchy. Maybe corporate policy says I have to put a woman on the mortgage desk, but that woman doesn't have to be you. I got Sue Marino breathing down your neck. Sue Marino's got fire in her eyes."

"Sue Marino can't hold a stick to me."

"She's gonna do twenty on the Romanians."

"Twenty? Who's she going to sell them to?"

"She'd do thirty if she had HonFed and AmeriBank."

"HonFed was nothing before I picked it up. Carol Manning didn't sell squat to Mike Kohanamoku. He doesn't even remember Antonia Zennario's name."

"So Mike K. has a thing for your cheerleader routine. So the fuck what? He's not going to buy the Romanians just because you kick over your head!"

"Fuck you, Coyote."

"Don't you ever talk to me like that unless you mean it, girl."

"Piss off."

Coyote Jack shook his head in mock regret. "You talk like that around your boyfriends? I hear they get turned on when you call Greenspan a peckerhead. Is that true? Does that get them going?"

Lisa Lisa stormed out. She ran to her desk, grabbed her purse, and ran into the bathroom, where she kicked out one of the Mexican maids, who was cleaning the grease skids off the mirror. As soon as she was alone she started to whimper, and then to cry. She sat down in one of the toilet stalls and took some time to get ahold of herself, taking several deep breaths and massaging her neck. Then Lisa Lisa went to the mirror and washed her face. She stripped off her makeup, set a wet paper towel on the back of her neck, and washed her hands thoroughly. Slowly and methodically, she began to reapply her foundation, then her eye shadow, eyeliner, and lipstick. She changed her earrings. She carried a small curling iron in her purse, and she began to fixate on how her hair turned out at its ends, rather than ducking under, so she plugged it in and spent the time waiting for it to warm up plucking the few hairs between her eyebrows. But she couldn't just pluck a few, and soon she had thinned the left eyebrow by half and had to balance the right eyebrow exactly, which was nearly impossible, and for a while she forgot all about the curling iron until she put her hand down on it and burned the skin a little. Finally she got everything back in her purse and reapplied her lipstick one more time and turned in the mirror to check herself one last time before she marched back out onto the sales floor primly and sat upright at her desk, fighting off the surge of exasperation that almost led her to fall apart again.

Everybody was eating breakfast, smacking lips and groaning in delight at the richness of the food. Nickel Sansome was wolfing down his smoked country sausages. He sucked them whole into his mouth, storing what he could not chew in his jowls, like a squirrel. His shirtsleeves were rolled up and he gripped his fork down near the tines. He bent his head over his plate and lapped at the crumbs of meat. Orange juice had spilled over the edge of his glass and soaked into his research report on the Romanians. Lisa Lisa watched him in horror, then she looked forlornly at Eggs Igino, who was sitting down for once at Regis Reed's desk, eating Raisin Bran out of a bowl, with a spoon, with a napkin hanging down from his neck. He chewed each bite for quite some time with his mouth closed while he cheerfully mused through the international section of the morning newspaper. When he went into the kitchen to refill Sidney Geeder's coffee thermos, she followed him. She was a woman in this business, and it was only getting harder for her.

She had given herself to this business, and she had given herself away. She tried to stop herself. He was just a kid. He was just a boy. But he had not yet given himself away. When Eggs Igino dumped another packet of grounds into Mr. Coffee, Lisa Lisa moved up behind him, brushing against his back and whispering, "Do you know what it's like to be a woman in this business?"

Eggs Igino turned around, and she was right against his chest. She reached up to his neck and straightened his tie. A sweet, seductive, playful grin came across her mouth. For a moment, all of what had made her head cheerleader for the Michigan Wolverines was right there, all of the charm and the radiance and the body.

"You're not supposed to be a woman," she said. "You're supposed to check it at the door. But it's not easy, Iggy," she said. "It's not easy, with you around."

He didn't back off. Her leg was pressed between his, or vice versa—he couldn't be sure. A moment passed between them, in which neither spoke, in which Lisa Lisa was pleased to realize that Eggs Igino was indeed attracted to her. Eggs Igino felt a great surge of energy through the fuses that held his life together, and he waited to see if the world he'd built came crumbling down. He waited to see if his hands reached out and landed on Lisa Lisa's ass. He waited to see what words came out of his mouth. He remembered what Nickel Sansome had said about the proximity of Lisa Lisa's apartment to the financial district, and he remembered what Sid Geeder had recently said about the men Lisa Lisa might have loved. Eggs Igino realized that someday in the future his fuses would eventually break, that all was not right in his universe, that he was far more tempted than he thought he would be. But this was not that day: All of what had made Lisa Lisa the head cheerleader at Michigan was no longer there, and she was just one of the poorer salespersons, on the bubble for termination, with a variety of addictions.

"Sidney Geeder needs his coffee."

11 · Machines

THE TIME HAD come. The salesforce hoofed out of their mission briefing and slogged down the aisles to take their places in their bunkers. They readied their pieces and gazed into the radar. They were soldiers in their twenties and early thirties. Mercenaries. Professionals. They were the front line of an economic superpower. They were the foot soldiers in the trenches of information warfare. The enemy was out there in the mist, behind the buildings, hidden in the computers, camouflaged by numbers, ready to ambush the wires and the cable and the wavelengths. They wore the uniform, they wore the face paint, they woke in the middle of the night and humped all day avowing the principles on which their great country was built. They were the last moving parts in a machine that could move money and redistribute wealth and manufacture consent and divert public attention and produce results and stall reform. It was the juice-o-matic of the new economy, a Swiss Army knife of the information age, a machine capable of multiple worthwhile functions of unquestionable commercial appeal. It came with two speed settings, Hectic and Burnout, and its moving parts needed frequent replacing. It was cheaper to replace the parts than to repair them, cheaper to install ambitious young bodies who were desperate to make a sale.

They eyed the clock. They rehearsed the research department's pitches. Paul DeShews tightened his elbow braces, pulled his floating keyboard to his thorax, cinched his knees to the sorbothane pads of his ergo chair, and adjusted the extensions on his telephone headset. Sid Geeder refilled his coffee thermos. Sue Marino was already on the phone, trying to convince her fiancé that their marriage would be fine, she was just under a little stress because of the deal, she would be her old self again soon. They all checked their

Quotron screens to make sure all markets were online and watch for urgent personal messages scrolling across the bottom. Eggs reprogrammed his Quotron to constantly display the live prices of bond futures, gold futures, oil futures, and dollar futures down the left column of his screen. Lisa Lisa used the reflection of her face in the green monochrome monitors to lengthen her eyelashes, which she then batted in Eggs Igino's direction. Nickel Sansome was anxiously searching the underside of his desk drawer for the nickel he had taped there.

They all increased the volume on their squawk boxes until the entire sales floor buzzed with static. Their stomachs churned and their muscles felt mushy with anxiety and their throats went dry until their mouths grew so cottony that their tongues went numb. Nelson Dicky poked his tongue out and flicked it with a pen to bring back its feeling. Lisa Lisa's feet were falling asleep and they hung below her chair like golf clubs, whapping against the file cabinet. Sue Marino had the urge to call her mother. She checked the clock. They all checked the clock constantly. The syndicate desk came over the squawk box with a few words of encouragement and a long, scathing threat to eliminate all salespersons who did not meet their quota by the afternoon closes. The firm had bet its reputation on this one.

Sidney Geeder tried hopelessly to block out all thoughts of Ivana Perkova and her family tales of growing up on the banks of the Danube. Sidney Geeder felt his sacroiliac knot up and start to tingle, then go numb. He couldn't hold his water and he had to piss frequently. He was furious, raging with hatred, and otherwise in a perfect mood to be selling bonds. There was only one thing that could make him feel better, so when the phones went red, Sidney ignored the calls from Wide World Savings and Franklin Mutual and Pacific Capital to call information for Santa Clara, get Kenny Whitlash's home phone number, and wake him up from bed. Whitlash's voice coughed with phlegm and croaked, "What the fuck?"

"Okay, asshole," Geeder rasped. "Time to pay."

"Who is this? Geeder? Sid—that you?"

"Hell yes, Whitlash. The Romanians are on the plate. I'm not taking no for an answer and I'm not writing a ticket for less than six million."

Whitlash coughed, then spat. He sighed. "I'll take twenty."

"Twenty? You don't have twenty million to sink like that. The government auditors will shut you down when they see that on your books."

"I'm getting the twenty next week. You're going to loan it to me, when we do the deal to finance the fax machines we're going to send to Romania."

"Next week! I haven't heard about next week! I thought your deal was going to be in six months!"

"Your management says the timing is too good to pass up, with all the positive publicity the Romanian deal is getting. Besides, now that the Finance Bank of Romania has all this money to loan to ROMTELECOM, we want to sell them our fax machines right away."

"I thought you were giving them the fax machines!" Sidney wailed, gasping for breath.

Kenny Whitlash cackled wretchedly. "Why give faxes to them now that they have money to buy them? I hear ROMTELECOM is swamped with cash. You ought to call them to see if they want to buy the Romanians."

"Ahhhh!" Sidney groaned, slamming the phone on the desktop to break Whitlash's eardrums before hanging up. There was no satisfaction in making Ingenesis pay for all of its crimes when it was going to come back to Sidney to borrow the money a week later. There was no enjoyment in seeing those big clods of bonds weighing down Ingenesis's quarterly financial balance sheets. There was no revenge when Sidney was on both sides of the market. He couldn't even feel the knot at the base of his tailbone anymore. It had been over a month since he'd seen Dr. Perkova.

He tried to get satisfaction out of the commission he'd just earned, but as big as it was, it was nothing compared to the 100,000 shares of corporate stock that had traded up to 47⅜ at the opening on the news of the Romanian deal. Sidney needed to lash out in frustration at how rich he'd undeservedly become, so he called Franklin Mutual back and confessed that the Romanian bonds had 10 percent *less* collateral, not 10 percent *more*. He explained that the dumb journalist at the *Journal* had got the whole story wrong, that the bonds were a piece of shit and that Romania still only had one political party and that some of the money would be siphoned off to arm the Serbs and that the Royal Princess Cruise Lines never got near the Black Sea.

The head trader at Franklin Mutual listened patiently. "Oh, I'll buy them anyway," he said, when Sidney had finished. "My boss really likes them. Besides, I sold fifteen million Freddie Macs at the opening to free up the cash. I have to do something with the money."

"Don't be so stupid," Sidney screamed. "You're being robbed."

"Oh, it's not my money," the head trader answered. "It's the bank's money, and the bank doesn't want to be left out of a deal that makes the front page of the *Journal*."

"You're going to regret it," Sidney warned feebly. It was one of those days when it didn't matter what he said, the Atlantic Pacific machine was working.

"Like I said, my boss wants the bank to do its part in rebuilding Europe. We stopped making inner-city loans in the late eighties, we stopped loaning to small businesses last year, and our profits have gone up since we closed those branches in rural towns. He's been taking a lot of heat and needs something to point to as evidence of our slogan 'Investing in Hope.' I'm under strict orders to buy."

"I'm begging you," Sidney pleaded. "You buy these bonds and you're only going to come back to me later as part of some bailout, needing money to finance your losses!"

"Oh, you'll be long gone by then," the head trader answered smoothly.

"No I won't," Sidney rebuffed. "I won't be able to hide. They'll come after me, they'll come after my money and give it to you to waste on space exploration bonds."

"Sidney, you don't sound right. Are you okay?"

"No! I'm not okay!" he hollered, unplugging the phone and burying his head in his arms. He had to piss like crazy, but instead he called Pacific Capital and admitted that the Princess Cruise Lines had never gone near the Black Sea.

"Sure they do," the fund manager laughed. "They've been getting so many calls from Wall Street types in New York asking about the cruise to Crimea that they've scheduled a maiden voyage in June. Sails out of Athens, through the Sea of Marmara. It was tough to get tickets but I pulled some strings. Got a room on the quarterdeck below the promenade pool. I'm surprised you're not going, the way you talked it up so heavily. Boy, whoever started that rumor ought to call them up and demand a cut—they're going to get rich off all the interest in Central Europe."

"It can't be . . ." Sidney whimpered, now balled up in the crawl space beneath his desk. He really had to piss. His bladder wasn't that full but he just couldn't control his urethra.

"Those Romanians are the talk of the street," the fund manager at Pacific Capital continued. "Salomon is tearing their hair out trying to figure how you turned one hundred dollars into one hundred and ten just like that. They still don't understand it."

"Ahhhhh . . ." Sidney sighed. He was up on one knee and pissing into a coffee cup that he had placed on the floor. With his back to the window and his desk shielding his front from everyone on the floor, nobody noticed.

"I hope they're not all gone already," the fund manager exclaimed. "I really need the yield. I haven't been able to find good yield for my total-return fund since the bottom fell out of the junk market a few years ago."

"Oh, I have plenty left for you," Sidney answered, jiggling himself and zipping up. "How many do you want?"

"At least ten million. I've got to save some money for the Bulgarian deal Solly is doing. It's not scheduled for several months, but they're trying to rush it up to next week to capitalize on the success of your deal."

"But our deal has just begun. It's only been half an hour!"

"Reuters put it out on a headline, said it's going smoothly. UPI picked it up, too. I hear there's retail interest. The retail salesforce at Merrill is dying of envy at the commissions you guys must be earning. Hey, is that guy Mark Igino a friend of yours?"

"Sure, he sits right next to me. Why?"

"Nothing much. Just tell him I think it's great what he's done for Eastern Europe. So many investment bankers could care less about contributing something of value to the world. He's a real inspiration."

"Arrrgghh!" Sidney screamed, smashing his handset against the mahogany trim of his desk and cracking the plastic into two pieces, still strung together by the wiring. "Jesus!" he hollered, picking up his second phone. But that one wasn't working either because it used the same wiring as the first. Sidney spun in a circle and slapped the desk and looked out over the sales floor. He ran around Nickel Sansome and Lisa Lisa to Regis Reed's old desk, but the phone was gone, along with the broker screens and Quotron. He dove under the desk to see if Regis kept a spare phone, then bumped his tailbone against the bottom of the drawer as he was getting back up. He felt a spike of pain jolt down his leg, and he limped around the floor to the three other empty desks, all of which were without phones and monitors. He limped downstairs to the supply room, where all the lights were still out because the lazy investment bankers hadn't arrived for work yet. In the supply room he grabbed a cardboard box with a handset inside, but the box was suspiciously light, so he ripped the top off the box, dumped out the packing Styrofoam and installation manuals, and found a piece of corporate letterhead, signed by Clark Kalinov, stating that because of budget pressures created by the purchase of a fifth fax machine, telephone handsets were temporarily unavailable. Sidney kicked out at the stack of empty handset boxes, causing them to tumble onto the floor. Sidney tried to gain his composure and think. It was such a simple little machine, the telephone, but without one Sidney was powerless. He went into another office and used that phone to call the syndicate desk via the inside line to report the three sales he had made for $45 million. He couldn't take that handset because it didn't have the special jack that plugged into the phone panels, unless he could somehow splice the wiring from one handset to another's jack. He ran back upstairs carrying the phone and found Eggs Igino eating breakfast and taking notes on a paper napkin.

"Why aren't you working?" Sidney asked.

"I'm done," Eggs answered, dipping a forkful of toast into the egg yolk on his plate. "I did my sixty. I could do more, but I really hate these bonds." It really had been that easy—when Sierra Prudential and the Bank of Sacramento learned that *the* Mark Igino was calling on them, they opened their wallets. They felt lucky to be buying their bonds from such a genius. They were proud to do their part investing in the future. Besides, they needed the yield.

They weren't allowed to invest in options or futures, and there just hadn't been this kind of yield in bonds since the bottom fell out of the junk market. Interest rates had been so low because of the constant recession that there just hadn't been anything to liven up a portfolio. Investing in bonds had been boring until the Romanians came along, and they wanted to be part of the excitement.

"Let me borrow your phone then," Sidney requested, holding up the broken handset.

"It's your own fault you busted it."

"I need a phone!" he howled. "I can't work without a phone. You don't need yours anymore."

Eggs patted his face with a napkin. "I was going to call my sister. She wakes up about now." He dug into a pink grapefruit with a serrated spoon. "Don't worry—I'll fix your phone." Eggs opened his drawer and pulled out the duct tape Wes Griffin had left there. He tore off twelve-inch strips, which he then ripped down the middle to be an inch wide. He put Sidney's broken phone on his desktop, looking at the wiring for a moment, then unscrewed the transmitter casing on the downstairs phone and removed a few spare parts. He shredded the wire coating between his teeth and patched in the new transmitter. He removed the mute button on the broken handle, then he taped the pieces together. He circled the handset numerous times, building it into the size of a football that sat like a beanbag on the shoulder without having to be pinched in the nook of Sidney's neck.

"That should help keep your back straight," he said, turning over the contraption to Geeder, who immediately plugged it in and answered the phone that had been ringing for fifteen seconds.

"Geeder!"

"Who's this? Coyote Jack?"

"Guess again, Geeder!"

Sidney recognized the man's voice from somewhere, but it wasn't a voice he knew from the phone—Sidney had memorized all of his customers' phone voices. The voice had a slightly Southern drawl and sounded young, certainly under thirty. There were other voices in the room of the speaker. "Reed? Regis Reed?" he guessed.

"Very good, Sidney. Thought you might have lost your touch."

"Where are you?" Sidney asked.

"Irvine Savings. Los Angeles. I'm the new pension trust manager, and I'm ready to do business. I need a quote on fifteen million Freddie Mac 11.5s in April."

"You looking to buy or sell? Wait a minute! Has the credit department cleared this? Irvine Savings was on credit hold!"

"We're off. We were just purchased by the Japanese, got it at a steal from the RTC."

Sidney flipped up the credit department updates on his Quotron. Sure enough, Irvine Savings had been moved into the sell column, but with a tight credit limit. "Does Coyote Jack know about this?" Sidney inquired.

"Of course he does," Regis responded.

"I don't like it," Sidney observed. "I'm suspicious. Shouldn't Eggs Igino be your salesman?"

"Eggs Igino doesn't want to do the kind of business I want to do," Reed snapped, coughing into the phone.

"What kind of business is that?!"

"Get real, Geeder. There's a lot of faster ways to get rich than by selling bonds year after year, taking a tiny slice each time. I know you kick back commission to Ingenesis every month."

"That's a lie! I'm clean!"

"Sure, right. You and Lisa Lisa."

"What's Lisa Lisa done?"

Regis laughed snidely. "Kohanamoku at Honolulu Federal gets half her commission on their business, that's what she's done. Why else do you think they buy your shit?"

Sidney looked over the top of the desk at Lisa Lisa, who was sniffing her underarm's wet spot. "Find another salesman, Reed. I'm too close to get mixed up in whatever you're talking about. And I don't want to know any more than you've already told me, which I don't believe anyway. You're dreaming if you think I made my money cheating. I've never kicked back a penny in my life. Why cheat when the accounts are so easy to fool?"

"Every man has a price, Geeder. I've got a lot of money to spend. I could do five million of the Romanians, plus I could churn mortgages as long as I cover my loss before the end of the month and the losses aren't too big. Give me forty-five percent."

"No deal. Call Nickel Sansome."

"I don't want Nickel. He's already dirty. I want you, Sidney. How about forty percent?"

"I said no deal!" Sidney unplugged him and ran off the sales floor to the bathroom, where he pissed again and washed his face and paused to get his breath. Then he ran back on the sales floor and retook his position at his desk, gulping down another cup of coffee to keep his edge up. Sixty-seven more days to go and he would be out of here. He had to watch it. He had to arrive on time, he had to stay clean. He couldn't slip up. He had to keep his hands off the women he worked with, and he had to keep his mind on the bonds. He had to stay away from any temptation to talk to Helmet Fisher.

"Quit while you're still young, kid," Sidney slurred at Eggs Igino nonchalantly.

Eggs Igino was amused. "Quit? Are you kidding me? The firm owes me sixty thousand dollars on my trades today. I'd sure like to quit, but not until the firm pays me what it owes."

"Well, *then* you should quit," Sidney agreed. "Quit before it squeezes the life out of you."

"But I couldn't quit *then*," Eggs Igino laughed, holding a hand over his grin, trying to stop himself from chuckling. "Because by then we'd have done another deal, and the firm would owe me another sixty thousand dollars."

"But seriously . . ." Sid tried to steer the subject to a more earnest inquiry. "What would you really do if you quit? Where would you go? What would you do with all your time?"

"Oh, I'll never be able to quit. The firm has got me locked in." Igino looked bemused by his words. "Chained to my seat. The only way I'll leave this place is in a coffin."

"That's the way I'll be going if my back doesn't relax soon."

"You ought to try standing up," Eggs suggested.

"I couldn't possibly stand all day."

"You'd build up your strength over time. It would only be hard for a week or so. Standing up makes it easier to move around, so you won't get as tight from being in one position constantly. Our bodies aren't made to stand still. Our bodies are made to move.

They're incredibly effective at moving, and they're horribly inept at standing still. Come on, get up out of that chair. It can't get any worse."

"You gotta be kidding. My legs are numb."

"Why shouldn't they be numb? You never use them. If you stood up, they wouldn't fall asleep on you."

"They're not asleep—the peroneal nerve is getting pinched at the sacral plexus."

"Stand up, Sidney! They want you to sit down all day."

"Who's *they*?" he shot back with excitement. "Who are you talking about?"

"How should I know?" Eggs Igino snipped.

After minutes of haranguing and persuasion, Sidney finally kicked his chair back to the window and tried to stand up straight. But his back was so stiff he leaned forward and his shoulders hunched up around his neck. Eggs put a box of research reports on the floor and got Sidney to stand with one foot planted squarely on the box, the other leg slightly bent. Eggs told him to rock his weight forward and backward and to swap leg positions every couple minutes. Sidney looked around. It was amazing how much he could see from up there that he couldn't see while sitting down: there was the "Go Fish!" bumper sticker adhered to the support axle of Sue Marino's chair, and Coyote Jack's secretary at her desk, filing her nails, and Lisa Lisa's bare feet, rubbing into the carpet.

Jokingly, Coyote Jack came out onto the floor and said a prayer over the Bible that Antonia Zennario had left behind. He then told the force that all the Romanians had been sold and the firm was throwing a party that evening in celebration at the Ming Garden. He was about to excuse them when John White came out on the floor and told them that the firm had rented a few suites across the street at the Excelsior for the party. He recommended that the lucky guys who lived in the East Bay or Marin call their wives and explain that they wouldn't be driving home tonight. If anyone wanted to clean up before the party, they were welcome to use the shower as long as they stayed out of the liquor cabinet—he didn't want any careless drunkards passing out before the food got served. Some top brass was flying in from New York and Los Angeles, and there was supposed to be at least one of the wire services present, so no snide remarks about the Romanians would be tolerated. For god's sakes, don't talk about work at all—Salomon Brothers never talked about work at their parties. There was nothing more pathetic than a salesman suffering from total eclipse of the brain. John White handed out photocopied pages from a joke book. If there was a dull spot in the conversation, they were to tell a joke. If they didn't know how to tell a joke, they were to practice in the bathroom until they were as smooth as Bob Hope. Deadpan. No giggling or cracking up before the punch line. Salomon Brothers never giggled before the punch line. There was nothing more childishly pathetic than a salesman laughing at his own jokes. Then John White began to comment on their attire. This was a dinner to celebrate the future—oxford-cloth button-downs would not be tolerated. Paisley ties were out. If they needed to go shopping before the dinner, so be it, but don't expect to be served at the bar in a paisley tie. And for the women—nothing hanging below the knees. The less the better. Get out of those wool suits and do something, anything, with the hair. When in doubt, verge on the risqué. John White was paternally strict, condescending, and blunt. He let them know that they were under strict orders to enjoy themselves, and anybody seen brooding solitarily in the dimly lit corners would get busted right back down to vice salesman on the spot.

Coyote Jack glared in heated outrage at John White's ploy to appear to be the host of the party and had to restrain himself from yanking obsessively on the new leather suspenders he had bought just for the occasion that were already too tight and chafing his wool trousers against his testicles. When the salesforce left the floor, Coyote Jack was so twisted up in resentment that he immediately drove to Dr. Vandivort's office and ordered the doctor to prescribe him a bottle of antidepressants and some depressants. Dr. Vandivort gave Coyote Jack the prescription, and then Coyote Jack leered knowingly at Dr. Vandivort's receptionist, who was just a baby and had plush, dumpling cheeks and blunt, fat fingers that clicked away at a computer keyboard. Coyote Jack handed her an embossed invitation, then he ordered Dr. Vandivort to order her to come to the party. Coyote Jack picked up his drugs at a local pharmacy, as well as a new kind of hair gel that added body to dry, limp hair. When he got to the Ming Garden he popped a couple of the blue-speckled depressants to loosen him up, then he chased those down with a couple of pink antidepressants to make sure no stray thoughts entered his head without permission. He immediately felt better and went to tell Tommy Fang all of the jokes John White had handed out so Tommy Fang would remember how charming and personable Coyote Jack was.

Some of the salesforce started to arrive. Nickel Sansome was chatting with Dave Rennaker, so he went over and slapped the boys on the back and told them to disperse and entertain the newcomers. Coyote Jack picked up a few of Tommy Fang's herbal medicine drinks made in highball glasses with a hunk of ginger. One he gave to Sue Marino as he told the story about how Carol Manning had flown to Cabo San Lucas with the trust manager from First Nationwide; the other he delivered to Eggs Igino, who was trying to describe the physics of a windsurfing sail to Dr. Vandivort's receptionist. Coyote Jack stood at their side, listening, until he'd seen Igino finish at least half the drink. Eggs Igino didn't really know how to sip a drink—he drank everything like it was soda pop, to quench his thirst. Dr. Vandivort's receptionist was staring up at Eggs Igino's blue eyes with dollfaced adoration. Eggs told her that he was a mortgage researcher up from the Los Angeles office here only for the evening, that he lived half a block from Manhattan Beach, where he surfed every afternoon. He added that he was writing a screenplay about a troop of rugged female surfers who go down to Baja for the weekend, sort of a *Deliverance* for women, et cetera.

The party had come into full swing. Eggs got his drink and then went into the bathroom. Dave Rennaker was snorting coke off the chrome housing of the hand dryer and trying to persuade Nickel Sansome to do just one line. Nickel kept pointing to his drink, saying that he was just fine, and sort of to prove his point he downed his entire highball glass. He was worried the coke might affect his breathing. But Rennaker only scoffed and made it sound like a personal insult that Nickel wasn't partaking in the heavy stuff. Nickel tried to change the subject by asking if Rennaker ever wondered if Sue Marino shaved her bikini lines meticulously, or if she just let it grow like a weed. Rennaker grunted and insinuated that he didn't have to wonder, that he might have some personal experience with the question at hand. Nickel doubted him, and so like a good salesman Rennaker exaggerated his claim, stating for a fact that Sue Marino did in fact shave her bikini lines constantly, but that she had a problem as a result with ingrown hairs that caused these pretty despicable dot-sized red rashes. Nickel pretended he didn't believe him, even though he wasn't sure. Then Rennaker said that if Nickel did just one itsy-bitsy line, he would provide absolute, verifiable, guaranteed proof that Sue Marino had an almost hairless crotch speckled with rashes. Nickel's mind tried to resist, really, but Rennaker had pushed his buttons.

"What kind of proof?" Nickel asked innocently.

"Absolute, verifiable, guaranteed proof."

"But what *kind* of proof? You got pictures?"

"Only one way to find out."

So Rennaker cut an itsy-bitsy thread of a line on the chrome of the hand dryer that was really a monstrous, gargantuan rope of uncut dope, but Nickel didn't know any better. It seemed crazy to Nickel that all that powder could go up his nose, but it did, and it didn't sting too bad.

"All right," he said, a happy giggle breaking his fat face into a stupid grin. "Give me your fucking evidence."

"What evidence?" Rennaker said, playing it a straight deadpan, as if he had no idea what Nickel was talking about.

"The evidence! I want to see Sue Marino's crotch!"

Rennaker couldn't help it, he began to laugh, and once he was laughing he really started to guffaw and hold his sides as he pointed at the bit of dust on Nickel's nose. He was laughing so hard he couldn't even tell Nickel to wipe his nose off.

"You motherfucker," Nickel Sansome swore as his sinuses kept inhaling in short blasts to try to absorb all the powder. "You goddamn motherfucker!"

"Hey, I did you a favor," Rennaker protested, snickering. "An hour from now, you'll be thanking me."

"Fuck you."

"An hour from now, we'll be right back here again, doing more. Hell, invite Sue Marino."

Nickel Sansome stormed out of the bathroom, trying to slam the door behind him, but the door was on an air-compression spring that resisted his efforts.

Tommy Fang's crew brought out dinner on huge, broad platters that they carried on their shoulders. Everyone sat down to the food. Lisa Lisa sat down next to the Executive Director of Internal Surveillance. Coyote Jack watched as many of the female customers tried to seat themselves at Eggs Igino's table. When he looked at Sidney Geeder's date, she snapped a military salute at Coyote Jack and then smirked and put her hand in Geeder's lap. They were all good and drunk, and it seemed like they had been there for hours. The Executive Director of Internal Surveillance stood up and made a joke about how everyone should enjoy themselves and take no prisoners and not to worry about indiscretion, because the firm already had a damn good reason to fire every one of them if it wanted to.

Nickel Sansome stood up and told the same joke that Coyote Jack had told everyone earlier, about Jesus, Mohammed, and the Dalai Lama trying to decide where to invest their money. People laughed again anyway. They all thought that Nickel knew they'd already heard it and was doing an imitation of Coyote Jack. It was a pretty good imitation, because Nickel was so depressed that his face was downcast in a gloomy, macabre scowl. When the wonton soup was served, the bowls were licked clean. The poached flounder was a hit, as were the flaming strawberries for dessert. Coyote Jack began to daydream about that Honolulu office. There was a whole lot of construction going on in Hawaii, and there were a whole lot of mortgages coming out of the islands. Coyote Jack imagined wearing a flowered shirt to work every day, learning to speak a little of the native language. On Fridays, he would order a whole pig to come in and get roasted over a pit right on the sales floor. They would break the meaty ribs right off the hog, slathered with pineapple sauce. If Eggs Igino had been milking Hawaii the past few months, then that Honolulu office would be open by now. Coyote Jack looked over and saw Dave Rennaker going into the bar with Lisa Lisa. Out of the pasty green light of the monochrome monitors, Lisa Lisa looked much younger. It was a shame she wasn't tougher and couldn't post big numbers on her accounts. She was really a pretty sexy gal, and Coyote Jack wouldn't have minded keeping her around just for decoration value if she weren't so damn tough, always carrying a chip on her shoulder about how hard it was to be a woman in this business. In Coyote Jack's opinion, female salesmen were given a pretty long leash already.

Nickel Sansome went into the bar when Coyote Jack lied to him that whores were in there. There were quite a few people there, though, and he had no idea which ones could be bought. He sat down next to Dave Rennaker at the bar rail and ordered one of Tommy's specials, then hunkered in to eavesdrop on Dave Rennaker and Lisa Lisa. She didn't seem that interested in him, even though he had shoulders like a yield sign, because she kept glancing across the room at where Eggs Igino was telling stories to a couple of women from the First Nationwide operations department. Pretty soon Nickel got bored, because he could see nothing was going to happen, so he nudged Dave Rennaker and started asking if he'd ever told him about his high school girlfriend. He kept asking, very nonchalantly, slowly butting in, and soon both Dave and Lisa Lisa had turned their attention to Nickel as he told them about how his old high school girlfriend had been this cheerleader with a flushed, vibrant, totally enthusiastic beauty that made Nickel the envy of his whole school. She had high pert breasts and pencil-thin legs that kicked above her head hundreds of times during a game. During sex, he said, she talked dirty and wanted to be told pornographic stories of Nickel screwing her best friends and younger sisters. Nickel said that his whole life had been downhill since then. During football games, he said, she would become totally enraptured by the action. She couldn't stand to see her men lose. Nickel was a tight end with bricks for hands, so they never threw the ball his way. He had plenty of time, between plays, to look over on the sidelines and see his girlfriend so tensed up. When they lost, she broke down in tears. Really started bawling. It was touching, but it was only a football game and it was embarrassing, too. But she was so damn cute! She could get several of the other girls to start bawling too. Nickel then admitted that she had been the highlight of his life and he still had a picture of her that he carried in his wallet. Rennaker laughed at how pathetic Nickel was to still be carrying a picture of his high school girlfriend in his wallet. Lisa Lisa eyed him suspiciously, wary of the resemblance. Nickel reached for his wallet and held it out in front of him. He made a fuss of pretending to have lost her picture, then he found it. It was a 5 × 7 color print, folded into quarters, with a low-resolution image, as if it had been taken from the television. He handed it to Rennaker, and Lisa Lisa leaned over Rennaker's big arm to get a glimpse.

"Oh my god," she cried, pushing both of them off their bar stools and grabbing for her purse.

"Hey, it's Lisa Lisa!" Dave Rennaker yelled out to the bar crowd, waving the picture above her head. "A fucking cheerleader!" He looked down at the picture again. She was on her knees on the sidelines, clutching her pompoms, bawling. "In tears!" he hollered.

People came wandering in from the dining room to see what all the shouting was about.

"Let's see a routine," Nickel suggested in a cheery, rah-rah tone that implied all his malicious, undermining, monstrous intentions, which conveyed all the deeper agony and humiliation he continually suffered. "Let's see you kick."

Lisa Lisa pouted and couldn't manage to defend herself. To no avail, she tried to hold off tears, and then, to no avail, she tried to hide her tears by running from the room before they fell from her eyes and streaked her makeup, but with her head down and her hand shielding her eyes she ran right into Coyote Jack, who was strolling into the room. She ran right smack into his tall, soft chest, and her arms fell away as she staggered backward. Coyote Jack took one look at the tears coming down her face, streaking her makeup, and grinned a sly, gratified grin. Coyote Jack was quite impressed by his own foresight and astute judgment of character. He knew that someday she would break down in tears, that she just couldn't hack it. He hated weakness.

People began to make plans for the rest of the evening. Nickel Sansome, who was still wide awake, invited the girls from First Nationwide over to his apartment. The Executive Director of Internal Surveillance went off to the Excelsior with one of the hired women. John White suggested a nightclub off Union Square where they could pay topless women to dance with them. Someone else suggested a boxing card in South San Francisco where they could bet on the fighters like horses. Eggs Igino went out into the street to comfort Lisa Lisa. She was standing in the cold, clutching her elbows, waiting for a cab. The streets were empty.

"I hate this job," he said.

Lisa Lisa wiped at the tears in her streaked makeup. She took a deep breath. "You're lucky," she said.

"Me? Why?"

"Hating your job is a luxury. I'm not good enough at it to rise above it like that."

Eggs looked at her. "I don't believe that. This job is not that hard. You answer the phone and tell people what they want to hear."

Lisa Lisa shook her head. "Maybe for you."

"Mmm . . ." He doubted her.

"Eggs, like when you were in grade school and learning algebra, y equals x squared, that sort of thing, and you looked across the room at everyone else who was doodling in the margins, you probably thought they were just lazy, didn't you?"

"Not necessarily."

"I used to hate people like you. You never believed how hard it is for some us."

"Do you hate me?" Eggs was confused. "I haven't done anything."

"No, I don't hate you. But upstairs I have cheat notes all over my desk, tiny little acronyms to help me keep straight a repo from a reverse-repo, or a put from a call. I've been working there three years and I still feel like I'm faking it."

"Yeah?"

"*Yeah*. And most of your accounts feel the same way. They don't understand what they're buying. They're not criminals, intent on cashing in on Romania, making a killing in emerging markets. They buy because they want you to approve of them."

They walked down a few blocks to where she might find a cab. Lisa Lisa reached out and put her hand on Eggs's forearm, stopping him. He was so young.

"Hey," she said. "I'm sorry about, you know, coming on to you at the coffee machine. I shouldn't have done that. I'd just, well . . . Coyote Jack had been giving me a hard time."

"Coyote Jack." He nodded.

"So . . ."

"Coyote Jack can be tough."

"Eggs?"

"What?"

"You know, I don't live far from here. Would you walk me home?"

Eggs nodded. They walked along Montgomery Street, below the Transamerica Pyramid.

"Isn't it weird," Eggs said. "We work with people all the time, and we think we know them—but it's just a convenient type of knowing."

Lisa Lisa nodded. "We learn just enough to make pleasant conversation."

"We don't *want* to know, really. We'd rather not. Sometimes it's like we'd *rather* work with a faceless computer. Isn't that *weird*?"

"That's a little naive, Eggs. I don't want to know what Coyote Jack does at night, who he sees, what he thinks about. I really don't want to know Paul DeShews any better than I already do. I think you think it's weird because you're a man, and there's no downside of trying to get to know someone."

"What do you mean?"

"When you're a woman, you always have to be a little afraid. It's safer not to be too friendly."

"Oh." He was a little ashamed for having to have it spelled out for him.

They walked some more. They came to the steep incline of Telegraph Hill. Lisa Lisa's apartment was a block away.

"Coyote Jack's been talking about a Hawaii office," Eggs said, trying to make conversation.

"Is that right?" Lisa Lisa said, from the far-off place in her mind.

"I can't tell if he's bullshitting me. He might just want me to have something to look forward to, something to stick around for."

"I go to Hawaii twice a year," she said softly. "It's nice."

"Would you work there?"

"Oh, yes, are you kidding? Sure, I'd go."

"It's a tempting thought, all right. Then again, he might just be fucking with my head."

"Eggs?"

"What?"

"Do you have a girlfriend?"

"Uh, no."

"You know, a lot of guys, they treat their girlfriends like princesses. Men have thoughts—all sorts of thoughts, dirty thoughts, mean thoughts, thoughts they're ashamed of, really—but they can't bear to share those thoughts with their girlfriend. They tell themselves that they don't want to hurt their girlfriend, or wife, or whoever. They think they want to protect her. But that's not it. You know what it really is?"

"What?"

"They're afraid. They're afraid of their own thoughts."

Eggs nodded slowly.

Lisa Lisa went on, "I didn't think you were the kind of man who was afraid of his own thoughts." She paused. "Are you the kind of man who's afraid of his thoughts?"

"What do you mean?" he asked, stalling, a little ashamed.

Lisa Lisa stopped and turned toward him. She rolled her shoulders back and tossed her hair. "I mean, what are you thinking about right now? Are you really thinking about Hawaii?"

Eggs just watched her. He didn't say anything. She caught his eyes and stared him down.

"Are you just looking at me, Eggs, or are you *looking* at me? Go ahead—if you can't tell me with your mouth, then tell me with your eyes."

So he looked at her, looked at her hard, set his neck, and gazed right into her eyes to tell her that yes, yes, he wanted her.

"Thank you," she said.

"For?"

"I just needed that." She stepped forward, then looked down, then looked up again at him. "You know," she said, "sometimes I look at you and I think you are just way too young, you're just a baby. But then there's times I'm just overwhelmed, because you're a baby, but, well, you're a really, really *beautiful* baby." Lisa Lisa kissed him on the lips very briefly, so that he would be left wanting more. His lips were big and soft and she had to kiss him a couple of times, actually, to cover all of his lips. They were so soft! She kept kissing them. She felt his hand moving around her breasts, and she gasped slightly. Her eyes were closed involuntarily; it was a spell. "Come on," she said, taking his hand.

They started talking about films. Eggs Igino watched only foreign-made films, and Lisa Lisa argued that he was missing good movies.

"Like which?" he asked.

Suddenly she couldn't remember any. She laughed nervously. "But if there was one," she said, "you would miss it."

When they got to her apartment she sat him down at the kitchen table and asked if he wanted a glass of water. She told him most people don't get enough water. Water and sleep. So he said okay and took a glass of water. She asked if he used salt on his food, and he said no. So she got out a vial of iodine and put a drop in his water, saying most people don't get iodine now that they don't salt their food. Then she went into the bathroom to touch up her makeup.

"I used to dream of being a cook somewhere, like at a resort or on a nice ship or something," she said when she got back. She was wearing blue jeans and a cardigan sweater over a T-shirt. When he stared at her, she got nervous and revived his interest by giving him another kiss. "But, you know, for a woman, being a cook is like giving in. It's what men want us to be, and I just can't accept that. But the funny thing is, I'd probably be happier, you know? As a cook, that is. Am I rambling?"

"Yes."

"Oh, gosh, I'm sorry, you'd probably like a glass of wine, wouldn't you?"

He said that he would, and he drank it quickly and gave himself another.

"Isn't this silly?" she asked. "I can't explain it." She touched a napkin to his face where a drop of wine had splashed. "I get so girlish. I mean, normally I'm tough, I'm strong, but once I know a man is interested then I just change."

They went into the living room and sat down on the couch. She put on Patsy Cline. It was dark outside, and the Transamerica Pyramid took up most of the view through her window. Eggs was much more comfortable seeing her in casual clothes—she was more familiar to him. She snuggled up against him and unbuttoned his dress shirt and slid her hand onto his chest. When he didn't reach back for her right away, she told him sometimes he just had to give in to his body. She told him it wasn't good for a man to always let his mind have control. She told him all men found this out sooner or later, even good men. She told him he was a good man and that he was only learning how to be a man, and then his hands began to knead her body firmly, her shoulders and back and butt and breasts and calves, and he kissed her hard as he gripped her, and she could suddenly feel the force of his energy, she could feel how strong he was, how determined suddenly. He unbuttoned her jeans and pulled them off her easily. He took off his shirt and his pants, then her cardigan and T-shirt, and pushed her down on her back.

"Wait," she said. "Put the sweater over my shoulders."

So she leaned forward and he draped the sweater over her back, pulling the arms over her shoulders. He looked at her eyes as his hand slid between her legs. She closed her eyes, not wanting to reveal her pleasure. When he lowered himself onto her, she clung to him dearly. She raised her legs slightly and pulled him into her, and they both groaned wildly with sudden exhilaration. How could so much pleasure come from a mere body? She envisioned herself soft, soft like a pillow of silk, let herself be shaped by him. They made love for an hour. They were on the rug in front of the window, with a quilt over their legs. She begged him to come. Eggs held her and rocked with his whole body, and though he didn't love her at all he wanted her to know how well he could love a woman, he wanted someone to know the secret inside him, which was that he was capable of a great love. Lisa Lisa mistook his love for her, and she grew giddy and overly endearing, kissing him too much. He was confused, and suddenly he just wanted it over, so he concentrated until he came. She whispered in his ear, "See, I'm not so tough. I'm not so tough at all." It felt so good she wanted to cry, and she did cry a little, just a tear or two.

"What's going on?" Eggs asked, stopping.

"Nothing," she said, looking away. "Please, don't stop."

"Why are you crying?"

"It's nothing," she said. "I'm just emotional."

"This isn't right," Eggs said. He sat up and stared at her and saw her again as the Lisa Lisa he worked with.

"Please, don't," she said.

"What do you think this is? I thought you just wanted to fuck. Now you're crying."

"I thought I did," she said, crying a little more and brushing away her tears with the back of her hand. "I can't help it. You're so nice, such a nice man. I can't help it."

"I think I'd better go. Christ, what am I doing here?" He pulled away and fumbled into his shirt. "Look, this is nothing personal, I've just never done this before, and you're very sweet but I just never thought it would feel like there was so much at stake here."

"What did you expect? I'm a thirty-year-old woman. You expected me not to have any feelings at all?" She buttoned the cardigan around her breasts, misbuttoning the loops at an angle.

"I'm sorry," Eggs said, hopping on one leg as he danced into his trousers and clasped his belt. "I'm really sorry."

"Don't be sorry for me, Eggs. Please, not that. I don't want your sympathy. That's the last thing I want. You ought to know that. All I want is your respect."

Eggs was in the other room, finding his shoes. "Okay, I'm sorry about being sorry. Damn, it's just me, I'm shy and I've never done this, okay?" His footsteps went down the corridor. The door opened. "I'll see you tomorrow, okay?" The door shut.

Lisa Lisa went into the bathroom. She looked at herself in the mirror.

"Such a child," she said aloud, and tried not to think about it.

She removed her makeup with cold cream and applied her low-lustre, firming-action moisture cream, which she let work while she used the toilet. Then she decided to take a shower and shampoo her hair, which she wouldn't have time to do in the morning. She lathered twice and shaved her legs, then took a pumice stone to the rough spots on her heels and elbows. While her skin was still wet from the shower, she rubbed all over her body a self-tanning milk so she would wake up in the morning with a healthy glow. Around her eyes she dabbed a hydrating eye gel. She combed sculpting fluid into her wet hair so she would be able to shape it in the morning. And she had to rub lemon-based hair-lightening cream on her sideburns. And she had to brush her teeth, then protect her lips. She'd really wanted Eggs Igino. She'd really looked forward to her huge, underwater breaths and her strobelight mind and the clench at the base of her spine and not sleeping a wink.

At four o'clock, Lisa Lisa dragged herself out of bed and forced herself into her clothes. She thought she should have a hangover—wished she had one, even—but she hadn't had much wine and she was completely lucid. She walked the cold downtown streets to work, sheltering herself against the breeze that swirled at the corners. The streets were peaceful, almost sympathetic, and for a moment knowing that she was alone in the world felt freeing rather than sad. On the way into the building, the security guards greeted her with a chipper "Good morning." They told her she looked awfully nice, and she smiled. She rode up the elevator and strolled out onto the sales floor. She went into the kitchen, poured herself a cup of coffee, picked up a copy of *The Wall Street Journal,* and moseyed to her desk as she glanced over the front page. She looked out the window, where the sun shone orange against the other towers. Light banter came over the squawk box, and she began to take down opening numbers and construct the story of overnight trading. Slowly, the others straggled into the office. She watched as Coyote Jack came out of his office with a huge, proud smirk to his face. He walked directly to her desk. He was smiling.

"You have fifteen minutes to collect your personal belongings," he announced sternly, crossing his arms across his chest. "The security guards will be here in a moment."

"What are you talking about?" She laughed nervously. "Coyote, don't joke around like that."

"Do I look like I'm joking?" he asked militantly, peering right into her eyes.

"Come on, Coyote," she pleaded, trying to reach out and touch his hand, which he jerked away. "Coyote, please. What's going on here?"

"You're being fired. You've already been fired."

"What in the world for?" she cried.

"I don't have to give you a reason," he snarled.

"Coyote, let's go into your office and talk this out. If this is about the Romanians, I really sold the hell out of them, I really did." She got up from her chair and started moving toward his office.

Coyote Jack grabbed her by the arm. "Don't go anywhere in this office. Don't touch a single research report or trading notebook or telephone call list. Those are the property of the firm. You have been fired, Lisa. You are no longer an employee of Atlantic Pacific. In another thirteen minutes you will be trespassing on the premises and will be forcibly removed."

"I'm going to talk to John White about it," she stammered, trying to pull away from Coyote Jack's grip.

"John White is on his way to New York."

"You *can't* fire me, Coyote. Please, Coyote, I need this job."

"For god's sakes, Lisa—take it like a man, will you?"

"Just let me stay through one more deal. I'll prove it to you. You can put me down for thirty million. I don't care if I have to suck their dicks to get them to buy."

"Forget it. Your accounts are Eggs Igino's accounts, now."

"Eggs Igino's accounts? He can't have my accounts! I built those accounts! HonFed was nothing before I came along!"

"You're wasting my time, Lisa." He waved over the security guards who had entered from the forty-first floor and come up through the internal staircase. They were the same security guards she had seen as she entered the building. Coyote Jack pointed to Lisa Lisa. "You know the routine, boys. No special privileges." Then he turned and walked back to his office to call the maids.

Lisa Lisa began to cry. She couldn't get ahold of herself, and she pawed at the belongings on her desk, knocking them toward a paper bag. She reached for her telephone and popped one of the direct lines to Honolulu Federal. The security guard grabbed the phone from her hand and hit her disconnect button. Lisa Lisa found a packet of tissues in her drawer and began to wipe at her eyes with the whole packet. She found her address book in the drawer and tried to throw that in the bag, but the highly trained security guard caught it in midair and put it back on top of her desk. She was really bawling and started pounding on the desktop. Then the security guards told her that her fifteen minutes were up and it was time to leave. "It can't be," she cried. Each put a hand on one of her elbows, and they guided her away. She clung to her one bag of personal belongings. "Fuck you all!" she yelled. They pushed her out the door and stood with her at the elevator. She tried to restrain herself, wanting to claw at the security men and tear off their uniforms. "Do you know how this feels?" she asked them with indignation. When the elevator opened, they pushed her in gently. "Get your hands off of me," she swore. "You take your own elevator!"

When the elevator closed, Lisa Lisa bent over hysterically, and then, knowing it would do no good, forced herself to stand up straight. When she left the building, Eggs Igino was just walking across the esplanade. She threw her bag of belongings at him.

"Fuck you, you little snot-nosed bastard!" She swung at him and missed.

"What the fuck?" Eggs jumped back.

"You knew all about this!" she cried. "Oh, you asshole, you knew all along that you were going to get my accounts, you just wanted one quick fuck before I disappeared. . . . I wouldn't give it to you, would I? I wouldn't let you use me like that, I wanted to make you pay with your heart, and you were afraid, you're such a little boy, you're so scared. . . ."

"What are you talking about?" Eggs stammered.

"Don't play dumb, you jerk. All that stuff about the Hawaii office—you knew damn well. This is really one for the record books. You'll never be forgotten, Eggs Igino—they'll be talking about you for years. 'Yeah, he knew she was getting cut loose, so he poked her the night before, gave it to her good, yeah.' Except you felt sorry for me, you bastard, you couldn't even go through with it, as if somehow your sympathy saves you from having done anything wrong."

"Did you get fired?"

"Right. Now you'll ask me who's going to get my accounts! I just can't believe you. I can't. Get away from me!"

Eggs tried to grab her arm, but she swung at him again and ran off, clutching at her elbows.

Eggs stood there a long time, sorting through what she had said. Slowly, the other salespeople climbed out from behind their bunkers and wandered over to Lisa Lisa's desk. Everything had been left behind. Nickel Sansome took a jar of low-lustre firming-action moisture cream and began to rub it into his scalp. Sue Marino took the address book and began to flip through the names, then headed toward the hallway closet to see if any suits had been left behind. In her desk they found three sheer spandex pantyhose, a pair of forest-colored T-strap pumps, a blow dryer, a curling iron, underarm pads, bra pads, shoulder pads, Tampax, and a broken umbrella. Behind all that, they found a stack of old First Boston business cards with the name Lisa A. Lisa printed on them. They were about to start a round of nervous jokes when Coyote Jack came out and yelled at them to get back to work.

"Let's go, let's go, you jarheads!" he screamed. "Don't get lazy on me now!" Coyote Jack went desk to desk, murmuring to each of the salespeople to put in a full day's work and not even to think about taking a lunch. He handed each of them a newly coded magnetic security card that they would need immediately to enter the floor. Then the maids arrived and Coyote Jack pointed them to Lisa Lisa's desk. They began to scour the desk. They scoured the green felt-tip ink off the linoleum. They puttied the scratches in the mahogany. They lifted the grease stains off the carpet, which had been worn bare in Lisa Lisa's three years. They touched up the paint on the file drawer. They entirely replaced the phone headset, which smelled of Aquanet. They had no sympathy for the rich white woman who had left. For three years, they had kept her clean, wiped the lipstick off her phone and picked the hardened drops of nail polish off the linoleum and straightened the piles of trading notes she'd made.

The salesmen watched the maids scour Lisa Lisa's desk. They were scared and hungover and felt completely powerless, and for all these reasons they began to feel famished. The coffee gurgled in empty stomachs. Nickel Sansome watched the maid with the long, straight dark hair in envy. He wondered what it would be like to have a labor job, where he wasn't always suffering from self-recrimination, fighting for status, and fending off the harassment of management. He wondered what it would be like to just show up at six and leave at three and not carry any concerns home. Or what it would be like to have a good excuse to have scorn for the wealthy, or to not have to pretend he was an insider when he never felt like one. Nickel Sansome gazed upon the maid with the long

straight dark hair and imagined what she would look like in a
short, sheer black nightgown and black heels. Nickel suffered from
a ringing in his ears that sometimes was also a sharp pain as an
aftereffect of the cocaine. He was also dehydrated from the alcohol. He leaned over toward Nelson Dicky.

"What do you think? I'll bet she was cheating the firm," Nickel
hypothesized. "She might have been trading on inside information."

Nelson Dicky shook his head. "Lisa Lisa was straight," he insisted.

"Well, what do *you* think?"

"I don't know," Nelson admitted. "She was number four on the
desk. She was doing her job okay."

"*I'm* number four," Nickel countered. "She was number five."

"Only recently."

"Who do you think will get her accounts? If I don't get her accounts, I'm going to Merrill."

"Sure, right. You at Merrill? Is the sky falling?"

"I need the accounts. A guy's got to eat."

Nelson Dicky shook his head in sad disbelief. "Aren't you going
to answer your phone?" he asked, pointing to Nickel's phone
panel.

"I'll answer it on my own schedule," Nickel stated proudly,
pausing a moment before picking up his phone.

"Get back to work!" Coyote Jack screamed, looking through his
window at where Nickel Sansome was slothfully padding about in
his bunker. "You lousy paste-for-brains cockroach! Do you feel
like being next?!" Coyote Jack slammed the phone back down and
paced his room in circles, pushing aside his furniture. Then he
stopped at the window again and stared out at Eggs Igino's desk.
He was dying to tell Igino that he would pick up HonFed and
Ameribank, Lisa Lisa's best accounts. He wanted to tell Igino more
about his plans for the Hawaii office; Igino was a visionary—he
would understand what could be done with Hawaii. Coyote Jack
dialed Sid Geeder's number, even though he could see that Sid
Geeder was already working two phones at once. That Sid. One
hell of a competitor.

Coyote Jack's secretary eventually answered the phone. "Good morning, Atlantic Pacific?" she responded.

"Get me Sid Geeder," he gruffed. Then he watched as his secretary strutted out onto the sales floor and all the hungry, hungover men gawked over the plush bosoms and rocking hips. She went out to Sid's desk and leaned over the edge and shouted something down into the crawl space. Sid reached up and tapped a button on his phone bank.

"Hurry, Coyote. I'm working a sale."

Coyote Jack found a loose thread on his new suspenders and began to tug at it. He kept pulling, but he couldn't see where the thread was coming from. "Where's Eggs Igino?" he asked.

"Who am I, the bellhop? I don't have any idea where he is."

"He hasn't called in?"

"Ahh, I gotta go." Sid Geeder popped off the line.

So Coyote Jack called the number for Eggs Igino's apartment. There was no answer. He left a message, asking Eggs to call in if there was anything wrong. Coyote Jack got anxious, and he could feel the tightening in his throat muscles that frequently preceded a bout of stuttering. He went into the kitchen to see if any breakfast had arrived. He found Clark Kalinov digging through the refrigerator. Clark Kalinov's hair was still wet and his face was flushed and he wasn't wearing a tie.

Clark Kalinov stepped away from the refrigerator holding a bottle of grapefruit juice with someone else's name on it. Kalinov saluted Coyote with a sharp nod.

"Where's breakfast?" Coyote Jack asked.

"Should be coming through the door any second," Kalinov assured him, looking down at his watch.

Coyote Jack nodded in acknowledgment. "Oh, by the way, Kalinov: You'll be getting a replacement for Lisa Lisa."

"That'll be fine."

"See my secretary for the details. Somewhere in her files she's got a report on the new class of hires that we can bid upon. She'll photocopy it for you."

"I'll look through it today."

"We should probably get a woman, someone we can groom to replace Sue Marino in another year."

"Very good, sir."

"I thought you said breakfast was coming through the door any second?" Coyote Jack charged grumpily. "I got a fucking hole in my gut I gotta plug up."

"It's a little late," Clark Kalinov admitted, again checking his watch.

"It's never late," Coyote Jack argued. "I could set my watch by those gals. In fact, I *do* set my watch by those gals."

"Maybe your watch is off, then."

"My watch isn't off!" Coyote Jack growled.

"I'll go ask Eggs Igino if he knows anything," Clark Kalinov suggested.

"Eggs Igino! Have you seen him?"

"He's not here?"

"I don't know where he is." Angry and upset and getting scared, Coyote Jack turned and walked back out to the edge of the sales pits. Clark Kalinov followed him. Together, they stood side by side, gazing across at the force, looking for Eggs Igino. It was not like him to be late for work. Not like him at all.

12 · Assets

EGGS IGINO HAD disappeared!

"They'll never find him," Sidney beamed proudly. "He's too smart to ever be caught."

"What did he steal?" Nelson Dicky asked, coming up to Sid.

"Steal? Hell, he stole one of the firm's greatest assets. Snuck it right out the front door when everybody was watching him. The firm will never be able to replace it."

"Jeez, I'll bet Coyote Jack's hopping mad. So what did he walk out of here with that was so irreplaceable?"

"Himself." Sidney snickered and clutched at his sides in amusement.

"*Himself?* That's not a crime, is it?"

"I never thought he'd do it," Sid went on, rubbing his hands together gleefully. "He was always joking with me about how we could never quit, how the firm always owed us tons of money. Christ, what *balls!*"

"He was crazy," Nelson surmised, casually burping out of the side of his mouth as he dug his hands into his pockets and jiggled their contents.

"So crazy that he walked right away from this place."

"That doesn't sound so crazy," admitted Sue Marino, who'd just walked up to see what Sid was so excited about.

"It's not!" agreed Sid Geeder, as he sat back down in his chair and reached under Eggs Igino's desk. He came back up with a pair of dirty, worn running shoes with tall waffled treads and criss-crossed laces that were tightened with a plastic clasp. "It doesn't sound crazy at all, does it? That's what's so absolutely grotesque about it, so peculiarly odd and brilliantly eccentric!" Sidney kicked off his double-welt-construction oxfords and slipped on Eggs Igino's shoes. They were made of Gore-Tex with a sponge tongue and air-cushioned heel; Sidney's feet spontaneously lifted into the air at their comfortable lightness. Energy surged into his legs as he stood up and clicked his heels. Sidney cracked off twenty jumping jacks, ripped off his tie, and jogged in place. "I've never heard of anything so shrewdly devastative! It's pure genius. Right when the firm needs him most—right when he's supposed to take over the accounts of a fourth salesperson—he walks!"

"You sure he didn't jump over to Shearson?" Nelson Dicky reasoned.

"I'm sure of it. Eggs Igino doesn't care about money. He's probably on some beach somewhere, having his stomach rubbed with coconut oil. Can you imagine what will happen to the salesforce when they hear that the most promising salesman in the firm has just walked out the front door and not come back?"

"Christ, they'll bolt," Sue Marino realized. "Not all of them, but some."

"That's right!" Sidney laughed. "They don't want anything but to be happy. One day, boom!—it'll hit them: 'Follow your heart.' The next day—*sayonara.*"

Nelson Dicky looked out the forty-second-floor window. "Ahhh, maybe he's just taking a few days' unannounced vacation."

"That's what management wants to think," Sidney Geeder countered. "But I have a good feeling about this one."

"Ahhh, maybe he's just taking a little surprise vacation," Coyote Jack whined to the Executive Director of Internal Surveillance, who had brought several henchmen into John White's office to talk it over.

"That's what I'd like to think," John White responded thoughtfully, resting his chin on his intertwined fingers. "But I have a bad feeling about this one."

"Doesn't Geeder know *something*?" the Executive Director of Internal Surveillance piped in.

"I don't know anything!" Sidney insisted, when they had brought him in after work that day and thrown him down on John White's couch. Two statuesque goons in navy-blue suits sat stiffly on either side of him. Whenever Sidney tried to stand up in frustration, they grabbed him by the arm and shoved him back down into the cushions.

"I don't think you know how serious this is, Geeder," growled the Executive Director of Internal Surveillance. "Don't you realize how important Igino was to the future of this firm?"

"I don't think *you* realize how much trouble you're in," Sid shot back, shaking his head in mock misery. "Don't you understand how important Eggs Igino has become in only a few short months? He's an *icon*. Christ, wait until the *Journal* hears."

"The *Journal*!" John White screeched in horror.

The Executive Director of Internal Surveillance stepped forward and put his hand in the air calmly. "We don't have to worry about the *Journal*. We run tombstone ads in there every day. They'd run our version if they run anything."

"So what's our version?" Coyote Jack stammered nervously.

The Executive Director of Internal Surveillance pondered his options.

"We could say we fired him," Coyote Jack suggested.

Sidney Geeder busted out laughing.

"You shut up, Geeder," Coyote Jack said.

"Hey, at least I know where he is," Sidney yelled in return.

"*Where?*" yelled John White, Coyote Jack, and the Executive Director of Internal Surveillance simultaneously, the last grabbing Sidney by the lapels of his suit coat and shaking him.

"He's *gone,*" Sidney answered. "He's not on vacation."

"I'm not convinced," the Executive Director of Internal Surveillance said. "He could be anywhere."

"Well, he has to be *somewhere,*" John White figured.

"Of course he's somewhere," Sidney hopped back in, confounding their capacity to think this through. "But that somewhere could be anywhere." He was hoping that if he caused them enough consternation, they'd let him go just to get rid of him.

The Executive Director of Internal Surveillance put his face only six inches from Sid's. Sid could smell his musk-scented aftershave, and it curdled his stomach. "When's the last time you saw him?" the Executive Director of Internal Surveillance asked.

Sid turned his head toward the window. "Same time as you did. Left the party three days ago, chasing Lisa Lisa."

The Executive Director of Internal Surveillance whirled around to look at Coyote Jack. "And so *she's* the last one to see him? Well then, why the hell aren't we grilling her?"

"She's been fired."

"What in the hell for? She had evidence. She was the last person to see him!"

"She wasn't performing."

"Wasn't performing?"

Sidney clucked his tongue mischievously, then chirped, "Coyote Jack was going to give her accounts to Eggs Igino."

"Look, I don't think Lisa Lisa had anything to do with Eggs Igino's taking a little sudden vacation," Coyote Jack defended himself.

"He's not on vacation," Sidney corrected them all once again. "He quit."

John White gritted his teeth and clenched his fists. "Nobody quits Atlantic Pacific, Geeder. Nobody. You tell your accounts that Eggs Igino quit and I'll put you out on the street in a second."

"All right," Sidney acquiesced, rolling his head onto his shoulder in John White's direction. "I forgot. I'll remember it this time: Nobody quits First Boston."

"Goddamnit! We're not First Boston anymore!" John White screamed, kicking at the support leg of his *méridienne* couch. "Fuck it!"

Sidney Geeder waited for the tension to build. "I'll tell you where Eggs Igino is if you tell me what you've done to Dr. Ivana Perkova."

"So you *do* know where he is!" the Executive Director of Internal Surveillance spat back into Sidney's face.

"He doesn't know," Coyote Jack said, narrowing his eyes and rocking back on his heels.

"What makes you think we know where Dr. Perkova is?" the Executive Director of Internal Surveillance bluffed.

"What makes you think that I know where Eggs Igino is?" Sidney shot back.

"Because you just said you would tell us!"

"No I didn't. I said I would tell you *if* you told me what you've done with Ivana."

"You were his best friend," John White said. "If anyone would know, it'd be you."

"Geeder's bluffing," Coyote Jack decreed. "He's a goddamn salesman. You can't trust him. Eggs Igino was too smart to tell anything to Geeder. We've got a file on Geeder thick as a phone book, not to mention those shares he's owed. If he knew something, he'd tell us."

"Maybe I would, maybe I wouldn't," Sid said proudly.

The three men stood there with their arms crossed, trying not to think about the deep shit they had gotten themselves into, or what would happen to them if the word got out that the firm's most promising young salesman in ten years had suddenly vanished without a trace. In the three days since he'd disappeared, the Executive Director of Internal Surveillance had tried all the obvious leads. There were no phone calls placed from his apartment. His bank account had been drained the day after the Romanians. NASDAQ confirmed that he hadn't yet reregistered at any other firm. It didn't add up. Finally, they'd broken into his apartment, but it was untouched, abandoned with all its meager contents. The kid lived like a monk; the kid wasn't at all afraid to be poor, and that scared the shit out of the Executive Director of Internal Surveillance, who'd never seen a rich man unafraid of being poor. He just didn't see what Eggs Igino had to gain from leaving the firm that had made him rich and famous in such a terrible lurch.

That was what Coyote Jack was trying to figure out, as he sat in his office the next day ruminating over options for replacing Eggs Igino. But Coyote Jack kept coming to the conclusion that Eggs Igino was irreplaceable, and therefore he kept returning to the necessity of finding the crackpot and putting him back into action. But finding Eggs Igino would require thinking like Eggs Igino, and Coyote Jack's pea brain couldn't conceive of one good reason for Eggs Igino's maliciously abandoning Coyote Jack in such a tremendous bind. Coyote Jack didn't even have the courage to ask John White what had happened to the firm's plans for Hawaii. The query sat in Coyote Jack's mind like a canker, constantly requiring his mental attention and distracting him from moving on to other thoughts. The more he gave it attention, though, the more it inflamed into an all-consuming panic that could only be alleviated momentarily by frantically scratching his neck by jamming a pencil under his starched collar.

"Oh, what the hell now!" Coyote Jack screamed when Clark Kalinov knocked on the glass window of his office, holding a piece of paper up to the glass.

Clark Kalinov pointed to the piece of paper and mouthed words Coyote could not hear. Coyote waved him away. Clark knocked again. Coyote Jack ignored him. Kalinov disappeared. A few minutes later, John White and Kalinov barged into his office.

"What the hell's going on?" Coyote Jack shouted.

"We could get our clocks cleaned," John White exclaimed. "He could be anywhere: Salomon, Merrill, Goldman."

"Who?" Coyote Jack demanded.

"Goldman," John White repeated. "Goldman Sachs."

"I know Goldman!" Coyote Jack bellowed. "Who the hell are we talking about?"

"We're talking about our competitors," Clark Kalinov stated superiorly.

"I know who our competitors are, you son of a bitch. You're wasting my time. Don't you know how busy I am?" Coyote Jack clenched his fist.

"Then why do you keep asking?" John White asked.

"Christ. Will you two start over?" Coyote Jack pleaded.

"It's Eggs Igino," John White pronounced.

"Eggs Igino! Have you heard from him?"

"In a way," Clark Kalinov affirmed.

"Not exactly," John White corrected.

"Draw your own conclusions," Clark Kalinov recoiled spitefully.

"We have reason to suspect," John White led in.

"That he might be at Goldman." Kalinov finished.

"It's a possibility," John White recanted. "No real evidence. But it's certainly feasible."

"Why?" Coyote Jack demanded, grabbing the piece of paper out of Kalinov's hand. "What's this?"

Clark Kalinov and John White looked at each other.

"It's a noncompete agreement," Clark answered. "It states that he won't leave Atlantic Pacific for employment at any other investment bank, bank, or investment fund of any sort."

Coyote Jack looked down at the stupid form printed meticulously on Atlantic Pacific stationery.

"But it's unsigned!" he screeched.

"Exactly," John White affirmed.

"I found it in his desk last night," Clark Kalinov explained. "He wouldn't not sign it without a reason."

"Not Eggs Igino," John White observed. "He had a reason for everything. He could see the future. He was prepared."

"I have several unanswered memos requesting that he complete the form and return it to me via Intermail in my files," Clark Kalinov argued. "It was standard procedure. He's the only salesman to ever refuse to sign the form. And he's the only salesman ever to just disappear into thin air."

"Well, what can we do?" Coyote asked. "It's not illegal, is it?"

"It's uncivil," Clark responded. "Pretty much the same thing. Our lawyers could get a restraining order to keep him from working in the opposing trenches. I've taken the initiative and already put in a call."

"The press will have a field day if he ends up at Salomon," Coyote Jack complained, banging his fist down on his desk in outrage.

"Maybe it's not Salomon or Goldman or anyone like them," Nickel Sansome conjectured, standing over Sid's desk and trying to draw him into conversation. Nickel crumpled a paper ball and tossed it in the direction of the Nerf hoop, which had been stuck to Lisa Lisa's Telerate monitor. "Maybe he's gone over to the Germans, the Bundesbankers. Or heck, the Japanese—maybe he's setting up shop with Nomura Securities, or Taio Kobe. That way he doesn't have to get reregistered through NASDAQ. The firm will never even know he's out there."

"Did you hear Nickel Sansome's theory?" said John White, as he strolled into Coyote Jack's office. "He thinks Igino is helping the Japanese."

"That traitor," Coyote Jack reacted spontaneously.

John White continued, "That way, he'll never show up on NAS-DAQ's databanks. He'll be out there cleaning our clocks, eating our shirts, and we won't even know it."

Instinctively, Coyote Jack and John White looked out the window into the mist that whipped by, as if they could get a glimpse of Eggs Igino in the fog. But it was a wall of gray, and they had no leads. It was a world where knowledge was power, and their complete ignorance of Eggs Igino's whereabouts was destroying their confidence and undermining their command of the office, which had been thrown into disarray by the failure of Clark Kalinov to deliver hot French toast with Vermont maple syrup right out onto the sales floor in the morning. The salesforce were grumbling with unease and were bound to catch on soon that the firm didn't have any idea where Igino was, and pretty soon the word would be all over the street.

"Let's just pretend that we *do* know where he is," the Senior Executive President for International Markets suggested when the top brass convened again in the penthouse to deliberate for hours on what bold, decisive action they would agree to take. "Let's say he's not missing at all. Let's say we sent him on a top-secret financial mission, and that he's incommunicado. He's undercover."

"But what if he turns out to be working for the Japanese?" the Chief of Internal Affairs asked. "Then everyone will know we've been lying."

"No they won't," the Senior Executive President for International Markets reasoned. "We'll just insist that he's a double agent, and that he's still working for us. Besides, at least this strategy might flush him out."

"I say we call the CIA," the Senior Director of Facilities chimed in. "When the Japanese steal one of our firm's greatest assets, I say that's a job for the guvvies."

"But he's *not* working for the Japanese."

"We don't know that. He might very well be working for the Japanese, and if anyone could find out, it's the CIA."

"You guys are getting way off track," the Senior Executive President for International Markets interrupted, waving his hands and trying to calm everyone down. "This is not that hard. Let's just say he's working on this deal we're putting together in the Dominican Republic. If anyone asks, we stonewall them, but then we slowly let on that he's undercover in Santo Domingo, doing recon on the deal. He was so effective on the Romanians that we've decided to give him a bigger role in this one."

"That won't work," insisted the Executive Director of Internal Surveillance. "Sidney Geeder already knows that we don't have any idea where Eggs Igino is."

John White cleared his throat. "We owe Geeder one hundred thousand shares of company stock. Geeder won't say anything."

"I'm not supposed to say anything," Sidney Geeder confessed to the private investigator as he entered the botanical gardens in Golden Gate Park, where they had agreed to meet. "But Eggs Igino is missing."

"But I thought they sent him on a secret mission somewhere."

"They're just pretending. They don't know anything."

They walked down one of the gravel paths into the exotic bushes from South America. Sid took the private investigator's hand. "I tried to trade them information on Igino for a lead on Dr. Perkova, but they didn't bite. Do you have any leads?"

The private investigator looked over her shoulder, up the pathway. "Look, Sid, I can't keep looking for your doctor. I haven't been able to find anything, and I have reason to suspect the firm has paid her to cut off contact with you."

"Why do you think that?"

"Because they offered me five thousand dollars to quit snooping on them."

"They did? Christ, what'd you do?"

"I took it."

"You took it!"

"Five thousand dollars is a lot of money, particularly when I wasn't coming up with anything anyway."

Sid stopped walking. "When did this happen?" he said, irritated.

"Yesterday, when I was at the medical library at UCSF, trying to find microfiche records. As I was leaving, two goons got on the elevator and threatened me, then handed me an envelope of bills. Look, Sid, I'm just a small-time PI. I don't do criminal work. I don't mess in the wrong people's business. Unless you've got something illegal to report to the police, I suggest you leave this alone. But the police are just going to laugh when you tell them that you can't find your girlfriend."

Sidney sat down on a stone bench. He sighed deeply. The private investigator sat beside him and leaned her head on his shoulder. Sid looked at her, and her eyes were wet.

"Selling bonds used to be so simple," Sidney observed with a recalcitrant remorse. "People didn't just disappear. You went to work in the morning and you came home at night and if you didn't want to be bothered, you weren't."

"I'm scared for you, Sid," said the private investigator.

Sidney hugged her, wanting wantonly at that very moment to be in her apartment on her king-size bed inside her closet, buried under batik sheets and lush pillows. Sidney was still in love with Ivana Perkova, but he was even more in need of comfort, wherever he could get it, and it was impossible for him to gaze down at the flesh of her inner forearm and not suffer a pang of deep longing. Her wavy dark brown hair was cut short in back, with bangs in front, and Sid loved to cup his hand on the back of her bare neck and casually run his fingers through her locks, and sometimes, when they were alone, to bury his hot face into the cool crook where her clavicle met her throat. In addition to the dog tags that jingled occasionally underneath her blouse, the private investigator customarily wore a black velvet band choker. She displayed great affection for Sidney constantly, despite his love for another woman, and her worry for his plight was so genuine that Sidney wanted to hug her fiercely in gratitude. Outside of the office, Sidney Geeder was quiet and resolute, resting for the next day's hypocrisies, and he liked that around her he didn't feel pressure to show off his intelligence or manhood. Now she was telling him that like Ivana Perkova, she had to back off. She wouldn't see him anymore, and in a corny way it broke Sid's heart. He had all the money in the world, but right now it wasn't money that he needed. The firm had no morals, no qualms about interfering in the affairs of an employee's heart. Sidney Geeder was just another firm asset that required shrewd and dispassionate management like all its other assets.

The Atlantic Pacific Corporation had over $7 billion in accumulated capital, which it leveraged into $130 billion in measurable assets. Assets were broken into the categories of current, long-term, and fixed, which included various unmeasurable intangible assets. As was the case with all financial institutions, almost all of its $130 billion was in the current category, consisting of thousands of contracts to sell bonds paired off against liabilities to buy those very same bonds. The corporation's goal was to remain as liquid as possible in order to remain flexible and respond to the opportunities and impasses of the market. It avoided purchasing any office buildings other than its 49th Street Manhattan tower, preferring short-term leases. It didn't buy cars for its executives or even country club memberships, preferring annual cash bonuses. A salesman could be fired without notice and even without cause, which was the risk salespeople took in order to be paid so highly. All of the offices, despite their lavishness, were still as cookie-cutter as a motel chain—no tolerance was permitted in carpeting, wallboardings, chairs, light fixtures, telephones, or desks. Atlantic Pacific could liquidate an office or erase a department or sever a portfolio in a matter of hours, and therefore it was a perfect corporate warrior.

Despite the enormousness of these measurable financial assets, the real engine of the firm was in its intangible assets, including its reputation for innovation, its network of contacts in Washington, and above all the know-how of its employees, without which the firm could not operate. The firm strategized incessantly to milk its employees' brainpower while simultaneously keeping them so strung out, addicted, and off-kilter that they didn't know how valuable they had become. In order to ensure a constant supply of talent to replace burned-out employees, the corporation raided the most esteemed graduate schools for their most honored students, promised them a chance to prove themselves quickly, and fed them into a mill. Various standardized tests ascertained a minimum standard, then various unstandardized tests sifted for those with the natural skills of investment banking. Among the standardized tests were the Scholastic Aptitude Test, the General Management Aptitude Test, the Series 7 general securities license, the Series 63 options license, a National Association of Securities Dealers and Exchanges background check, an internal surveillance security clearance, and a lie detector test given every other year, in which the salespeople were asked to testify that they hadn't illicitly sold confidential corporate information. Among the unstandardized tests were the Freddie Mac Adjustables, the Euro-Floaters, the Resolutions, the Romanians, and the Lincoln Convertibles, which was the big new deal that had something to do with the Dominican Republic. So when the corporate legal department found out that Eggs Igino, who had passed all of these tests with ease, had skipped out on his implicit promise to hang around long enough to collect the $60,000 the firm owed him, they took the position that Eggs Igino had stolen one of the firm's most valuable intangible assets, and they put out a warrant for his arrest. It was all fine and good that top brass put out the word that Eggs Igino was on an undercover mission in Santo Domingo, but if you looked at it with a perverted legal mind-set, Eggs Igino could be considered to have broken the law, and the law had to be enforced. So they called in Stormin' Norman Walker, the lawyer for the San Francisco salesforce, and got copies of all paperwork concerning Eggs Igino, Inc., which was a wholly owned subsidiary of the Mark Igino Corporation, established to avoid paying California sales tax on the breakfasts he had delivered out onto the floor. One unit of the Atlantic

Pacific legal department was all for attempting a hostile takeover of Eggs Igino, Inc., by snatching up his single share of stock, but that would require approval from the attorneys general of California and New York. Another unit attempted to push Eggs Igino, Inc., into involuntary Chapter 7 receivership by virtue of its failure to show up and collect the $60,000 that it was owed. But then it was surprisingly discovered by a top-notch anal-retentive associate that none of the paperwork regarding the Mark Igino Corporation or Eggs Igino, Inc., had ever actually been signed by Eggs Igino. For a few minutes, as the word spread through the mahogany-walled corridors of the department, there were great sighs of relief and shouts of celebration, but then another hotshot associate looking for a promotion asked the obvious question of whether the Mark Igino Corporation existed if its paperwork hadn't been signed. But of course it existed, because while everyone stood around the conference table with brows furrowed, Stormin' Norman Walker pulled out his gold Cross pen and signed his own name in the blanks at the bottom of every page. Suddenly, just like that, Stormin' Norman Walker was the chairman of the board, chief executive officer, and sole shareholder of the Mark Igino Corporation and all of its subsidiaries.

"I *own* him," Stormin' Norman grinned in a bastardly way that caused a ripple of applause to circle the room. They had done it! Now Eggs Igino was a mere employee of Eggs Igino, Inc., and was completely in their control. Stormin' Norman Walker, in his first action as chief executive, drew up the board resolution to send its one employee, Mr. Mark Igino, on a top-secret financial recon mission to Santo Domingo. Now Eggs Igino really *was* in the Dominican Republic, and they had the paperwork to prove it in case Sidney Geeder or anyone else doubted it.

"That's pretty dangerous, isn't it?" Nickel Sansome wondered aloud, as he stood by the coffee machine watching the door for any sign of Coyote Jack. "I mean, the *Dominican Republic*. I can think of a lot safer places to be."

Sue Marino was digging through the cupboards, hoping to find some microwavable popcorn or anything else she could eat. "Oh, it couldn't be *that* dangerous. This is finance, not gunrunning. He's probably in the basement vault of some offshore bank, poring through transaction ledgers, plugging away on an adding machine."

"Sure, but there's practically a revolution going on in the Dominican Republic. Aren't there all these militarized factions fighting for power? Heck, you'd never catch me going to Santo Domingo. No fucking way."

"That's why he's Eggs Igino. He's not afraid of anything." Sue Marino got a dreamy look in her eyes.

"He was a genius, all right," Nickel Sansome tittered anxiously.

"With nice legs," Sue Marino added, lusciously turning her shoulders away from the cupboard.

"All I remember was his hair," Nickel admitted ponderously, looking at the reflection of his own wispy tufts in the glass of the microwave door.

"I've been using his parking place in the garage," Sue Marino confessed. "Just until he gets back."

"And I've been using his watch," Nickel acknowledged, pulling up his left sleeve to show the gold corporate timepiece the firm had awarded Igino. "I found it in his desk."

"I just hope Eggs gets back soon. We need him here to pull us through the deal."

The government of the Dominican Republic, which had transferred hands many times in the previous twenty years and was currently controlled by the head of the military, had real assets of over $7 billion, which was minuscule for a government but pretty good-sized for a nonservice corporation. The Dominican Republic was about as big as John Deere, the tractor company, or Weyerhauser, the lumber company. Among these real assets were the capitol building in Santo Domingo, the treasury and all of its currency-printing facilities, several bridges, all of the roads (which were in grave disrepair and grossly overvalued on Dominican Republic financial statements submitted to the World Bank), some sugar plantations from the days of nationalization in the early part of the century, all of the minerals in the soil on that land, all of the fish within six miles of the shoreline, some beaches, and all of the military weaponry, vehicles, and ammunition that hadn't already been consumed in the various coups d'état and attempted coups d'état in the past twenty years. Against those fixed, unsellable assets, the government of the Dominican Republic owed the World Bank $1.5 billion, the International Monetary Fund $800 million, the United States government $600 million (and unpaid customs duties going back sixty-five years), and a consortium of U.S. money banks $900 million, which it had lent to them in the mid-eighties at the urging of President Reagan.

In short, the Dominican Republic had the assets to cover the liabilities, but it just wasn't liquid: it couldn't turn those assets into cash. This was preventing it from getting *more* loans that it couldn't pay back. Nobody had ever really tried to collect on the loans very hard. Heck, it was a foreign government: what could be done—invade with a military and seize the assets? Such an action would be an act of war, and require the sanction of Congress and the United Nations. Those money banks that got stiffed nearly a billion bucks were out of luck, at least until Atlantic Pacific got the idea of putting all those bad loans together in a syndicate and selling them to a shell company from Delaware called New Lincoln, Inc. New Lincoln was going to purchase the bad loans with money it raised in the bond market. The salesmen were going to sell convertible bonds for New Lincoln, Inc. That's all the salesmen knew so far, but they were sufficiently entertained by the idea that they would be selling Lincoln Convertibles. It was an idea rife with metaphor, and the salesmen had a ball making jokes about test drives, plaid suits, and car bombs.

"It's not funny," Sid Geeder protested, when everyone started chuckling during the morning briefing after Coyote Jack promised that the Lincoln Convertibles had chrome trim, whitewall tires, and leather upholstery.

"Stop laughing!" he grunted, elbowing Paul DeShews in the ribs. "We don't know anything about these bonds!"

"Shut up, Geeder!" Coyote Jack snapped, glowering across the table in disgust at Geeder's liberal whimpering.

Sidney put a lid on it for the rest of the sales meeting, hovering over his thermos of coffee, forcefully breathing through clenched teeth as the caffeine gurgled in his empty stomach.

Atlantic Pacific might have already taken over and sold for scrap every possible corporation in the 1980s, but it had found something else to take over, such as small Caribbean countries. With the military getting involved in economics and entertainment, it made perfect sense for the investment banks to dabble in conventional warfare. As the salesforce slowly learned, New Lincoln, Inc. was partially owned by a consortium of military contractors who had far more missiles and attack vehicles than could reasonably be used by the U.S. government. They intended to foreclose on the Dominican Republic's bad debts and take control of the assets of the Dominican government. As a Delaware corporation, the Dominican Republic would then fall under the jurisdiction of Delaware corporate law. The firm was very cagey in describing this to the salesforce, who sometimes couldn't be sure if it wasn't a bad joke. When they realized that it wasn't a joke at all, Sidney Geeder balked. The Dominican Republic was a country, for god's sakes, and Sidney just wanted it left alone. When too many salesmen balked at the intent to sell the bonds, Coyote Jack just raised the commissions until enough salesmen fell in line to create a critical mass that swept up even the stragglers. There was always a price at which the salesmen would sell. There was a market for their better intentions, a market that suffered jolts of greed that were countered by sieges of guilt, leading to forays of independence that were met with escalades of peer pressure.

"They haven't done any good governing themselves," Coyote Jack yammered meanly to Sidney Geeder later that day. "The place is a shambles. AIDS is rampant, the forests are destroyed, corruption is everywhere. I can't even keep track of who's in charge now. The only reason we don't hear about it is their troubles are overshadowed by Haiti. They can't do any worse under Delaware law than they've done under self-rule."

Sid Geeder dropped his head. "It's a *country*! They're a democracy! You can't interfere with it!"

"We'll have elections," Coyote Jack countered. "It'll be a perfectly democratic election of the board of directors. One vote per share."

"One vote per *share*? One vote per *share*? You gotta be kidding! What about one vote per *person*?"

"Per person? Boy, Sid, that's not the way corporations work. The shareholders vote by proxy for the board of directors, who elect a CEO. It's really a lot cleaner than government, with all that congress/president/constitution bullshit. Governments are broke. If they ran the Dominican Republic like a corporation, it wouldn't be in such deep shit. We're going to put capitalism to work down there, turn it around, and then sell it. We'll make a killing."

Sidney clenched his fists. "And what's next? Honduras? Samoa? Tahiti? Mexico?"

"Sure, why not?" Coyote Jack asked. He was bored. "Government is really obsolete as a means of management. They're frozen by gridlock. In a few years, the world is going to thank us for getting rid of government. Governments played a useful role in civilization for a few thousand years, but they're like the slide rule. We don't need them anymore."

"You can't be serious?" Sidney said. "We're just going to point missiles at the capitol building and tell them to come out with their hands up?"

"We'll be heroes," Coyote Jack beamed. "I hear the citizens really hate this tyrant they've got. Boy, will he ever be surprised."

"It's illegal!" Sidney wailed. "It's an act of war! The United Nations will never allow it."

"Quit whining, Geeder. You're getting on my nerves. You'll sell your quota in half an hour, then be done with it."

"I don't want a quota," Sidney said anxiously. "I'm laying low for the next fifty-three days. I'm not taking any more risks. You can do it without me."

"Get off your high horse. Quit making such a big deal about it. Remember the Third Law of Information Economics."

"What's that? The *Third Law*?" Sidney asked.

Coyote Jack cleared his throat. " 'We're all working temp jobs.' You, too, Geeder: a temp job. So do what you're told."

"A temp job? Christ, Coyote, I've worked here five years. Where did you hear a cockamamy idea like that?"

"Eggs Igino, the horse's mouth. The Laws of Economics don't lie. Your stay on earth is brief, Sid."

"So is yours!"

"Exactly. That's why I don't pass judgment over these Lincoln Convertibles. Don't be so prejudiced."

Sidney shook his head adamantly. "I'm skipping this deal."

"Don't even think about it."

"What if I'm sick that day? What if I have the flu? No big deal."

Coyote Jack's face was stone. "Skip this deal and you're out on the street."

"You can't fire me. You need me for the Sprint deal, and then the Canadian Petroleum deal."

"Why do we need you? Everyone wants to invest in Romania now. A rhesus monkey could sell those Sprints. You son of a bitch, Geeder. Do you really think we're going to let a tiny little sprocket like you bring us to a halt? You've really got a fucking big head, you know that? One hell of an ego. You think I need you? I can fire you right now and have another warm body in your seat tomorrow. I can get any kind I want. We've got salespeople on the back burner all over the world. I can put a lesbian Creole paraplegic there, if I thought she'd move the Lincoln Convertibles. Now you get out of my fucking office and think it over for a while, and you think hard about how come I'm sitting here as sales manager and you're sitting there eating shit on the phone all day."

Sidney scrambled for a defense. "You can't fire me for getting the flu. That's illegal."

Coyote Jack smirked, then clucked his tongue and leaned back in his chair, sliding his fingers up and down his suspender straps. A wide grin came over his face. "You're really thinking about it, aren't you?" he asked. "You're thinking of calling in sick."

"I'm thinking about it," Sid answered somewhat defiantly.

"You would do that? Over just these bonds?" Coyote Jack pressed.

"I might," Sidney repeated less affirmatively.

"You would just stay home, hang out in bed with your girlfriend, watch soap operas and drink ginger ale and stuff your mouth with saltines? The whole long, excruciatingly boring day? No way. You'd never make it. You'd last two hours."

"I'd last the whole day. I mean it, Coyote: I'm not selling these bonds."

"You really want me to let you skip them?"

"Yes. Yes I do."

"In that case, I think I should double your quota. You never learn, do you, Geeder? The same thing happens every time. For being such a smart aleck, you're really an idiot."

"Thank you, Coyote. I really appreciate the encouragement and your esteemed opinion."

"Get this, Geeder. Unless you're going to quit, you're going to do everything I tell you. You're going to be a loyal foot soldier to the end. You're going to sell these bonds just like you sold every other bond. Lather. Rinse. Repeat. You hear me? Now get out of my office, Geeder. Go back to work, and that's an order."

But Sid couldn't go back to work, and instead he ran out of the office and sped across the sales floor to his desk, where he hid in the crawl space until three o'clock, at which point he jumped in his pickup and drove across the city to City Hall, where he stormed into the district attorney's office and fell in love again.

Sid Geeder had run away to the assistant district attorney that he used to date in order to discuss with her whether anything could be done about the firm's payoff to Ivana Perkova and the private investigator. The assistant district attorney was beautiful, but she was also an uptight professional woman constantly on a diet and too embroiled in the politics of being promoted to associate district attorney for Sidney Geeder to fall in love with her. Sid Geeder loved to eat and he hated to talk about work, while she was the exact opposite. When they had dated in the past, they had done nothing exceptional. They ate at the finest restaurants, chatted amicably about criminal procedure and the Fourth Amendment, went for a stroll through the streets of his neighborhood, and then eased their way noncommittally into his bedroom, where they had sex without pinching, moaning, swearing, slapping, sweating, or rolling off the bed. The assistant district attorney had a hard, skinny body with very little to grab onto. She had shiny straight blond hair that she knotted behind her head before getting into bed. She was taller than Sid by an inch, and they refrained from gazing penetratingly into each other's eyes. Afterward, Sidney avoided asking any questions that might endear her to him, such as what her family had done on Sundays growing up or if she had owned any pets or if she'd ever been married.

He was never at risk of falling in love until the day he ran into

her office howling about the Lincoln Convertibles right when the
assistant district attorney had been burned by interoffice politics
and needed an escape. They picked up a bottle and drove down the
peninsula carelessly in Sidney's pickup, with the windows rolled
down so their angry shouts were lifted away by the oncoming air.
She compared interoffice politics to the time the neighborhood
boys had once cheated her in a spontaneous game of strip poker.
They had each previously put on ten pairs of underwear, and every
time she thought she was going to win, another pair of briefs was
underneath. Sid Geeder laughed at that and howled some more
into the wind. They stopped to get gas thirty miles south of the city
and ended up playing putt-putt golf at a theme park across from
the gas station. On the second tee the assistant district attorney
challenged Sidney to a match of strip golf, and Sidney, quickly
counting the pieces of his attire, felt his heart go. By the sixteenth
green, when they were ordered unkindly to leave, he was down to
his pants and she had to sink a bank shot around a water trap to
keep her camisole and half-slip. An hour later, they were at the
door of her house, where three scrappy mutts leaped on his leg and
sniffed his hand and licked the wax from his shoes and chewed on
his pant leg. They went across the street to throw a Frisbee for the
dogs, and when they returned to the house they resumed strip golf
with her ex-husband's Pro-Staffs and neon-orange balls, creating
impossible holes down staircases and under couches and banking
around the toilet. The game went on titillatingly, long past the
point of nakedness, until they finally went weak and attacked each
other on a pile of dirty laundry beside the washer-dryer set in the
basement, swearing and sweating and going miserable with love.

"So did you love her?" the assistant district attorney asked, leaning up on her elbow, after Sid had explained how the firm had paid
off the private investigator.

"I don't see how that has anything to do with it."

The assistant district attorney nuzzled herself into Sid's chest.
"Oh, it has everything to do with it, doesn't it? You want me to
help you rescue your lovers from their own greed? I think I'd prefer
if they stayed away from you."

"But you have to do something," Sid argued.

"Why?"

"Because it's your job!"

"Oh, now I see why you came to see me. You're not interested in me at all," she said, making a fuss and rolling away from him. "Well, you could have said something about this *before* we made love, don't you think? Or were you just trying to soften me up?" She looked over her shoulder at him, her face a sour frown.

"Please, please," Sid begged. "Look, they're friends of mine, and the company is overstepping its role, and it's scaring me. I just want to get Atlantic Pacific out of my life! They have no business watching over me like I'm some federal witness—I just want to go to work in the morning, come home at night, and have the rest of the day to myself!"

"Why don't you just quit?"

"Because it's not fair, that's why! They're not going to beat me."

"Do you think they *want* you to quit?"

"Probably. If I last nine more weeks, then they owe me about four million dollars. But they need me, too, particularly with Eggs Igino gone."

"*Four million!* My god! That's so much money! Why don't you just shut up and do what they say and get your money? Then I'll help you find anything you want."

"I'm not going to shut up! I have rights!"

"Sure, but wow, why risk the money? You're crazy, Sid. If I were you, I'd just take a backseat and cruise for a while."

"Of course I'm crazy! You'd be crazy too if your employer was snooping on your phone calls, stealing your medical files, and paying off your boyfriends! If I wasn't crazy after all this, then I'd really be worried about myself. Going crazy is the only sane reaction to all that's happened."

"It's worth it, though. I mean, four *million*. Wow. What are you ever going to do with all that money?"

"I don't have the faintest idea," Sid said. "It's not that much, really."

"Surely you must have some plans?"

Sid shook his head. He didn't think the money was the point.

"I can't quite figure you, Sid. It doesn't really make sense that you'd be selling money for all these years, waiting for your payoff, but now that you're close you don't really care."

"Of course I don't make sense! Not making sense is the only sensible way to behave. Crap. And I thought you would help me."

"I *am* helping you. I'm trying to help you realize that your firm is a huge multinational financial conglomerate deep in cahoots with every agency of the government and every corporation in the Fortune 500. You can't fight them, and if they're offering you four million dollars, then I'm going to try to help you reach out and take it."

Sid rolled on his back and contemplated what she was saying. "They offered Wes Griffin four million too, but he never made it. They sent him to the firm shrink, who somehow convinced him to quit early."

After one too many trips to Helmet Fisher, Wes Griffin had retired to his suburban garage and spent his days fine-tuning the contact point dwell angle on his classic '72 350 GTO. He was thirty-four, a millionaire, and suffering bouts of powerlessness, which he tried to overcome by racing the rural blacktops in the East Bay at night. He still woke at 3:45 A.M. as he had done for four and a half years at Atlantic Pacific. He opened the garage by hand so as not to wake his wife. The roads were slick with dew, but they were empty of traffic. He gunned out toward the Central Valley or the Sacramento Delta, testing the suspension in the curves, hitting top speeds when the roads straightened. It wasn't a very fast car, because Wes had geared it for acceleration. Wes got to know all the county police officers when they took him in to the courthouse. He sat in the front seat with them, chatting about the stresses of life. Wes paid his fines and was back out on the road a few days later. Eventually, the police just ignored him as long as he stayed out of residential areas and slowed down near farms. Wes Griffin was a tall, wiry man with a thick neck, sloped shoulders, and a mane of glossy blond hair. He had been the King of Mortgages during the CMO craze in the late eighties, when the yield curve was steep and the market was gullible for high-concept bonds. CMOs, or collateralized mortgage obligations, were pools of mortgages that were cut into new cash streams to make them perform differently from mortgages. According to Sid Geeder, mortgages were like zucchini in the late summer: coming out the ears. In order to keep prices up, Atlantic Pacific found dozens of recipes for its mortgages, the financial equivalents of zucchini bread, zucchini soup, zucchini tortillas, et cetera, which it tried to palm off on the markets. Wes Griffin was the green thumb. He was the corner grocer, sitting there at his desk, grinning at nature's bounty. Mother Earth had given him many gullible customers who were crazy to own the next new thing. "Stealing candy from a baby," he used to smack, until he went to see Helmet Fisher for his wandering eye and ended up taking apart the engine on his car.

"I always wanted to learn more about engines," Wes Griffin had murmured in a monotone, vacuous inflection that made him seem as hollow as a ghost. He had stood at the window, staring. "It's time I really devoted myself to what truly interests me."

"That's a bunch of crap," Sidney Geeder had countered. "Engines just sound good after four and a half years working on intangible numbers. Their physicality appeals to you, oil dripping and parts connecting. You're fantasizing. You're projecting. You'd be bored stiff."

"I really want to take the engine apart. I want to take it apart and put it back together. I think it's a good way to get my life in order."

"Your life will still be as fucked up after you reassemble a car engine as it was before you took it apart. Helmet Fisher has got you trusting words again. Watch out: words are how you sold the Euro-Floaters."

"He fixed my wandering eye."

"So why do you want to quit? Your eye's fine now. You've got six months."

Wes was still subdued and distant. "I don't want it to start wandering again. It's scary, Sid. Lots of people have bad backs. Not many people's eye starts darting about in its socket."

That was nine months ago, and Wes Griffin's eye was steady on the double yellow line dividing the county highways. When Coyote Jack invited him to come in for lunch, his wife had begged him not to go. She'd never trusted Coyote Jack, and knew he was up to something. But Wes Griffin wanted to brag about the 82 he'd shot at the Pleasanton Country Club, and his behind-the-dugout box seats at Oakland A's day games. Wes wanted to show off his suntan and the shine to his blond hair and the muscles in his forearms.

Wes Griffin was a multimillionaire who only felt powerful around other millionaires, and so he drove down to the office, took Eggs Igino's parking spot, and came into the office through the main entrance on the forty-first floor.

"Uh-oh," Nickel Sansome sirened, when he saw Wes strolling down the aisle with Coyote Jack. "The kiss of death is here."

"What's the matter?" Sue Marino asked, looking up from a list she was making of the assets and liabilities of being married.

"He's bad luck. He's contagious. Stay away." Nickel grabbed a stack of research reports and hustled off to hide in the bathroom.

"I don't get it," Sue Marino said, turning to Paul DeShews. "Why is Nickel so afraid of Wes Griffin?"

"Wes Griffin's here?" Paul DeShews remarked with a sudden panic. He glanced around until he saw him chatting with Coyote Jack and Sidney Geeder. Paul DeShews grabbed his phone and dove into a crouch, covering his face as if he were making a pivotal sale.

"Why is everyone avoiding Wes Griffin?" Sue Marino implored Nelson Dicky, who sat calmly in his chair.

"It's just pagan superstition," Nelson explained, brushing away his fears. "It's considered bad luck to come in contact with someone who's gone to hell. They're like vampires. But, hey—who believes it? Not me."

"Me neither," Sue agreed, standing close to Nelson for protection.

"It's self-fulfilling," Nelson went on. "If you believe it, you're hexed. Carol Manning believed it, and look at her."

"Who's Carol Manning?"

"She was the token woman before Lisa Lisa. She got pregnant and went to the clinic for a checkup sometime in the second trimester, and Antonia Zennario was chained to a fire hydrant on the sidewalk, protesting with the Mothers for Life Coalition."

"Who was Antonia Zennario?"

"She was the token woman before Carol Manning."

"What happened to Carol Manning?"

"Miscarried," Nelson answered.

"She *miscarried*?" Sue Marino repeated in a surprised tone. Nelson was firm. "Right then and there."

"And she quit?"

"Yup. Went straight to hell. Could barely work. Finally John White put her to sleep."

"What does that mean?!"

"Like a racehorse."

"What's like a racehorse?" Coyote Jack interrupted, introducing Wes to them.

Nelson turned and improvised. "My oldest son. Thirteen years old, a natural point guard. Can run forever."

"Wes here shot an eight-eight-eighty-eighty-two at Pleasanton," Coyote Jack countered. "Which hole was that eagle, Wes?"

Wes looked down at his shoes uncomfortably. His shoulders ached and his eyes skirted the sales floor nervously. "Fifteen," he responded finally.

"A dogleg," Coyote Jack said proudly. "Think of that, huh, Nelson? Retirement doesn't sound so bad."

"Doesn't sound bad at all," Nelson lied. "Heck, I'd retire if I could just hit a green in two."

Wes started to stammer and then stopped.

"What was that, Wes?" Coyote Jack beckoned gruffly, slapping Wes on the back.

"You have to retire first," Wes clarified meekly. "Then you start to hit the greens."

Nelson laughed as if it were a joke, and then Coyote Jack laughed too. "Well, I guess I won't be hitting greens for a while," Nelson chuckled, looking at Coyote Jack knowingly.

"Let's go bug Jack White," Coyote Jack suggested, ushering Wes Griffin off the floor and down the corridor of offices.

"See?" Nelson Dicky remarked to Sue Marino after they had strolled out of earshot. "Was I struck by lightning? Did my tongue swell up and clog my throat? Black-magic nonsense. Wes Griffin's just an ordinary guy."

"Luck has nothing to do with this job," Sue Marino observed. "We're too smart to be victims of bad luck."

"You got it," Nelson Dicky affirmed.

"We're Atlantic Pacific," Sue Marino puffed, heading back to her desk. "We're top dog," she continued, then answered her phone and fell into miserable despair when Stormin' Norman

Walker informed her that he had received notice from her fiancé's lawyer that her fiancé was pulling out of the proposed merger of his limited partnership and her corporation.

"What are you trying to tell me?" Sue Marino cried.

"He's not going to marry you."

"He's not?"

"He says you're not the person he proposed to in Scotland. You're lucky he's not suing you for misrepresentation."

For months, Stormin' Norman Walker and her fiancé's lawyer had been arguing over the arrangements of a prenuptial agreement. Eventually they concluded that family law was much too limiting, and they should merge their corporations rather than actually get married, keeping their partnership in the more flexible domain of corporate law. There was a long list of tax writeoffs for acquiring a company but practically none at all for marrying a man. And in case anything went wrong with their relationship, it was much easier to break apart two corporations than to go through the messy legal hassles of divorce. But in the meantime, Sue Marino's obstetrician boyfriend had come to the conclusion that he was making a big, big mistake in getting involved with a bond sales-woman. Norman Walker's only advice was that she hang out with her friends that evening.

"What friends?" Sue Marino demanded angrily. "Who has friends?"

"Well, then go out on a date," Norman Walker suggested in his throaty, phlegmy voice.

"With who?" Sue Marino screamed, tossing the phone into the garbage pail below her desk and heading off toward the bathroom.

Then the rumors began. Nickel Sansome overheard Sue on the phone with Norman Walker. Nickel Sansome was so struck with compassion for her plight that he mercifully phoned the corporate desk in New York and informed the cocky AA industrials trader that Sue Marino was hard up and needed some action. The cocky AA industrials trader spread the word around the corporate desk, whence it leaked onto the Miami sales floor, then spread to the Cayman Island wire room, causing a twenty-nine-year-old money market salesman who had gone through training with Sue Marino suddenly to remember her hoarse cowgirl hey-y'alls and sweet giggles, her shiny chocolate hair and the flowered print dresses with a long slit that had kept him distracted from Weston Bank's lectures all summer. He called friends in the London Eurobond market, where the rumor flew through a sales manager in Paris to a managing director in Bonn who was still hanging out at the office late at night worrying how to keep his job after the Germans ignored the Romanians and threatened to ignore every other Romanian-related deal coming down the pipes. He was glad for the interruption and got out the trainee directory from two years previous, which had a picture of Sue Marino taken on the back porch of her parents' ranch in Casper, Wyoming. She was young and buoyant and it thrilled the Bonn managing director to think that she needed a great fuck to get her mind off her ex-fiancé. He knew a salesman in Singapore who spent a lot of time with exotic prostitutes in Thailand and was just coming in to work for the morning, but since the Singapore salesman had no plans to come to the West Coast, he called the treasury bond trader in Tokyo, who often did. The treasury bond trader called the Los Angeles desk to ask if it was true that this woman in San Francisco was a real looker and whether he should book a flight, but the people at the Los Angeles desk were too curious, so they called Dave Rennaker on the San Francisco equities desk to ask if it was true what they had heard, that Sue Marino was single again and needed a date for the evening.

"That's news to me," Dave Rennaker admitted. He looked across the sales floor at Sue Marino, who was just coming in from the bathroom. She fell down onto her chair despondently and reached into her garbage can and fished out her telephone. "She sure looks upset, though."

"Go get her, stud," the Los Angeles desk urged him on in unison. "Make her forget her fiancé."

Dave Rennaker only scoffed at the thought. "Never wipe your butt with your eating hand," he warned them. "Never piss in your drinking water."

"Aww, c'mon. You're equities, she's mortgages—that's not inbreeding."

"It's bad luck."

"Hey, speaking of bad luck, is it true what we hear?"

"What's that?"

"About Wes Griffin."

"What about him?"

"Coyote Jack wants to bring him back. An encore perform-ance."

"Is he really coming back?" Dave Rennaker said, approaching Sidney Geeder's desk carefully.

Sidney held Wes Griffin's old field binoculars up to his eyes as he peered through Coyote Jack's fishbowl window and tried in vain to read John White's lips. Wes was scrunched up in his chair. Sid could see the individual beads of sweat forming at his hairline. Wes's eyes jittered back and forth from John White to Coyote Jack and then out onto the sales floor.

"I can't tell," Sidney said.

"That's really pathetic, trying to yank a guy out of retirement. Let him rest in peace, why don't they?"

"Robbing the grave," Sidney agreed. "Merciless."

"He doesn't look too good."

"He's the walking dead. Take a good look—we'll all end up that way one day." Sid held out the binoculars.

"Not me," Dave Rennaker said proudly, thumping his chest. "I'm getting out clean."

"That's what Wes Griffin used to say. Then his right eye went goofy."

Sidney, now bored with snooping on their meeting, swung the binoculars around to Coyote Jack's secretary, who was coming down the hallway waving a piece of fax paper, and settled on her great motherly breasts, the image of which filled Sid with a sudden pang of longing for the assistant district attorney's slender body. She stopped at Coyote Jack's office and knocked on the door ur-gently, and then to Sid's surprise she burst in on their meeting. He watched as Coyote Jack jumped out of his chair in rage and let fly a barrage of insults. Coyote Jack's secretary cowered and then turned to John White, handing him the piece of fax paper as she slipped back out into the hallway. She ran down to her desk and fell over the desktop in a defeated and sorrowful heap. John White stared at the piece of fax paper for a while, muttering to himself, and then he passed it to Coyote Jack as he slipped out into the hallway and ran down to his office, where he fell onto his couch in a miserable lump. Coyote Jack scanned the page with his eyebrows raised and his eyes bugging out. Wes Griffin said something to him, but Coyote Jack didn't answer. Finally, Coyote Jack struggled out of his chair and wearily tromped out of his office and down the hallway to his secretary's desk. He handed the piece of paper back to her and pointed across the sales floor to the copy room. Brushing back her tears with a tissue, Coyote Jack's secretary pinched the awful piece of paper between her fingertips and carried it in front of her as she crossed the sales floor and descended the opposite corridor to the monster photocopier.

"All right, what the hell's going on?" Sidney Geeder demanded, popping into the copy room just behind her and slamming the door shut.

"Oh, Sid!" she cried, turning to hug Sid and pout on his shoulder. "They've captured Eggs Igino!"

"There there," Sid said, patting her on the back and brushing down wisps of her hair that tickled his nostrils. "We were bound to find him sooner or later," he assured her.

"But they've got him first!" she wailed.

"Who's *they*?"

Her head shook with sobs. "I knew we never should have sent him to Santo Domingo."

Sidney pushed her away and held her by the shoulders. "All right, pull yourself together. Now who in the hell has found Eggs Igino?"

"The Dominicans!"

"The *Dominicans*?" Sidney repeated in disbelief.

"He's been kidnapped!" she sniffled, thrusting into Sidney's hands the sheet of fax paper, which was on the letterhead of the Dominican Liberation Party and stated that they had captured the famous financier Mr. Mark Igino and would return him only if Atlantic Pacific ceased its attempt to turn the Dominican Republic into a Delaware corporation.

"They're fighting back!" Coyote Jack's secretary screamed.

"I find this hard to believe," Sid muttered, reading the fax over and over again.

But *The Wall Street Journal,* which had already been leaked that

Eggs Igino was on a recon mission in Santo Domingo, found it quite easy to believe that a group of militant Dominican nationalists known for their car bombs and strongarm tactics would kidnap Atlantic Pacific's most promising young salesman. Considering how much high finance had meddled in international politics over the years, it made perfect sense that someone had finally decided to fight back. And it was impossible to keep the *Journal* from hearing that Eggs Igino had been kidnapped once Sid Geeder notified all the salespeople in the Atlantic Pacific offices around the world. Sidney Geeder wasn't really sure what to believe, but if spreading the rumor would derail the Lincoln Convertible deal, then he was all for it and thought it was part of his patriotic duty to fax the ransom note to every number on the speed dial. In just a few days the entire financial machinery of the Atlantic Pacific Corporation nearly stalled as every conceivable meeting was held and every relevant government agency was called in for a briefing. Atlantic Pacific had come across all sorts of methods of blocking a takeover—golden parachutes, greenmail, nonvoting stock—but this was hitting below the belt. The surveillance department and the SEC and the FDIC were well equipped to crack down on white-collar criminals, but they didn't have the faintest idea what to do about people with guns.

13 · Patriotism

THE FINANCIAL MARKETS had replaced elections as the barometer of the country's mood. The financial markets were a constant, real-time, reliable national opinion poll about the state of the economy and the plight of the common shareholder. Democracy was indeed an obsolete form of management, and time and again the American public had voted for less of its tiresome workings. In its place they proposed the orthodoxy of Capitalism, and they rallied for their cause like devout patriots. The principle of free trade gave the average investor something to shout about, and like all mass movements it made the oxymoronic promise that it would fill their personal, individual pocketbooks. In Capitalist ideology, inefficiency was the greatest sin and needed to be exorcised from the economy via a stiff dose of competition. The followers were riled up and looking for a good fight. Rather than causing a collective scare, the boldness of the Dominican Liberation Party merely raised the firm's hackles and further entrenched the top brass in its firm belief that the Dominican Republic should be rescued from government. Hell, the French sold us Louisiana and the Russians sold us Alaska—what was so strange about the Dominicans selling us their country at a discount? Those ungrateful squirts deserved to be taken over. What did that unmanaged band of undercapitalized military guerrillas think it was doing, taking on a rich multinational corporation and a storm of market opinion? The Atlantic Pacific Corporation printed up millions of red, white, and blue bumper stickers that said "One Vote per Share" and stuffed them inside the Monday edition of the *Institutional Investor*. Then it manufactured hundreds of thousands of sturdy silk flag sticks that flew the corporate logo of New Lincoln, Inc., several of which got planted along the mortgage desk in San Francisco in an attempt to inspire the salesforce to sell the heck out of these bonds for the good of the country. The firm was dreadfully sorry that Eggs Igino had to be sacrificed, but they refused to negotiate with terrorists, and it was Eggs Igino's patriotic part to die a martyr for the good of the market.

Besides, it turned out that he wasn't irreplaceable after all, because in the training program they found a red-cheeked, innocent-looking goofus with fat jowls, naive grin, and wiry hair that sort of looked a whole lot like Eggs Igino. The next day he was sitting in Eggs Igino's chair looking overly civic-minded and enthused. Sidney Geeder ignored him and tried not to watch as he obediently wrote down every last irrelevant detail that was announced over the squawk box by traders hoping to be heard by some bone-headed salesman out there in the universe stupid enough to listen. The goofus had no idea what was important and what was inconsequential, and Sidney could tell just from looking at his buck teeth that he would never think for himself. He wouldn't last two years, and Sidney Geeder had the irresistible urge to go kick his teeth in, just to smarten him up. Sidney watched in astonished amazement for a while until he couldn't stand it any longer and curled his upper lip back so his teeth hung down like buck teeth. He flared his nostrils and furled his forehead in mock concentration. He stood that way for a while, leaning over the goofus, but the kid didn't even notice. Then Sidney dug into Eggs Igino's file drawer and found the sack of strawberry danishes. He began to attack it voraciously, spilling crumbs onto the kid's trading notebook and almost dumping them into his hair.

"Hey," Sidney interrupted. "Hey, kid. You hungry?"

The kid looked up. "I ate before I came to work."

"But this is strawberry."

"No it's not. It's just a dab of red-dyed glycerin, flavored with a squirt of strawberry oil. And that danish is baked with unrefined animal fats. Those molasses-tasting crumb nuts sprinkled on top are just raw sugar stirred in coconut oil. You're that much closer to the grave with every bite." He bent his head and went back to work.

"I wasn't going to give you one anyway," Sidney mumbled, falling back into his seat and grabbing his thermos of coffee. The danishes were always so sweet that he needed to gargle with bitter black coffee immediately after eating them. In truth, he hated strawberry danishes almost as much as cream-cheese ones, and the only reason he still ate them was to keep alive Igino's presence on the floor. But Sid's supply was dwindling, and he wished Eggs had told him who his contact was in New York.

"See, I told you so," Paul DeShews sniggered, warily approaching Sidney's desk an hour later to needle him. He gripped a flag stick in his hand and tauntingly waved it in Sidney Geeder's line of vision. "Ho, ho, you'll really be spreading the gospel now. I know how much it kills you to be an advocate of the American system, but there's nothing like a fat commission to overcome your sense of restraint. Boy, I'd really like to hear it when you swear to your accounts about how the Dominican Republic will be so much better off under Atlantic Pacific rule."

Sidney swatted at the flag, snapping the silk New Lincoln logo back toward Paul's face. "Rule? If you think there's havoc down there now, wait until we take over."

"Not so," Paul continued, undaunted. "We're a terrific role model. This company was built on the backs of those who were willing to fight for the right to make their fortune. We have a long legacy of rescuing people from mismanagement and bureaucracy."

"You expect your accounts to believe that?" Sid shouted. "This deal is doomed."

"Just beautiful," Paul commended. "With that act, I'll bet Coyote Jack will boost the commission in no time."

"You scare me, Goody. You really frighten me. Coyote Jack gives you an order to sell these bonds, and you just salute like one of your micronazi Cub Scouts. Don't you realize that this country is founded on rebellion?"

"No it's not. This country is built on discipline!"

"Discipline?" Sidney mocked a hearty laugh. "Discipline was an idea invented to control boredom."

"I can't believe you have something against discipline! Discipline is everything. Without discipline, you have chaos!"

"And what's wrong with that? Chaos is vastly underrated by the critics, considering how popular and prevalent it is."

"But chaos is—chaos is, well, *chaos*!" Paul howled, crisply snapping his flag stick down on the mahogany trim of Nelson Dicky's desk, nearly crushing one of Nelson's fingers.

But the chaos had only just begun, and it was nothing compared to the bedlam that erupted when a German shepherd was brought onto the floor later that day to sniff for bombs.

"Oh, it's nothing," Coyote Jack yawned. "Just a little bomb scare."

"Don't mind her," John White added, pointing to the dog. "She can work right around you. Go back to work."

But the salespeople couldn't go back to work once they'd heard that a bomb threat had just been faxed in. The German shepherd entered their sales pit and put her snout up to everything, alternating a tinny whine with a low, rumbling growl as she encountered different scents. Her fierce hazel eyes guided her up and down the aisles as Coyote Jack hollered at the sales floor to ignore her and to stay on the phone. It took an hour for the dog to sniff every nook and cranny of all forty foxholes before it moved on to the management offices. The suspense was unbearable, and the salesforce crumbled into nervous maniacs. Several of them hid in the bathrooms, lining up for the stalls. But then the shepherd was escorted in there, too, and the salesforce came stampeding out of the bathrooms like a herd of wild horses and ran into the monster photocopier room, huddling behind the machinery, until the shepherd followed her nose right into that room, too, and the salesforce trampled each other trying to squeeze out the door before they galloped back onto the floor and cowered under their desks, shivering with fear, wondering why there were guards with pistols on their belts attending all the exits.

The guards with pistols on their belts had been posted by John White as a security measure. All incoming phone calls, including those to the fax machines, were set up to be traced. Coyote Jack, John White, and Clark Kalinov were given their own personal fax machines, so they would never interrupt an incoming threat. No nonemployee personnel would be allowed on the floor. Breakfast service was cut off, as was maid service, and soon the salesforce could barely read their trading monitors through the thick layer of dust that clung to their screens. The salespeople kicked up the dust and the air grew dirty, sticking to their sweaty foreheads and causing several of them to sneeze repeatedly. The mahogany oozed Lemon Fresh wax, which, unpolished, turned pale yellow and got on their hands and ended up everywhere. The piles of paper on their desks went unstraightened and soon toppled, causing the nervous salesforce to jump and twirl at the unexpected sound. Every morning, as they came onto the floor, they showed their badges, gave a thumbprint, and scoured their desks for signs that someone had been there during the night. They were afraid to go to the bathroom, or at the end of the day even to leave the building. When Sidney Geeder got home, he went straight to the local tavern to get plastered and carouse with strangers he could trust. Sidney was hopping mad that the firm didn't just forget about the Lincoln Convertibles and go back to its old business of selling straight debt for American industry. He missed the good old days like crazy, when a salesman was just the grease of the financial machine and not such an important cog that he became a target for industrial espionage. The more complex and risky bonds had become over the past ten years, the more fell onto the shoulders of the salesmen, who were supposed to convince their accounts that these bonds were no more complex or risky than the bonds they'd been taught to buy back when they were in business school. Sidney Geeder felt the weight of the entire financial system on his shoulders. He was one of the biggest salesmen at one of the biggest firms, attempting the riskiest and most dangerous financial shenanigan in years. If it succeeded, there would likely be a storm of takeovers of small mismanaged nations, and if it failed, the name of Atlantic Pacific would be mud on the street, which would have suited Sidney Geeder just fine except he all but owned 100,000 shares in the Atlantic Pacific Corporation. As a shareholder it was in his interest to lie through his teeth. Goddamn self-interest—the firm really had him where it wanted him, and there was practically nothing he could do about it.

Sid felt like just calling in to the firm, saying that he, too, had been kidnapped, and hiding out until the whole thing blew over. He hobbled out of his local tavern and lumbered down the street, and when he passed a phone booth the idea teased him again. He took off his tie and wrapped it over the mouthpiece of the phone and dialed the office number, hoping that the security staff were still around.

The security staff were indeed still around, and when the phone rang long after hours they stared at each other in surprise.

"Geeder's next," the muffled voice coughed. "Call off the deal or more of your salesmen will die." Then it hung up.

"Jesus!" the Executive Director of Internal Surveillance shouted, putting down the phone. "Did you hear that? We've got to find Geeder before they do."

Sid knew they would come looking for him. On Geary he hailed a cab outside a hospital, and in minutes he was downtown, in the lobby of the Excelsior Hotel, across the street from the offices of the Atlantic Pacific Corporation. He asked for a room on the forty-second floor facing the street. The desk attendant made a fuss, but money was no obstacle for Sid, and they found a room. A moment later Sid was flopped on his bed, gazing across forty yards of sky to the sales floor of his firm, with a decent view of his own desk, which was open to the window. Instinctively, Sid phoned the assistant district attorney.

"Where have you been?" she exclaimed. "I figured you had written me off."

"I'll explain it when you get here," Sid responded, trying to speak in a calm voice. He gave her the room number and asked her to bring binoculars. He begged her to come right away. Then he called room service and ordered champagne and some dinner and a huge pot of coffee. Sid took a shower and changed into the terry-cloth bathrobe they gave to guests.

When the assistant district attorney arrived, Sid hugged her fiercely and ran his fingers through her hair and kissed her all over her face as he pushed her onto the bed. She fell back laughing, her arms up at her side, happy that Sid hadn't entirely written her off. She wore a yellow trapeze dress under her coat, which gave Sid ample room to slide his hands over her slender body.

"Ohh, where have you been?" she moaned.

"You'll never believe it," he said, his hands creeping back up her legs. Sid slowly explained what had happened.

"Sid, you could get arrested if they find out it was you who gave the bomb threat."

"Oh, they couldn't arrest me," Sid said merrily. "They need me to sell their bonds." Sid rolled over on the bed and stared at the ceiling. "The thing is, anybody could be making them. It makes you wonder how many will come from salesmen like me who just don't want to sell these bonds."

Just then a light flickered on the sales floor across the street. Sid jumped up and grabbed the binoculars out of the assistant district attorney's purse. He stood at the window, naked, and surveyed the scene. Someone was walking down the hallway from the kitchen. The person walked into Coyote Jack's office and went behind his desk, sat down, and turned on Coyote Jack's desk lamp.

It was Coyote Jack. He had a glass of ice. He opened his desk drawer and pulled out a fifth of scotch, with which he filled his glass. He popped his suspenders off his shoulders and untucked his shirt and kicked his feet up on his desk.

"You think I should give him a phone call?"

"Why?"

"Tell him he's next. Put the fear of God in him."

Sid handed the binoculars to the assistant district attorney, and as she spied on Coyote Jack, Sid swept the smooth back of his hand up and down the insides of her arms. Sid was so delirious with exhaustion that all he could think about was his own physical body and how good it would feel to crawl under the sheets with the assistant district attorney. He offered her some champagne and went to pour a glass. There was a steak of sautéed swordfish and baby asparagus on a plate. Sid couldn't resist a little nibble, the taste of which immediately reminded him that all he'd eaten lately was potato chips and Polish hot dogs with sauerkraut from the local bar. He wheeled the tray of food over to the window and pulled up a chair. Coyote Jack had drained half the bottle.

"Makes you wonder how often he does this," Sid said.

"It's creepy," the assistant district attorney said. "Is he married?"

Sid nodded. "I know it's hard to believe."

Suddenly, Coyote Jack stood up and seemed to go to the window, but stopped a few feet short. His pudgy fingers moved down his shirt, undoing the buttons. He slid out of his shirt and folded it delicately over the back of a chair. His blubbery, heavy, pale chest was bare, and he poked at his sides and grabbed fistfuls of fat. He was looking at himself in the reflection of the window glass. A roll of fat hung over the waistband of his trousers. Coyote Jack sucked in his gut and thrust forward his chest, then clenched his arms and flexed. His thick neck became even broader. He held the pose for ten seconds, then relaxed and got himself another drink. He came back and went into the pose again, this time until veins rose on his neck and his face became flushed with blood.

"I really hope he doesn't start jacking off," the assistant district attorney said. "I don't think I could take that."

Coyote Jack was now doing push-ups. Sid counted them out loud.

The assistant district attorney left her station at the window and stretched out on the king-size bed. "Do you think the Dominicans really have Eggs Igino?" she asked.

Sid sat down on the corner of the bed and thought out loud. "No, of course I don't. But that's the thing with finance—it's not what's true that's important. What drives the market is what people think is true, and right now they think Eggs Igino is a hostage. The firm wants the market to think he's a Dominican hostage so nobody will feel guilty for taking over the country. Anybody could have sent those faxes—Christ, those faxes could have been sent from the PR department just to position the deal. A whole lot of money is made in the market by predicting what people will think is true, rather than what actually comes true."

"But doesn't it eventually come around to the truth? If you stuck with the truth, wouldn't the market eventually come around to your opinion?"

"Maybe. But what's the truth? I don't know where Eggs Igino is. He disappeared. I know he lived in Mexico for a while; I know there was a woman that he used to love very dearly. I don't have the slightest bit of proof, but I'd guess he's with her. I don't have a better explanation. I sure would like to disappear like that. Just poof, gone."

"But you *have* disappeared," the assistant district attorney reminded him. "They're probably tearing their hair out trying to find you."

Sid crawled toward her on the bed. "Oh, I'm not going anywhere. Where would I go? As soon as I use my credit card in the morning to pay for this room, they'll be here within the hour. Besides . . ."

"You've got those shares."

"Right."

Sid was absolutely right; when he paid for the hotel room at five o'clock the next morning, the security team that had taken over Atlantic Pacific's forty-second floor got a call from the credit card company and found that Sidney was right across the street. They sighed with relief and jumped into an elevator as Sidney kissed the assistant district attorney goodbye and crossed the empty street and waited for an elevator. The security team were so intent on getting over to the Excelsior that they bowled right past Sid as he stepped into their elevator. When they got to his hotel room, they found the bedsheets tossed on the floor, the bathtub still full of soapy lilac-scented bathwater, and leftovers of a breakfast of *huevos rancheros* with strawberries in cream on the side. But Sidney was gone.

"He slipped us!" the Executive Director of Internal Surveillance raged, swinging his fist and smashing one of his lieutenants in the chest. They filed out of the room and took the elevator back downstairs, where they accosted the desk attendant and bellhop, who had just come on duty. Feeling humiliated and fearing the wrath of the firm's top brass, the security team trudged back across the street and into John White's office, which they had turned into a command central. They slid out of their sport coats, uncinched their gun holsters, and ran their fingers through their hair. Then they sheepishly slunk down the hall to the kitchen to get a cup of coffee, and found Sid busy filling his thermos.

"Hey, boys," Sid smiled maliciously. "Get a good night's sleep?"

Sid retook his position at his desk, feeling better than he had in days. Never had the sight of his fellow salespeople cheered him so much. For a few hours, life seemed like the good old days: the traders in New York announced their daily business on the Hoot 'n' Holler, the salesforce wrote down whatever they thought would make a good story, and the phone lights went red with chatter. Nickel Sansome made a feeble joke about the global financial village. Sue Marino took out of her desk Lisa Lisa's pancake of lowlustre, firming-action moisture cream and began to dab it at her crow's-feet. The goofus who had taken Eggs Igino's place got his trading ticket jammed in the time stamper and spent fifteen minutes attempting to clear it of stray paper. Coyote Jack's secretary yawned as she came in the front door, stretching her arms out to her sides and pushing her chest up where it could be seen by all. Sid Geeder went to the forty-second-floor window and stared out at the awakening city, imagining what it would be like to have to ride a bus or find a parking space.

"So I guess it's not true," Nickel Sansome said, sliding up beside Sid.

"What's that?"

"What they're saying in L.A."

Sid tried to find his room at the Excelsior across the street. "What do they say in L.A.?"

"It's just a rumor," Nickel giggled.

"Well, what the hell is it?" Sid demanded angrily, although he was secretly enjoying the good old way Nickel tormented him.

"That the Dominicans got you last night. What do you think I should tell them?"

"Why do you have to tell them anything?"

"We traded," Nickel whispered. "They told me their quotas on the Lincoln Convertibles, and I'm supposed to tell them the low-down on why you've disappeared."

"But I haven't disappeared!" Sid said.

"You haven't?"

"I'm right here!"

Nickel shrugged. "But that's not what's important. They *think* you've disappeared, and so I've really got to run with it. Like I said, I'm working a trade with them. If you don't want to know what their quotas are, then I suppose you don't have to tell me where the hell you've disappeared to."

"That's idiotic!"

"They'll be really disappointed to hear that you're standing right here. Boy, couldn't you just take a long lunch or something? I've got a reputation to protect."

"I don't care."

"Aren't you dying to find out what their quotas are? Mine's twenty-five. What's yours?"

"None of your business! And no, I'm not dying to know what their quotas are. I don't care. There's too many other things to care about."

Nickel was persistent. "I'm really dying to tell you. It's really going to rile you. You'll be mad as hell and you'll probably run right into Coyote Jack's office to complain, and then he'll double yours on the spot for good measure."

"That's exactly why I don't want to know," Sid agreed, even though by now he was damn curious what the quotas were in L.A. "It doesn't matter anyway, because I'm skipping this deal. I hate these bonds."

"Boy, I'd sure like to skip this deal, too. Of all of the deals we've done, this one's the dirtiest. When are we going to go back to just selling regular old corporate ten-years and T-notes?"

"We'll never go back," Sid predicted. "The monster's out of its cage."

Nickel paused. He tilted back on his heels and clicked his toes together. "How about I tell you what the L.A. quotas are, and you agree to tell me something unspecified but worthwhile in the future. I'd like just to tell you, but I've got my reputation as a shrewd negotiator of dirt to protect."

"Oh, all right," Sid said, finally giving in.

And so Nickel ran down the list of salespeople in L.A., giving their quotas. It wasn't a complete list, but it gave a clear picture: nobody was higher than thirty, and the average was around fifteen. Sid's was fifty. It made Sid so hopping mad that he immediately wished Nickel hadn't told him. Knowledge was power, but this kind of knowledge only incensed him, so much so that he wanted to rage against the firm. Suddenly inspired, Sid sat down at his Quotron and typed out another bomb threat, which he downloaded to the central laser printer. He tried to use the same margins and page placement as the original faxed ransom note, of which he had a copy. Then Sid clipped off the letterhead of the Dominican Liberation Party and taped it above his bomb threat. He carried this over to the bank of fax machines, intending to fax it into John White's office, where the security team was holed up. But all the fax machines were busy sending and receiving prospectuses to and from each other. This made Sid so outraged that he stormed into Clark Kalinov's office. But Clark Kalinov was testing new health clubs again and his room was empty except for his desk and personal fax machine. Relieved, Sid placed his bomb threat in Kalinov's fax and coded in the number of John White's fax. The paper slid through, then spit out a receipt. Sid neatly placed the receipt on top of Kalinov's stack of receipts. He heard a commotion down the hall and skipped out of the office. A minute later, he saw the crowd of security men go storming into Kalinov's office, where they camped out until Clark Kalinov showed up.

When Clark Kalinov showed up, he was feeling so fresh and revived from his workout that he had decided to reward himself with three chocolate-glazed bear-claw danishes for breakfast, which he carried inside an Intermail envelope so nobody would see. He poured a mug of coffee and came down the hall. Because his hands were full, he pushed open his door with his rear. Suddenly he was grabbed from behind by the tail of his suit coat and thrown up against the wall. Skilled hands patted him down from behind. Clark tried to cry out for help, but his face was so smashed into the wallboard that only a squeak came out. Then they cuffed him.

"What are you guys doing this for?" he wept, going soft in their fierce grip.

"Don't play dumb with us!" the Executive Director of Internal Surveillance shouted back angrily, rearing back and socking Kalinov in the chest, then slapping him across the face, causing a wad of coffee-colored saliva to drool down his chin. Clark coughed in his throat and his stomach pumped in and out, attempting to vomit.

"Please, please, tell me what I've done wrong," he mumbled.

"Do you think we're stupid, Kalinov? We've got your receipt!" He turned to his men. "Let's move out!"

In under an hour, the security team had moved its command of operations down the hall to Clark Kalinov's old office. Clark Kalinov had been turned over to the Feds, who threw him in jail and charged him with obstruction of justice, fraud, and assault.

"All right," Sid said, coming into Coyote Jack's office. "So we know it was all a hoax. You can call off your guard dogs now."

Coyote Jack crossed off a notation on his daily reminder. "Geeder. I was just about to call you. I'm giving you Eggs Igino's quota. It'll put you at one hundred million."

"Is this a joke?"

"Not at all. Those bonds look cheap now that the bomb scare is over. You'll move a hundred easy."

"Aww, c'mon, Coyote, put a cork in it. I haven't slept in days. Think about it. You don't want to give me Eggs's quota. That gives me too much power. What if I disappear like Eggs Igino? You'd really be screwed."

"You won't disappear. You're not at all like Eggs Igino."

"Maybe I'm more like him than you think," Sid said.

"Maybe you'd *like* to think you're more like him than you really are."

"Don't psychoanalyze me," Sid warned.

"You know what I'd like to know?" Coyote Jack wondered. "I'd like to know if you're as high-maintenance to your girlfriends as you are to me. Are you the kind of guy who needs to be stroked every day? Huh? You get jealous when your girlfriends talk to the waiter, that sort of thing?"

"I wouldn't know," Sid said. "You stole my girlfriend."

"That's not the way I heard it," Coyote Jack said. "The way I heard it is, she was fed up with her job: fed up with all of you salesmen's constant sob stories, making half a million every year and still complaining. She knew you'd try to find her, knew you're Mr. Obsessive. So she comes to John White, asks him to help her disappear without any obvious traces."

Sid steeled his jaw. "And this just happened to coincide with the impending Romanian deal."

"Lisa Lisa told her about the deal. Ivana didn't want to hang around and hear all your whining about Romania this and Romania that."

"You're just fucking with my head, Coyote."

"You used to be Mr. Know-It-All, Geeder. You used to know the shot. Nothing slipped past you. Now you don't have any better sense of reality than ole Paul DeShews out there."

"I'm just tired," Sid admitted. "I'm just really tired. I'm going to go home and sleep."

"You do that," Coyote Jack said.

"Then you're calling off the guards?"

"Absolutely," Coyote Jack said, grinning.

Everyone was gone, and it seemed impossible for Sid to hang in there even another week. That night, he slouched in his pink chair and stared off into space, trying to keep track of the events that had led him here. His back was beyond stiffness—it was so frozen and numb he didn't notice it anymore. His eyes itched from dryness, and there were full sacks of fluid hanging below them. He'd been sleeping only an hour or two a night, a feat he'd managed mostly out of fear, although he was also drinking an insane amount of black coffee. As he sat in his chair he could not sleep. His nerves were too jumpy and strung-out. He couldn't relax. Whenever he closed his eyes, he had visions of being chased by strange men. He made himself pot after pot of coffee, and sometimes his mood managed to improve after a few cups, which only meant he was that much more depressed when he came off his high. Over the next few days, work gave him no satisfaction at all, and the morning briefings seemed increasingly absurd. Meanwhile, the news about bomb threats forced the legal departments at all of their customer banks to take a serious look at what these Lincoln Convertibles were really about, and some of them were coming back and taking the bold position that as prestigious as Atlantic Pacific was, it might have made a mistake on this one. They just weren't sure that it was entirely permissible to foreclose on the Dominican Republic and seize its assets, even though the transaction followed the laws of accounting very strictly, as well as the laws governing bankruptcy and interstate commerce. It probably also adhered to several laws of economics, the law of natural selection, a few laws of thermodynamics, and the Law of the Wild. But there were other things to consider, such as peace plans, United Nations resolutions, and human rights agreements. An investment bank had never been subject to a peace plan before, but with the direction things were headed, it was very darn likely that Atlantic Pacific would be at the peace table sometime before the Lincoln Convertible bonds came due in ten years. Sid could tell that the deal was on shaky ground because his accounts took longer to answer their phones. Those few that indicated they were likely to buy were talking about quantities of just a couple of million, and none of the salesmen were confident of their capacity to meet their quota except for Nickel Sansome, who'd begun to kick back his commissions to Regis Reed at Irvine Savings. They'd struck an agreement that Reed would buy $12 million of the Lincoln Convertibles, which caused such a bout of self-recrimination and guilt that Nickel wanted to call his father and cry out his sins. Finally Nickel gave in and went to see the firm psychiatrist, Helmet Fisher.

"Tell me more about your father," Helmet Fisher instructed.

"What about him?" Nickel Sansome asked, sweating uncomfortably on an enormous leather couch. Helmet Fisher's office was built like a library, with bookshelves to the ceiling on all four sides, and on those bookshelves were thousands of upright toy soldiers of dozens of kinds.

"Tell me about *his* father. Was he the one who started the family corporation?"

"No, that was his father's father's father."

"I see. Your great-great-grandfather."

"No. My great-great-great-grandfather."

"That's quite a lineage you have. Every single one of you has repeated in your father's footsteps. Is that couch uncomfortable for you?"

"It's just fine," Nickel responded fearfully as the skin on his arms stuck to the leather.

"Is it too hot in here?"

"Just right, actually," Nickel answered cheerfully as a bead of sweat plunged down his brow and stung his eye.

Helmet Fisher shifted his weight in his chair, creating a squeak that caused Nickel to flinch. "Let me tell you a little tidbit of mythology," Helmet Fisher said. "Then you tell me if it has any meaning for you. This is the myth of the goat-man, which comes via ancient Arabia. For years and years there was a great line of goats that ruled the forest. They had strong legs and tough foreheads good for knocking over old trees, as well as double stomachs that could digest anything poisonous. One year, a big goat was born that stood upright on his hind legs, which had very little hair and hooves with five little useless digits. The older goats almost killed him at birth, but they let him live. This goat had a soft forehead and a finicky digestion and he went about hating himself for most of his life. He was always cold and hungry and spent his time pondering."

"That's it?" Nickel asked.

"What do you think it means, this goat-man myth?" Helmet Fisher inquired pretentiously, scratching at his beard and widening his eyes quizzically.

"That I'm not a goat," Nickel answered.

"Precisely," Helmet Fisher continued. "You need to think of this myth and you need to say to yourself ten times each day, 'I am not a goat.'"

"I am not a goat," Nickel repeated, several times over. "Do you think this will help my baldness?" he asked.

"I have noticed that you have very little hair for a man your age," Helmet Fisher observed. "Let me tell you another little myth. This is from mainland China, up near the Wei River. A little boy went down to the river one day for some water and saw the most magnificent flying beetle making music with its wings as it danced from pad to pad. It was a very glorious beetle that everyone would want to see. He caught the beetle in his ceramic water jar and took it home. But he was so afraid that the beetle might fly out when he showed it to someone that he never did. He grew paranoid, fearing that if he did reveal it, someone would steal it. He never even looked at it himself, for years, but all the while he walked about the village proudly. One day, when he was ready for marriage, he took the jar to his wife's father as a dowry, and when he opened it there was only dust in the bottom."

"I could see that coming," Nickel stated.

"It is a very universal myth," Helmet Fisher responded. "The endings are not meant to be a surprise. Now, which character do you relate to in the story—the boy, the beetle, or the wife's father?"

Nickel considered it for a moment. He really wanted to tell Helmet Fisher that the source of his great guilt was that he was kicking back commissions to Regis Reed. But Helmet Fisher was on the firm's payroll, and word would no doubt get back to Coyote Jack or John White and he would be out of a job. "The beetle, I guess," he said finally.

"Aha!" Helmet Fisher piped, jotting down notes in a lab book.

"Why 'Aha'?" Nickel asked fretfully.

"The beetle/goat-man combination is quite rare," Helmet Fisher explained in an authoritarian, scientific tone that didn't hide his glee. "I've read about a few cases, but never met one in person."

"Is it bad?" Nickel asked, slightly confused.

"Not at all, not at all," Helmet Fisher consoled him. "It just means we have a lot of work to do. While you go through the wolf/purple-star phase you might suffer some side effects."

"Wolf/purple-star phase?"

Helmet Fisher nodded. "Some people find it scary, having all those deep feelings brought to the surface. You probably won't sleep much at night."

"I'm not sleeping at all," Sidney Geeder admitted to Sue Marino, who'd come by his desk to ask if he was okay. His face was gaunt and his eyelids were swollen. "Whenever I wake up, I think there's a man with a gun in my room."

"It's just a bad dream," Sue Marino assured him.

"Let me ask you something, Sue. Did you ever go see Ivana Perkova, back when she was the doctor?"

"Sometimes. My boyfriend was a doctor, though."

"But you did go to her?"

"Yeah, sometimes."

"Did she seem nice to you? I mean, was she empathic, or was she more like, like *bored* by you?"

Sue looked at Sid and tried to figure out what he was asking. "Let me tell you something about doctors, Sid. That empathy they give you? It's an act. They're like Southern women—it's a gift they have of making everyone seem special. But the truth is, you're just another warm body. And that's the truth whether your doctor is taking your temperature or doing the dirty deed with you. When they're around a live body, they've got one thing on their minds. You know what that is?"

Sid shook his head.

"AIDS," Sue said. "I'll ask you this. You thought you had a thing going with the Romanian girl, right? So, not to pry, but did she make you wear a condom? My fiancé, he wore a condom every time. He said he would take it off when we got married. Like he was saving himself."

Sid admitted that he hadn't worn a condom.

"Well, then maybe it was love." Sue shrugged.

Sid left work at three, on the dot. He stumbled out the door with his shirt collar open and his sleeves rolled to the elbows. When he got to his apartment he took four aspirin, put hot water on the stove, and fell down on the couch and tried to sleep. He tried every possible trick he could think of. He imagined that the pain in his head was bright sunshine in his eyes making him hot and faint. Every time he neared sleep, it occurred to him that he had a $100 million quota and no chance in hell of selling so many bonds. Sidney buried his head under a pillow and tried to think about sex, tried to think about Ivana Perkova's slender calves and the way she would purr deep in her throat when he massaged her shoulders.

This only made him worry and wonder even more about whether she might really have tried to leave him. So he tried the opposite tactic: he tried to recite the entire alphabetical index to Fabozzi's *Fixed Income Securities* textbook, and the dates of the Chinese dynasties, and the U.S. presidents of the nineteenth century, until he was so bored that he would have to fall asleep to escape the drone. But he didn't sleep. He had nothing to do with his time. He didn't care. Around dinnertime, he ordered out for a pizza, which he didn't eat when it arrived. Finally, he fell asleep briefly, and when he awoke it was dark outside and he wasn't thinking straight. He was still so tired that he thought it was morning and he had to get to work. He didn't change his clothes. He looked for his briefcase for twenty minutes, checking the same places over and over in mindless frustration until he gave in and called a cab. He fell down in the backseat and didn't notice that there was too much traffic for it to be four in the morning. Downtown, it was quiet and normal. He saluted the security guard, rode up the elevator, waved his magnetic card-key over the security eye, and clumped across the sales floor. The place was empty. He was the first one there, which wasn't unusual. The others would stroll in soon. Sidney popped up his Telerate screen and jotted down notes on the price movements since the afternoon closes. Then he went into the kitchen and turned on Mr. Coffee. Eventually, he climbed back down under his desk where he could think a little better. His eyelids began to twitch shut, flickering uncontrollably. He couldn't keep his eyes open or closed. When he tipped his head back, it felt like he was falling backward into a deep cavern. Time passed. He forgot what he was doing there and quit expecting the others to show up. The maids came through and vacuumed, and for a while Sidney sat in the kitchen until they were done. Suddenly it occurred to him that it was the middle of the night.

"Arrrgghh!" he grunted, falling into a coughing fit from exhaling all his air too quickly.

Sidney gathered himself and made his way back down to the street. He hailed a cab and gave uncertain directions to the assistant district attorney's house. They drove around her neighborhood for ten minutes before he remembered which place was hers. He sat down on her doorstep and pushed her bell five times. After a while, he did it again. She opened the front door for him. She was wearing a navy-blue teddy that made her seem like a deep pool of mountain river water. He stumbled to her couch and fell into her arms and begged her to tell him whether there were wires in his mouth or sticks in his legs.

"What?" she said, slapping at his face to keep him awake. "Sidney, you don't make any sense."

"I never make any sense," he mumbled, his eyes twittering as if going through rapid-eye-movement dreaming, but with the lids open.

"You said you have wires in your mouth."

"I have everybody's quota on the Lincoln Convertibles," he gasped as a little drool slid down his chin.

"You're having a bad dream again," she warned him, shaking his shoulder.

"Look at my legs," he begged. "God, I can't feel anything anymore."

The assistant district attorney pulled up the cuffs on Sidney's trouser and massaged his calves. "Your legs are fine," she assured him.

"It's not a dream," he warned her in a slurred voice she could barely make out. "Everyone's gone and I have everyone's quota on the Lincolns and I can't feel anything anymore." His arms suddenly jerked and batted around at the pillow that his head was resting upon. "The wires!" he screamed. He suddenly twitched frantically and tried to stand up.

He didn't look good. His eyes were twitching and he was breathing as if through a straw, sucking the air hard but not getting much. His clothes were soaked right through with sweat. His face was pale and bloodless and clammy. She took a throw blanket off the couch and put it across his chest, petting his forehead and trying to get him to relax. He kept mumbling, not making any sense, crying for help. She went into the kitchen and poured a glass of ice water. He took only a sip, so she placed the cool glass against his forehead. Hundred million, he babbled. Hundred million. Then he sat up for a moment and began to herky-jerk his arms and shoulders and head around like a loose puppet. He stood up and tried to dance or something, then he fell forward. She wasn't quick enough

to catch him. He landed with his head against the edge of the coffee
table, spinning upon impact and ending up on his back on the carpet. There was a burst wound splitting open his eyebrow, which
hung down over his eye like a flap. Blood started pouring out, but
not nearly as fast as she would have thought, considering the gash.
The assistant district attorney began to cry from panic and exhaustion. She fished out an ice cube from the water glass and put it on
the wound. Sidney was out for a moment, but he came back to a
groggy state, saying he didn't feel very good. He wanted to know
what day it was. Was it Friday? She got a stocking from her dresser
and tied it about Sidney's head, pressing the flap of skin back into
place and cinching it down to keep it from bleeding. She pulled
Sidney up and saw that there was a lot more blood on the carpet
than she had thought. She was still in her teddy, so she put Sidney
back down and got a pair of athletic shorts on, then dragged Sidney over her shoulder down to her car in the garage. He could
walk, but not straight. She drove to the nearest hospital. On the
way, he kept trying to get a look at his wound in the vanity mirror
on the sun visor. He was pulling down the stocking, and she had to
keep screaming at him to stop and to lean back and close his eyes.
They got to the emergency room. She took Sidney's wallet and
filled out the forms and tried to tell them that he might be on drugs
as well as having the wound. This led to another series of forms.
The nurses ushered Sidney through big white swinging doors.

When Sidney Geeder didn't show up for work the next morning,
Coyote Jack was horrified and the office was thrown into a panic
until his secretary sauntered into his office and informed him that
the hospital had called to verify that the firm was covering all costs.
Coyote Jack jumped on the horn and called the hospital and demanded to talk to Sidney. They wouldn't let him do that, so he got
the nurse to tell him that Sidney had received eleven stitches for a
contusion of the temporal and orbicular epidermis.

"What the hell does that mean?" Coyote Jack screamed angrily.

"He cut his head. He'll be fine."

"Then let him out! What's he still doing there? We need him at
the front!" It was for exactly this reason that the firm had a self-
insurance system: so they could order around the doctors. Coyote

Jack couldn't understand how Sidney had ended up at a hospital instead of at one of the firm's doctors.

"We'll let him out as soon as we get his plasma rotated and he gets some rest."

"What in the hell does he need that for? He's got a cut on the head!"

"He's also been suffering from severe caffeine poisoning."

"Caffeine poisoning!"

"His kidneys were barely functioning. If they'd gone into arrest, it could have been fatal."

"Fatal!" screamed Coyote Jack's secretary, who was listening in from her desk outside his office.

"He'll be fine now," the nurse continued. "Once we get the plasma flushed, he'll be able to sleep. We'll monitor him just to be sure, but once he gets some rest and he seems coherent, we'll let him out."

"How long will that take?" Coyote Jack demanded.

"We don't know. We don't want to wake him up. He might sleep for a few hours or a few days."

"Days!" Coyote Jack hung up the phone in shock. He dug into his desk and found an open-ended round-trip airplane ticket to Hawaii. He couldn't take any chances. He stormed out onto the sales floor, yanked the phone out of Sue Marino's hand, and told the account that she would call him back.

"Coyote! What in the world's going on?"

"You're getting Lisa Lisa's big accounts. Nickel will cover the rest. I want you on the next plane to Honolulu." He looked at his watch. "It's a f-f-fi—a long flight. You'll get there around t-t-t-ten A.M. A room will be ready for you at the F-F-Four Seasons. Go get familiar with Mike Kohanamoku. Spend today and tomorrow with him. Suck his dick if you have to. Then take the red-eye back here the day after tomorrow in time for the Lincoln Convertibles. Any questions?"

"Well . . ."

"Don't you dare go soft on me now, Marino. Call Kohanamoku from the airport. Let's go! Get out of here."

"I need some clothes . . ."

"There's a shop at the hotel. Now damnit, let's go—the next plane leaves at nine. You've got half an hour to get to the airport. If you miss that flight, don't bother to come back here."

Sue Marino grabbed her purse and headed for the door. Coyote Jack whirled and reached across the aisle, clamping down on Nelson Dicky's shoulder.

"Let's go, Nelson. My office."

Nelson Dicky obediently slid from his chair and followed Coyote back into his fishbowl. "Where's Sid?" he clucked.

"He's at the hospital. He poisoned himself drinking too much coffee. They say he could be out for a couple hours or a couple days, they don't know yet. Look, Nelson: He'll make it back in time. Hell, he's Sidney Geeder. He's the iron man. He's terra firma. You and I, we've known Sid a long time. He'll be here for the Lincolns. But just in case—I've got to assume the worst. I need to deputize you. Until Sidney gets back, you're the King of Mortgages."

"Me? But I only sell treasuries."

"You're an honest guy, Nelson. You've got country drawl in your voice. Maybe you don't know shit about mortgages, but the accounts don't know that. They'll trust you. You're a religious man—religious men don't lie. I have complete faith in you that you'll be able to pull it off."

"Pull what off?" Nelson quivered.

"I'm giving you Eggs Igino's accounts."

"Oh no."

"Sierra and Bank of Sacto."

"Oh jeez."

"Just keep them warm until Geeder or Igino gets back. Talk to them three times a day. You know the routine." He clapped his hands in encouragement. "Let's go, you're the king."

But Nelson Dicky was no king. Nelson Dicky was a soft-spoken, honest fellow who donated almost all of his commissions to his church and considered himself under God's orders to like his job. He was the kindest, sweetest, most selfless person on the floor. He couldn't yell at his customers or order other salespeople to get him coffee. He couldn't earn the salesforce's favor by complaining until the commissions were raised. Most of all, Nelson Dicky couldn't muster the ruthlessness to testify to his accounts that the best place to put their money was in these newly designed, highly speculative bonds. The only place he felt comfortable putting money was in United States Treasury securities, and when the salesforce learned that Nelson Dicky had been deputized the new King of Mortgages, their spirits sank and the success of the Lincoln Convertible deal seemed in jeopardy.

Sid Geeder had just woken up beside the woman in white.

"Wow," he said to the woman in white. "I feel like I slept for twenty-four hours straight."

"You did sleep for twenty-four hours straight," the woman in white answered casually.

Sidney looked at her again. She had dry, crackled skin and a slight mustache and spindly dyed-brown hair yanked tight underneath a cap made of paper. Sid's wrists were strapped to the armrails of his bed. There was a mouth guard on his lower teeth, which he spit out onto his chest. His room had only a small window in the corner covered by a grate. Oh my god, he thought. I've gone and done it. I've finally cracked. They locked me up and drugged me and strapped me to a bed.

"I'm in the loony bin!" he shouted in a burst of realization.

"Don't be silly," the nurse glowered. "You're in the hospital."

"What are my arms strapped down for then?" he demanded.

The nurse gave him an unsympathetic stare. "So you wouldn't tear the stitches out of your head during your sleep."

"You operated on my head!" They had really done it now. They'd cut him open and stolen his knowledge.

"Where in the world did you get that idea?" the nurse spat, trying to shove the mouth guard back onto Sidney's lower teeth. "You came in here with a laceration to your eyebrow."

Sidney spit the mouth guard out again. "Then why did you drug me up for twenty-four hours?"

"We didn't do anything of the kind. You came in here high as a kite. You could have killed yourself, you know. You're awfully lucky you gashed your head open, or you might have died."

"That doesn't make any sense!"

"Of course it makes sense," the nurse insisted. "If you hadn't nearly killed yourself by slicing open your eyebrow, we might never have been able to drain out your blood plasma."

"My blood plasma!"

"It was toxic," she snickered.

"It was mine!" he hollered. "They're trying to steal everything from me now."

"Who?"

"Them!"

"You're paranoid," the nurse scoffed maliciously.

"For good reason!"

"You really are crazy if you think you're crazy, because you're not crazy at all. You just have a cut on your head and were about to die from caffeine poisoning."

"Caffeine poisoning? That's the craziest thing I've ever heard! Nobody's ever killed himself from drinking too much coffee."

"No, but quite a few people have almost killed themselves from drinking too much coffee. You, for one."

"But I feel fine!" Sidney yelled. "I haven't felt better in months!"

"That's because you have somebody else's blood plasma in you."

"Whose blood plasma?"

"I don't know whose," she sneered. "How would I know whose blood plasma you have?"

"I was just hoping you'd know where I could get some more. This stuff is really quite sensational. I feel like a million bucks. You really ought to try it."

"You're crazy."

"Aha!"

"Not that again. Here, look at your chart." The nurse pulled his chart off the end of the bed and showed him the scribbles made on the hospital sheets.

"You mean I'm really not crazy?" he shouted, wiggling his toes and fingers with glee.

"Of course not!" she repeated. "Whatever gave you that idea?"

"Oh my god!" he shouted, his face suddenly turning downcast in horror as he realized that now he had woken up he had to go back to work and sell the Lincoln Convertibles.

"What?" the nurse said in alarm. "Are you all right?" She grabbed his arm and took his pulse and put her crinkly hand on his forehead.

"Oh, I'll survive," Sid said in misery, falling back against his pillow.

The nurse made a note on his chart.

"What are you writing?" Sid asked.

"Just that you've woken up and seem lucid. In a couple of hours, we can check you out of here and you can go back to work. They seem very anxious to have you back."

"Are you sure it's okay?" Sid said. "I mean, I've only been awake a couple of minutes. I mean, what if I fell right back asleep for another twenty-four hours?"

"Well," the nurse said rudely, not enjoying Sid's sarcasm, "then we probably wouldn't release you, would we?"

"I don't think you would," Sid said, a plan forming in his mind. "I think it would be improper to kick a patient out of his bed while he's sleeping. Particularly if he's recovering from caffeine poisoning, which can be fatal." Sid's eyes flickered and then closed. "In fact," he said, "this conversation has exhausted me, and I'm feeling sort of dizzy. Quite dizzy, actually." His head rolled into his pillow, and he tried to slow his breathing and make himself fall asleep again. He tried not to move a muscle. But Sid's body felt so energetic with this new plasma that he was wide awake behind his closed eyelids and still body. Sidney realized that all he had to do now to skip the Lincoln Convertible deal was to remain perfectly inert for a few days and never open his eyes. It was a perfect plan, and there was nothing the firm could do to stop him.

"We've got to stop him!" Coyote Jack growled, pounding his fist on his desk as he spoke into the phone to Dr. Vandivort, the firm physician. "Can't you do something?"

"I can't do anything," Dr. Vandivort mumbled in dismay. "It's the hospital rules. If we could get him transferred to my custody, then I could do something."

"Well, let's do it!" Coyote Jack ordered. "What are we waiting for?"

"We're waiting for him to wake up and sign the forms authorizing his transfer."

Coyote Jack spluttered into his phone in agony. "But if he wakes up, then we wouldn't have to do anything, you idiot!"

"Well, then, there's nothing else I can do," Dr. Vandivort said smugly.

"Can't you do anything?"

"Oh, sure, I could do something," answered Helmet Fisher, the firm psychiatrist, when Coyote Jack explained the situation. "We could go in there during visiting hours and hypnotize him."

"That's brilliant," Coyote Jack agreed, and an hour later they were leaning over Sid's supine body, whispering in his ear. Helmet Fisher gave his voice a melodious, confident inflection and described to Sid a black closet, in which there was a staircase of one hundred steps descending into the subconscious. Slowly, rhythmically, Helmet Fisher led Sid down all one hundred steps. Sid had been so bored by remaining still for so long that he couldn't resist the shrink's imagery. When Helmet Fisher opened the door at the bottom of the staircase onto a lava field, where a river of warm blue water ran by, Sid felt himself losing control. He fought back.

"What did he say?" Helmet Fisher turned to Coyote Jack.

"I couldn't make it out," Coyote Jack answered, leaning farther over Sid.

"I think he's asking for help," Coyote Jack mumbled, watching Sid's lips very carefully.

"It's all right," Helmet Fisher said calmly. "You're just fine."

"Now, by the count of ten, you're going to wade ashore, and you're going to climb out of the water. Then the sky is going to open up overhead, and it's going to be day up ahead, and you're going to wake up," Helmet Fisher said smoothly.

"Get up!" Coyote Jack yelled, shaking Sidney by the shoulders.

"What if we just unplugged one of these tubes?" Coyote Jack suggested, and before Helmet Fisher could advise him against it, Coyote Jack had yanked out Sid's intravenous. Fluid began to run out all over the floor and the monitoring computer began to beep loudly. Suddenly a nurse burst through the door and pushed between the two men and saw what was happening. She reattached Sid's intravenous. A moment later two orderlies ran in. The nurse ordered them to escort Coyote Jack and Helmet Fisher out of the hospital. A minute later the orderlies were back, and the nurse ordered them to wheel Sidney Geeder down to the high-security ward, where he would be monitored on camera. Sid smelled the sour stink of antiseptic mopping, heard his wheels squealing as he rounded a corner, felt his gut sink as the elevator dropped, but he kept his eyes closed through all of it. He was overjoyed to overhear that he was being taken to a ward where the firm couldn't get at him. The effort of trying to stay asleep all the time was exhausting Sid, and he crashed into unconsciousness as soon as he reached his new room.

When he woke, he was dying to open his eyes and look around, but he assumed that there was a camera on him and he didn't dare. He tried to keep his breathing slow and steady. In the next room he could faintly hear the sound of a television, and he focused his mind on trying to make out the words, in vain. The antiseptic smell of the room made him want to vomit. Very slowly, he rolled onto his side and pulled his legs up to support his lower back, which, after all this time in the hospital, felt like one hot blister. He isolated the heat and tried to use it to relax his muscles, but that didn't make any difference to the numbness. So he switched to pretending that there was a huge block of ice melting in the bed right beside him. On reflex, Sid urinated into the bedpan. Sid began to wonder if maybe all of his muscles had gone numb, or if they had lost all of their strength. It seemed to him that he could barely move even if he wanted to. He wondered how we know our bodies exist—do we define them through their movement, through change? Does the body that remains immobile all day no longer exist until it changes? This seemed true—Lisa Lisa never noticed her body until she saw that her feet had swollen. Then Sid began to wonder what he would be like if he had to lie like this not just for a few days, but for the rest of his life. What if he were paralyzed and couldn't hear or speak? Or what if he didn't have a body at all, and the hospital merely kept his mind alive by plugging it into an electrode and setting it in a bath of sugar water? What if that were all there was to life—what if we were only brain? Sid imagined a future where people went to work and lay down in saltwater isolation tanks. Electrodes would be hooked up to their brains, which would be hooked up to superfast computers, and then you'd put your seven hours in. It would be seven hours rather than eight because we would have advanced as a society and become more humane.

Sidney stopped thinking about this as he realized that all of his limbs had fallen asleep and were tingling. Even the muscles in his neck. He was being stabbed with pins and needles everywhere, right up to his ears. Suddenly he worried that one of the nurses might have forgotten to change his IV, and that he was running on bad juice. Paranoid, Sid quickly became convinced that mildly toxic fluid was being pumped into his wrist and causing all of his skin to tingle. He desperately wanted to jump up and shout out at the nurses on the camera to come in and save him. Perhaps his flask was empty and air was being sucked into his arteries. Then he would be getting the bends, like underwater compression, or his body would stall, like a car that gets air in its gas line. Sid was in misery worrying over the fate of his body. He listened for a dry sucking sound of an empty flask coming from the side, but he heard nothing. He waited for his body to seize up and spasm. He huddled in his bed and hoped to hell that his body would survive. He felt himself growing exhausted again with worry as he drifted off into his dreams.

He was shaken awake. "Get up, get up," a voice said. "Your government needs you."

Sid thought he must be dreaming.

"Hey, buddy," the voice came again, sometime later. "Your government needs you." The voice paused. "You think he can hear us? They might have him on some drugs."

Someone played with the paperwork on the chart hung on the foot of his bed. "Naw, he's not on drugs."

"We know you're listening," the voice said. "Fuck—is that videocamera on?"

"The camera's off," the other voice said.

"We're the NIA," the first voice went.

"The National Information Agency," the other voice clarified. "You've never heard of us."

"We report to the President. The President's been trying to solve this Dominican Republic problem since he got elected. If you guys are finally going to save the Dominican Republic from the Dominicans, then you can be damn sure we're going to be there to take credit for it. There's a whole new movement to privatize foreign policy."

"The President's all for it," the second voice chipped in. "As long as it works seamlessly and doesn't come back to bite him in the butt. We don't want another Haiti on our hands."

"The economy depends on people like you, Geeder. These bond deals Atlantic Pacific's been working the past few years are vital to our national interest. A third of the salesforce take their clues from you. When you sell, they sell."

"We've read your sales pitches," the strong, gruff second voice said. "Brilliant. Just brilliant."

The first man shook him again. "Think of it like this. Fifty years ago, every nuclear physicist was as closely guarded as you are right now. You're safe in here until the day of the deal. They'll never get you like they got Eggs Igino."

"We're watching you," the other man repeated.

Then they left. Sid fell back asleep, and they woke him again. "Your government needs you," they said once. Sid refused to open his eyes. He had no intention of helping his country anymore. When he woke up again, it occurred to him that he must be close—that it must almost be past the time for the Lincoln Convertibles. He really had no way of knowing, but he grew excited as he imagined how pissed off Coyote Jack must be. He couldn't keep a smile from breaking the stillness of his face as he imagined Coyote Jack tromping up and down the aisles, trying to bludgeon the salesforce into dumping those Lincolns into the market. Then Sid heard the door to his room open and a cart being wheeled up to his bed. It was probably the physical therapist who every afternoon gave Sid's body such a thorough massage that he absolutely hated it. The massage was so relaxing that it was practically impossible not to be sharply reminded of the massages Ivana Perkova had given him. Each afternoon the physical therapist worked up and down all of Sid's muscles and joints, and each afternoon Sid fell into a glum, bitter mood fueled by what the firm had done to squelch Ivana Perkova.

Today's massage was even more like Ivana Perkova's than the others—it was as if she were right there with him. This massage was a whole lot more endearing than the other massages, and Sid wondered if the physical therapist was coming on to him. Her hands caressed his skin and ran through his hair.

"Sid," she whispered. It seemed like it was coming from very close to his ear, but Sid had so lost his sense of space that it could have been from across the room.

"Sid," she said again, and this time Sid felt the blow of her words on his ear. Sid resisted, just scrunching up into a tighter ball and burying his head in his pillow.

"Oh, Sid," she said again. "I was so worried about you all these times." Her voice was inflected with a guttural, heavy-on-the-vowels accent. It was Ivana Perkova's voice! At least he thought it was Ivana Perkova's voice. But he could be projecting her voice onto one of the nurses' voice. It could be that he so wanted to hear her voice that he was hearing it regardless of reality. Sid kept his eyes closed.

Then this woman was giving Sid a hug, clutching at his gown and kissing his shoulder and quietly weeping.

Sid rolled over and flicked open his eyes for just a flash and met Ivana Perkova's worried gaze.

"It's you!" Sid jumped up, grabbed Ivana Perkova fiercely, tugged her onto his bed, and kissed her mouth. He began to cry with relief at the sight and smell of her and the feel of her in his arms. She wiped away his tears and he wiped away hers, and then they sighed with relief and hugged each other more.

"Oh, where have you been?" Sid cried.

"They told me not to see you anymore." She rolled under Sid and felt his weight on her body. "I didn't want to get you into more trouble. I thought I just had to stay away."

"You could have told me first."

"You would have just argued with me."

"No I wouldn't," Sid said coyly, kissing her on the nose. Sid felt incredibly elated and shocked. He took great lungfuls of air and scratched the sleep from his eyes and kicked his legs in pleasure. He was alive! And being alive had never felt so good. Ivana was alive! And she'd never felt so good in his arms. He babbled nonsensically, then laughed at his own idiocy. "But—but where have you been? I even hired a private investigator to look for you."

"You did? You really missed me, didn't you?"

Sid nodded.

"I had to move out of that apartment so fast that I moved into a boardinghouse rather than getting a new apartment. It's a very nice place in Pacific Heights, and they serve breakfast and dinner, so I don't have to cook. But I don't have a phone in my room, so if you tried to track me down that way I'm not surprised it didn't work."

"Are you working?"

"Not much," she answered slowly. "I'm teaching a couple of classes at an institute here and in Marin."

Sid was relieved that she was safe. It suddenly seemed silly how much he'd worried. "How did you get in here?" Sid asked.

"Well, at first they wouldn't let me in. No visitors, they said. But I know my way around hospitals. I put on a nurse's uniform and nobody paid attention to me."

Sid considered that, then he suddenly realized something and felt a terrible letdown. "How did you know I was here?" he asked, grabbing her by the shoulders. "How did you know I was in the hospital?"

"What do you mean?" Ivana said, grabbing Sid by the collar of his gown and shaking him in return playfully. "John White told me. I was really sorry to hear about your appendicitis. In fact, we shouldn't be rolling around like this, with your stitches."

"But I don't have appendicitis!" Sid yelled.

"You don't?" Ivana Perkova pulled up the bottom of Sid's gown to see for herself. There were no stitches anywhere. "Then what are you doing in the hospital?"

"I was hiding," Sid said somberly, realizing that the firm had sent Ivana Perkova to wake him up.

"Oh, I don't think those Dominicans will get you in here. This is a security ward."

Sid shook his head. "I wasn't hiding from the Dominicans. I don't even know if there are any Dominicans."

"Then who are you hiding from?"

"I was hiding from Coyòte Jack!" Sid wailed, rolling off the bed as he realized that they needed to escape. But it was too late, because the door opened and Coyote Jack marched in, followed by a swarm of security men. They grabbed Ivana Perkova and pulled her from the room. Others pushed Sid back down on his bed. Coyote Jack leered menacingly at Sid and grabbed Sid by his chin, pushing his head back into the pillow.

"You want me to fire you, Sid?" Coyote Jack asked. "Is that what you want? You don't have the guts to just quit, so you're trying to get yourself fired?"

"I've been sick," Sid said.

"Sick, my ass."

"I nearly killed myself!"

"That was three days ago. Shit, I should have fired you long ago."

Sid's eyes scanned the room. "You can't fire me," he said nervously. "I've got a hundred million quota, and without me your deal is doomed."

"Yeah, well, if you don't show up tomorrow and fill that quota, then you can kiss your four million goodbye."

"I'm in the hospital—you can't fire me for getting sick; that'll never hold up in court."

"According to the hospital, your vital signs have been normal for seventy-two hours. That makes you AWOL, Geeder. I'm warning you—four A.M. tomorrow, I want you at your desk. If you're a no-show, then you might as well call Paine Webber and beg for a job washing windows. You'll be rotten meat when the word gets out that you skipped a deal. Nobody will even return your call."

"I'll consider it," Sid said.

"You do that."

When they were gone, Sid Geeder got out of his bed and stood up and stretched out his body. He went to the window and stuck his leg out behind him to stretch his calves. He could see the trees of the Presidio from his window. He tried to think back and remember when life was simple, when he was just nine months from retirement and all he had to do was lie low to get there. Why, why, he wondered—why did he try to fight it? Why didn't he just go with the flow and last it out, why couldn't he just go to work in the morning and make it just another day on the job, just another deal, and go get drunk tomorrow night and find Ivana Perkova and be happy? It was Eggs Igino, that's what had happened. Sid stared out the window and wondered what had become of him.

Eggs Igino looked out the window, wondering if the light rain outside would rinse the sky of any of its smog. He hated the familiarity of this hotel room, hated Mexico City's crowds, hated that when he tried to run in Chapultepec Park his lungs seized up in pain. His body was testy with anger and untapped energy and tequila.

"I wasn't the only one to blame," he said to the window.

Katie sat up against the headboard of the bed. She had a glass of tequila over ice beside her. Her hair was blond and there were sun freckles on her shoulders. "I didn't go fuck those women."

"You stopped caring about me. You used to fall asleep when I was talking. You wouldn't go to parties, you didn't like my friends. I was lonely. I was trying to save myself."

"Save yourself? You jerk. You were just trying to get your dick wet."

"I was trying to make you hate me. I wanted you to leave me. I didn't have the strength to leave you."

"You didn't have the strength to leave me? What do you call living in Mexico for a year?"

"I didn't have the strength to be near you. I had to be as far away as possible if I was going to leave you at all."

"Am I supposed to forgive you for that? That's your explanation? That's the best you can do? You have two affairs and the reason is you were trying to get me to leave you. Then you take off to Mexico and your reason is you didn't have the strength to just get another apartment. That's good, Mark. Real good."

"I felt so guilty . . . I was running from myself, trying to punish myself . . ."

"Some punishment, living on a beach three hours north of Acapulco. Tell me, Mark—when you were there, did you give it to the tourist girls?"

"No."

"Why don't I believe you?"

Eggs turned from the window and went to the refrigerator and got himself a beer. He sat down on the edge of the bed. "You're not the same person anymore."

"It's because of you! *It's because of you!* You did this to me!"

"We've done nothing but fight since we got here."

"What's wrong with fighting? Maybe if we had fought when we were living together, none of this would ever have happened."

Eggs put his hand on Katie's foot, which she withdrew. "I'm tired of fighting, Katie. We've only got one more day here."

"Well, what do you want?"

"I want you to let me show you that I love you."

"I'm not sure I can take that."

He put his hand on her leg again, and this time she didn't move it away. He moved up onto the bed beside her. She finished her drink and set it down on the nightstand.

"Watch out, I'm drunk," she said.

"You never used to drink before. Certainly not tequila."

"Well, I've never been locked up with a strange man in a hotel room in Mexico City before."

Eggs rubbed his hand down her thighs. "I'm not really a strange man, am I?"

"Just strange enough," Katie said.

They made love like people who'd just met, and they lay in bed for a while and when they got restless again they went to the roof of the hotel, where there was a pool that was too shallow to swim in. They were the only people there. They played tag in the water, and then raced each other back and forth, like children, and for the first time all week they laughed.

14 · Natural Resources

IN AN INDUSTRIAL economy, natural resources included minerals, timber, oil, and human labor, all of which were used in the manufacturing of product. In the information economy, the main raw materials were intellect and time, both of which were used in the drumming up of deals. Of the two, time was considered more valuable, because once it was used it was gone forever. So when an opportunity was spotted, the accustomed management practice was to throw a whole bunch of bright minds at the problem and tell them to get it done by morning. The assumption was that brainpower was not like water, or timber, and heavy misuse of it would not pollute the minds of an entire generation of employees. The premise was that their lives could afford to give away five or ten years of time without damaging the natural habitat of the mind. They didn't wonder whether their jobs might be squandering their most important natural resources, that the changes in their personalities might be irreparable. So when Coyote Jack ordered Sue Marino to warm up Honolulu Federal to the Lincoln Convertibles in just two days, Coyote Jack assumed that Sue Marino would not question whether the past few years of her life had been wasted in the reckless pursuit of material gain. Coyote Jack assumed that Sue Marino's addiction to the fulfillment work gave her would hold, that she wouldn't end up on some beach somewhere with her toes in the sand contemplating the purpose of her existence.

Sue Marino sat with her feet buried in the coarse white sand, watching Mike Kohanamoku surf the fifteen-foot Blue Monster at Molokai. He had worked two hours in the early morning, then taken the day off to show her the islands. Mike Kohanamoku was as big as a tree, with wrists as thick as Sue Marino's knees, glossy hair to his shoulders, and teeth discolored white, like oysters. His smooth skin was completely hairless, as if he had been raised by fish. By unanimous election, Mike was tribal chieftain of the Hoolehua natives, who were a gang of middle-aged small business owners who pooled their resources to strengthen the local economy between tides of tourism. They gathered in a bar in the afternoons and played dominos, which is where Sue Marino tracked him down after she had arrived the day before. He had laughed at her gray suit. As he introduced her to the members of his tribe, they all chuckled over her suit. One of them went across the street to his shop and returned with a short sundress and cartwheel hat. Mike took her for a drive. She was exhausted. She let herself sweat. Mike wanted to know her personal history. She told him about the obstetrician, and about Scotland, and about how when she was in ninth grade she had come to Waikiki with her family. She asked her younger sister to take some pictures of her standing in the waves with her bikini top off. The pictures were going to be for her boyfriend. A wave knocked her over, dragged her out, and then spit her back, leaving her nearly unconscious on the sand. Her bikini top was gone. Her younger sister was gone. She was somewhere else on the beach, but she didn't know what direction her family was in. Ever since then, she had been afraid of waves. Mike Kohanamoku grinned the whitest grin Sue Marino had seen in a long, long time.

They'd had dinner outdoors, at a roadside shack serving sharkburgers and roasted coconut chunks on skewers. She never went back to Oahu to her hotel; Mike found her a bungalow near the beach, where she fell asleep on top of her bed in her sundress as she listened to the Blue Monster pound the sand. She slept forever, and when she woke up she cried. She didn't know why she cried—it could have been joy over being waked up by the sound of water, or it could have been the dread of having to return home that night. She'd lost her suit and her shoes somewhere. The paint on her toenails was chipping off. She went outside onto the warm patio. On the door to her bungalow was taped a note from Mike that he was surfing on the beach and to come find him. The sand was already hot—she walked under the shade of the coconut trees lining the beach. The few adventurous surfers congregated at one outside break. When Mike stood on his board, he was unmistakable because of his size. He didn't cut back and forth, he just zipped across the face of the wave, staying comparatively safely away from the curl. Sue Marino sat down and watched. When Mike took a spill, she felt her heart sink in fright, and when he reappeared spouting water from his mouth like a whale, she giggled.

"The Hoolehua have a piece of ancient wisdom," he told her later, trying to stifle a smile. "It translates loosely as 'Don't eat thirty minutes before surfing.' " He laughed at his own foolishness, then went back to sucking a stick of sugarcane.

At the end of the day she took a plane back to Honolulu, then another back to San Francisco. The plane was nearly empty. Sue lay across the middle seats with a blanket over her shoulders. Whenever she closed her eyes she saw Mike Kohanamoku's giggling grin. She'd never even had a chance to ask him whether he would buy the Lincoln Convertibles. She fell asleep for a while. When she woke up, her throat was sore and the flight attendants were marching up and down the aisles preparing the cabin for landing. It was four o'clock in the morning. Still in her sundress, Sue took a cab straight to the office and had just enough time to change her clothes before the final sales mission briefing on the Lincoln Convertibles. There was no time to grow despondent, no time for remorse. No time to think. She gave a thumbprint for identity to the guard at the door, then she was frisked by two others before she was allowed into the teleconference room. Two new kids were sitting next to the two-way video screen, flicking a small, triangular piece of paper back and forth across the table through field goals of opposing hands and upright thumbs like a couple of clowns. Next to Coyote Jack was a woman in a wheelchair with a stunted, dog-shaped body: long trunk extending through a thick neck into a pointy head, but very small, flipperish legs and arms. She was drinking coffee through a long straw from a mug resting on the arm of her wheelchair. Beside her was that naive-looking blond-haired kid chewing on a pencil with his buck teeth like a beaver, and next to him was old Wes Griffin, who'd been brought back from the dead. Wes sat there quietly, looking a little tense, dutifully studying his prospectus on the Lincolns. Sue Marino did a double take on Nickel Sansome. He had gone totally bald and had grown the beginning of a mustache. On second look, she realized that he had shaved his head in preparation for the battle. His speckled and bumpy skull made the bile in her stomach rise. Paul DeShews sat meditatively still like a wax figure; not even his eyes blinked. It was a goddamn circus—a freak show.

The two-way video screen cut to the syndicate desk, where the syndicate manager leered into the camera so that in San Francisco his face was four feet across and five feet tall. They could see the clipped hairs in his nose, the pale corporate-blue veins running through his eyelids when he blinked, the gold crowns on his molars. He shouted at every salesman in every Atlantic Pacific office in the world. He bitched, he bribed, he tried to make them feel like a tiny bit of lint stuck to a wad of tissue paper being used to wipe the hemorrhoidal butt of a foreign dictator. Low. They'd been through it before, so many times, and it never failed to make them feel as if they were going into battle nailed to the tread of a tank. There was nothing new in the way they began to scratch their armpits and pick at the calluses on their elbows and feel a painful gurgle in their stomachs that made them bend over and hyperventilate as they took the verbal abuse. Then the two-way video screen blinked to the research department, and they were bombarded with last-minute irrelevant data: the minimum wage in the Dominican Republic was $3 a day; more than 150 U.S. companies already had industrial plants on the island; when the United States occupied the Dominican Republic from 1916 to 1924, it was a time of great harmony and prosperity. The purpose was to make it seem that behind the few tidbits of Dominican history was a real country full of real people all dying to enlist in the capitalist war machine. Financial capitalism was a highly exportable information commodity: it was an idea that sold, and sold well, and everyone bought it, and kept buying it. The salesforce slunk low in their chairs. Coyote Jack mopped the sweat off his brow with a napkin that left crumbs of cream-cheese danish clinging above his eyebrows. It wasn't the same without Eggs Igino and Sidney Geeder around to act cocky in the face of so much pressure. Nobody in the conference room whispered under his breath, or passed food under the table, or broke out laughing when the Research Manager for Caribbean Ecosystems postulated that the once-lush Dominican rain forests could be regrown in six years. Then the screen cut away to a video assembled from various national news broadcasts about the disputed elections in the Republic, including a press conference in which the President stressed how important the Dominican Republic was to long-term stability in the region. Then the big syndicate head came on again and yelled at them some more and promised a gold corporate watch to anyone who sold more than $15 million in bonds. Then he cackled in derision and showed every salesman in every Atlantic Pacific office in the world his tonsils.

"Double-time! Double-time!" Coyote Jack chanted when the screen blipped off. "Hustle. Hustle, you jarheads!"

The salesforce emerged from the briefing room trepidly. The security forces had installed huge manila-colored blinds that covered the windows. They came down the aisles armed with hyperbole and accounting regulations, computer printouts and legal interpretations. They wiped their monitors clean, sat down in a cloud of dust. They plugged into their cockpits and took off into the electronic cyberspace, through the fiber-optic cables, into a world where information was power. They flew in a cluster, hovering near each other for security, but not so near that their own thoughts could be overheard. When they neared their targets, they began firing. Paul DeShews climbed into his antigravity apparatus and tipped back until he was facing the ceiling. The air was dank and the men were hungry. Their garbage cans were overflowing with the rotten remains of the past days' fast-food lunches, and the smell recirculated evenly throughout the floor so there was nowhere to hide from it. As the sun came up and the light began to filter through the blinds, it framed stark silhouettes of guardsmen standing in the space between the blinds and the windows. The thump-thump of a helicopter passing by caused the force to hunch up tighter to their desks. As the central laser printer clicked on automatically, the security guard marching down the aisle spun around, dropped to a knee, and drew his gun.

"It's like buying Apple in '78, or Boeing in '52, or Ford in '27," Wes Griffin assured his old account Sierra Prudential. "In fifteen years, New Lincoln will be like Hawaii. It will be a major tourist attraction of the first order. Even a small investment now would be worth the risk, considering the potential return."

"Ahh, I won't be around in fifteen years to take the credit," Sierra Prudential responded.

"Fifteen years was an exaggeration," Wes countered. "Five years is more like it. Development is the rage. Over one hundred and fifty U.S. companies already have industrial plants established there. We've applied for an NBA expansion team. The lush Lincoln rain forests that once covered sixty percent of the island will be fully regrown in six years."

Sierra Prudential broke out laughing.

"It's true!" Wes cried, stretching for material. "They've isolated the genome on the chromosome that controls these things. In Florida, they've got palm trees that grow ten feet a year and drop coconuts the size of watermelons. I'll fax you over the article. Listen, it's a new world out there. If you want to make a buck, you've got to think about the future. You've got to get in on the ground floor."

"It just doesn't fit our portfolio specifications," Sierra Prudential stalled.

"Well, let's talk about that," Wes Griffin rambled. "I have to respect your portfolio specifications. Generally speaking, is Sierra bullish or bearish on this market?"

"A little bearish," Sierra admitted. "The fundamentals have been soft for a long time."

"Exactly," Wes said. "And these Lincoln Convertibles are the perfect bearish investment. Let me explain. When inflation and interest rates go up, what investments go up in value?"

"Gold, land, real estate."

"Bingo! Land. You said it yourself. Mother Earth. And these Lincoln Convertibles, do you know what they buy you?"

"Let me guess," Sierra said. "Land."

"Prime Caribbean real estate," Wesley said.

Sierra Prudential broke out laughing again and hung up.

"Are you bullish or bearish?" Nickel Sansome asked Bonnie Hsiao at the Bank of Canton.

"Bullish, really," she answered. "The Fed would never tighten with such soft fundamentals."

"Exactly," Nickel agreed. "If rates are going anywhere, they're going down. And when rates go down, what goes up?"

"Stocks," Bonnie answered. "But I can't buy stocks."

"You can now. Buy the bond that becomes a stock after you buy it. It's the only convertible bond that becomes a stock when rates go down."

"But why would I want to buy a government?" Bonnie asked innocently. "Governments are broke."

"You're not buying a government," Nickel countered. "You're buying a piece of corporation that's taking over the assets of the government. There'll be no messy lobbying, no lousy conference committees, no tricky constitution to adhere to. No red tape. There'll be a completely democratic election by the shareholders to elect a CEO, who will then be given free reign to rule the corporation."

"It sounds too good to be true," Bonnie Hsiao observed. "What's the catch?"

"The catch is that if you don't buy now you'll be shit out of luck. These bonds are moving like drugs in a ghetto."

"I really have to check with the bank president," Bonnie stalled.

"When does he get in?"

"About nine-thirty."

"Nine-thirty! That's afternoon in New York. I'll try to hold a block of bonds for you, but I can't make any promises. You'd better check with the president the moment he comes in. I'll call you at nine-thirty."

Nickel popped off the line and poked his head out over the edge of his desk to survey the situation. Wes Griffin, on the other side of the desk, had wrapped a bandanna around his forehead and then pushed it down until it covered his bad eye.

"It's psychosomatic," Nickel jeered. "Quit using that hankie, Green Thumb. It's a crutch."

"It's self-defense," Wes muttered, waiting for another account to answer its phone.

"Sure, right. But Sid Geeder's already using that excuse. You'll have to come up with something better," Nickel said. He opened his desk drawer, found some coins, and wandered off to the kitchen to get a snack, leaving his desk drawer open.

Angered, Wes Griffin immediately switched over to Nickel's desk and sat down in his chair. He found Nickel's steroid inhaler. He popped its plastic top off and dumped out the aerosol canister, which he turned upside down in the wastebasket and sprayed until it was empty. Then he replaced the plastic top and returned the inhaler to its previous position. He looked over his shoulder suddenly, fearing that Coyote Jack had seen the whole thing.

Coyote Jack was on the phone to the Bank of Sacramento, which had been one of his accounts long, long ago, back in the days when customers barely had computers and couldn't independently analyze their purchases. He sat at Lisa Lisa's old desk, embarrassingly crunched down in her low chair with his knees in his chest.

"I don't know," Bank of Sacramento replied to Coyote Jack's exaggerated estimates of the Lincolns' performance in a static environment. "I put them on my computer and I show the strike yield holds flat as the conversional infraratios trend toward the center of the Gaussian curve. In a trend-line analysis, the derivative of the beta has to hang above zero to expect positive income in less than seven years. In effect, the bonds have a duration double the long bond."

"You really have to take that computer analysis stuff with a grain of salt," Coyote Jack responded.

"Oh, I do," Bank of Sacramento clarified. "When my uncertainty ratio exceeds the square of the credit risk, I ignore the computer completely and rely entirely upon those old-fashioned financial wisdoms: prudence and moderation."

"Jeez, don't be a wimp," Coyote Jack said. "Sometimes you just have to hold your balls and jump."

"Oh, I do hold my balls and jump whenever Eggs Igino tells me to. He's never been wrong, and he trained me to use my computer whenever other salesmen call and try to confuse me with exaggerated promises. If he told me to buy these bonds, I'd be all over them, in size."

"But Eggs Igino put this deal together!" Coyote Jack lied. "How can you have a stronger endorsement than that?"

"Oh, I don't know. I just would feel a whole lot better waiting until I could talk to him myself. Maybe if the deal falls apart, those Dominicans will let him go. Then he could tell me whether to buy them or not."

"But if the deal falls apart, there won't be any bonds anymore!" Coyote Jack gasped with humiliating agony. It didn't use to be this hard to get his accounts to buy.

"Well, then I'd sure be glad I didn't buy them, wouldn't I?" the Bank of Sacramento concluded thoughtfully. "There's nothing that makes me look more foolish to my board than buying bonds that no longer exist."

"But they do exist!" Coyote Jack tried to explain. But it was no use. His face was red and his neck was hot as a blister and his innate fear of numbers was undermining his confidence. When he slicked his hair back over his head, his hand came down discolored slightly orange. Coyote Jack's self-tanning lotion was sweating out of his scalp, or peeling off, and dripping into his hair. He mopped at his mane with napkin after napkin, hoping his gray hair hadn't changed hue. He gazed at his reflection amid the greenish tint of his Quotron monitor, wondering where the hell was Sidney Geeder.

"Where the hell is Sid Geeder?" John White said, sliding up beside Coyote Jack. "Jesus, what the fuck—are you bleeding?"

"Lemme alone," Coyote Jack snapped back. "I'm not bleeding. How's it going in New York? I don't hear a lot of activity on the Hoot."

John White lied, "It's going fine, but mostly in small lots, so salesmen are calling in their kills on the inside line."

"Small lots? Like, how small? Fives?"

"Sure," John White readily agreed. "There's some fives. A lot of ones and twos. But once retail realizes they can move this, we'll see it go in chunks."

"It's gonna be a long day," Coyote Jack muttered to himself.

A commotion broke out near the staircase leading downstairs. One of the firm security men and an NIA guy were frisking a tiny man in a navy-blue suit carrying a briefcase while two other NIA men pinned someone else to the ground and were looking through the guy's wallet. Coyote Jack and John White hurried over to talk with Cornwell, the NIA man.

"It looks legit," one of the other NIA men reported to Cornwell. "He's got the right ID."

"What do I care if he has the right ID? Anyone can fake an ID. If there were supposed to be SEC observers here this morning, then I surely would have heard about it."

The man on the ground mumbled something.

"What's going on?" John White said. "Who are these men?"

"They're SEC," Cornwell explained. "But NIA's got jurisdiction on this one, and I say SEC's not allowed."

"You can't tell us what to do!" shouted the man pinned to the floor with his feet and hands spread apart. "Either we're allowed to observe this deal or I radio out and a hit squad will shut you down within the hour!"

Cornwell paced up and down the aisle considering. "Okay," he caved. "But you're just observers. I don't want to see you talking to the salesmen. I don't want to see you picking up any phone lines. This is too goddamn important of a deal to our government interests to let the goddamn government interfere with it."

The SEC observers were released, and they brushed themselves off and wandered down the aisle with their briefcases looking for a place to sit. One of them eyed Sid's desk near the window.

"Don't even think about it," Coyote Jack said, following closely behind.

Eventually they had to go back downstairs and get chairs of their own. They sat down at either end of the aisle between the mortgage desk and the total return desk and tried to overhear what lies the salesmen were telling their accounts. The SEC observers were quiet and careful not to interrupt. They were straitlaced, boring men who knew the rules and nothing else, but there just weren't that many rules that applied to a bunch of companies taking over a country. All they cared about was that the hostile takeover of the Dominican Republic go smoothly and peacefully and not violate any international peace agreements. They sat there obediently, yellow legal pads on their laps, crafting the opening sentences of the report they would file at the end of the day. The SEC observers were entirely powerless in the situation. They had been sent in mostly for show because the SEC director had seen on television how UN observers had been sent to Kenya to make sure that country's first democratic presidential election wasn't rigged. The election *was* rigged, of course, and the UN observers had no way at all to stop it, but it sure looked good to have them there, because it gave the world the impression that the election wasn't quite as rigged as it might have been. It looked so good, in fact, that Atlantic Pacific had invited UN observers to watch them take over the Dominican Republic, and the SEC observers had barely jotted down the opening paragraphs of their standard reports when they had to cross it all out and start over, making mention of the men in powder-blue helmets who sat beside them.

John White and Cornwell had expected the UN observers, and so they got the royal treatment while the SEC men were ignored and made to feel inconsequential. The UN observers were given padded roller chairs, and Coyote Jack's secretary brought them cappuccinos from downstairs. John White explained his operation proudly and otherwise fed them a lot of bullshit. The UN men didn't care, of course. All they wanted was for this hostile takeover of the Dominican Republic to go smoothly and peacefully and not violate any laws of interstate commerce or bankruptcy proceedings. With all the internal security men, NIA men, SEC observers, and UN observers, the sales pits were so overflowing with bodies that it was nearly impossible to move about without pissing someone off. The salesforce had never been subjected to this kind of scrutiny, and if they'd thought it was hard to sell these bonds before, it was nearly impossible to sell them with all manner of government agency breathing down their necks. They became despondent and resigned to defeat. It seemed that nothing could save this deal unless Sid Geeder showed up.

Nelson Dicky tapped the direct line to another account as he watched the door, waiting for Sid Geeder to appear and make sense of it all. They all watched the door and waited for Sidney Geeder to arrive. It was just like the morning that Eggs Igino disappeared, when the salesforce, hungry for something warm to put a dent in their hangovers, watched the back door like a dog at its empty bowl, big puffy eyes staring wimpishly at the brass handle, waiting for it to turn.

The brass handle of the back door turned, and just like that, Sidney Geeder burst through in bare feet, his gown open at the back and flying behind him like a cape, a big cheery smile on his face, bantering and saluting everyone. Immediately he was tackled to the carpet from behind by one of the security goons. The goon got on top of him and tried to push his face to the floor with one hand while reaching behind him for his handcuffs with the other, which was a big mistake, because Sidney Geeder had been a wrestler for two years in college, and as soon as he felt the goon's weight transfer, Sid shrugged in that direction and toppled him off. Sid swung his legs around in a leg whip and rolled the goon onto his stomach and then drove one arm up behind his shoulder blade. When the goon persisted in fighting, Sid hammer-chopped him to the throat, causing the security guard to go limp as he coughed saliva into the carpet. Sid was sweaty and raging with physical pleasure, amazed at how terrific his body felt, disappointed that the goon didn't give him a longer fight. Sid smiled, stood up, brushed the lint off his hospital gown, and came waddling down the aisle, his hairy bowlegged legs visible to all.

"Stand up!" he said to the amazed salespeople, who gawked back at him. "Stretch your legs!"

Sue Marino looked up with great relief. Nelson Dicky got wet in the eye. Wes Griffin trotted over to the edge of Sidney's desk.

"What are you on?" Wes asked. "You're really wired."

"Blood!" Sidney preached. "The wonder drug! Plasma! Shot myself up with Type O Positive!" His voice softened into a mock surreptitious tone. "You really ought to try it, man. It's some serious shit. I'm hooked, and I don't think I'll ever be able to live without it."

Wes chuckled. Sidney slapped him on the arm.

"So one more for the road, is that it?" Sid asked. "Or are you making a comeback, going to do the seniors' circuit?"

Wes Griffin shrugged and looked down uncomfortably.

"What'd you do with your hair?" Sid asked.

Wes ran his hands through his long blond locks. "I'm a test case for a miracle hair-growth product made from mustard greens. My mane grows like a weed now."

Sidney laughed. Good old Wes. It was good to be back. Coyote Jack's secretary dug around in Clark Kalinov's old utilities closet and found a pink pinpoint oxford-cloth button-down, and then in the hallway closet she discovered a tropical wool suit that had belonged to Regis Reed.

"I hope you don't mind pink," she said, sidling up to Sid and holding the shirt up to his chest to check its size as Sid stepped into Reed's old trousers. Coyote Jack's secretary bent down to pin under the cuffs with a stapler. Nelson Dicky reached into his drawer and came up with a spare tie.

"What about shoes?" Coyote Jack's secretary worried, looking up as Sid bared his hairy upper body and tried squeezing into Kalinov's old shirt.

"They're under my desk," Sid answered. "Can you reach them?"

"These?" Coyote Jack's secretary said, holding up Eggs Igino's ratty sneakers. Sid nodded, and as long as she was down on the floor she helped him into them like a shoe salesperson, knotting the laces for him.

"You're all set," she said happily, cinching Sid's tie a little tighter for him.

"Who the hell are you?" Sid said, turning to the observer sitting off to his right.

"SEC," the naive goofus sitting to Sid's left told him.

"Well," Sid said, speaking to the SEC man. "Fasten your seat belt, because you're going for a ride."

The mood turned. The force returned to their phones, inspired by the bravery of their leader, the king, the King of Mortgages, and for a while they became confident that the Lincoln Convertibles really could be sold.

"Whatever gave you that idea?" Sidney shouted when the trust manager at World Savings asked if Congress had to approve the takeover of the Dominican Republic under the War Powers Act. "Does World Savings need congressional authorization to hire security guards to watch the vault? Do you need a congressional mandate to chain a dog up in your front yard? It's protection of private property. If Lincoln hires a few military contractors to defend its new acquisitions and clear out the trespassers, so be it. Not only is it perfectly legal, but it won't cost the taxpayers of Delaware a dime."

"It's just not in our bylaws to loan money to foreign governments. We're a savings and loan. The FSLIC and the Resolution Trust will slap us with a big penalty if we take a risk like this."

"Since when is investing in corporate bonds not in your bylaws?" Sidney reasoned. "You just have to get it out of your head that this has anything to do with foreign governments. New Lincoln, Inc. is a United States corporation that will be listed on the New York Stock Exchange, file 10Ks with the IRS, and adhere to all regulations governing interstate commerce. It's partly owned by blue-chip companies such as Ingenesis, Martin Marietta, and General Electric, which guarantees you I'm not selling you junk. Look, I can understand how you feel: the bonds are unusual, no question. It even took me a few days to get used to them, to see how much sense they made. Twenty years ago, they weren't even selling mortgage-backed securities in the open markets, but it took some visionary people to realize how much more efficient the market would be if we did. Ten years ago, nobody would touch junk bonds with a ten-foot pole. But along came the visionaries. You have got to do a little soul-searching here. You have got to ask yourself whether you're a visionary investor, or whether you're just another sheep in the flock. That's really the question here. The question is not whether these bonds would outperform CMOs in a down-rate environment, or whether Moody's labels these AA or AAA. The question at hand here—the question you have to ask yourself—is whether you've been studying portfolio investments all your life over there so that you can play it safe. I mean, do you really go to cocktail parties and brag about not having posted a loss in thirty-four consecutive quarters? Or do you brag about buying Microsoft in '84? That's what we've got here. We've got Microsoft in '84, and the ball is in your hands. You can play, or you can take a seat and watch. I'll say it again—you can play, or you can take a nosebleed seat in row ZZ next to a fat lady dumping popcorn down her throat. I said soul-searching, and I meant it. Men have only a few opportunities like this in their life. Men dream about chances like this. I'm talking not just being a part of financial history. You've got a chance to be part of *world* history. I'll lay it out for you. All these foreign governments around the world are suddenly picking up on democracy and turning themselves around. But democracy is an American invention, and we ought to be the ones capitalizing on it. We really should be charging a royalty. We should be licensing democracy. But until someone figures out how to accomplish that, the best thing we can do is turn these countries around ourselves. Why let someone else profit from it? Look, in the eighties, for a while this technique became really popular to buy a shitty company with bonds and turn the company around real quick to pay off the bonds. We kept doing it and we kept doing it until there weren't any shitty companies anymore. And then it occurred to us, 'Hey! Why limit ourselves just to companies?' Why not scoop up shitty countries, fix 'em up, and sell for a big profit? And I'm telling you, there's some real dogs out there that need a face-lift. And you've got to ask yourself whether you've got the balls to play this game. Have you got the gonads to be a part of history? Are you a man who, when the opportunity arises, can let them all hang out? In ancient Greece, they used to have eunuchs guard the women, because the eunuchs were safe. They didn't take risks. When the men went off to war, when the men charged into battle, the eunuchs were at home combing the women's hair and sipping tea. And you've got to ask yourself: you've got to ask yourself whether you're a eunuch, or whether you're a man. There's no middle ground here. Eunuch or man. Man or eunuch. Are you on earth to comb hair and sip tea, or are you on earth to fuck?"

There was a long pause on the line.

"I'm no eunuch," the trust manager responded shyly.

"I didn't think you were," Sidney assured him. "Nope. I knew you had it in you to make the call. You're in the club now. Don't be shy about it. I want you to go out to some cocktail party tonight and boast about the shrewd move you've made today. Pat yourself on the back."

The trust manager coughed. "I'm a little uneasy . . ."

"Sure you are," Sid agreed. "But don't be ashamed. Be proud! Now, what are we going to write on this ticket?"

"Jeez, Sid, uh . . ."

"Hey, once I start writing a ticket I can't stop. It's just like the meter lady. Let me read it to you. Across the top, it says the New Lincoln Convertible Preferred 9s of 2001. Customer: World Savings, that's you. Salesman: eight dash one one, that's me. There's only one box left. Now what do you say? Ten?"

There was a pause. "I was thinking of more like just a couple," the trust manager said timidly.

"Well, all right. This time I'm going to put you down for a piddly little fiver. But I don't want you coming back to me at the end of the day begging for more when you start reading in the afternoon *Examiner* how Wall Street entered a whole new era today. Because this is your last chance. Is it going to be a ten, or do you have just one testicle hanging there today?"

"Just a five, Sid." The trust manager was practically crying he wanted to hang up the phone so bad before the trade was confirmed. But nobody hung up the phone on the King of Mortgages. Nobody.

"Five million Lincoln Convertibles to World. You're done, babe. Go have a drink."

Sid popped off the line and took a huge deep breath, then shook his head and shook his shoulders loose. "Done!" Sidney howled across the sales floor. "Dead! I could smell his breath, he was so close! I could see the whiteness of his eyes!" He reached over and grabbed Nelson Dicky by the scruff of his collar to get his attention. "I'm telling you, Nellie: I sank the hook! I had him thrashing helplessly at the side of the boat. Then I reached down with the net and rescued him. I showed him the light. I breathed life back into the guy. I gave him a new lease. I gave him something to believe in." Sid exhaled slowly and waggled his fingers with excitement. "So how's it going for you? What have you done for me lately?"

Nelson shook his head. "I think on my second round of calls, I might bring a few in."

Sidney whistled. "Hang in there, soldier. Rome wasn't crushed in a day."

"I'm not going to make it," Nelson warned.

"You'll pull through," Sidney encouraged. "Remember the Freddie Mac Adjustables? We pulled through then."

Nelson nodded his head, but his words didn't change. "I'm not going to make it," he mumbled wretchedly.

"You guys are pathetic," Nickel Sansome said from across the desk. "A couple of driveling choirboys. Whiners. This deal isn't that hard to sell."

Sidney was surprised by Nickel's confidence. "How many have you done?" he asked.

"Twelve," Nickel answered smugly.

"Twelve!"

"Twelve!" Nelson echoed. "Wow."

It wasn't quite true, not yet. Regis Reed was a little late getting to work today for some reason, but the trade was a lock. A done deal. Reed had said as much just yesterday. Nickel was so confident, in fact, that he decided that he had a hankering for a Coke and a candy bar. He knew of this pharmacy two blocks down where he could get the Coke and the candy bar for one dollar. Thinking of the way Eggs Igino used to do it, Nickel stood up and strolled off the floor complacently, with his hands tucked in his pockets and his shoulders rolled back. Rather than avoiding Coyote Jack,

Nickel whistled a little tune as he walked right behind Coyote, who was grilling the guy who had taken Thom Slavonika's place.

Nelson Dicky watched forlornly as Nickel slid through the door. He punched his phone button for Inter-Power Authority, his bread and butter. Inter-Power would buy anything Nelson told them to buy. Nelson had been the fund manager at Inter-Power for three years before he came to Atlantic Pacific—they trusted Nelson more than they trusted themselves. Nelson had never, ever sold them a dog. Nelson had kept Inter-Power on the moral high ground. Inter-Power Authority provided all of the natural gas and electricity to the State of Utah. It would have been sacrilegious to sell them, for instance, the Freddie Mac Adjustables, or more than a few million Resolutions.

When Inter-Power answered the phone, Nelson chatted amicably for a while about wives and children. He blabbered a little about overnight trading. Then he dove in.

"Have I ever told you about these New Lincoln Convertibles?" he asked nonchalantly.

"Nope, but I read something about them on Reuters. It's like raising money for Dominican contras to infiltrate Haiti or something. We got a big laugh out of it over here when it came across the wire."

Nelson's hopes began to crumble. He forced a laugh, went with it. "That's exactly what I thought at first," he agreed. "I got a big laugh out of it over here, too. But then I got to thinking, and I saw some of the numbers on this bond, and I had to ask myself: Where's the downside? How can a guy possibly lose on a bond like this? Let's say the worst happens: They don't foreclose on the Dominican Republic. They just don't. They think about it and realize it's too complicated. Then the bond doesn't convert. The bond stays a bond, issued by a consortium of military contractors, all with high-grade credit ratings and blue-chip status. They're not going to default and destroy their own credit ratings. You've got AAA credit paying you single-A yield. Think of that: AAA credit paying single-A yield. Tell me you wouldn't buy a bond like that."

"I wouldn't buy a bond like that."

"Sure you would," Nelson insisted. "Look, times have changed.

The market is so much more sophisticated now. You're never going to become The Man just by swapping five-year treasuries for ten-years anymore. You have to look for the big play."

"Heck, Nelson, you sound like you want me to buy those Lincoln Convertibles."

"Well, you should seriously consider it. I just didn't want this great opportunity to pass you by."

"You're actually serious. You want me to buy those bonds."

"The yield is a little hard to overlook," Nelson said.

"I can't believe it. You're really trying to sell me."

"I'm not pushing," Nelson said. "If I knew that you should buy these bonds, I would tell you to cover your eyes and jump."

"Nelson, you know darn well the church wouldn't sanction the purchase of any bond used to fund warfare. That's against our religion. We can only invest in peace."

"I know that," Nelson insisted. "I know the rules. But the Dominican Republic has been in trouble for a long time. The church has sent missionaries down there for years with almost no luck. People are dying, and the military doesn't care. We have to think about bringing peace to the island. We're going to clean it up, take care of it. These aren't war bonds—they're *peace* bonds."

"Shucks, Nelson, you sound like a salesman. Even your voice has changed. Are you sure everything's all right?"

"I'm under a little pressure," Nelson admitted.

"You sound like you're selling vacuum cleaners."

"Just think about the bonds, please," Nelson said. "Talk about them with the CFO for me, at least. You owe me that."

"We did talk about it. Like I said, we got a big hearty guffaw out of it. We're not even going to sniff at those bonds, and I don't want to hear any more about it. Hey, you're under pressure, I understand. You need some volume—I'll call Solly and dump some five-years, then I'll call you right back and buy some seven-years. How's that? Nobody can say you didn't get some business today."

"Uh, hang on . . ." Nelson said.

"I'll be right back to you," Inter-Power said, and then the phone went dead. Nelson looked up at Sid Geeder for more support, but Sid had dropped down below his desk to concentrate on his call to Ingenesis.

"What do you mean you can't buy these bonds?" Sid wondered aloud, mocking a Socratic dialectic.

Kenny Whitlash sighed. "It's because we're one of the military contractors that owns New Lincoln, you idiot. The proceeds from the bonds are supposed to go to us. What would the boys at General Electric think if I bought bonds just to pay it right back to myself? They'd think I was crazy."

Sid faked an amused laugh. "You didn't have any trouble buying the FB Romanians when the money was going to buy your fax machines. Why is this any different?"

"I can't believe you're even calling me on this one. Asking me to buy bonds for my own subsidiary is like a dealer snorting his product up his nose. The math don't work on that one."

"Oh, I don't think I'm that crazy asking for you to buy just a tiny slice of ten million. You see, if people like you don't step in and save this deal, then there won't be any deal at all. There'll be no proceeds for you to get. So here's the math: It's a two-billion-dollar deal for a company in which you will hold a ten percent share. If you invest ten million dollars now, you'll get back two hundred million at the end of the day. That sounds like a pretty darned good return to me."

"What you're saying is illegal, Sid. It's worse than illegal—it's stupid."

"Well, how stupid will you look when we have to call you at the end of the day and say the deal ain't gonna fly?"

"You think I believe that? You're Sid Geeder—you'll figure it out."

"Oh, I've already figured it out. I figured it out quite easily, and you happen to be my answer. In fact, if you don't buy ten million of your own bonds, then I'll just stop selling for the rest of the day. I'll take a nap under my desk. I don't need to sell these bonds. I've got four weeks left, then I'm cashing in my pension and I'm out of here. These bonds are nothing to me."

"You're bluffing. Sid, you can't be serious."

"I'm feeling sort of woozy, anyway. I could really use a nap."

"Fuck you, Sid. Don't do this to me. You know the hell I'm going to catch?"

"Will you call me around two o'clock this afternoon and wake me up? I want to be awake when the shit hits the fan."

"Damn, damn."

"Sing me a lullaby, will you?"

"Oh, all right!" Kenny Whitlash finally gave in. "Ten million is done. But don't call me for a month, you hear me? Stay away."

"Night-night," Sid whispered, hopping off the line. He turned to Wes Griffin. "These bonds are easy. Connect-the-dots is what I'm saying. Two for two. Compared to the Euro-Floaters, this is like selling newspaper subscriptions. It's all a matter of confidence. *Be the bond,* that's my motto. Be the bond, Wes. You hear me? Be the bond."

Wes nodded his head as he made notes in a new trading notebook.

Sid continued, "You don't look so good, Wes. You seen a ghost?"

Wes looked up, squinting out of one eye. "I'm all right. I'm having a little trouble focusing." He opened his bad eye for Sid to get a look. "How's it look? Does it look okay?"

"Oh, it's just fine," Sid lied, turning away from the gruesome way Wes both did and did not look at him. "It's not wandering at all. You just go ahead and get right back on the phone."

"I'm having a little bit of a hard time reading the monitors," Wes admitted. "The numbers are slightly out of focus."

Sid looked down at his Quotron, then made a disgusted face and tapped on his keyboard. "I don't think it's just you," he lied. "My Quotron screen's a little fuzzy, too. They haven't replaced Clark Kalinov yet. The office has been going to hell."

"I'm hungry," Wes pouted.

Sid slid around in his wheeled chair to Eggs Igino's old desk and shoved the blond-haired goofus aside so he could dig through Eggs's drawer and find the old sack of strawberry danishes. He was angry at the blond-haired goofus merely for existing, and to humiliate him Sid told him that as soon as Eggs Igino got back from Santo Domingo the kid would be good as gone.

"Dogmeat," Sid hissed. "You won't make it five weeks." Then he wheeled back to his side of their foxhole and climbed out of his chair and humped down the aisle to the kitchen, where he threw the sack of danishes in the microwave. At the beep he carried the sack back to his desk, waving it in front of the hungry noses of all the salespeople up and down the aisle. They all looked up hopelessly. Sid sat down again and pulled out a danish and began to gnaw through its gummy dough as if it were the freshest, tastiest, most delectable swirl of pastry his palate had ever encountered. The other salespeople eyed his breakfast forlornly, mumbling to themselves about their own lack of foresight in not bringing breakfast or lunch on a day when they would surely be here working the phones till the market closed. Benevolently, Sid set a danish out on a paper napkin and cut it into little squares with his envelope opener. He encouraged the force to take a cube of danish. They were tiny tidbits, not much bigger than a crumb, and each member of the mortgage desk knew in advance how humiliated he would feel if he dropped the speck of stale dough into his empty stomach while Sid stood there feasting on danish after entire danish. But Sid was the King of Mortgages, and they were used to feeling inferior to him.

"The King of the Jungle," Sid reminded them as one by one they snuck up to the edge of Sid's desk and pinched a cube off the napkin. Nobody wanted to admit how Sid had fooled them into compromising themselves for such an unsatisfying smidgen of food, and so they all hummed happily as they chewed their bite, patting their stomachs and burping. Nickel Sansome even loosened his belt a notch.

"What in the hell do you think you're doing?" Coyote Jack screamed, running out onto the floor and breaking up their party, pushing the salesmen away from Sid's desk.

"Feeding the masses," Sidney said. "Let them eat cake!"

"Goddamnit—don't you realize these people need to be selling bonds? What do you think they're here for, an all-you-can-eat buffet?" Coyote Jack swept the remains of Sid's danishes off his desk and into the aisle, then stomped on them. He was incensed. He spun around, looking for someone to attack, then caught sight of Wes Griffin with his bandanna knotted around his head to cover his bad eye. Coyote Jack strolled up behind Wes and flicked at the long locks of Wes's golden hair.

"Are you a surfer, Wes?"

Wes didn't turn around to look at him. "What?"

Coyote Jack crouched behind Wes and yelled into the back of his head. "You got a bad ear on top of a bad eye? You heard me. I thought only surfers and rock stars had hair like that. You a rock star?"

"No, sir."

"So you're a surfer. You'd probably rather be out there on the waves right now than selling these bonds, wouldn't you, Wes? Isn't that the truth?"

"C'mon, Coyote."

"No? Well, if you would rather be here selling bonds, then why haven't you sold any? Why have you, in the past four hours, managed to move a grand total of zero million, zero hundred thousand, point zero zero Lincoln Convertibles? I mean, I didn't give you another chance so you could just stand here like a lampshade and soak up the old atmosphere. You're probably thinking of quitting again. Are you thinking of quitting again, Wes?"

"I didn't quit. I never quit. I retired."

"Oh—pardon me. You *retired*. Then why did you tell Sid Geeder here that you quit?"

"I didn't tell him I quit. I never said that."

"Then why else did he tell all of his accounts that you had quit?"

"You'd have to ask him."

"I did ask him. He says you quit." Coyote Jack stepped forward and ripped Wes's bandanna off, jerking Wes's head backward. Wes whirled and stood up, his fists clenched, trying to look Coyote Jack in the eye and stare him down. But Wes Griffin couldn't, because his eye was a little off to the side. "Having a little eye trouble again, Wes? Boy, that must really sink your gut. Only four hours you've been back, and already the old peeper is astray. Who's it looking at, Wes? Has your eyeball got a thing for Sue Marino? Has it got just an incurable longing to gaze down upon her hemline? Maybe that's why you wanted to come back for one more fling with us, because it sure doesn't seem like you came back to sell any bonds. Oh, what's this?" Coyote Jack looked down at Wes's clenched fists. "Getting ready to take a swing, are you, Wes? You've probably been thinking about doing that for five years, haven't you? So that's why you volunteered for another tour of duty—you're here to take a swing at me. Somehow you got it in your head that your whole life would work itself out if you could just drop me to the carpet, is that it? Well, go ahead. I can take it. I'm a rock. Take a swing."

"You're a scumbag, Coyote."

"Take it!"

"Fuck you!"

"Take it, you wimp!"

Wes Griffin's hands shot forward and caught Coyote Jack below the chest, catching him off balance and sending him crashing into the municipal desk behind him, where the side of his head caught the edge of a hard plastic trash can. There was a cracking sound on impact, and Coyote Jack fell between two roller chairs. Instantly, the security guards circled Wes, watching him like a dangerous criminal, waiting for him to make a move on one of them. From behind, a guard delivered a shot to the kidney area with a billy club. When he bent over in pain, the others grabbed his arms and legs and lifted him into the air, then rushed him down the aisle and off the floor as he screamed obscenities. As soon as he was out the door, all attention went back to Coyote Jack, who had climbed back to his feet and stood with one hand on the side of his head. A crack ran along the side of the trash can at his feet.

"Let's go! Let's go!" Coyote Jack shouted, as the salesforce drew blank, frightened scares. "Sue Marino—you take his accounts! Make another round!"

"Fuck you, Coyote," Sue Marino returned.

"You sell some bonds and then you can talk like that." Coyote Jack walked toward her, clenching his fists.

"That was horrible! You treated him like dirt! You can't do that to people! This place is fucking crazy!"

"Shut up, Marino. I don't have time for wimps like you."

"Fine! Find someone else to sacrifice herself to your cause. Find someone else to lay down her body. Fuck you, Coyote."

"I don't care what you say, Marino. You can say all you want today. I don't give a shit. All I'm going to pay attention to is the charts at the end of the day. You go cry in your corner if you have to. Whatever it takes. But when the dust clears, your accounts better have a twenty in their column." Coyote Jack whipped around and stalked off the floor, slamming his door behind him.

Sue Marino glared. She'd had it. She really had. No way was she going to beg Mike Kohanamoku to buy the Lincolns just to save Coyote Jack's ass. She would never stoop that low. And she was never going to give that asshole a chance to fire her as he had Lisa Lisa, humiliating her in front of everyone like that. No fucking way. Sue Marino pulled the plastic sack out of her wastebasket and started dumping out her file drawer into the sack. She pulled her desk drawer all the way out and just dumped it indiscriminately. It took her less than a minute. Two years of work collected in less than a minute. She threw her Rolodex in there and some corporate stationery with John White's name printed on it, in case she needed to forge some recommendation letters. Then she shook her hair straight and stood up and dragged the plastic sack down the aisle. She stopped at the closet to steal a raincoat and someone's umbrella, which she hooked on her arm. She left without looking back.

Nickel sauntered down the aisle nervously, chewing the last hunk of his candy bar. Few of the salesforce were on the phone. They stared blankly off at the walls. "Hey, what's going on around here?" he inquired in a forced jolly tone. "Hey, cheer up. We've been here before," Nickel said.

Nobody answered him. There were so many new people on the floor it was a house of strangers.

Nickel pulled a chair over to Sidney's foxhole and kicked the goofus out. He sat down in Eggs Igino's old place. Sidney was buried in the crawl space, hiding.

"I guess it's just you and me left, old man," Nickel attempted to banter. "You probably didn't think I would last more than a year when you first saw me, huh? You probably took one look at the chrome dome and said to yourself, 'That meat won't last twelve weeks.' Am I right?"

Sidney glared back, squinting his eyes and steeling his jaw. "You'd better get back on the phone," he said.

"What are you so tense for?" Nickel said.

"You know what I fucking mean. Sell these bonds."

Nickel giggled frantically and started rubbing his brow. "Hey, Sid, come on. Who are you talking to? Like I said, I'm covered."

"Get out of my sight, Sansome. I have a hankering to smash your face in."

"Oh, no need for that, Sid. Everybody is so stressed out! What is everyone so stressed about?"

Sidney's leg shot out from the crawl space and kicked the underside of Nickel's chair seat, causing Nickel to tip back in his chair, reach behind him for balance, and go tumbling over backward, banging his elbow on the edge of the file cabinet. Like a snake, Sidney's leg slowly retracted into place. Nickel scrambled to his feet as he rubbed his elbow and swore back at Sidney. He threw a stack of research reports toward Sidney's hole, which opened in midair and fell harmlessly short. Nickel limped back to his desk, scowling at the goofus and the dog-lady, scuffing his shoes loudly against the worn carpet.

"You're all hopeless scum!" he swore, waving his arms to include the entire room in his comments. "You're bacteria leeching off a fungus growing on the underside of a dogfish swimming in the toxic waters off a crime-ridden and polluted city. You couldn't sell canned rations during a nuclear attack! You couldn't sell missiles to the Iranians!" Nickel sat down at his desk and popped the phone line to Irvine Savings. He barked at whoever answered to put Regis Reed on the line.

"I think it's time to write that ticket," Nickel suggested when Reed finally picked up.

"Oh, sure," Regis Reed agreed. "Let's see: twelve million Lincolns at a commission of four dollars a bond. That makes my share twenty-four thousand dollars. Boy, it sure would be crazy for me to turn down that kind of easy money."

"You're damn right," Nickel said. "And we all know you're not crazy."

Regis Reed paused. "I'm feeling kind of woozy, though. A little delirious, actually."

"Cut it out, Reed. Let's write this ticket and go celebrate. I'm buying."

Regis Reed gave a witch's cackle. "I'm hearing voices. Uh-oh. They're talking to me. It sounds like the ghost of Abraham Lincoln. They're coming to get me," he joked.

"Cut it out, will you?" Nickel said, sweating heavily now and picking at the fresh roots of hair on his scalp.

"Just think how fucked Atlantic Pacific would be if I *didn't* buy these bonds. I'll bet Coyote Jack's got his job on the line over this deal. I bet the whole goddamn firm has got its international reputation at stake over this one. Tell me, Nickel, how fucked would Atlantic Pacific be if I *didn't* buy twelve million Lincolns? How fucked would they be if instead of buying twelve, for instance, I bought, say, *zero*?"

Nickel humored him. "Oh, we'd be royally screwed. We'd be reamed up the ass."

"With a broom handle, Sansome."

"Fuck it, Reed. Let's just write this ticket. Twelve million New Lincoln Convertible AA-Grade notes in July at par. Just say 'Done' and let's go celebrate."

"What if I didn't say the D-word?"

"Come on! Just say it."

"You know what I'm thinking about right now, Nickel? I'm thinking about how I used to be the Prince of Mortgages over there, until I got screwed. I'm thinking about that time Coyote Jack humiliated me out on the sales floor in front of all those people who I used to think were my friends but who never spoke out on my behalf. I'm thinking about those four months' worth of sales commissions that Atlantic Pacific never paid me. I swore to myself I would get you all back. I can't believe how stupid you are, Nickel. You walked right into the spider's web, and you didn't have any fucking clue. You thought you were relaxing in a nice hammock. I can't believe Coyote Jack would fall for it. You're so fucking greedy, you saw what you wanted to see. Irvine Savings can't buy Lincoln Convertibles. Those bonds are illegal. They're moonshine. They're street drugs. You knew that, but you chose to overlook it. You're miserable, Sansome. You're really fucking pitiful. You won't have a job tomorrow. Tomorrow morning, New York is going to look at the charts and see a big goose egg next to your twenty million quota. You might as well not even show up. You might as well just go to your dad's club and play backgammon tomorrow and take a nap on those fat leather chairs with your mouth open and drool sliding out onto your tie. You suck, Sansome. Your brain is too small to operate in this world. I have no sympathy for you. None at all." Regis Reed blinked off the line, leaving Nickel listening to a dial tone.

"Aww, crap," Nickel said, trying not to start crying. His lungs felt as if they would seize up. He pulled the inhaler out of his drawer and sucked in a huge blast. Still, he felt his windpipes constricting. He told himself that it was just psychosomatic, and tried to laugh at the stupidness of it.

"It's not like I have asthma," he said to Nelson Dicky, who wasn't listening. "I just need to relax, that's all." He tried to chuckle, but his lungs wouldn't release any precious air, and though his shoulders jiggled no sound came from his mouth. He got up and strolled toward the kitchen, where he could relax for a moment. Coyote Jack stopped him in the aisles.

"Where the hell are you going? Who's watching your phones?"

Nickel whispered. "I've got to relax." He pointed toward his neck. "Just going to get a Coke."

"Relax on your own time. Get back to your desk and get on the horn. Do you think these bonds are going to walk out of here on their own?"

Rather than confront Coyote, Nickel turned around and headed back to his desk. Sidney Geeder was screaming at someone. The overhead air duct had a bad filter and was rattling against the vent frame. The phones were ringing all over the floor. The time stamp beside his desk was ticking.

"Go ahead! Get on the horn! Sell!" Coyote Jack yelled.

Nickel picked up the phone and pretended to talk, but he only dialed the weather lady. He fished in his file drawer to see if he'd brought another respirator. It occurred to him that if his breathing problem was only psychosomatic, it was no wonder that the steroids did no good. He needed a psychosomatic solution.

"Aw, crap, please," he said, throwing the empty inhaler into his wastebasket. He was hissing now, trying to get oxygen. The more he thought about it, the less he got. He just had to relax. It was all in the mind. Meanwhile, his face was turning blue. He felt a bubbly

sensation behind his eyes, and his lungs felt bruised and swollen—
it hurt terribly to try to use them. Then he could feel his eyes bugging out and a headache forming in the back of his brain. He was
hot, sweating suddenly everywhere. His phones started ringing.
Both Irvine lines were red and flashing. Nickel suddenly realized
that it must be Regis Reed calling back, that it was all a joke, that
he was going to buy those bonds now. He reached for the phone
button. His fingers were sticky and swollen.

"I can't breathe," he murmured, like a leaf landing in the grass.

"Bid fifteen million Fannie Mae 11s in July," someone not Regis
Reed barked.

No, Nickel thought. Not the Fannie Maes. The Lincolns. You're
done. Fifteen million Lincolns. "I can't breathe," he gasped. He
suddenly started thinking about his Korean girlfriend, and how, as
she was dressing this morning, he had noticed on the waistband of
her white cotton underwear a tiny pink ribboned bow.

"What's your bid?" Irvine yammered. "July! July!"

July. The phone slid from Nickel's hand and fell into the wastebasket. Nickel had a monstrous headache. He was so tired. He was
just going to shut his eyes and lie down on the carpet here for a
while, get a rest.

Nickel landed in the aisle, his arms bent askew as if he'd fallen
from a great height.

"Hey," observed the naive, blond-haired goofus. "Is he faking
it?"

The woman in the wheelchair scooted back from the desk for a
moment and rolled up by Nickel's head. She rolled into his shoulders to nudge him. "I think he's dead," she decided. "This happens
all the time in Japan. They drop like flies over there. Walking down
the street one day, then splat! Dead."

"Someone better call Coyote Jack," the goofus suggested.

They stayed there for a while, just looking. Then the woman in
the wheelchair called Coyote Jack and got Coyote Jack's secretary
on the phone. The secretary took the message that Nickel Sansome
was dead, wrote it down on a pink slip, and carried it in to Coyote
Jack. He came sprinting out of his room onto the sales floor and
dove down by Nickel's face. There was still a light pulse in his
neck.

"Somebody do something!" he yelled. "Doesn't anybody know CPR?"

One of the NIA men stepped through the growing crowd, surveyed the situation, and grabbed Nickel and lifted him up, holding him tight against his chest. The NIA man made his hands into fists and placed them at the base of Nickel's sternum. Then he hopped up and down, with each landing giving Nickel a huge squeeze. "C'mon, boy!" he said assuredly. "Cough it up! Spit it out!" Seven, eight times he squeezed, but nothing came out. "What did he swallow?" the NIA man asked the observers. The crowd parted around Nickel's desk, as everyone turned to see what Nickel had been eating. A half-finished Snickers bar was melting on his trading notebook.

"Jesus," one of the UN observers whistled. "I'm never eating one of those things again."

The NIA man who had a grip on Nickel stuck his finger down Nickel's throat and fished around, poking past the tonsils. "It must be lodged way down there," he observed, wiping his finger on the breast of Nickel's shirt. "He's going to have to go to the hospital."

They hauled him off the floor.

They were dropping like flies, and the corporate stock was dropping, too, on rumors that the deal was soft and demand was slight and Atlantic Pacific was running out of troops to sell the bonds. Accounts all over the world could see on their trading monitors that Atlantic Pacific stock had dropped from yesterday's 49 to a midday 35, and they could put two and two together, and many of them didn't want anything to do with it. When their Atlantic Pacific phone line went red, they chose not to answer it. It was increasingly obvious to everyone that Atlantic Pacific would get stuck with whatever portion of the $2 billion it didn't manage to sell, which would eat so much of its capital that its other operations would freeze. Atlantic Pacific traders in New York were told to start dumping their positions in other bonds in order to free up capital. The market grew testy and nervous. Every investor and dealer and broker in the world watched the market on his screens and prayed that the whole goddamn system wouldn't come tumbling down. The SEC observers put down their pens and tried to figure out why all the salespeople were pounding on their desks and cabinets and swearing at their phones.

"I can't get through!" Dave Rennaker screamed from across the floor.

"Answer the fucking phone!" the Creole paraplegic lesbian doglady yelled.

"Screw it!" hollered the guy who had taken Thom Slavonika's place, and he threw his phone at his Quotron screen, which exploded on impact, causing a huge vacuum *kaboom!* to echo across the floor and green glass to scatter across his desk, a piece of which sliced open a tiny notch in the meaty underside of Paul DeShews's thumb. Paul DeShews was afraid of the sight of blood, and he had spent his life trying to avoid the fact that underneath our skin we are mostly fluid.

"I'm bleeding!" Paul screamed, going faint.

All the Quotron screens were connected on a single SCSI cable, making them like those old-fashioned Christmas-tree lights: if one went out, none of them would work. Their screens didn't go blank, but the images on them froze as the computer crashed.

"What the fuck!" Sid said, pounding the F5 button of his Quotron, trying to find a bid price on a security he wanted a customer to swap out of. "What the hell happened?" He looked up and everyone pointed down the aisle to the guy who had taken Thom Slavonika's place. "I can't see!" Sid yelled. "I'm blind! How can a guy fight when he's blind? Will you answer me that?"

But there was no answer to his question. Blinded, Sid didn't give up. He'd moved $27 million so far, and he still had a couple of hours before the market closed. He crawled back under his desk with his phone and his trading notebook and reentered the fray.

The room stank. The shouting intensified, and then it waned. The trading monitors were useless. The research reports were ignored. The phones were of little help. The squawk box cackled as traders in New York tried to hold the firm together. Coyote Jack stomped up and down the aisles, yammering in their ears, and then he was joined in the same activity by Cornwell, who was on strict orders from on high to make sure the market didn't balk at this deal. The salesforce were burned out on the yelling and it failed to motivate them or anger them. They rolled up their sleeves and loosened their ties and folded sheets of their trading notebooks into paper airplanes, placing bets on whose plane could travel the farthest.

"Can't you control your salesforce?" Cornwell yelled at John White. "Get them back on the phone!"

John White sat in his office, tilted back in his chair, staring out at the clouds of fog that clung to the building. "Don't tell me what to do," he said slowly. "They're just blowing off a little steam. They'll get back in it soon."

"They're wasting valuable time!"

"Have you ever been on a sales floor before, Cornwell? Do you have any idea what it's like to sell bullshit like these convertibles? It's hell, man. Have a little respect."

"Respect, my ass. Your salesforce is weak. Weak! We should have moved this deal over to Merrill before it was too late. You can't even keep bodies on the line! You've got a half-dozen empty seats out there, and another half-dozen are rookies who couldn't sell drugs in a ghetto. I could sell bonds better than the imbeciles you have out there. We were told you had the best salesforce in the country! We were told Atlantic Pacific was the finest fighting machine in the world! You're a bunch of lardasses!"

John White pulled his feet off his desk and leaned forward. "If you're so brilliant, Cornwell, you go do it yourself."

So Cornwell went to try for himself. But not just Cornwell—he ordered all of his NIA men to pick up a phone and start talking, say anything, just try to find out why whoever answered the phone wasn't going to buy the Lincoln Convertibles. They'd all read the file on the deal as part of their briefing for this mission—they knew these bonds as well as anybody. Then, to prove that the NIA men weren't any tougher than they were, the Atlantic Pacific internal security men picked up the phones, too, and tried to weave their way into the datanet of information. They sat in the foxholes with their rifles leaning against the desks and screamed at each other, trying to figure which buttons to push to make the phone ring. They couldn't get anywhere. Their backs began to hurt and they grew tired easily; they just weren't accustomed to long periods of sitting. The SEC men were appalled, and they began to write furiously into their yellow legal pads that all of the security laws of the

U.S. government were being violated, until they realized that it was the U.S. government that was breaking its own laws, which might not be entirely illegal at all. The UN observers were horrified that the deal wasn't going smoothly, and they worried that New Lincoln, Inc. might not have such an easy time assaulting the capitol building in Santo Domingo next week. Everyone began to wonder whether it really made any sense that a few corporations could just get together and do a leveraged buyout on an entire nation.

"But it's not an *entire* nation," Cornwell explained to the person who picked up the line he had punched. "It's just the assets of the Dominican government itself. We're not touching any of the people or any of the private land that's held there. The government of the Dominican Republic contributes only a small portion of its GNP."

But it was no use. Against everyone's expectations and all the conventional wisdom, common sense seemed to be prevailing. Common sense had never won out before, at least not this early in a deal, and it made no sense to the pundits why all of a sudden common sense would rear its ugly head and rain down upon their party.

"It's not that bad," Coyote Jack said, trying a little spin control. "New York says they've moved three-quarters of the deal. That only sticks us with half a billion. Besides, hey—so what? We're the biggest shareholder in the Dominican Republic. What's so bad about that?"

"What's so bad about it is that their island is a worthless scrap of land that only has value as a future nuclear dump site," John White shot back. "We've fucked up royally, and you can be damned sure I'm not going to be blamed for it."

"Me neither," Coyote Jack said quickly.

"Oh yes you will. I'm going to lay this one down on your neck, Coyote. You took a quota twice what we've managed to sell. You overextended this office and mismanaged the salesforce. I'm going to take so much shit tomorrow I'll be lucky if I survive."

"How was I supposed to know they wouldn't find Eggs Igino?" Coyote Jack defended himself. "Am I to blame for him just disappearing?"

"You're the sales manager, Coyote." John White reached out

and popped Coyote Jack in the middle of his soft chest with a hard forefinger. "You've fucked up. We haven't sold half our quota. New York's going to come down awfully hard on us. I've got a conference call with the syndicate in an hour. I'm not sticking up for you any longer. You're on your own."

Coyote Jack got mad. He stood chest to chest with John White, yammering back that the deal never should have been released with so much havoc going on. It wasn't his fault that the bonds were a piece of shit.

Suddenly the squawk box behind them went dead quiet. It had never happened before. John White changed the channel, but he still received only fuzz.

"The Hoot's dead!" Sidney shouted across the floor. He punched the direct lines to New York, but the phones didn't even ring. "We're cut off! What the hell's going on out there?"

"We're surrounded!" someone else yelled back.

They rushed to the windows and tore down the blinds, as if they would be able to see what was happening out there.

John White looked out his window at the helicopter that was circling the building. The door to John White's office opened and Cornwell popped his head in. "John White!" he yelled at the two men.

"What?" John White said.

"Come with me," Cornwell ordered.

"I haven't done anything wrong. It was him." John White pointed at Coyote Jack.

"Let's go, let's go," Cornwell barked. "We don't have much time."

"What's going on?"

"I'll tell you about it on the way."

John White was deeply afraid of Cornwell and his men's guns. "I'm not going anywhere until you tell me where you're taking me."

"Your deal's fallen apart. I just got a call from Washington. They're pissed. We can't afford to have our military contractors take a loss like this. Something's got to be done. Now come with me!" Cornwell ran out.

John White stepped through the door in a rush to catch up with

Cornwell. He carried a briefcase full of paper napkins and a spare shirt and tie. They went out the back door and got in the elevator, which they rode to the top floor. There were several men waiting for him. They ran up to him. He expected them to strike him in the gut and cuff him, but instead they guided him by the shoulders to the end of the hall, where a staircase ascended to the roof. A helicopter was touched down across the rooftop. John White imitated Cornwell's hunched-over walk across the heliport. A door opened and a helping hand was thrust out. Cornwell climbed aboard, and then John White, and then the bird rose up into the sky.

15 · Power Is Temporary

IT WAS A filthy profession, but the money was addicting, and one addiction led to another, and they had all gone to hell. Regis Reed had gone to hell, and so had Green Thumb Griffin. Nickel Sansome lost his hair and stopped breathing, while Lisa Lisa's feet swelled three sizes. Sue Marino lost her slow, drawn-out voice, and then her smile, and then her fiancé. Thom Slavonika was put out to pasture. Eggs Igino, who had arrived like an apparition, had simply vanished. Coyote Jack overextended himself and was removed forcibly from the floor.

They had all gone to hell, but they had all learned a valuable lesson. They learned that knowledge is power, and then they learned that in some cases, knowledge had absolutely no use at all. Some kinds of knowledge had value in the marketplace; self-knowledge was not one of them. Nor was the knowledge that one was loved. In the market for knowledge, certain forms of knowledge were encouraged, and others were left unrewarded until they died off. Some kinds of knowledge were deemed efficient and convenient. Others were deemed too abstract and difficult to sell. The knowledge that was convenient and efficient was stored in the employees' heads, where it could be accessed quickly, on demand. To make room for so much convenient thinking, old and useless knowledge was cleaned out and discarded. According to Eggs Igino, who had studied psychology before he had studied economics, sanity was often thought to be a clear distinction between one's inner world and the outer world. When he applied this to the workplace, a sane employee was one who had a clear distinction between self and employer. But when a firm's greatest assets are the minds of its employees, one would have to classify this arrangement as insane, almost by definition. The line between employee and employer was blurred. Wealth was allocated to the mentally efficient, to those who could stave off psychological malfunction with justifications, promises, and excuses. Wealth went to the crazy, to those who gave their lives in service to the firm, to those who found beauty in the pristine columns of balance sheets and could express their creativity through the small tolerances of FIFO, LIFO, and U-Cap adjustments.

There was the small cost of being miserable, but that could be momentarily relieved by a change in title. If you were young and could read numbers like a crystal ball, you had bargaining power but were not immune to the process. If you were a woman, you were allowed a little valuable space for your feminine mystique—perhaps half of your desk drawer, your purse, and a posterior lobe of the cerebral cortex. If you were a man, the labor market rewarded you for ignoring your extracurricular hobbies, such as your family. Men weren't stiff and distant by nature—they had just been subjected to the market process for 130 years. They were just worn down by a market that pays a lawyer 300 percent the salary of a high school English teacher. Their lives went past them so fast that little of it sank in. It was impossible to keep track of it all. They wanted it all to slow down, but life was not a story; it didn't slow down conveniently right before the end and it never came to a clean resolution. As a matter of survival, they learned to joke about it. They joked about the teeth of the guy who took Thom Slavonika's place, which were rotting. And Paul "Goody" DeShews, who was going to defy gravity. And Nelson Dicky, who had been saved by

God. And the handicapped dog-lady's testicles, which were made of steel and clanged when she sold the flip from mortgages to high-yield corporates.

They joked about these things and they wondered what it would be like to shine their own shoes, and though it wasn't easy, they all survived. They never left their trenches and they did as they were told; they didn't do anything except go to work eleven hours a day, five days a week, for a few years of their lives. In the end, when the dust cleared, only Sidney Geeder was left standing, and everything was different except the market, which was the same, because it was normal to rub out everything human and leave only those who can defy gravity and those who were made of steel. Sid Geeder slurped his coffee and watched a crew of contractors remove the oil paintings of battleships from the 1787 New York Navy, which had been Atlantic Pacific's corporate symbol. Then they removed the brass Atlantic Pacific lettering that hung on the far wall, and when that was done they began to roll up the corporate-baby-blue carpet in long strips. They worked methodically, quickly, barely interrupting the remaining members of the salesforce, who, out of habit, wrote down the opening prices in the treasury market and began to call their accounts and brief them on overnight trading in Tokyo and Bonn. One of the contractors went desk to desk picking up all the Atlantic Pacific ballpoint pens. It took them about an hour to strip the office of all the main signs of the Atlantic Pacific Corporation, whose name was mud on the street.

Sidney began to suspect that he'd finally succeeded in bringing down the firm. He punched up the company stock price on his Quotron, but to his surprise the stock had traded back up to 38 overnight. It didn't make sense. Then the workmen came back in. They brought new rolls of plush forest-green carpeting with them and unfurled it into the aisleways. Carpet tackers crawled around stapling it into position, barely disturbing the remaining members of the salesforce, who, out of habit, went to the kitchen and scrounged around for food. Other delivery men brought in new oil paintings of fine Arabian warhorses decorated in armor. They popped the canvases out of the old gilded frames and replaced them with the new canvases, then rehung them so the unfaded wallpaper behind couldn't be seen. Some of the horses were galloping at high speed; others were rearing up on their hind legs. They were all in action and had fierce, militant eyes. The contractors stood in front of them admiring the detail in the horses' coats.

Then they went back into the hallway and returned carrying an ornately welded stainless-steel sign for Allegiant Securities, which was the new name the firm had chosen for itself during the night. Coyote Jack's secretary came out on the floor and passed around new forest-green-ink corporate ballpoint pens, which had a logo of a white horse imprinted at their base. She introduced herself to the new salespeople all down the row who had been flown out from New York to replace those who had gone to hell as well as those who, in yesterday's activity, had failed to fulfill at least 75 percent of their quota. It was a little harsh to fire people for not making a quota that wasn't realistic in the first place, but the firm made the tough choice that it was better the salespeople be taught that the quotas were strict and not to be taken lightly. The next time the firm overextended itself and set impossible quotas, the government might not be there to bail them out. Sidney Geeder had sold $38 million, which was more than double what anyone else in San Francisco had sold, but it still wasn't even close to 75 percent of his target. Sid Geeder nursed his mug of coffee and waited for John White to come out on the sales floor and ask him into the office.

John White came out on the sales floor and asked Sid Geeder into his office and told everyone to go back to work. *This is it*, Sid Geeder thought to himself, as John White's secretary poured him a fresh cup of coffee. *Now I'm gone too*.

But it was worse than that. "The NIA decided that this deal was too important to our national interest, and it bailed us out. It bought the last half billion of bonds to make sure it's a success. They can't afford to have all of their main military contractors take a loss on this deal. It's not that unusual, really. They step in and give jet fighter contracts to Martin Marietta all the time to keep them from going out of business. Half a billion in bonds is not much more than a couple of stealth bombers."

"You mean the firm's not dead?" Sid said. "This is terrible."

"On the contrary. We're stronger than ever."

"You're lying," Sid accused him. "Our name is mud."

"Oh, but we're not Atlantic Pacific anymore. We're Allegiant Securities. Not a bad name, huh? A computer spit out that appellation. Allegiant Securities is the finest selling machine on the street."

"Give me a break," Sid shot back.

John White paused for that to sink in. "Anyway, now that Coyote Jack's gone, I want to give you a promotion," John White said.

"I don't want a promotion," Sid Geeder said. "I've only got four more weeks till I cash out those shares. Then I'm never working another day in my life."

"You can keep the shares if you take the promotion."

"But can I cash them out?"

"In two years."

"Two years!"

"Unless you get another promotion," John White added. "Then it would be *another* two years. But you'd be a managing director, and the work is easy. In fact, there's no work for us at all. You barely have to show up."

"What if I don't take the promotion?" Sid Geeder asked.

"If you don't take the promotion, then I have to fire you."

"So I never even get the shares?"

"Those shares are worth a lot of money to the firm. We can't let people have them who want to cash them out. If we wanted you to cash them out, then we would have given you cash in the first place. You've been a valuable employee to us, Sid. So valuable that I have to fire you. We can't let people become invaluable to us."

"That's crazy."

"It's not crazy. It's the Third Law of Information Economics."

"What's that? What's the Third Law?"

"Never hire someone you can't fire."

"Where did you hear that? Did someone teach it to you?" Sidney jumped out of his chair.

"Eggs Igino. He taught it to me."

"Eggs Igino! Have you heard from him?"

John White looked down at his shoes. "I haven't heard anything. Management still worries he's going to show up at Shearson or Merrill and clean our clocks. We never should have hired him. He was way too valuable."

Sid looked out John White's forty-second-floor window. There was nothing but fog and they were the only spaceship in the sky. "I never should have come back. I should have disappeared for good like Eggs Igino."

"What are you whining about? I'm giving you a promotion."

"Some promotion," Sid muttered.

"Hey, there's guys out on the sales floor who would give their right arm for a promotion like this."

"Good for them," Sid said. "Why don't you give Nelson Dicky my promotion and let me take his shares?"

"Are you kidding? Nelson Dicky is the kindest, sweetest guy on the floor. Everybody loves him and nobody respects him."

"I don't see why you're singling me out this way. What have I done for the past five years except make this firm a ton of money?"

"Who's singling you out? Nobody in management is allowed to cash out their shares. Sid, do you realize what would happen if we let them? Don't you know what would happen if all of a sudden we allowed management to swap stock for cash?"

"Christ, they'd bolt. Not all of them, but most."

"There'd be no money left."

"Would you? Would you bolt?"

"I'd be out the door in an hour," John White confessed. "I'm up to two hundred thousand shares by now."

"That's eight million dollars!"

"Like a painting I can't sell. I'll never see a dime of it."

"Then why do you stay?" Sid gasped.

"What? And throw away eight million in stock? I'd have to be crazy to walk away from money like that."

"But that doesn't make any sense!"

"Who says it has to make sense? Making sense has never been a prerequisite for this business. You really shouldn't try to make sense of it after all this time. You did just fine for four years and eleven months ignoring the obvious contradictions. Look at Eggs Igino. He tried to make sense of it, and what's happened to him?"

"What's happened to him?" Sid asked.

"How the hell do I know? Ask him yourself if you're so anxious to find out."

"But how can I ask him if I don't know where he is?" Sid screamed in frenetic bewilderment as all of what John White had just told him began to sink in. Sid batted at a stack of research reports on John White's desk and sent them flying. He tore out of John White's office with his head down, stomping his footprints in the new forest-green plush carpet, the sight of which only made Sid angrier. Sid didn't even look where he was going, and he bowled into someone, knocking him backward. Sid looked up.

"Who the hell are you?" he screamed at the unfamiliar tall man in a pink shirt who stood before him.

"I'm the New Clark Kalinov," the man answered angrily. "And who the hell are *you*?"

"I'm the New Sid Geeder," Sidney answered disgustedly.

"Oh—I wasn't expecting you until tomorrow. You've got some forms to fill out."

"Fuck your forms!" Sid pushed past the New Clark Kalinov and went back to his familiar territory at his desk. He tried just to read the newspaper, but there were so many new faces down the aisle, staring at him all dopey-eyed, looking for advice on how to be a salesman. They were waiting for him to get on the phone and give them ideas on how to sell bonds.

"What the hell are you looking at?" he hollered. "Shoo! Leave me alone!"

They kept staring at him. Several of them started to read their papers, kicking their heels up on their desks just as he was doing. When Sidney saw something interesting on his Telerate screen, they all turned to their Telerate screens to see if they could tell what he was looking at.

"Stop that!" he howled. "Think for yourselves!"

The dog-lady in the wheelchair scooted over to the edge of his desk. "I'd be happy to think for myself," she said. "If you'd just tell me what to think about."

Sid Geeder slapped his forehead in frustration. "I can't tell you what to think about!"

"Why not?" the dog-lady in the wheelchair asked disrespectfully.

"Because then you wouldn't be thinking for yourself!" he wailed, throwing the newspaper in the dog-lady's face. He immediately decided to call his accountant, Stormin' Norman Walker, and explain what John White had done.

"Can they *do* that?" Sid asked. "It's got to be illegal."

"What's illegal about it?" Norman Walker asked.

"But they promised me those shares!"

"Only if you last five years."

"But it's practically been five years," Sid argued.

"It won't be if they fire you."

"They can't just fire me, can they? I've held up my side of the bargain. I haven't done anything wrong. I'm the best salesman they've got. Don't they have to have a valid reason to fire me? Isn't that the law?"

"Oh, but they do have a reason," Norman Walker answered. "You didn't sell your quota of the Lincolns."

"But that quota was ridiculous! Nobody could have sold a hundred million."

"That's exactly why they gave it to you. To make sure they had a reason to fire you."

"Then why don't they just fire me?"

Norman Walker coughed into his phone line. "Because they don't *want* to fire you. Once they've got a good reason to fire you, they'd much rather promote you instead. You'd be a great sales manager."

"Then why don't they give me those shares? If they let me keep the shares, then I'd take the promotion."

"You're lying and they know it," Norman Walker accused him. "You'd cash those shares out and the next day you'd quit. You wouldn't put up with being sales manager one week."

"Norman, we're talking about four million dollars the firm promised me! And you're telling me there's no way I can get it?"

"Well, you could take the promotion. In two years, you'd get the shares."

"I can't wait two years."

"You're only thirty-four. What's two more years?" Norman Walker reasoned.

"Everything," Sid answered. "Two years is everything. Two more years would be the straw that broke my back."

"You just think that. You've been under stress. Take a few days off, come back. It'll all seem much more reasonable then."

"Forget it," Sid said. "I don't want it to seem reasonable."

Sidney Geeder was relieved when Ricky brought the mail and he could go through it, dumping the pieces one by one into the waste-basket with flourishing satisfaction. He threw away the research reports, and he threw away the price listings, and he threw away the trade confirmations. He threw away everything of waste on his entire desk until his wastebasket was overbrimming. Sid was nearly in tears of despair and frustration. All those years, and they added up to nothing. He got so angry he wanted to bash John White's face in with a stapler, but Sid Geeder knew that in the firm of Allegiant Securities there were a hundred men ready to take John White's place, none of whom would say anything different. The individuals just didn't matter—the organization lived on. Sid Geeder tucked his wastebasket under his arm and went off to empty it. One of the contractors in white overalls followed him down the hall, and as Sid ducked into the monster photocopier room the contractor slipped in behind him and closed the door.

"What the hell do you want?" Sid screamed, whirling around.

The contractor was grinning mysteriously. He wore a paper baseball cap and circular glasses. Freckles came up out of his red-dish-brown beard. He didn't say anything. He just giggled and clucked his tongue, then shoved his hands into his pockets. He raised his eyebrows knowingly.

"Where the hell did you come from?" Sid yelled again.

"What will you give me for it?" the contractor smiled.

"For what?" Sid said, dropping his wastebasket to the floor.

"For the information. The information about where I've been for the past seven weeks. I can't just give you that for free. It's valuable information that most of the world would be willing to pay for."

"Holy shit," Sid whistled, trying to look past the glare in the contractor's glasses.

"You ought to be willing to pay for it. Do you realize what kind of havoc you could cause if you knew how to just vanish into thin air? You and I could be on some island, dipping our toes in the hot sand, while everyone else is at his desk slaving away. You would drive everyone crazy, even John White, and suddenly your life wouldn't seem so imposing." Eggs Igino leaned his hip against the monster photocopier and stretched his leg out behind him. "You would be in control."

"It's you! It's really you!" Sidney Geeder blabbered in unstoppable delight, hugging Eggs Igino like a puppy and pinching his cheek. A flush of joy crept up Sid's back and made him feel as if all the hairs on his head were standing on end. "It's really you!" Sidney roared with frenetic laughter and held his arms high in a triumphant gesture. A great rush of exhilaration swept over Sidney Geeder, and out of his mouth popped a hilarious guffaw, followed by an incoherent mumbling pause. Ensnared in a ranting frenzy of joy, all he could do was scream.

"He's alive!" Sidney bellowed, spinning in a circle and hopping up and down. "He's escaped! He's free!"

"Not so loud," Eggs Igino whispered.

"Where'd you go?" Sid cried.

"I went to see someone I had to see."

"This place has really gone to hell."

"It had always gone to hell."

"They had everyone thinking you were captured by the Dominicans."

"People believed that?" Eggs laughed. "Amazing what a fax can do."

"It was you? You sent those faxes?"

"One of them. There were others?"

"Sure," Sid said excitedly. "I sent some myself! You would have been proud of me. I even made a phone call!"

"Well, see—it wasn't just me."

"You nearly brought down the entire company! You *did* bring down the entire company! We don't even have the same name anymore. Everybody's gone to hell except Nelson Dicky and Paul De-Shews. They're all gone. Boy, do I miss some of them." Sid paused for a moment out of respect. "How the heck did you get in here?"

"The maids. I snuck in on a cart."

"But what the hell did you come back for?"

Eggs squinted his face up on one side and jiggled the change in his pocket. "I came to rescue you," he said.

"Rescue me? From what?"

Eggs Igino shrugged. He looked off into space. "Just to rescue you. You know, from all of this. It can be done, you know. You can just disappear entirely. We can make an escape."

"To where? Where would I go? What would I do with myself? I've been working here so long I don't know anything else." Sid pressed his fingers against his forehead in thought. "John White sucker-punched me on those corporate shares. He says I have to stay two more years to keep them, otherwise I'm dead meat. I'd never last two years. I wouldn't! But what else can I do? Everything I know is about selling bonds. My head is entirely empty of anything that might be of some use in getting another job. I'm invaluable to this firm, but to any other industry I'm completely worthless. I can't work a computer—the only software I understand is stuff we invented to price bonds. I don't even have any contacts. Where can I go? I'm worthless."

"Aww, come on. You're not worthless. You're Sid Geeder. *The* Sid Geeder. The only model and make in the whole world. You're rarer than diamonds. Scarcer than uranium. You're priceless, Sid. Nobody can buy you. Four million doesn't even come close."

Sid looked up. "You're right. I like that. They can't buy me."

"Hell no."

"I'm Sid Geeder. *The* Sid Geeder."

"No more selling ice to the Eskimos."

"No more selling sand to the Arabs," Sid agreed happily. "Who knows what might happen to me once I turn my life around! Anything could happen!"

"That's right. You're only thirty-four years old and you're smart as a whip. Buy a company, I don't know. Coach wrestling if you have to."

"Something will turn up," Sid stated optimistically.

"That's it."

"It all starts with me quitting."

Eggs shook his head. "Don't quit. *Escape.*"

"Escape? Why would I want to escape? If I'm going to quit, then I'm walking out the front door."

"They'll fire you before you take two steps. At the door they'll find a way to humiliate you. They'll strip-search you, do a nut check, make sure you don't walk out with anything that belongs to the firm. They won't even let you take a ballpoint pen. They won't even let you take one of your own business cards. There's no way you're going to win, Sid. There's no way you're going to show them up in front of the new salesforce. It's best if you just disappear."

Eggs Igino was right, and Sid could picture all of it. "But how?" Sid asked. "Do I just not come back tomorrow?"

"Why wait until tomorrow?" Eggs said.

Sid put his head down in thought. "You know, if I'm really going to disappear, then there's one thing I'd like to do before I go."

"Then go do it," Eggs agreed.

Sid flew out of the room, ran down the hall, and crossed the sales floor, entering the opposite corridor and bursting into John White's office.

"This better be important," John White said, looking up from a stack of paperwork.

Sid leered in a sneaky, blissful way. "Do I look like I'm flush with the newest wonder drug? Do I look like I've discovered the secret to youth?"

"I'll say. You look like superman, bursting out of your clothes. What gives?"

"It's about the promotion," Sid said.

"You don't want it?" John White guessed.

"Oh, no, I do want it!"

"You do?"

"Oh, yes, yes," Sid said. "Are you kidding? Put me down for another two years. Call New York. Call the *Journal*. Tell the whole salesforce. Tell 'em right now. Tell all the accounts. Put out the word! I'm gonna be the best sales manager you've ever seen!"

"Well, that's terrific," John White said, caught up in Sid's excitement. "Welcome aboard. But get yourself a decent suit and some shoes, will you? You dress like a goddamn salesman."

"Roger that," Sid said, trying not to laugh. He closed the door and ran back across the sales floor to the door of the monster photocopier room, which he opened, only to find that Eggs Igino had disappeared.

Vanished. "Oh shit," Sid said, sitting down on a box of copier paper and putting his face in his hands. "Aww crap, not again." There was a commotion going on out on the sales floor, and a round of applause and whoops, probably as John White told the news of Sid's promotion to the salesforce. There was no sign of Eggs Igino at all, not even a note. Gone, just as quickly as he'd appeared. In a moment, everyone on the floor would come looking for him.

"What's going on?" Coyote Jack's secretary cried when she found him sitting there on a box of copier paper. "Aren't you coming to celebrate your promotion?"

"I'm not taking the promotion."

"You're not taking your promotion?"

"Are you kidding? I can't work here anymore. I just told John White I'd take it to throw a wrench in his plans."

"You're leaving us?" She began to sniffle.

"Don't tell anyone," Sid asked. "Just let them figure it out."

"But I'll be all alone," she responded, pulling a tissue out of her bra strap and dabbing at her eyes.

"There, there," Sid reassured her. "I'll be happier this way."

Then she toughened up and squared her shoulders. "Well, we'll miss you," she said.

"I'll miss you too," Sid agreed. "Do me a favor, will you? Watch the hallway while I go out the back door?"

Coyote Jack's secretary stepped out into the hallway. Sid crouched at the doorway.

"Well, watch out," she advised him. "There's a lot of mean people out there."

"I'll watch out," Sid said.

"Well, good luck."

"And good luck to you," Sid returned. "You be careful." He turned and sprinted down the hallway and popped through the back door, which he then closed gently behind him. He strolled out toward the elevators. One of the internal security men stood there yawning. He barely noticed Sid.

"Left my wallet in my car," Sid said, patting his rear pocket.

The guard's eyes shifted over to Sid momentarily, then sleepily returned to their half-mast fixation on the carpet.

A "bing" announced the arrival of the elevator. Sid stepped in, turned, and automatically reached to the lobby button without having to watch his hand. He stepped to the back of the elevator as it dropped through the shaft. He tried to think of where he could go, what he would do. He wanted to see Ivana. That seemed to be the only thing he could think of. It was the only thing left that seemed important. When the doors opened, Sid hesitated. A crowd of other building occupants pushed aboard. Sid had to fight through them to get off.

The lobby was humid from a team of gardeners misting the tall, leafy, junglelike trees that grew along the glass walls. The sun was just coming up, and morning light refracted through the mist and sparkled. Trying not to look conspicuous, Sid waved at the building security staff who kept an eye on the elevator to the basement. It was three more floors down, three long, slow floors. He fished in his pocket and came out with his keys, which he readied in his hands for a quick getaway. He walked fast, skipping almost, past aisles of cars fancier than his, then stopped and froze as he saw that Coyote Jack's silver sedan was in its regular slot.

On instinct, Sid bent into a crouch, as if the car were going to attack him. Then, slowly, he stepped along the car to its side windows. The driver's seat was tilted back as far as it would go, and reclining there was Coyote Jack, wearing his white-on-white striped tab-collar shirt, without a tie. He seemed half asleep but bolted upright when Sid's body cast a shadow over his eyes.

"I've got a gun," Coyote Jack yelled, reaching for his glove compartment. "Get away!"

Sid ducked and flipped down against the rear tire of the sedan.

"Jesus Christ, Coyote! It's me! It's Geeder! Don't shoot!"

Sid heard the sliding release of the car's door lock. The driver's door opened, and Coyote Jack's legs swung out.

"Goddamn, Geeder. You scared the shit out of me."

"Do you really have a gun?" Sid asked.

"Nope."

Carefully, Sid stood up and dusted off his pants. "What are you doing here?" he asked.

Coyote Jack's face was pasty and swollen. His eyes were squinting. "I don't know," he answered.

"Did you tell your wife?" Sid asked.

"Not yet," Coyote Jack answered, and that seemed to explain everything. But he went on, "I don't quite know where to go."

Sid looked down at the cement. He pressed on a pebble with the toe of his shoe. "Well . . ."

"Well." Coyote Jack nodded, as if they had agreed on something.

Sid cleared his throat. "Quit moping. There's always plenty of jobs for hatchet men like you," he said.

"Is that what you think?" Coyote Jack asked defensively. "A hatchet man?"

"That's as kind as I can say it."

"Fuck you."

"Yeah, well, fuck you too," Sid responded. He turned and started walking away.

"Goddamnit, Geeder, don't you walk out on me like that! I spent five years putting up with your bullshit! Five years, Geeder, and you never thought about anyone but yourself."

Sid walked backward in small steps, facing Coyote Jack. "You deserve what you got. You got what you deserve."

"Nobody else counted. You looked down on every one of us! Damnit, Geeder, you listen to me for once!"

"Go cry to your wife about it, asshole." Sid continued marching, trying to walk out of earshot.

"Goddamnit, Geeder! You never listened to me!"

Sid softened his footsteps, trying to just disappear. He turned a corner down another row and the din quieted. When Sid reached his truck, Eggs Igino was reclining against the passenger door with his face hidden behind an open newspaper.

Sid Geeder tried to downplay his relief. He ambled up and stuck his key in the door, then climbed in. Eggs got in beside him. Sid turned the motor over.

"So, what's the word, kid?"

"The word?"

"The word of the day."

Eggs chuckled. "The word," he mumbled, thinking to himself but coming up with nothing. Sid wheeled through the garage. Eggs wanted to say something inspiring. Finally, he turned it back to Sid. "I give up," he answered. "What's the word?"

Amused, Sid grinned, then shrugged. "Let's go find out." He gunned his truck up the ramp, making sharp, familiar turns, waving his pass one last time at the parking attendant. They came out into the street. It was before the rush of morning traffic, and the yellow light from the sun filtered through waves of heavy white mist. A few blocks away they looked back one last time, but their building had already disappeared.

About the Type

This book was set in Sabon, a typeface designed by the well-known German typographer Jan Tschichold (1902–74). Sabon's design is based upon the original letter forms of Claude Garamond and was created specifically to be used for three sources: foundry type for hand composition, Linotype, and Monotype. Tschichold named his typeface for the famous Frankfurt typefounder Jacques Sabon, who died in 1580.

FOR THE BEST IN PAPERBACKS, LOOK FOR THE

In every corner of the world, on every subject under the sun, Penguin represents quality and variety—the very best in publishing today.

For complete information about books available from Penguin—including Puffins, Penguin Classics, and Arkana—and how to order them, write to us at the appropriate address below. Please note that for copyright reasons the selection of books varies from country to country.

In the United Kingdom: Please write to *Dept. JC, Penguin Books Ltd, FREEPOST, West Drayton, Middlesex UB7 0BR*.

If you have any difficulty in obtaining a title, please send your order with the correct money, plus ten percent for postage and packaging, to *P.O. Box No. 11, West Drayton, Middlesex UB7 0BR*

In the United States: Please write to *Consumer Sales, Penguin USA, P.O. Box 999, Dept. 17109, Bergenfield, New Jersey 07621-0120.* VISA and MasterCard holders call 1-800-253-6476 to order all Penguin titles

In Canada: Please write to *Penguin Books Canada Ltd, 10 Alcorn Avenue, Suite 300, Toronto, Ontario M4V 3B2*

In Australia: Please write to *Penguin Books Australia Ltd, P.O. Box 257, Ringwood, Victoria 3134*

In New Zealand: Please write to *Penguin Books (NZ) Ltd, Private Bag 102902, North Shore Mail Centre, Auckland 10*

In India: Please write to *Penguin Books India Pvt Ltd, 706 Eros Apartments, 56 Nehru Place, New Delhi 110 019*

In the Netherlands: Please write to *Penguin Books Netherlands bv, Postbus 3507, NL-1001 AH Amsterdam*

In Germany: Please write to *Penguin Books Deutschland GmbH, Metzlerstrasse 26, 60594 Frankfurt am Main*

In Spain: Please write to *Penguin Books S. A., Bravo Murillo 19, 1° B, 28015 Madrid*

In Italy: Please write to *Penguin Italia s.r.l., Via Felice Casati 20, I-20124 Milano*

In France: Please write to *Penguin France S. A., 17 rue Lejeune, F–31000 Toulouse*

In Japan: Please write to *Penguin Books Japan, Ishikiribashi Building, 2–5–4, Suido, Bunkyo-ku, Tokyo 112*

In Greece: Please write to *Penguin Hellas Ltd, Dimocritou 3, GR–106 71 Athens*

In South Africa: Please write to *Longman Penguin Southern Africa (Pty) Ltd, Private Bag X08, Bertsham 2013*